MATCH *POINTE*

...go Bloome is the international best-selling author of the Avalon
...ogy. The series, including the books *Destined to Play*, *Destined*
...el and *Destined to Fly*, reached the *Sunday Times* best-seller
...and they have been published globally.

...Indigo has lived and worked in Australia and the United
...gdom with a successful career in the finance industry. Having
...ed hectic city life for a move to inspirational Tasmania with
...husband and two children, she was able to explore her previ-
...ly undiscovered love for storytelling.

...Match *Pointe* is her first stand-alone novel.

...ow Indigo on:
...facebook.com/IndigoBloomeBooks
...@Indigobloome
...digobloome.com

Also by Indigo Bloome

The Avalon series

Destined to Play
Destined to Feel
Destined to Fly

INDIGO BLOOME

MATCH *POINTE*

HARPER

Harper
An imprint of HarperCollins*Publishers*
1 London Bridge Street,
London SE1 9GF

www.harpercollins.co.uk

A Paperback Original 2015
1

A catalogue record for this book
is available from the British Library

ISBN: 978-0-00-759757-4

Printed and bound in Great Britain by
Clays Ltd, St Ives plc

MIX
Paper from
responsible sources
FSC® C007454

For all those who read the Avalon Trilogy,
my most sincere thanks.
This one's for you!
xo

Prologue

Caesar

Antony 'Caesar' King was one of the wealthiest men in the United Kingdom. Casino and hotel management were his business staples, but he was equally notorious for his ruthless dealings in property investments and high-end gambling. The crowning glory of his business empire – on which he spent a disproportionate amount of his limited time – was the firm he had built from scratch: The Edge. It was the world's leading sports agency, responsible for managing the global careers of the most influential and brand-conscious athletes. Caesar had a natural instinct for identifying emerging talent, and the financial resources to back those he happened to tap on the shoulder.

Athletes knew that if The Edge represented them, they were on the path to greatness. To say 'No' to Caesar was akin to kissing your sports career goodbye and fading into oblivion. Not only was the business highly lucrative, but it also ensured Caesar was the pre-eminent 'mover and shaker' in the industry. At elite sports venues the world over he was immediately recognisable for his flamboyant dress sense, and he had the personality to match. Whether people loved him or hated him, such was his magnetism that they were drawn to him like moths to a flame. Power and superiority emanated from every gesture he made and the tone of every word he spoke. And rest assured that he relished the authority he wielded and the attention he attracted. Indeed, he depended on it for his continued success.

* * *

His father, Antonio 'Tony' King, was a self-made man. From humble beginnings in Italy, Tony had emigrated to America after the war. He had hocked his few valuables for several hands of blackjack, and won enough to kick-start his life in the new world. He was a conscientious gambler, willing to bet on high-risk ventures. And against all odds, he won significantly more than he ever lost.

Antony junior's middle name was a direct tribute to an exceptionally lucky night at Caesar's Palace in Las Vegas. During a few raucous rounds of poker, Tony was challenged to risk all of his winnings on the roulette table.

With all the careless arrogance of a man who had nothing to lose, he barely glanced at the spinning wheel, where the numbers and colours swirled towards the potential gain or loss of such a huge sum. Instead, the beauty of a tall young blonde a few feet away captured his eye. With a sly wink he beckoned her close, whispering in her ear that she was his good luck charm. It was only when she returned his smile that he let his eyes focus on the tiny silver ball slowing towards black thirteen as if it were magnetically attracted to the number.

The ball fell into place, and the crowd who had gathered around the table erupted into applause as Tony walked away $1 million richer. He graciously accepted the envious congratulations of those around him, and the gratis upgrade to the Emperor's Suite proffered by hotel management. Needless to say, he wasted no time in bedding the stunning babe, who had more than happily accompanied him and his newly acquired funds to the suite.

At first Tony was shocked by the news of her pregnancy, but given that the conception had occurred on the luckiest night of his life, it seemed fate was sending him a definite sign. The woman had no interest in becoming a mother at the peak of her youth and beauty, so he made her an offer any young student with a substantial college debt would find difficult to refuse. A healthy, strong baby boy was delivered into the world, and once the obligatory paternity tests were completed, the biological mother willingly accepted the bonus money they had agreed on, granting Tony full custody of his only son and disappearing from their lives forever.

Caesar had wanted for nothing during his youth as he was groomed to be the heir of his father's financial throne. He became the only true love of his father's life. Tony was determined that Caesar would have all the refinements he'd lacked in his humble upbringing in Italy. So it was inevitable that Tony would choose the prestigious six-centuries-old Eton College to educate his only son. Fortunately the college had no problem accepting Tony's ostentatious new money.

Caesar excelled academically, more so in mathematics than in any other subject. Although he won several mathematics awards across Europe and was the youngest player ever to represent Britain in bridge, Caesar didn't necessarily understand what all the fuss was about. It all came so easily to him that it was as natural as breathing.

It was only after he discovered the game of tennis in his first year of secondary school that his true passion was ignited. In his mind, tennis was the ultimate sport, dwarfing all others. The idea that a grand slam was all down to two players after a fortnight of competition intrigued him. Only one player could outplay, outsmart, outwit and out-hit the other. There were no teammates to confer with, rely on or blame; two solo players were left to fight it out on court, bound only by the rules of the game.

To win you had to have everything – the physical and mental stamina, skill, consistency, tenacity and most importantly the absolute belief in yourself, that you deserved to win and had the capacity to do so. At the end of the day only one person would take all the glory.

Tennis appealed to Caesar in a way that other sports didn't. It got under his skin. He felt more alive watching Wimbledon than at any other time during his schooling. It was as though he belonged there in some way.

From that point on Caesar channelled much of his energy into the game of tennis, and even managed to crack into the top one hundred on the junior tennis circuit when he was fifteen years old – albeit briefly. Unfortunately, a bad skiing accident left his knee structurally damaged and unable to live up to the relentless demands of the game. Though he was bitterly disappointed, the accident neither deterred nor diluted his interest in the game. He hadn't missed a tournament at Wimbledon since his first year at Eton, and he didn't plan on missing any in the future.

In fact, the accident spurred him on to become involved in the sport in other ways, and sparked his interest in the players moving up through the rank and file. He knew many of the players personally, and he began to learn what motivated them, when they had their off days and on days, and where they derived their desire to win.

Suddenly he was intrigued by the game for completely different reasons, as his mathematical brain took over and he developed a program called 'Junior Jousts' for betting on each of the players. His father fully supported and funded his first foray into sports gambling. It was so successful his father applied a similar mathematical model to identify arbitrage opportunities for professional sports and the money came rolling in. Why? some asked. His father responded simply. 'Because it is Caesar's destiny.

He was born under a star where winning is the only way.' Caesar revered Tony, and the most important thing in his life was to continue to make his father proud.

* * *

Caesar was now in his forties, and still attended every grand slam, never short of a jaunty handkerchief and cravat to complement his impeccable hand-tailored suits and glistening polished shoes. He made a point of establishing a connection with each of the top ten players in the world at any given time, engineering reasons to meet up with them more regularly. That way he came to know them very personally – just as some horse-racing punters build steam rooms in their homes to become better acquainted with jockeys. This close association was the reason why he was able to sign most of the top players up with his elite agency.

Even though The Edge employed dedicated staff to look after his clients' every whim and sponsorship deals, Caesar liked to provide a more personalised service. It was important to him that the players had direct access to him – not a relationship per se but certainly an identifiable association. So he offered them excellent rates to stay in his luxurious hotels and to be seen in his glamorous entertainment and gambling establishments, usually in his company.

His motive was undeniably twofold. Not only did he derive great personal pleasure from being directly connected with the greats of tennis stardom, but at the end of the day, it also made good business sense and gave him ultimate control over the players he endorsed.

Yet most of all, he was passionate about testing his automated betting models against his personal insights into each player's capabilities and state of mind. And that was why he so enjoyed the obscenely sized individual bets he made with his billionaire friends in their secretive 'Club Zero' aptly named for the number of zeroes that accompanied each transaction – often on par with the size of the egos placing them! Caesar's gambling was as highly informed as it could be, since on some occasions the bets placed entire companies at stake. Companies Caesar strategically pursued for his ever-expanding empire.

The only other part of his life that kept him engaged – in a non-business sense – was his philanthropic interest in the Royal Ballet. Some called it his hobby. The beauty and graceful movement of the dancers provided him with a sense of serenity he didn't experience elsewhere. Perhaps it was a way to make up for the lack of feminine energy in his father's male-dominated world? No one was sure … nevertheless, his substantial contributions to the Ballet's Benevolent Fund had secured his prestigious invitation to become a member of the Board of Trustees. Accepting this role meant he had access to the ears of London's high society, not to mention association with the aristocracy – lords, baronesses and even HRH the Prince of Wales and Her Majesty the Queen (who disappointingly had no interest in tennis whatsoever, but fortunately was an avid patron of the arts).

To know Caesar, you had to know three things. First, his father was the ultimate role model in his life. Second, tennis was his absolute passion. And third, his love of ballet was his greatest pastime. Other than the finer things in life his bank balance could afford, he treated everything else with absolute disdain.

Eloise

To those in the know, Eloise Lawrance was the latest up-and-coming star on Britain's ballet scene, and had just been chosen to dance the lead in *Swan Lake*. Her movements were technically perfect, her timing precise, and due to her young age perhaps she could be forgiven for lacking a little passion or soul in her otherwise flawless performances.

Eloise was uniquely beautiful, though she only ever saw the imperfections in herself. Men and women alike were attracted to her fragile radiance, but she never noticed their attentions. She wished her fingers were a little longer and her feet were more delicate, but most of all she longed for her hair to be manageable and straight – which was why she seldom wore it out. Her soft translucent skin only caused her frustration, as she could never go out in the sun without it freckling, and she believed her aquamarine eyes were too big for her heart-shaped face, instead of seeing them as her most distinctive feature. At least her body proved to have excellent proportions for a ballerina, though she would have preferred a tad more height.

Yet Eloise had long ago relinquished all rights to her own body. Her diet was strictly controlled so she maintained the delicate balance between her fear of putting on even one additional pound of weight, and ensuring she had the stamina to endure the demanding twelve-hour days. Adept at being weighed, pinched, probed and analysed on a regular basis, she was more than skilled at detaching herself from her physical form. Every measurement had to be recorded in detail; even 'point to point' (the distance between her nipples) was noted for each new ballet performance. She liked the way others took control so she could focus solely on her craft, her one creative outlet. In her mind, her body was only a means to an end; merely an instrument to enable her to dance.

She was a quiet, reserved person, not exactly shy but certainly not outgoing. Although she was friendly enough when spoken to, she preferred to keep to herself and didn't have many friends. Being in the ballet meant that her opportunity to form any real friendships was limited, for in her mind the other ballerinas were all potential threats who could unravel her dream – something she was fiercely determined to protect. She had been ensconced within the realm of ballet for more than a decade and it had protected her from the harsh realities of the outside world. She had experienced this world in her youth, and had no desire to revisit such a heartless place again.

So she never raised her voice or caused any trouble, instead choosing to focus on listening intently to what was required of her. She appreciated the calm passivity of conforming with her ballet masters' strict requirements – with the aim of always exceeding their demanding standards. And from her perspective, this compliance had finally paid off.

Earlier this year, Eloise had been proudly announced as Principal of the Royal Ballet. Everything she had worked for with utmost focus and physical dedication had finally been acclaimed by her esteemed ballet mistresses and masters, and endorsed by the Board. Striving for such recognition had given her the drive to ensure she was as close to perfect as she could be since arriving as a student at the Royal Ballet School aged twelve. Throughout her teenage years, she had never socialised if it interfered with her studies, rarely succumbing to potential suitors, who would no doubt distract her from achieving her dream.

Now she – and everyone else – knew that her dedication to the art of ballet had been worth it. For she was the best; she was Number One. All of the other girls would aspire to be like her, to act like her, dance like her, *be* her. It provided her with an identity she had never had before. And she loved it!

But even though she had reached the pinnacle of all she'd ever wanted to achieve, before each performance, the fear of losing everything crept insidiously into her thoughts. Fortunately, she had become adept at forcing her mind outwards – to focus on the rapt applause she would hear from all over the darkened theatre at the end of each act, and the beautiful flowers she would receive at the end of the performance, rather than on the lonely holes in her emotional life. After all, to show fear was to admit weakness, which she saw as a dreadful imperfection. Imperfect was something a prima ballerina would never be.

Staring into the mirror on the opening night of *Swan Lake*, she saw a vision of what she was about to become onstage. She had discarded the loose grey sweats that usually covered every inch of her feminine body, and her wild auburn mane was now tightly restrained and unrecognisable beneath an elaborate headpiece. She liked the fact that her pert lips were artificially red and her aquamarine eyes were buried beneath a swathe of dramatic black make-up. The headpiece accentuated her neck – long and supple, as a swan's should be – and her striking costume and feathers miraculously gave her the birdlike qualities that would see her fly onstage. And though she was petite, at five foot four, she knew she would become larger than life in order to do whatever the ballet required of her.

She had come from nothing to being the most revered person in every performance. She lived for this feeling and for this feeling alone. When she danced beneath the heady lights, she was as close to home as she had ever been. It was the only sense of belonging she had ever experienced, and she would cling to it for dear life. For to fail now, when she had reached the peak of her career at twenty-two, would destroy her. To fail was intolerable. She had dedicated her life to perfection and there would be no turning back.

So, drawing her dramatic eyes away from the vision in the mirror as the announcement was made for her to make her way to the stage, she completed the ritual she performed before every performance. She sat down, placed both her hands on top of a small, worn music box and closed her eyes. After a moment of quiet meditation, she opened the box and watched as the tiny ballerina swirled around and around, to the tune of 'Music Box Dancer'.

Eloise imagined herself as the ballerina, who only ever truly came to life when the box was open and provided her with an opportunity to dance. Absorbed by the music and the tiny dancer's pirouettes, Eloise transformed into the tragic heroine Odette, losing all sense of self in the process.

She turned and made her way to the stage, to give the performance of a lifetime to her many admirers – knowing the music box would only be closed after the final curtain was drawn, and be safely packed away until next time.

Ballet

Caesar's relationship with Ivan Borisov dated back to the days when Ivan was a junior tennis champion. Now Ivan was Number One in the rankings of the Association of Tennis Professionals (ATP), and had been for the past two and a half years. Ivan was a client of The Edge, but his passion for ballet – as insatiable as Caesar's own – ensured their friendship went much deeper than the connection Caesar shared with the other top players.

Ballet was in Ivan's blood, which was why Caesar found their discussions on the topic so engaging. Ivan's mother had been a prima ballerina in her youth, and still taught ballet in St Petersburg. Ivan had grown up around dance and could easily have made it his career, had his tennis not been identified as such a strength; comparatively, ballet was a new discovery for Caesar.

The two men met up at performances of the Royal Ballet as often as their schedules allowed. It was on one such evening, after the final curtain call of Tchaikovsky's *Swan Lake* at the Royal Opera House in Covent Garden, that Ivan turned to Caesar and commented: 'I've seen this ballet on many occasions around the world, and never have I been so captivated by the ballerina dancing the lead roles of Odette and Odile. Yet she seems so young.'

Caesar nodded. 'Indeed. *Swan Lake* is her first performance as Principal of the Royal Ballet. Her name is Eloise Lawrance. She's one of our own, actually; studied at the Royal Ballet School.'

Ivan's eyes shone with enthusiasm. 'She is just beautiful; she illuminates the entire stage. The precision of her movements is a joy to watch, simply bewitching.'

'It appears you are attracted in ballet to what you illustrate on the court, Ivan.' Caesar's features creased into a smile, which Ivan returned.

'You're being way too kind, Caesar. My mother, perhaps, but I'm afraid I have no such elegance.'

'Until recently, no one could even get close to winning against you,' Caesar observed, moving the conversation on to his other favourite subject.

'I know, Caesar, you're right.' Ivan sighed. 'It all depends on motivation, and I seem to have lost mine recently – which is why I didn't compete in the Australian Open this year.'

'You know better than I that it was a huge risk to take with your ranking; luckily your sponsors didn't ask too many questions. The other top seeded players are all hungry to close in on you like a pack of wolves. Any thoughts on what you're going to do to stay on top?'

'In all honesty I'm not sure. All I know is these days, if I have to choose between training and ballet … well, as you can see, I'm here, aren't I? Which is not such a good thing for the world Number One, is it?'

He shook his head as if to answer his own words.

'Please understand,' he went on, 'I still enjoy it, but the monotony of training is getting to me. I go through the motions but my mind is in another world – like a swimmer focusing on the relentless black line at the bottom of the pool, no longer able to see the big picture. And all my commitments *off* the court … You know I dislike having to appear smiling in front of cameras for sponsors – making sure my watch is positioned just so – I'm just bored with all of it. I feel like I've already achieved what I set out to do.'

'If you like, I can organise to reduce your commitments and free up more of your time – if that's what it'll take to get you back on form. Just a couple of calls, no problem.'

'Believe me, I know if anyone can, you can, Caesar. But it's not just that …' Ivan reflected a moment longer then gestured towards the stage. 'My heart is in *this* world, in dance and music and beauty, just what I have witnessed tonight. Now that I have seen Eloise – that was her name, yes?'

Caesar nodded.

'Well, now that I've seen her onstage, it makes me want to attend every one of her performances. I know I shouldn't feel this way – I should be focusing on my training – but there's something about that exactness, that discipline she has over her mind and body …' His thoughts meandered before he added, 'If I could only capture a performance like that before I play – you know, bottle it up somehow – I have no doubt that my motivation would be sky-high.' He sighed again, suddenly disheartened by the absurdity of his own suggestion. 'But instead I must wait until her next performance like everyone else.'

Caesar looked thoughtful. 'Are you saying you believe watching her dance before you play would improve your motivation?'

'How could it not? Look at her! I'm sure I'm not the only one who would feel this way. There's something captivating about the way she moves, like she brings the essence of the music to life … Well, if I could just bottle up a bit of ballet for my own personal use, that would be perfect.' Ivan laughed, then added with a wink, 'I know you are a resourceful man who is capable of many things, Mr King, but I doubt this is a problem you can solve. If you do come up with the answer, let me know; I'd love to hear about it.' He chuckled at the path their conversation had taken, amiably patting Caesar on the back.

'A fascinating challenge, just fascinating. In the meantime, my friend, come backstage with me, and I'll see if I can introduce you to Eloise and the rest of the *corps de ballet*.'

'Thank you but unfortunately I must be on my way, yet another plane to catch. Thanks for the chat. I shall look forward to seeing you again at another one of her performances.'

As the two men bid each other farewell, Caesar's intrigued mind was clicking into gear, working on a variety of scenarios based on Ivan's sketchy idea.

If Ivan could not manage to consolidate his position as the world's Number One, men's tennis would enter one of its most unpredictable eras. The Edge currently managed the top six male players in the world, which provided Caesar with tremendous insights into what was happening on the circuit – leading to substantial business opportunities.

The more inside information Caesar had, the more money he stood to make. And once an idea had seeded in his mind, it was rarely dislodged – particularly if it was coupled with a fire in his belly. There was no doubt this conversation had ignited the flame of an idea for Caesar and it was usually only ever a matter of time before it came to full fruition.

The Offer

Manon

All the dancers of the Royal Ballet had eagerly gathered in the narrow corridor, anxiously awaiting the announcement of their roles in Sir Kenneth MacMillan's *Manon*, widely acclaimed as one of the company's signature ballets. For most ballerinas, dancing the coveted role of *Manon* was deemed to be one of the highlights of their career. The ballet told the story of a young woman torn between the man she loves and a wealthy older suitor who promises her the luxury she craves. The character must exhibit various states of emotion – ranging from shy to flirtatious, from desperate love to the agonies of an eventual wretched death – all captured within the realms of dance. The demands on the ballet dancer were extreme, requiring almost exhaustive physical and emotional stamina.

Eloise was returning from the ballet's physiotherapist, having been dismissed by Madame Alana from the morning class when she landed badly on her ankle during her *sissonne* jumps, and was immediately drawn to the buzz of activity surrounding the notice board. When she approached the other dancers, the bustle around her immediately faded to silence as the weight of her reaction hung heavily in the air.

As she registered the black names listed on the white paper, she stared uncomprehendingly at the notice board, her eyes anchored to it as though she were paralysed in the worst nightmare of her life.

Not a sound could be heard other than Eloise's breath slowly inhaling and exhaling through her nostrils ... until a muffled, strangled scream passed through her pursed lips.

The dancers scattered in panic as though a large stone had been thrown amidst a flock of flamingos, their scarves and tutus fluttering and floating to the floor like feathers post-flight. They dispersed as quickly as they had assembled in an attempt to avoid what they all knew would be the eye of the foreboding storm.

In what should have been the triumph of her career, Eloise had been usurped by a Russian impostor.

Principal: Natalia Karsavina
Soloist: Eloise Lawrance

Eloise noticed her hands trembling, before she actually felt them lightly touch the bold print where she had expected to see her name. Her entire body went numb, not allowing her to feel the emotion she knew was brewing beneath her skin. Life swirled on around her, but it didn't seem to touch her. She was present, but in her mind she was not really there. This had to be false – a prank perhaps? But no one could be that cruel; ballet dancers were finely honed creatures, physically strong yet their self-esteem so very fragile.

How could it be? Her life's work – had it honestly come to this? How could she face her peers in light of this demotion? How could she face the world? *She* was the Principal of the Royal Ballet, not Natalia! They might as well have broken her legs, such was the pain in her heart.

The force that had driven her for years to study, to practise, to hone her skills hour after hour, day after day, all ultimately heading to the role of top ballerina at one of the greatest ballet companies the world had known, all had come to nothing, because the role she had aspired to had been cruelly snatched from beneath her wings. Although she had always loved *Swan Lake*, *Sleeping Beauty* and *The Nutcracker*, she had done them all to death, the movements so deeply entrenched in her muscles that she barely needed to engage her brain as they toured around the world doing one performance after another. *Manon* had been her opportunity to challenge, interpret and ultimately shine – to firmly establish herself in the history of the Royal Ballet as Number One for this day and age.

Eloise fell in a crumpled heap onto the cold concrete floor, as the pain of disappointment crashed over her limbs. They had finally broken her spirit, snapped it in half.

Though she was so often complimented on her demure presence, controlled emotions and grace, both on and offstage, suddenly uncontainable anger ripped through her veins and she got up and tore the menacing announcement from the notice board then charged along the corridor and up the stairs.

The futility of her years of silence, acquiescence and unswerving commitment suddenly seemed to burst the synapses of her brain. How dare some young Russian upstart from the Bolshoi Ballet replace her! Just because the company had recently appointed a new renegade choreographer, Xavier, who preferred the Russian dancer's style and chutzpah! It was *she* who was the lead ballerina of this company, *she* who had been classically trained at this very school for more than a decade, *she* who had only just been promoted to the iconic position of Principal. Unfortunately, it was also *she* who had nothing else to live for now the role of her career had been snatched away …

Unaccustomed to not being in control of her emotions, Eloise was seething as she threw open the door of the company director's office unannounced. Her slight frame trembled as she stared daggers at Sir Lloyd Barclay.

He could barely make eye contact as he shifted hastily from behind his desk to close the door discreetly behind her.

'Ah, Eloise, I'm assuming you have seen the cast sheet.'

As he uttered the words she saw her life shatter into tiny pieces before her eyes.

'That was *my* role, Lloyd! It was promised to *me*!'

With uncharacteristic vengefulness she pinned the piece of paper to his chest with her finger, though it merely floated to the floor as he stepped back behind his desk, which provided him with a physical barrier of authority and immediately diluted the emotive force between them.

Lloyd still avoided looking at her. 'That's nonsense, my dear. You know as well as I that nothing is guaranteed in this business, and that disappointment is part and parcel of being a dancer. Someone with your experience knows that anything can change at a moment's notice. Naturally, this is hard news for you to take in, but you will still be Natalia's understudy, of course, and –'

His words permeated her thoughts. *But the Royal Ballet isn't business; it is art, culture and beauty. It's my entire life!*

For the first time ever, she wasted not a moment in interrupting him.

'I will *not* tolerate being the understudy or a soloist. You know I don't deserve such a demotion. The role of Manon was mine, anything less is insulting!'

She furiously spat the words towards him, astounding herself with her aggressive behaviour. She had never spoken an angry word to anyone in her life, having always kept a tight lid on her emotions until they could be expressed onstage via another character.

Lloyd seemed to change tack. 'Under normal circumstances I would agree with you, Eloise. But you know as well as I that this role is demanding – both emotionally and physically. It will put your ankle under too much strain. We can't take the risk, and, well, decisions have to be made and, ah, well, have been, I'm afraid – as you have seen.' His facial expression tensed then softened in an attempt to placate her fury.

'My ankle has nothing to do with this!'

'You need to be patient, my dear – give Xavier some time to understand your true talent and your body time to heal.'

'Then why isn't he giving me the chance to prove that the role should be mine? You know I can dance through pain. It has *never* affected my performance.'

Even though they weren't particularly close, Eloise had always considered Sir Lloyd her ally, her dancing guardian, almost like the grandfather she had never known. Now the person before her seemed nothing more than a condescending old man determined to destroy her career.

Eloise took a deep breath to ensure her voice was measured. She could barely whisper her next words, her anger – or was it fear? – barely contained beneath the surface of her skin.

'I know my ankle isn't the real reason, Lloyd. *You owe me the truth.*'

'Well … you have to understand that this is Xavier's first ballet with us. He is looking for more depth and emotion, I suppose, for a role like this. He believes Natalia has your technical ability … but also dances with more passion and verve. It's in her genes. She has more life experience to draw upon for the complex role of Manon.'

He rose from behind his desk and placed his hand on her shoulder, which she deftly shrugged off. He shook his head, not sure what to do next. He, like everyone else, had never encountered this side of Eloise. Up until now she had always addressed him with deference.

The more Lloyd tried to convince her of the wisdom of Xavier's decision, the more blurred his words became to Eloise as his voice faded into the background of her mind.

'Natalia has more grit … edge … emotional depth …

'We know you are technically brilliant but your desire for perfection and control is inhibiting your performance …

'Ballet has been your entire life for more than a decade … Perhaps you should take a break if you're not content with being a soloist … explore something new for a while … get some perspective … At twenty-two there's still time to find yourself, discover who you really are, what you truly want in life … I'd be more than happy to approve a leave of absence given how upset you are …'

I am a ballerina.

It's who I am.

It's all I ever want to be.

I am a ballerina.

This mantra was on replay in her head like an old-fashioned broken record as his monologue continued chipping away at her depleted ego.

'There are so many bright, talented dancers currently rising through the ranks, and oh, the Russians, their skill, their grace, their exquisite beauty …'

Eloise imploded emotionally. Her deeply rooted feelings of never having truly belonged were allowed free rein to retranslate his words in her brain.

I am ugly!

I am imperfect!

I lack grace!

Ballet was all Eloise knew. Since before she could remember she had devoted every waking moment to becoming the perfect ballerina. *Prima Ballerina!* she screamed in her mind. *Not Number*

Two, not Number Three. Number One! The Principal Ballerina of the Royal Ballet and she made it, only to have it abruptly snatched away because one man – Xavier Gemmel – preferred Russian dancers over her.

Her peers sometimes thought her myopic mindset was a little naive and unrealistic and they encouraged her to socialise more with them, live a little. She became determined to prove to them that dedication such as hers was what enabled success, and anything less would result in failure – and she had proved exactly that. Until now!

How could she face them now? What would they think? Would they agree with Sir Lloyd's and Xavier's decision to demote her, sniggering behind her back, thankful that they hadn't been as invested as she? Of course they would! Long ago she had removed herself from the pettiness of their discussions to focus on perfecting her craft so she could turn it into majestic art. She was a child when she arrived and now it was as though the only family she had ever known were rejecting her – spitting her out of the only place she had ever belonged.

Her mind closed down, blocking out the last of Sir Lloyd's words, and her body took over.

She was unaware of her own movements as she held her head high, refusing to cast her eyes back on the life she was heartbreakingly leaving behind. She gathered her few belongings as if on autopilot, not noticing any of the commotion around her as she reached the corridor. The voices pleading with her to stay, to calm down and talk to them might as well have been thousands of miles away, they were so muffled in her mind.

She gingerly placed her beloved music box in her bag, not daring to capture a glimpse of herself in the mirror, lest she embed the image of the broken failure she had become.

The doors slammed behind her as the London chill slapped her face, colouring her cheeks. It was cold enough for the tears her heart had been trying to keep at bay to freeze like crystals on her face.

Even as she maintained her outward composure, she could feel herself shattering further on the inside as each moment passed. She defensively wrapped her faux fur jacket around her body and hailed the first cab she saw, directing the driver to Russell Square to her empty, lonely apartment – desperate to distance herself as quickly as possible from the complete betrayal by those she had once trusted so completely.

The steaming hot shower did nothing to diminish the chill in her bones. What was she to do now? She was used to a life of travel, going to the most beautiful cities the world had to offer, dancing in theatres steeped in history. Admittedly, the busy, nomadic lifestyle sounded more luxurious than it was in reality, but it suited her perfectly. It provided her with her only opportunity to feel truly alive – when she was dancing centre stage.

Her life as a ballet dancer had given her a reason to wake up each morning and ensured she went to bed exhausted each night. It had protected, cherished and disciplined her. Now, she felt the enormity of how alone she truly was in the world. She had no one and belonged nowhere. She was left with nothing but a crushed heart and the vast nothingness of the wasted dreams of her youth.

In the depths of despair, she felt herself slip away from the world in the days that followed. Time was of no consequence, as she lay bereft in her minuscule apartment. There was no food in her fridge, nothing of substance in her barely used kitchen cupboard – not that she cared to eat anything. She could starve to death and not a single person in the world would be any the wiser about her now insignificant existence. She felt more alone than she had in her entire life.

The only thing that eventually managed to distract her from her desolation was the incessant ringing of the phone somewhere in the background of her clouded mind. When she finally went to answer it, she noticed a shiny pale gold envelope almost lost amidst the pile of scattered mail near the front door.

Both the envelope and the phone call had the potential to signify the end of her old life, and catapult her into an entirely unfathomable new world.

Tate

'Caesar King requests the pleasure of your company for lunch at the Tate Modern,' his personal assistant explained rather pompously to Eloise over the phone. When she opened the gold envelope, it contained a formal invitation along with the personal flurry of his distinctive signature.

Eloise had no idea what to expect when she dressed that morning. Her entire wardrobe consisted of the baggy trousers and sweat shirts she wore over her ballet clothes, some jeans and T-shirts for Sundays – her only day off each week – a denim jacket, her faux fur coat and a few evening dresses for when she changed after performances to meet visiting dignitaries.

Given she had no idea what the dress code would be, she was forced out of the house to quickly purchase a formal knee-length skirt and neat floral blouse from Zara, as well as a small attaché case. She loosely pulled her unruly hair into a braid, grabbed her jacket from the hook by the door, then set out for her mysterious meeting with the renowned billionaire.

After a short Tube ride Eloise arrived at the Tate Modern more than an hour before her scheduled meeting, hoping that wandering around the magnificent works of art would provide the necessary distraction to calm her rising apprehension. She would have given anything to have had something else on today, anything rather than meeting Caesar King at this famous art gallery on the Thames …

But she didn't have an excuse *not* to go, and what was worse was that he knew she didn't.

Even beyond his connection with the Royal Ballet, she knew of the illustrious Caesar King. And everyone knew that when Caesar called, you answered. The only problem was that neither the phone call nor the gold-embossed invitation she had received had provided any clue as to why he would want to meet with her. Although it did manage to pique her interest enough to temporarily suspend her state of misery.

Deep down she secretly hoped Sir Lloyd had asked him to check up on her, maybe even offer her her position back, but she knew she was hoping against hope and that Natalia would be Principal for the foreseeable future. Unless she was prepared to play second fiddle – which she most certainly was not – her future with the Royal Ballet seemed doomed.

As the time of the meeting approached she was sorely tempted to run in the opposite direction. She hadn't seen or spoken to anyone since her demise and was still in a precarious emotional state. But just as she was considering retreating back home, the great man himself appeared, saying farewell to his guests from his previous meeting. He cheerfully greeted a nervous Eloise, whose palms had suddenly broken into a warm sweat.

As far as she could remember, she had only briefly made Caesar's acquaintance at one of the Royal Ballet's gala performances where the senior dancers were required to socialise with benefactors and the Board of Trustees. His well-known Italian–American heritage contrasted with his upper-crust English accent, and he was better looking, fitter and more polished in real life than the way he was portrayed in the tabloids (which was usually with a drink in his hand). But more than anything it was his charisma that was evident from the moment he walked into the entrance hall. It took her by storm.

'Thank you so much for meeting me, Eloise. After you.' He gestured for her to precede him into the lift. 'We'll go up to the restaurant on the seventh floor.'

Although she had visited the gallery, Eloise had never dined on the seventh floor. The views of London over the Millennium Bridge were breathtaking as she settled into her plush seat in the private room. She was pleased she had worn a formal skirt and blouse rather than more casual attire, given that Caesar was dressed in a navy suit with his trademark cravat and handkerchief; today's colour was cerise.

'I hope you don't mind, I've ordered lunch for us. Would you like a cocktail to start, or perhaps some champagne?' He raised his eyebrows, awaiting her answer.

If Eloise had been nervous before, she was practically speechless now. Apparently a cup of tea wasn't on the agenda, she thought anxiously, still unable to believe she was meeting with Caesar *alone* and still hadn't so much as uttered a word.

'I, ah, I'm not sure ...'

'We'll start with two bellinis, I think, Max, and take it from there.'

'Certainly, sir.' The waiter silently disappeared, closing the door behind him.

'Now, I suppose you're wondering why I've asked you here,' he began, his smile broadening.

'The thought *has* crossed my mind, Mr King.' Eloise was relieved when her first words came out more smoothly in reality than she'd imagined them in her mind.

'Please, call me Caesar. I've no doubt it has. But before I get to that matter, let me just say how sorry I am that you're not currently dancing with the Royal Ballet. You are such an extraordinary ballerina; it is definitely our loss.'

Eloise had been dreading discussing this, but had known it would be unavoidable given Caesar's active involvement in the company.

'Thank you,' was all she said in reply.

'So tell me, do you have any plans for your immediate future?'

It took Eloise a moment or two to answer. 'To be honest, I haven't given anything much thought since walking out. I realise I'll need to soon …'

'I know this is out of left field, but your future is the very subject I'd like to discuss over the course of this lunch. I have a proposal I want you to consider. But let's get to know each other a little better first, shall we?'

Eloise agreed, still unsure where any of this was headed.

'How about I start with a little bit about me?'

'Sure, sounds good.' Eloise was grateful he was taking charge, given her level of discomfort with the whole setting.

If there was one thing Caesar was great at – and loved – it was talking about himself until other people relaxed around him, and he didn't mind how long it took. He was a patient man when it served him to be.

Eloise listened attentively, politely at first and then with fascination at the twists and turns his life had taken. Caesar's passion for tennis and ballet was obvious, as his eyes lit up and his gestures became more animated whenever he mentioned these topics. Before long, Eloise was completely engaged, laughing at his stories and hanging on his every word. Looking down at her plate, she was surprised to see that she had already finished her lunch. Caesar filled up her glass for the second time with a crisp Pouilly-Fuissé, which she found delicious even though she rarely drank. It didn't take her long to realise that it was far simpler to go with the flow of all things Caesar, and he was never slow in taking the lead in the conversation – which suited her no end.

'So, tell me about yourself now that I've disclosed most of my life to you.'

'Mine isn't nearly as interesting. Up until recently it was pretty much ballet, ballet, ballet … Now I don't know what it is.' She forced herself to swallow the tears these words evoked.

'Tell me more, I'm all ears.'

As stoically as she could, Eloise described her childhood of foster care and her thrill of being accepted at age twelve to study ballet at White Lodge, home of the Royal Ballet School: something that had changed her life. It was the first time she had verbalised her bitter disappointment about *Manon*, and once she'd started she couldn't stop.

Caesar observed her as she disclosed the bare bones of her life story, knowing they were nothing more than scraps. He already had a file compiled on her life, so didn't press for the details she avoided, and which he already knew. He merely took notice of what she left out and her mannerisms as she spoke, which fascinated him.

The poor child had nothing in her life other than ballet. There were times when she was fighting back her tears and he felt like holding her hand to help her through the pain, but he quickly checked himself. He was depending on her feeling completely abandoned and the plan he had developed hinged entirely on that premise.

'Do you plan to return to the Royal Ballet, Eloise?

She shook her head solemnly, knowing that words might break her.

'But you said yourself, you were given the role of Soloist. It's not as if you were sacked.'

'I will *not* return as Soloist.' Eloise spoke quietly but firmly, and felt anger and disappointment cascading over her crushed heart all over again. She made an effort to rein in her tumultuous emotions; the last thing she wanted was for Caesar to see her like this, though she feared it was already too late.

'So what are you going to do? You must have some idea. You're too gifted to simply walk away. Perhaps you just need some more time to think things through.'

'Dancing is all I have, Caesar. My pride won't let me go back – not after the argument I had with Sir Lloyd. It was made very clear to me that the Russians are the next big thing to hit the ballet world and that being "home grown" is now seen as second-rate.'

'I'm sorry you feel that way, but I understand what you're saying. As you know, our new choreographer, the world-renowned Xavier Gemmel, is on a two-year contract and has the full support of the Board. I'm afraid he has scope to bring in more dancers from Russia, which doesn't help your situation either.'

Caesar watched as Eloise shuffled uncomfortably in her seat, confirming the truth of his words. He often found that succinctly stating the reality of a situation, although difficult for people to hear at the time, had a profound impact on their decisions. It was a strategy he often used to his advantage.

'Maybe I should apply to another company overseas … I'm not sure. I'm not skilled in anything else. And I can't imagine a day without dance in my life.'

'You could apply overseas, but you would need the Board's approval to do so.'

'What do you mean?'

'I'm assuming you've read your contract, Eloise …'

'My contract with the Royal Ballet?'

'It states clearly that you do not have the right to accept a position at another ballet company without the Board's approval. From what I can ascertain from the other trustees, they're looking forward to having you back – albeit as Soloist. In the meantime, I believe Lloyd has approved an extended leave of absence, and you should receive a letter shortly.'

'If Xavier doesn't believe I am good enough to be Principal, I can't return under his leadership. I worked hard to be in that position, but to pretend I can return when Natalia has been promoted to my role is impossible. Xavier is well known in the industry for his nepotism and I'm sure it will only get worse during his tenure.'

'Unfortunately I can't disagree with you there. This issue was discussed at length before he was appointed. We all knew what we were getting into. So let me ask you this: if you *aren't* returning to the Royal Ballet under the current conditions and you are unable to dance elsewhere, what exactly are you going to do, pray tell?'

Caesar couldn't deny that right now he felt like the cat circling the canary whose cage door was open – she was such a delicate little bird – but he'd learnt from experience that it was far more effective to let people work through their feelings. At least then they believed they were making their own decision rather than being masterfully manipulated towards his end game, as was usually the case.

Eloise felt as desolate as she had the day she walked out of the ballet on hearing Caesar's words. Her current situation was almost too much for her to bear.

'I just want to dance,' she replied at last. 'I do think I need some distance from the Royal Ballet, but I have no idea how to go about it.'

That was the cue Caesar had been waiting for, and if truth be told, he'd had enough theatrics for one day. So he wasted no time in cutting to the chase.

'Then I'm hoping that's where *I* may be able to help. I would like to make you an offer and I'm hoping you'll consider it very seriously. It is something I have put much thought into and I hope it is of equal advantage to both of us. It will guarantee your financial independence – but I won't lie to you: nothing in this life comes without a price.'

He took a moment to open his Italian leather briefcase, removed a manila envelope with her name on it and slid it across the table towards her.

'Essentially it means that you would contract yourself to *me* for the next two years.'

If Eloise had been desolate a moment ago, she was in shock now.

'What?' She stared at him wide-eyed. 'Why me?'

'Because you are financially vulnerable, and you are a magnificent dancer whose skills should be allowed to develop – even if away from structured ballet. You are a beautiful young woman whose life has barely begun – even though you think it is over. I am in a position to provide you with a lifestyle that surpasses what you had with the ballet and surrounds you with athletes who are the top of their field. But I need your personal commitment for two years. After that, Xavier's term with the Royal Ballet will be complete, you will have just turned twenty-four, with more life experience than you've ever imagined and, well, let's just say who knows what your future may hold?'

He looked directly into her enormous, dewy eyes, giving her time for his words to sink in.

'I don't know what to say ...' Eloise wondered whether she was trapped in a warped dream or perhaps it was a nightmare; she couldn't decide which.

'I completely understand this may come as a surprise, so let me explain my proposal, the specific details of which are inside that envelope.'

Eloise's dessert – once again, pre-ordered by Caesar – arrived just as he was relating his discussion with Ivan Borisov. Eloise had vaguely heard of Ivan on the sports news, but was far more impressed that his mother was the famous ballerina Anna Alexandrava.

'Ivan is Number One in the tennis world, and for the moment, it's not in my interests to see him lose that coveted position. He believes that having you dance for him before every match would bring back his motivation and passion for the game. It may or it may not; only time will tell. I know that you are feeling dejected about losing your own role as Principal, but I'm hoping I can make you an offer too good to refuse. I'm calling it my "Number One Strategy". Although I'd oversee the arrangement, to cover all expenses and ensure that the conditions of the contract were being met, you would become accountable to the top-ranked male tennis player. You would travel with him around the world and essentially he would become your new "Master" – to use a term familiar to you. It would be up to both of you to agree on the terms of your relationship.' He paused. 'Do you have any questions so far?'

'My new Master?' She couldn't remotely fathom why this piqued her interest.

'In my opinion, the most successful tennis players tend to be dominant and controlling – the game demands these characteristics of its champions. Just as you, to the best of my knowledge, are submissive by nature, which drives your perfection in ballet. Professional ballet dancers must adhere to the rules of the dance and depend on certain boundaries. By all reports, you perform at your best under the strict demands of your masters and mistresses.'

There was no doubting Caesar had certainly done his research thoroughly as he paused to watch all the colour drain from Eloise's face, when just moments ago it had been flushed. He smiled as he continued, congratulating himself again on his choice. She was even more perfect for the role than she had appeared on paper, and so very easy to read – an open book in every sense.

'It will be up to both of you to negotiate the parameters of your relationship. This will be an important discussion, as your respective lawyers would then draw up the terms of your agreement, which of course I would require you to uphold.'

'And by parameters you mean what exactly?'

'The rules that define and determine your relationship.'

'So I would negotiate this with Ivan?'

'You would negotiate this with whoever was Number One, as per the ATP's – the Association of Tennis Professionals – rankings. Currently this is Ivan, and he is very keen for you to be his private ballerina.'

'Oh, I see. So the contract would be with you for two years but my agreement would be negotiated separately with each Number One during that timeframe?'

'Exactly.' Caesar was pleased she seemed to be catching on.

'And would my relationship with the Number One ever be more than dancing?'

She had to ask; it needed to be clarified.

'That would be entirely up to you, but you should be prepared for the possibility. It is certainly not my aim to place you in a situation that isn't consensual. That is why the agreement between you is such an important step in the process. Of course I can't speak for each Number One; it would be for them to negotiate the boundaries with you. Only then would the specifics form part of the contract.'

'And how do you know they would even agree to such a proposal?'

'I manage the top six male players in the world. I know their lives inside out, more than their nearest and dearest ever will. If Ivan doesn't maintain that position, one of the other five will be Number One. I have included a brief dossier on each of them for you to review before making your decision. I think you will be pleasantly surprised.'

He smiled, almost like the cat that had already swallowed the canary.

'But how do you know that they would even want me in their lives?'

'Believe me, Eloise, I know every one of these men would welcome you into their life in whatever shape the relationship takes. As you know better than anyone, being at the top is lonely and isolating. To have someone who doesn't judge them and understands the pressure of their lives, the need to perform on cue over and over, would be invaluable. It became abundantly obvious to me after my discussion with Ivan. If these elite athletes don't have a partner one hundred per cent dedicated to their career, it's only a matter of time before the stress cracks show and their relationship fails, often affecting every part of their life. I see it time and again. Should you come into their lives, understanding what drives them to be Number One, as you know first-hand, supporting them to achieve, with no strings attached ... do you think they'll knock all that back? You'd be a dream come true!'

The entire situation was too much for Eloise to take in.

'I know it's a lot to absorb, and probably the last thing you were expecting from our meeting today. So I'd really appreciate it if you could read through the information when you go home, consider what I've offered and let me know within the next two days if you are remotely interested. I'd be more than comfortable if you feel you need to experience the lifestyle I'm proposing before committing to anything. If you decide to proceed, the contract between us will be legally binding for the next eight grand slams; there are four a year. You'd start with the French Open in May, then Wimbledon, followed by the US Open, and finally the Australian in January.

'It's a big decision, which I encourage you to consider seriously. And I need to be clear: should you proceed, your life for the next two years will not be your own.' His eyes became lethal for a flicker of a second, right before his tone lightened. 'If you have any more questions whatsoever, just call my direct line.' He handed her his business card.

'Unfortunately, my next meeting is across town and I need to get going. As I said earlier, Eloise, I hope you will consider my offer seriously over the next day or two. I've really enjoyed our time together today and hope we can continue getting to know each other in the near future.'

He stood up, so Eloise followed his lead, and he shook her hand again. Instead of having warm, sweaty palms, now all blood had drained from her fingers, leaving them stone-cold.

'Please feel free to stay here longer if you wish to.' He smiled. 'I'll look forward to hearing from you.'

As he reached the door, he stopped and turned back to face her. 'Don't look so scared, Eloise; life is meant to be an adventure. I hope I've just added to yours.'

'Thank you, Caesar. For lunch, for the chat, for everything.' As she said the words she realised her life now had options she hadn't even imagined a few hours ago. 'I'll be in touch.'

'Good. I'm counting on it!'

On that note, Caesar exited the room, leaving a befuddled Eloise standing in his wake.

Pub

Eloise found a pub just around the corner from the Tate Modern and made the spontaneous decision to pop in: something entirely out of character for her. She needed to calm her nerves and reflect on the puzzling meeting she had just left, and she wasn't ready to go back and sit in her tiny apartment by herself just yet. Though she tried to seem like she belonged in this environment, she looked quite out of place sitting at the bar, and the pint she was hiding behind could not conceal her incongruous elegance and grace.

She told herself that everything in her life was still as miserable as it had been an hour ago, but knew deep down this just wasn't the case. In fact, her life had just become far more intriguing than it had ever been – not that she would openly admit that to herself.

She sat in a daze a million miles away, not quite believing what had just happened to her. She was trying to assimilate the bizarre proposition sitting inside the manila envelope he had given her, when her reverie was interrupted by an unfamiliar voice next to her.

'Penny for your thoughts?'

She looked up into the eyes of a young guy with a mass of brown, shoulder-length, curly hair, a caramel tan and an adorable smile that exposed perfect white teeth and a dimple on each cheek.

'I'm sure you'd rather not know,' Eloise responded flatly, unaccustomed to being spoken to by strange men in public, and preferring not to be disturbed.

'Try me, I'm a good listener. May I?'

Eloise couldn't disguise her shock as he slid his seat closer to hers and ordered a pint from the bar.

'What …? Well … I suppose … why not?'

'Thanks! I'm Liam by the way.'

He extended his hand, and rather than averting her eyes and not responding as would be her usual practice, she couldn't help but smile. His casual friendliness was somewhat contagious. She looked into his honey-coloured eyes and was surprised to see nothing but kindness.

'I'm Eloise. Are you usually like this?'

'I suppose it depends on what you think I'm usually like.'

'I suppose it does!' She laughed, a sound she hadn't heard escape from her mouth for quite some time. It was an unusual sensation. 'I mean, do you usually just sidle up to people you don't know and sit down for a chat?' Eloise knew she had never acquired the social confidence for such outgoing behaviour.

'Why not? Life's short,' he answered simply, before looking at her a little more thoughtfully, noticing her bright aquamarine eyes and long auburn locks, pulled neatly away from her face and secured in a long plait that rested on her shoulder.

'I was just about to leave when you caught my eye. You look a little lost and very alone – and stunning!' She immediately blushed at his directness. 'If we can't reach out to each other as human beings, then what's the point in being alive?'

She was taken aback, both by his outspoken words and by the kind-heartedness they portrayed.

'How do I know you're not Jack the Ripper?'

'To the best of my knowledge Jack the Ripper lived about a hundred years ago, although ...' He paused, pretending to consider ... 'I suppose I *could* be a distant relative.' He took a sip of his beer, taking time to lick the foam from his upper lip. 'But I don't think I have his genes, because I'm one hundred per cent against violence – it goes against my Zen nature – and besides, there are many other things I would prefer to do with a woman, I can assure you, particularly one as beautiful as you.' His cheeky, light-hearted grin returned, along with his dimples.

Eloise caught herself returning the smile. Something about him drew her in, causing goosebumps to appear on her skin, and she shifted in her seat to deflect his searching gaze. In the past, it had only ever been dance that had stirred such arousal in her, but her immediate attraction to him was undeniable. He was gorgeous!

Even though his intentions could be taken as sexual, she felt surprisingly comfortable in his presence and found herself easing into conversation with this flirtatious stranger. The freedom of anonymity was taking her mind off the massive decision she had to make within the next two days.

'So, as I said before: penny for your thoughts?'

'Oh, it's just too complicated and surreal for me to even begin to explain – and anyway, I should really get going. I have a lot I need to work out.'

She stood up from the bar, not really wanting to leave but feeling like she could now face going home to start thinking through Caesar's offer. She could hardly have explained the details of his proposal to a complete stranger, nor even to someone she knew well. So she carefully placed the envelope back in her attaché case.

'You're not finishing your beer?'

'I don't really drink beer – and I don't usually go to pubs either. I just ordered it to fit in.' She smiled sheepishly.

'Right.' He placed some money on the bar and stood up with her. 'Are you walking across the Millennium Bridge?'

She nodded.

'Mind if I join you?'

'You're persistent, aren't you?'

'When I like something I see, absolutely.'

The more Eloise looked at Liam, the cuter he became – like a delicious milky chocolate bar, without the fat content. She gathered up her jacket and attaché case and pondered: *What harm could it do?* She hadn't felt anything like this for a long time, if ever.

'All right, then, why not?'

They both reached for the door handle at the same time, their fingers colliding. He stood firm, holding the door until she'd gone out before him. She noticed he was over six feet tall, and more athletic and muscled than she'd realised when they'd been seated.

'You look like you're dressed for a job interview.' He slipped into an easy stride next to her, even though she was much smaller and wearing heals that slowed her pace.

'I suppose, in hindsight, I could say yes to that.' She shook her head at the thought, wondering if she should consider Caesar's offer that way. She had never had a *real* job before.

'But you're having trouble deciding what to do? Can't be that hard, can it? All of life is an opportunity. Have you talked it over with friends, family?'

'No, not really ...'

She reflected on this. Outside the ballet, she didn't have anyone to confide in or to ask for advice, nor had she ever needed to – her only goal had been to become Principal Ballerina of the Royal Ballet, and everything she'd required to achieve that goal had fallen into place. All she'd ever needed was discipline, dedication, physical and mental stamina and to follow the instructions she was given. That was her entire world: to lose her mind to her body in dance. Her acknowledgment of this reality was disturbing, and suddenly she felt like a very young, inexperienced twenty-two year old who had been thrust into the harsh reality of an unknown world, in which dance played no part.

'It's just that I'm not sure if this is a risk I'm willing to take.'

'Ah, I see. But does the job involve doing something you enjoy?'

'Well, yes, I suppose it does. Just in a different way from what I'm used to.'

'Then how much of a risk can it be? Everything in life is a risk waiting to be turned into an opportunity. Change can be great for us, it can challenge us in unexpected ways. Tell me, what are the upsides of this new role?'

They walked across the steel footbridge and over the Thames as they continued their conversation.

'Dance, travel, lifestyle, security, diversity ...'

'Does it pay well?'

'It would probably set me up for life.'

'So what's the problem?'

'*That's* the problem: I think it's almost too much, that maybe I'm missing something ... and it would mean giving up my ultimate dream of performing on stage for a while.'

'There are many roads to achieving your dreams; I reckon the key is to choose the path that is flowing freely right now and be open to adapting as needed. All you can commit to is to be the best you can be, right now.'

'Are you always so positive?' His sunny attitude was infectious and she couldn't help but let some of it rub off on her.

'Trust me, it's the easiest way to live life. It helps smooth out all the bumps so you can sit back and enjoy the ride.'

'Sounds like you've had some experience at this.'

He nodded, still smiling at her.

'And if it *doesn't* smooth out the bumps?' she asked, suddenly tentative.

He stopped as they came to a crossroads and turned to look into her eyes. 'Then let me know. I'll come and save you.'

His thumb gently caressed her chin, causing her lips to part ever so slightly. The intimacy of his touch astounded her, caught her breath. She shook her head in an attempt to clear it – his gorgeous face staring down at her momentarily clouding her mind.

'I don't even know you; all we've done is talk about me.'

'And I've enjoyed that very much … but unfortunately I'm going to have to dash. I fly to the US tonight.'

'Oh! OK, well have a safe flight.' Disappointment washed over her as the special moment they'd shared evaporated. 'Liam?'

'Yes?'

'Thanks for the chat to a confused stranger.' As she smiled her face lit up, before the concern crept in once again.

'The pleasure has been all mine.' He smiled back. 'Best of luck with your decision.'

'Well, thanks.' She was flummoxed by him. 'And best of luck with the rest of your life.'

'That's the attitude, Elle!' he said with a wink and a smile. No one had ever called her that before. 'Until we meet again …'

He said it as if he were certain they would, deftly placing a European-style kiss on each of her flushed cheeks.

Their eyes met briefly before he winked, turned away and jogged off into the swell of London's human tide, promptly disappearing from her life.

Decision

That night, Eloise couldn't shift the unusual events of the day from her mind. Meeting with Caesar and his bizarre proposal. Her fortuitous albeit brief encounter with Liam. It was as though she had been cast out into the real world for the first time. Her tiny apartment didn't feel quite so lonely and she was surprised that her appetite was back; even after the lunch at the Tate Modern, she was ravenous.

With that thought, she ordered some home delivery of tom yum soup and honey-steamed fish with Asian greens and completely tidied her messy apartment while awaiting the food's arrival, something she hadn't done for weeks while she'd been wallowing in misery.

With food in her stomach, and feeling more emotionally stable than she had for some time, she settled herself onto her bed to read the contents of the offer in detail.

Eight grand slams.

Two years. She could do that. If she was lucky the Russian dominance of ballet would have dissipated by then …

All accommodation and expenses included.

No problems with that, and she could save on London rent.

A three-bedroom apartment in Belgravia, fully transferred into your name at the completion of the contract.

That was really quite unbelievable. After her childhood in foster care, she had never imagined such luxury could be hers without the safety net of ballet. Actually, she hadn't believed she would *ever* own her own place in London, so this was simply incredible. But as she'd said to Liam, what was the catch? She wondered …

An annual payment of £100,000, indexed to inflation for twenty years.

This sounded obscene! Only the best of the best dancers in the world could ever hope to aspire to such a salary, and that would be with endorsements. She wondered whether Caesar had more money than sense.

These two years would give her complete independence.

To realise her dream.

To follow her passion.

To dance!

On *her* terms …

For the rest of her life!

This was the reason she must seriously consider this outrageous offer – even if it was risky…

She suspected that Caesar had more information than he acknowledged about her career and life, and that she had played nicely into his hands. He seemed authentic enough on the surface, but she also sensed – as, she suspected, did many others – an underlying danger that meant the idea of signing a contract with Caesar should never be taken lightly. His influence in Great Britain, at least, was a sticky web entrenched both wide and deep in the business community and beyond. She had no doubt that he was adept at perfecting any number of masks during negotiations, to gain the outcome he desired.

But what did it matter when his offer was so generous? It would more than provide her with a cushioned transition from the secluded world of ballet into the upper echelons of society's elite – so long as she remained locked in his genie bottle for two complete years, to be set free just after her twenty-fourth birthday.

She couldn't deny the feeling that there was also something about his proposal that made her feel special, essentially 'chosen' above all others. Although she didn't understand why Caesar wanted her and only her, there was something about being specifically sought after and needed that soothed her dented soul. More significantly, she would *belong* somewhere – however temporarily – and she needed that more than anything right now, while she felt like she was in freefall.

Eloise had a restless night tossing and turning, imagining the direction her life might take should she accept Caesar's offer. Liam's words continued to penetrate her dreams, intertwined with Caesar's convincing monologue.

The most crystallising of these dreams occurred just before dawn.

The Répétiteur was casting his eagle eyes onstage as Eloise performed her first solo during the final dress rehearsal of Swan Lake. *As she commenced her pirouettes, she felt like she could fly; the flow of the music had taken over her body and she was free from all anxiety as she continued* en pointe. *Around and around her body swirled, her eyes fixated on the small light she used to anchor her spins. Her execution was flawless.*

This was why she danced; when she became the dance she was free from the world. Free from pain and hurt and abandonment, intrinsically connected to the music. Knowing that at last she belonged. Her body was awash with acceptance and love. She was, at long last, at peace with herself.

So absorbed was she in these feelings, feelings she had been searching for her entire life, that she hadn't noticed that the ballet had spontaneously changed from Swan Lake *to* Manon *and she* was suddenly being torn between the wealthy Monsieur G.M. and her lover Des Grieux. She had forgotten the moves as her body was pulled and pushed by the two men fighting over her. She didn't understand the dance, because this wasn't the ballet she had rehearsed over and over for so many years. This dance was different and she had no way of predicting what would come next. She felt as if she were being torn in half by these characters, a pawn in their play. Her arms were stretched painfully in opposite directions as she oscillated between both men, the suddenly violent music tensing her movements as she was thrust into the air by the four strong hands controlling her body.

Time was momentarily frozen, allowing her to perfect her position mid-flight – her legs stretched into a grand jeté with her arms held beautifully in fifth position. Her training kept her mouth closed, as though no physical exertion were required to perform this move. Suddenly the music became ominous as she began her descent. Floating downwards in slow motion, which gave her time to glance towards the floor, she discovered to her horror that no one was there to catch her fall; she was once again alone onstage. She desperately flapped her swan-like wings, before crashing violently onto the floor, her body shattering into a thousand tiny pieces.

The Répétiteur's voice bellowed from the back of the auditorium. 'Get someone from maintenance to clean up this mess and find me the understudy, now! Everyone prepare for the next act.' And clapped his hands loudly.

Eloise watched from afar as the pieces of her broken body were efficiently swept up and discarded in the commercial waste bin in the back alley.

She woke in a panic, her sheets soaked in perspiration. The dream had been as foreboding as it had been nightmarish – and it had rocked her to the core.

She instantly knew she needed to distance herself from the ballet. Taking time for her decision to settle in her bones, she went for a brisk early morning walk before having a shower and eating a light breakfast. Content that her mind was made up, she collected herself and made two phone calls. One was to set up a meeting with a lawyer – Caesar had provided a comprehensive list – and the other was to Caesar himself. It went straight through to voicemail, so she left a message, verbally accepting his offer prior to written consent.

Her life would not be her own for the next two years – but she was forced to acknowledge that it never really had been.

Memories

With a week to prepare for her new life, Eloise gave notice on her studio apartment, accepted the unconditional leave of absence offered to her by the Royal Ballet by post – as she still couldn't bring herself to walk through the doors – and packed up her entire life into a suitcase and two storage boxes. It was a weird sensation seeing all of her belongings crammed into such a small, neat space.

It was almost ten years to the day since Eloise had packed up her life as a child in Australia and moved to London. She'd been both nervous and excited back then, and now she was doing the same thing, but on Caesar's terms. Other than becoming a ballerina, nothing much had changed; she still felt alone, and detached from the world.

As she had many times during her young life, she desperately wished she had someone close to confide in, to share the decision she was making, which would no doubt have a momentous impact on the course of her life. For a brief moment, she allowed her heart to yearn for the mother and father she never had, for the sense of belonging they might have provided, and which she'd never experienced. She opened the lid of her music box, and listened to the familiar melody as the memories of her past played in her mind …

There had barely been a night when the box hadn't been by her bedside, inspiring her to continued greatness as a dancer, and reminding her of the only times when she felt free from the heaviness of her narrow life. Her music box was the only possession that had been with her since she was a baby, and it anchored her to the world. She had treasured it as she went from one foster home to another – until the day she discovered ballet.

From that point on, Eloise had focused on dancing above all else in her life; it was the only love she knew. Her dedication had finally been repaid when she was offered a place at the prestigious White Lodge, on the outskirts of London. The scholarship she was awarded gave her a real chance to pursue her dream of becoming a principal ballerina. She remembered walking up the grandiose stairs of the beautiful Georgian house in Richmond Park, at the tender age of twelve, and determinedly heading through the large glass doors, leaving her loveless childhood behind her and throwing herself into dance and academic training as a full-time boarder.

Since then, up until a few weeks ago, her life as a ballerina had followed a perfect trajectory. But now everything had changed. She knew she had to be strong; it was time to grow up and face the real world. It was the only way, for there was no one else to cushion her fall.

She remembered all the times she had gone to sleep listening to her music box as she watched the tiny, spinning ballerina with tears in her eyes. Reluctantly, she closed the lid, trapping the tiny dancer in darkness for the foreseeable future. For the first time ever, she was leaving the box behind, breaking the bonds of her past and starting life anew. As she packaged it up carefully, she couldn't bring herself to place it in storage, so she decided to send it to Caesar with a brief note asking him to look after her most precious possession, hoping it might help make their connection to each other a little more personal than a business deal.

She reflected that she herself was just like the tiny ballerina, giving Caesar custody of her life for the next two years. She would reopen the box at the end of those two years, as her life began a new chapter – whatever that might be. The symbol of her past would be the bridge to her future.

Discipline had ensured that she overcame the feelings of grief that had threatened her over the years, and it would do the same today. She took three deep breaths, and forced herself to control her emotions. Finally she was brave enough to close the book on her childhood and embark on her journey into adulthood – or at least, the journey she had allowed Caesar to map out for her.

The black Mercedes was waiting for her on the kerb as she left her apartment for the last time. Without looking back, she politely acknowledged the chauffeur and stepped into the car that would transport her to Heathrow and thrust her into her new world. The practice run in her contract became effective from the moment the car door slammed shut.

Cognac

The past few months had provided Caesar with the perfect opportunity to implement his Number One Strategy. Sir Lloyd's idea of appointing Xavier Gemmel, the exciting new choreographer, and allowing him to bring three ballet dancers with him – one of them being the widely acclaimed Russian Natalia Karsavina – was a random stroke of luck that played right into Caesar's hands. Caesar had used his considerable powers to persuade the other Board members to endorse the proposal, then it had only taken a few phone calls to indirectly threaten the withdrawal of funding should Natalia not be offered the role of Principal in *Manon*. After all, it made sound artistic sense, given that Xavier and Natalia had worked together many times before. It would be far less risky for the Royal Ballet and provide for a smoother transition into the new season. Of course, Sir Lloyd and the Board concurred. The entire operation had been seamless and had taken very little effort to coordinate. Time well spent, from Caesar's point of view.

The fact that Eloise had stormed out of the ballet, emotionally distraught after not having been given the role of *Manon*, had been no surprise to him whatsoever. After all, he had done his research on her life – or at least his people had – and it had become abundantly clear that she was an anchorless ship, cast into the vastness of the ocean with no land in sight. Presenting his offer had been like fishing with a scoop in a goldfish bowl. Some might have thought such a plan heartless and cruel, and perhaps it was, but after all, you don't become rich in this world by caring about other people's feelings.

As Caesar gazed at the music box that had just been delivered to his office, he wondered what the future might hold for Eloise – a young lady with such focus, yet so dependent on the approval of others. He did honestly hope she managed to find more meaning in her life over two years of being thrown into the volatile, competitive world of men's tennis, where there was much to gain and everything to lose. But then again, he could almost say the same of himself, which was why he had the tiniest soft spot for the loneliness that pervaded her life. If he hadn't had his father as such a strong presence, he could see his life might have turned out exactly like that of Eloise Lawrance.

Suddenly he hoped that she might find an anchor, a partner to love – something that he had never managed to secure. He had tried once, failed and been left heartbroken, and he never wanted to experience such pain again.

But if her affections didn't align with his overall strategy, well, naturally there would be consequences. Her life was now in his hands, and as long as she played by his rules all would be well. He hadn't achieved such success by being weaker than his opponents, and anyone who was contracted to him was on a tight leash until they proved they were worthy of his trust, particularly when the stakes were so high. The amount of money he had riding on this strategy was obscene, but it needed to be to make him feel personally vested and inherently alive. For other than the thrill of winning, not too much did these days!

Power and information were the only vices he allowed himself. He'd seen too many men destroy their lives and their fortunes because of their lack of control over their weaknesses – sex, booze, gambling or drugs. He enjoyed all of these, but only on his terms and only ever in moderation.

Reflecting on this, Caesar poured a modest portion of cognac into a crystal balloon and took a rare quiet moment to reflect on how the seeds of an idea had blossomed into this reality. He had shuffled all the cards, dealt his best hand and would now wait patiently to reap the rewards.

THE GRAND SLAMS
Round One

A Peak Performance Creed

If you think you are beaten, you are;
If you think you dare not, you don't;
If you like to win but think you can't, it's almost a cinch you
  won't.
If you think you'll lose, you're lost;
For out in the world we find success begins with a person's
  will;
It's all in the mind.
Life's battles don't always go to the stronger or the faster
  hand;
But sooner or later the person who wins is the one who
  thinks, I can.

FRENCH OPEN I
May–June

Change

Eloise was nonplussed to discover that one of Caesar's staff would accompany her on her first-class flight to meet Ivan in St Petersburg. Her thoughts oscillated between wondering whether Caesar thought she might flee and not fulfil the legal requirements of the contract, and speculating that he now considered her such precious cargo she required one of his keepers to guard her.

It was only when the plane arrived on schedule at Pulkovo Airport that she began to grow curious about what might happen next in her now unpredictable life. She was both excited and nervous about what the future might hold. Other than being aware of Ivan's passion for ballet, she really had no idea what he was like as a person. She couldn't help but ponder whether he was experiencing the same apprehension about her arrival. The only certainty she had was to expect the unexpected as her life unfolded over the coming days, weeks and months.

She watched her suitcase, containing everything she needed for the foreseeable future, being loaded into the car. When the boot slammed shut with a loud thud, she couldn't help but think her fate was being sealed in with it. She was pleased Caesar's people had organised a luxury limousine to collect her rather than the coach that had last taken her through the streets of this majestic city. She had loved performing here, and hoped this time she might have more opportunity to explore its rich history than the ballet tour had allowed.

Caesar had assured Eloise it wasn't important for her to know much about tennis, which was a relief, because she didn't. She had only ever been vaguely aware of the players in the finals of Wimbledon, mainly because she lived in London. What she did know was that from today she would be Ivan's private ballerina. In return, he would be her new Master, for want of a better word, and most importantly, her first Number One.

Any confidence she had had leaving London suddenly evaporated when she alighted from the limousine. She composed herself as best she could before stepping through the doors of Ivan's vast apartment, overlooking the River Neva.

Ivan's maid showed her to her room and she settled in quietly, awaiting further instructions. Eventually she was called to join him for some tea in the lounge room.

Ivan was dressed entirely in black and seemed polished and urbane as he greeted Eloise with a respectful nod, barely brushing her hand with his lips. He was not an ugly man, though his nose was a little too big for his face and his eyes a little too close together. At just under five foot eleven, he was by no means the tallest player on the circuit but he was as lean and athletic as any top sportsman. Eloise wondered where he hid the killer instinct required to win match after match, when there was no such aggression to be found in his personality off court. He appeared to be rather shy by nature, and the perfect gentleman.

Their discussion about her role in his life was simple and succinct. 'Caesar has sent through your details, Eloise,' he told her in his heavy Russian accent. 'I'm so pleased you decided to accept his offer to dance for me.'

'Thank you, sir.' She expected him to continue but he gazed idly out the window. 'I'd appreciate it if you could outline your expectations of my role.'

'Oh, yes, of course. It's simple, really. You will dance for me before each match I play. I'm not sure how long each performance will last; it will depend on the day. I'll be playing in quite a few tournaments leading up to the French Open and you will travel with my team. The schedule is on the table. Other than before my matches, your time is your own unless I let you know otherwise.'

'Nothing else? Only dancing?'

'Yes, that's right.' He turned to look at her as if he were missing something. 'I'm sure Caesar explained it to you. I've also informed my mother of your arrival and she is hoping you might dance some scenes from her favourite ballet, *Cinderella*. We'd both like to watch.'

'Yes, of course, sir!' she said with genuine excitement. 'It would be my pleasure.'

'Excellent. The maid has prepared lunch for you in the kitchen. I'll see you at 4pm in the studio.'

He then promptly left the room to go about his own business.

Eloise had had no idea of what to expect on her arrival, but even so it all seemed rather formal and distant. She wondered whether she had managed to do something to upset Ivan – though she couldn't imagine what in such a short space of time – or whether it was just his personality. Perhaps this would change as they got to know each other. She did her best to swallow her disappointment – if that was what it was – knowing that her job wasn't to question, it was to adapt to his needs. If this was how he preferred it – minimal interaction at best – then she would fulfil his wishes graciously.

That afternoon was the first time she danced for Ivan and his mother, Anna. It would be the first of many times, and they whispered in Russian as they watched her perform with enthusiasm. Occasionally Ivan asked her to stop and repeat certain elements of her scene, after which his mother would applaud and blow kisses towards her in appreciation, saying 'Beautiful' or 'Perfect', which Ivan translated from Russian to English for her. At times Eloise and Anna danced together, and it was then that Eloise enjoyed seeing Ivan's smile light up his face, making him look friendly and relaxed, in place of his usual austere disposition. It was obvious that he adored his mother and she appeared thrilled to have Eloise as an addition to their daily lives.

From the outset Ivan showed no real interest in Eloise other than her dancing. Eloise learnt that his preference was to keep communication between them to a bare minimum. His manager generally left notes informing her when and where she was needed to perform for him. The rest of the time, as he had said, she was free to do as she wished. So Eloise revelled in her lengthy explorations of the beautiful palaces, museums and cathedrals and majestic gardens of St Petersburg. There was no shortage of attractions in a city with such a rich heritage.

The only event Ivan and Eloise attended together publicly was a surprise trip to the Bolshoi Ballet in Moscow to see *Don Quixote*. Eloise forced the memory of Natalia's face from her mind, knowing this was where Natalia had trained, though she couldn't deny that she was on high alert, critiquing the performances and keen to absorb improvements that could be made to her own repertoire.

It was the first evening that she and Ivan had spoken at length; Ivan was attentive to Eloise's observations about how she felt as a member of the audience rather than as a dancer onstage. The next evening he had her perform for more than three hours in his studio as he wandered around the room, his eyes silently studying the intricacy of her movements at close range. At the end of her exhausting routine he smiled and clapped his hands, declaring, 'Bravo! Simply exquisite!'

Then he promptly left the room. As was often the case.

Eloise often hoped her relationship with Ivan would become a tad more communicative than it was, but she adored the meticulous way he studied her body when she danced for him. Even though she was alone more often than not, as long as he needed her to dance for him, she was content to fulfil her role.

Eloise knew her contract ensured that she was Ivan's responsibility, and this at least gave her comfort that she belonged somewhere. In many respects it was no different from her previous life – she was still paid to dance, she maintained her former nomadic lifestyle – but at the same time, she was no longer competing in the stressful world of ballet, the hotels were five star, her travel first class (if not private jet) and her expense account indulgent, even if she never took advantage of it and always asked for permission to spend regardless (for instance, to purchase clothes more suited to her new lifestyle). Having her needs completely catered for and her whole life organised on her behalf was more than satisfactory.

Yet what she hadn't realised was how accustomed she had become to interacting with a bevy of virile male ballet dancers. She might not have had many sexual relationships, but she desperately missed the physicality of men and the feeling of their muscled limbs against her own, their hands sliding along her taut curves and over her legs, neck and face. Their sheer strength in lifting her petite form into the air as though she were a feather, and effortlessly catching her as she fell. The physicality of dance was the part that made her feel connected, like she belonged. Suddenly she'd been removed from this overtly sensate world and thrust into a life where no one touched her at all, and her longing for more had taken her completely by surprise.

Ivan appeared absorbed in her beauty and grace but never once approached her. Although their contract clearly facilitated, among other things, a sexual relationship should they be so inclined, she was comfortable with the fact that it was all about dancing, as she wasn't exactly attracted to him. The contract also stipulated that she should not be sexually intimate with anyone else – not that she had the opportunity for that. So she accepted her enforced celibacy without complaint, knowing that going against Caesar's rules was never an option she could consider.

Lifestyle

Ivan never asked Eloise to watch him play, but she did learn first-hand that tennis was one of the busiest sports in the world. Whereas soccer had one World Cup every four years, tennis had four grand slams every year. And the top players were also required to compete in mandatory ATP World Tour Masters 1000 series that added to their ATP rankings each year in Asia, America and Europe.

Eloise soon grew accustomed to the heavy demands of the tennis calendar as Ivan competed in Monte Carlo, Munich, Madrid, Rome ... It was a never-ending whirlwind of airports, stadiums, crowds, cars and hotels and she danced for him before every match he played. He always chose the particular ballet and the precise scene he wished her to perform. Sometimes it was for as little as ten minutes, at other times it was for a couple of hours. During some tournaments he would have her perform the same scene before each match.

It allowed little time for her to reflect on what she might be missing back in London. If the truth were told, Eloise felt like her previous lifestyle was in ultra-slow motion compared with this – like comparing a snail with Usain Bolt. She had no concerns about keeping physically active when they were on tour, particularly as Ivan often asked her to dance again after he'd won a match to help him unwind, which she did willingly.

All of these tournaments led up to the French Open: the true beginning of her eight-grand-slam commitment to Caesar, and the end of her one and only escape clause. Everything up until this point had been preliminary, allowing her time to adjust to her new lifestyle. Once the grand slam commenced, there was no turning back. But although she appreciated the gesture of Caesar's 'trial run', in her mind the clause was superfluous. Once she had committed to something, her disciplined self would always see it through.

Before the French Open, Ivan asked her to perform the final scene of *Swan Lake*. She wondered whether he envisaged his opponent as the dying white swan and himself as the victorious black swan. She had read that some athletes used the soundtrack of movies like *Rocky* to psych themselves up before a major match, and perhaps this was Ivan's version of the same thing.

Being the perfectionist she was, she took her job seriously and aimed at improving her performance with each match Ivan played – just as he did. The philosophy seemed to be working, since the more she danced, the more he won, including the title of Number One for the third consecutive year. Ivan was in top form and Eloise was confident he would continue to win, ensuring her position as his private ballerina – she liked to think of herself as his lucky charm and felt she was contributing to his success.

After Ivan won the title in Paris, Caesar hosted an elaborate private dinner for Ivan, his coach, his manager, Anna and Eloise to celebrate. At the end of the evening he asked if he could have a private word with Eloise and agreed to escort her back to her hotel.

As they sat down at a table in the hotel bar, he began, 'So, how is everything going, Eloise?'

'Very well, Caesar. I'm really pleased for him.'

'And how are you adjusting to your new life?'

'Pretty well, actually. It's certainly busy, but I do feel that Ivan appreciates my dancing for him.'

'There's no doubting that. He has told me himself on many occasions the motivating impact your dancing has on his game. I believe we both have you to thank for helping secure his Number One world ranking. From my perspective you are fulfilling your role perfectly, Eloise. I couldn't hope for more.'

Eloise blushed at his words of praise. 'Thank you, Caesar. I've certainly tried to do my best.'

'So you will commit to the entire term of the contract?'

'I always had every intention of doing so.'

He smiled at her conviction.

'You do realise there is no guarantee that Ivan will remain Number One?'

She hadn't given much thought to the other players on the circuit, other than briefly flicking through the profiles Caesar had provided her with after their initial meeting.

'Are there ever any guarantees in life?' She laughed. 'It's OK, I'll take my chances.'

'I like your style, Eloise.' He noted that she seemed much more relaxed than when they had last met, not as emotionally distraught. It seemed this lifestyle *was* working for her.

'And are you still comfortable with the contract as is?'

'Yes, I am.'

'Then let's get the formalities out of the way, shall we?' He handed her a thick black pen, which she accepted, and she signed the document he placed in front of her.

'Let me welcome you officially to my world, Eloise. I believe you've made an excellent choice.' He signed his flamboyant signature below hers, sealing her fate, then immediately called the waiter over and ordered them both a celebratory glass of 1996 Dom Pérignon.

Two chilled flutes of champagne swiftly arrived at their table. 'Cheers to the game!' he toasted.

Caesar was thrilled that his combined love of ballet and tennis was proving to be a formidable formula, and one that had the potential of making him wealthier with each title. Ivan's victory in the French Open was simply icing on the proverbial cake if his forecasts proved to be correct.

WIMBLEDON I
June–July

Surprise

Given his recent form, it was only to be expected that Ivan should have a smooth run through to the semifinals of Wimbledon. But he met a glitch in his comfortable winning streak when playing against a young, up-and-coming Australian who took everyone by surprise. This opponent proved a worthy competitor, pushing Ivan into extensive rallies and forcing him to hit winners even he was a little shocked to have executed. The Australian's tenacity and self-confidence certainly captured the eye of sports commentators, and there were lengthy discussions about whether he had the skill and drive to become the next big drawcard of the tennis world.

The crowd was thrilled with the five-set marathon, which, after many hours, saw the top seed proceed to the final – just as the bookmakers, including Caesar, had predicted he would. Although Ivan was pleased with his performance and eventual win, there was no doubting his thirty-one-year-old body felt the additional strain of such a challenging match. It ensured his personal physiotherapist was more than occupied for the next thirty-six hours leading up the final.

In keeping with the noble traditions of Wimbledon, the atmosphere at the gentlemen's championship final was cordially electric. Ivan's opponent was the twenty-six-year-old Swede Stephan Nordstrom.

Nordstrom had never been in a final at the All England Club, even though he had convincingly won the Australian Open earlier in the year, his first ever grand-slam victory. His form could be erratic and nobody was sure whether he was a one-slam wonder or set to settle in for the long haul, given that his win had occurred when the world's Number One was absent from Melbourne Park. One thing was certain, however: the truth would be discovered by the end of the day.

There was not much time for Eloise to dance for Ivan before the final, as his coach took complete responsibility for orchestrating his every movement before he walked onto centre court. Eloise did her best in the twelve minutes she had been allocated, but she could tell he was distracted by nerves as he prepared to defend his Wimbledon title for the third time. His coach seemed as nervous as Ivan, so she assumed this tournament meant more to them than any of those he played leading up to it. After all, the Championships at Wimbledon were the most prestigious of all the grand slams – the slam all players dreamt of winning the moment the game of tennis took their lives hostage.

Right in the middle of Eloise's performance, the coach opened the door, declaring that her time with Ivan was over.

Ivan looked a little flustered as he walked over to her. 'Thank you, Eloise. Unfortunately my time is running out. I have a ticket for you, should you be interested in watching the final.'

It was unusual enough for him to speak to her after she danced for him, let alone offer her a ticket to one of his matches.

'Thank you, Ivan, that is very thoughtful. *Bonne chance*.'

And with that she was immediately guided away so his coach could have final words with him before the match.

It was a warm, sunny day so Eloise wore a tailored emerald dress with mid-length sleeves that came to just above her knees, pairing it with court shoes and a matching handbag. She had changed her outfit when she found a guide to sartorial standards included with her ticket. It amounted to 'No riffraff, please, we're Wimbledon'. Apparently short skirts, bare midriffs, jeans, trainers, bomber jackets and sleeveless tops were all deemed inappropriate attire. She also opted to wear her hair in a sensible low braid, just in case her unruly flowing curls were deemed unacceptable and she was refused entry. She would hate to cause a scene and any embarrassment to Ivan.

Even after reading the sartorial guide, Eloise was surprised at the formal attire of some of the people bustling around the Wimbledon members' enclosure. As she attempted to blend in, she felt like she was walking around inside a Burberry catalogue.

Staring at her ticket to ensure she was in the right place, she suddenly heard a vaguely familiar voice calling from behind her.

'Elle, over here! Eloise?'

Elle? Only one person had ever called her that. She turned around and came face to face with Liam's warm eyes and friendly smile.

'My goodness, hi! I didn't think I'd ever see you again!'

'The universe works in mysterious ways! How *are* you?'

'I'm really well, thanks. How about you?'

'Same, although I'd prefer to be playing in the final.'

'You *play*?'

'I do.' He laughed.

'I'm sorry, I had no idea.'

'No need for apologies, you didn't ask and I didn't say. Besides, most people hadn't heard of me before yesterday. If Borisov hadn't had the stamina and experience to last five sets in the semis, I'd be playing Nordstrom on centre court today. But that's how the cookie crumbles.'

'You played Ivan?' She was astonished.

'Yeah, you know, world Number One, presumably the person you are here to watch,' he said with a cheeky grin.

She wasn't sure how to answer, and thought it best to keep their conversation focused on him. 'You certainly take losing well.'

'I gave it my all on the day, that's as much as I can expect from myself. It was a strong effort but he's a great player – obviously. It's just a game – admittedly a game I would have loved to win – but I had a good run, and made it much further than I've done here before, so I can't complain.'

She remembered his positive attitude from when she met him in the pub, but still found herself shaking her head in surprise. 'I wish I could be more like that.'

'I know my day will come; I didn't reach the Wimbledon final this year, but maybe next year, who knows?' His high-voltage smile was on full display. 'Hey, are you going to be around later? I'd love to catch up with you, but right now my coach is waiting for me in the stands. We need to be able to analyse my opposition in detail.'

'Oh, sure, of course, I'd love to catch up. Sounds great!' Spending some time with someone other than herself sounded like too good an opportunity to miss – especially someone like Liam.

'Excellent!' He pulled a card out of his back pocket and handed it to her. 'Call me after the match and I'll see if we can find something more potent to drink than an untouched pint – I have the next week off so I can let loose.' His grin exploded into a heartfelt smile.

'Sure!' Eloise looked down at the card. 'Noah?'

'Yeah, that's me. Liam Noah Levique. Not using my real name makes it easier for me to stay incognito when I meet beautiful strangers, and my nan always called me Noah, so it sort of stuck as my tennis name.'

'Well, that makes sense. I'm not great at the whole tennis thing but at least I've heard of Noah Levique. You really did give Ivan a hard time.' She knew more than anyone how flustered and aching Ivan had been after such a brutal match. Noah had put up a mammoth fight.

'And I hope to do it again, only next time I'll win.' He winked at her as a flustered man began approaching from the stands. 'Gotta go – see ya, Elle! Call me. Tonight!' He held his forefinger and thumb to the side of his face as once again he jogged away from her with the boundless energy of an excitable puppy.

Eloise held the card to her chest and couldn't help but smile as she considered the amazing coincidence that Liam was actually Noah Levique, a professional tennis player – and obviously a good one at that. Never in a million years …

She heard the polite announcement asking everyone to find their seats as soon as possible and settled in to watch her first ever professional tennis match.

The young woman next to her was dressed in blue, with her face covered in blue and yellow zinc.

'Who are you going for, Russia or Sweden?' the woman asked, in an American accent.

'Russia – how about you?' Eloise asked with a smile, given the answer was so obvious.

'Who do you think? Sweden – of course. With him in the game, tennis has just got a whole lot hotter. He could do me any time!' With that she screamed and waved her arms in the air as Stephan Nordstrom was introduced and walked onto centre court for his first Wimbledon final.

There was something overwhelmingly charismatic about Stephan Nordstrom, everyone else in view almost diminished as he took centre stage. Eloise felt a strong attraction seed in her belly. And suddenly she had far greater interest in the match about to be played. Like the rest of the crowd, she watched in absolute awe as the two players shook hands and commenced their first game.

Today, on centre court at the All England Club, it was abundantly clear that each player wanted this title as desperately as the other. And by all accounts, they would fight to the death to have it.

Eloise could barely sit still in her seat. The pangs of guilt were like shards of glass penetrating her skin as she found herself continually drawn to Nordstrom more than Ivan; it was difficult not to be. Her remorse deepened when she caught herself spontaneously clapping as Nordstrom sent a backhand winner flying down the line after an epic rally, almost knocking out a linesperson as the ball continued its destructive path.

Nordstrom's response was electrifying as he pumped his fists into the air and released what sounded like a lion's roar. Ivan continued on smoothly, undeterred by the Swede's momentum on the other side of the net, maintaining his trademark cool, calm and collected persona while the fifth set climbed into double digits. Both players remained supreme professionals in front of an utterly engrossed crowd. Decorum was apparently everything at Wimbledon, and the umpire's reminders of 'Quiet, please' felt like a restraining order on a ball of energy. Not one person could tell which way the match would go and all were literally sitting on the edge of their seats, gasping at the force and stamina behind each point.

The battle of the titans was won in four hours and fifty-three minutes … by first-time Wimbledon champion Stephan Nordstrom. Both players collapsed in sheer exhaustion before hauling their tortured bodies to the net to shake hands with each other and the umpire.

Stephan stripped off his shirt, flaunting his bronzed and superbly defined chest and abdominals, pumping both clenched fists high in the air and unleashing another almighty roar to the global audience. The power of his voice reverberated around the arena, causing the crowd to roar in return as he flung his shirt and sweatbands into the stands.

Eloise was as engaged as anyone, her hands becoming numb from clapping so hard. Discovering Noah had made the semifinals only added to her now undeniable interest in the game, and more particularly in its ranking system. Ivan's failure to win didn't result in his losing his status as Number One, but it did mean it was definitely under threat.

Carefree

Ivan went into complete hibernation after losing the momentous match. His coach informed Eloise that she would not see him for at least two days. Therefore she eagerly called Noah, knowing she wouldn't be letting anyone down and thrilled to have an opportunity to see him again.

She was staying at the Dorchester, and was delighted to see a very funky Noah arrive in the foyer wearing faded red jeans, a white V-neck T-shirt and a fitted navy blazer with the sleeves pushed up above his elbows. She found herself staring at him, more than a little mesmerised, drawn towards his confident, casual stride and muscled body. She was caught a little off guard when he rushed up and scooped her off the ground in a bear hug, swinging her around before kissing her on both cheeks.

'You look hot!' were his first words as he returned her feet to the ground.

Eloise hadn't been sure what to wear and had changed outfits five times, before deciding at the last minute to be bold, choosing a deep burgundy lace bodycon mini-dress with a boat neckline, a gathered front and, most importantly, a plunging scooped back. She wasn't big-breasted, but she felt good in the dress because it showed off her slender, toned legs and the muscular definition of her back.

Before she had the opportunity to respond to his compliment he took hold of her hand. 'Let's get you out of here to some place more in our age bracket.'

The uniformed doorman motioned for a black cab to approach and held the door open for Eloise while Noah bounded around to the cabbie, handing him a card.

'Right you are, sir,' came the confirmation from the driver's seat as Noah settled in beside Eloise.

'So, Liam – Noah – where are you from?'

'Ah, the inquisition begins. You know I much prefer talking about you,' he countered with a grin.

'No way – it's time for *you* to answer some questions! It's only fair.'

'OK, OK, I give in. My dad is French and my mum is Australian. They divorced when I was young and I lived with my mum in Townsville but spent my holidays with Dad in Europe which was handy for competing as a junior.'

'Right – but you, well, I'm not sure how I should say this …'

'You're asking about my perpetual suntan? Are you sure that's politically correct?' His dimples showed that he didn't mind talking about it and was just having some fun.

'Let's just say you are beautifully bronzed compared with me.'

'No doubt about it. But that's not to say there is anything wrong with your delicate alabaster skin. You just need to keep out of the sun more than me.' As he held her hand in the back of the cab, his thumb caressed her palm and she could feel his warmth as tingles raced up her arm. 'My nan is Aboriginal, and just in case you hadn't worked it out, that's where I get my exceptional sense of tribal rhythm.'

She couldn't help but laugh.

'Well, of course! I'd like to see some of that rhythm one day.'

She had never been so comfortable talking to a member of the opposite sex. He was so easygoing that she felt completely relaxed, laughing and chatting to him without any self-consciousness or pretence.

'I'm hoping you'll get that chance tonight when we hit the dance floor – unless you're referring to my tennis?'

'So cheeky! I'd love to see both.'

They looked at each other and smiled, both sensing their relationship was set to move way beyond their last fleeting yet fortuitous meeting.

The driver turned off Kensington High Street onto Derry Street and pulled over. Noah promptly paid and jumped out to open Eloise's door, and they made their way up in the lift to The Roof Gardens, Virgin's rooftop club.

She had heard about the club from some of the other dancers, but had never been there before. It was weird having lived in London for so long yet realising there was still so much to discover and experience.

'Normally it wouldn't be open tonight. One of the perks of being sponsored by Virgin, I guess,' he said with a cheeky wink.

'Ah, I see!' She smiled back.

'Come on.' He grabbed hold of her hand and excitedly headed towards the bar. 'Tommy makes awesome cocktails. I'll introduce you.'

Eloise couldn't believe the size and lushness of the rooftop garden. The flora looked almost technicoloured against the somewhat monochromatic landscape of London.

They found a table for two within the garden, and just as they had settled in, two French pear martinis arrived along with some canapés, compliments of the chef. Just as Noah had promised, they would be drinking something stronger than a pint. Eloise was not used to spirits, but the fresh-tasting vodka and champagne concoction slid down her throat all too easily, while their discussion flowed effortlessly amidst interruptions of congratulations from the staff, who obviously knew Noah well.

The grey clouds in the sky turned a vivid orange as the sun finally began to set on the mild evening. Eloise couldn't remember a night out when she had felt so at ease; this was one of the rare occasions when she was able to have a few drinks without having to worry about a performance the next day. It was on this basis that she happily reached for her second martini when another round of drinks arrived at their table as if by magic.

'So, what's next for you in the tennis schedule?'

'I'm hanging around London for a week to catch up with some friends, before heading to Hamburg for the German Championships. Then it's off to America to prepare for the US Open.'

'You don't get too much downtime after something as major as Wimbledon.'

'I suppose not, though it would be much the same for you, wouldn't it? With your performances and travel.'

Eloise shifted slightly in her seat. She hadn't spoken to anyone about having left the Royal Ballet and wasn't sure exactly what to say.

'I'm sorry, have I said something wrong? It's just that when we met you mentioned dance, travel …' His voice trailed off. 'Are you no longer performing?'

'Well, I'm no longer with the Royal Ballet, so I'm not performing quite like I used to …'

'And are you going to elaborate on that, or will I have to ply you with straight martinis to get to the truth?' he asked jokingly, just as she noticed the delicious impact of vodka filtering through her body.

She deliberately placed her glass back on the table and picked up a coconut crumbed prawn to dip into the tangy sauce alongside it. 'You know how I mentioned a decision the afternoon we met?'

'Sure, and talked about taking risks.'

'Well, I ended up accepting the risks and everything else that came with them. And here I am, now indirectly part of the tennis world.'

'Whoa, wait up! Really? You weren't just there for the final like thousands of other fans?'

'Not exactly …' She wasn't sure how much she should mention with her mind already feeling a little blurred. She had signed a confidentiality agreement as part of Caesar's requirements and didn't want to jeopardise anything by having loose lips.

'At the moment, I only perform for Ivan,' she said rather sheepishly as she glanced towards Noah, who had raised his eyebrows at this admission. 'He loves ballet,' she added, as if that disclosure should explain everything.

'Wow. I've never heard of anything like that.'

'Yeah, it was weird for me at first, but now I really enjoy it. Each time I've danced for him, he's won. That is, up until today.' She absently wondered how he was taking the loss.

'So, if I become Number One in the world, will you dance for me too?'

So thrown was Eloise by the accuracy of his mischievous offhand query that she quickly reached for her martini and drank the remainder down in one gulp.

Noah could sense her unease. 'Hey, it's OK. As long as you're happy, it's none of my business. Honestly.' He squeezed her hand as she tried to compose herself.

'Nothing makes me happier than when I'm dancing. But tonight, I'm *very* happy that I'm out with you,' she added sincerely.

Noah sensed she wanted to drop the subject, so he dabbed his mouth with a serviette and readily accepted her compliment. 'Well, if dancing makes you happy and I do too, let's go get some groove on to the music.'

If anyone else had said the words, she would have thought they were nerdy, but coming from Noah they felt exactly right. There was no denying he was gorgeous and lovable, and he made her feel as light and carefree as a feather. She knew she could never deny anything that kept him smiling. She accepted his hand graciously, and the next few hours slipped into a fun-loving blur.

* * *

The next morning she awoke in her suite at the Dorchester to find two envelopes under the door. She opened the top one first, recognising Ivan's crisp white stationery. Fleetingly she wondered whether she might be in some trouble, then immediately pushed the thought from her mind.

I have returned to St Petersburg and will not be requiring any performances from you for the next ten days.

The impersonal nature of the note felt like a punch in the gut, though she shouldn't have been surprised; he was never one for small talk, or much talk at all, for that matter.

It meant she had over a week to herself. She had no idea what she would do with the time, since an opportunity like this had never arisen before.

The second envelope was on Dorchester stationery.

Hey Elle,
I hated saying goodbye to you last night. So I was thinking
you might want to spend a bit more time together in
London – too much too soon, maybe? I'll never know if
I don't ask! Either way, give me a call. I'd love to see you
again, and sooner rather than later.
Noah xox

Eloise couldn't contain her excitement as she called him to make arrangements. Problem solved. As he'd said, the universe worked in strange ways and right now it seemed to be doing exactly that – in their favour!

Friends?

Noah and Eloise spent the next week cruising around the canals of greater London. She met his friends, 'the lads' as he called them, in various pubs along the waterways, and found them just as easygoing and unpretentious as he was. No one would have guessed Noah was one of the top tennis players in the world, and rapidly rising further up the ranks thanks to his Wimbledon performance.

Eloise was privy to a world she'd never imagined could be possible for a professional athlete. Her life with the ballet had ensured she was strict and disciplined with herself around the clock – regardless of whether she had the day off or not – and her enforced breaks over summer had only meant an opportunity to train harder to ensure she was always better than her peers. Noah, on the other hand, happily drank with his friends as though tennis was the furthest thing from his mind. She had to wonder how someone so nonchalant had the stamina for the demands of the game.

On their first afternoon together, lazing in the sunshine, it was impossible for Eloise not to admire his loose locks tickling his shoulders and delectable shirtless body as his feet dangled over the side of the boat. She didn't even bother to hide her sideways glances towards him.

When he casually lit a cigarette as though it weren't an issue at all, the look on her face sent him into a fit of laughter. She watched, frankly aghast, as he deeply inhaled.

'What? Don't tell me you've never had a smoke before?' He took another drag and began puffing smoke rings towards the water.

Eloise was speechless. Even more so when he offered it to her!

'Well ...?' He paused to look at her more intently. 'My God, you haven't, have you? You've never had a single puff of a cigarette!' He shook his head in disbelief, smiling nonetheless. 'It's not illegal, you know ...'

She had no idea whether it was the look of horror he saw on her face that eventually made him reluctantly stub it out. Next, in one swift move, he grabbed her, dangling her upper body over the water while keeping a grip on her thighs and legs, a giant grin on his face all the while.

'No, Noah, don't ...!' she shrieked, for the first time not thinking about who was around or what people might think.

'Have you or not?' he insisted, threatening to cleanse her of her prim and proper attitude, completely ignoring her shrieks as her mass of loose hair dangled precariously close to the murky water.

'Noah, please – you could drop me!' she panted as he gave in and hauled her back up.

'I promise you, I would never, ever drop you, Elle.'

Instead of letting her be, he carried her into the cabin, tossing her easily onto the bed and pinning her arms by her sides as he straddled her body. He tickled her mercilessly until she couldn't hold back any longer, her hysteria eventually replacing any trace of nervousness as she begged him to stop. She had never been treated that way, not having grown up with any siblings or cousins of her own.

They stared into each other's eyes as they both took a moment to catch their breath.

'I'd give anything to kiss you right now.' He lowered his face towards her, and just as his soft lips touched hers she reluctantly turned away. He guided her face back to meet his questioning gaze.

'I'm sorry, I just can't ... It might go too far ...'

Their attraction to each other had been all too obvious since their first night out, but until this point had remained unspoken. Although

Eloise's desire had been supercharged since meeting up with Noah again, she had done her best to bury it. She had never made the first move in the few relationships she'd had – it just wasn't her style and the potential for rejection caused her no end of fear – but this time she knew she couldn't have even if she'd wanted to. Being well aware that nothing would ever happen with Ivan anyway, she would have given anything to say yes to Noah, right here, right now, and take their relationship to the next level. But heaven forbid the wrath of Caesar, not to mention the thought of kissing her future financial freedom goodbye. The clause in her contract about sexual relations with anyone other than her Number One was abundantly clear and always top of her mind; it just wasn't worth the risk.

With a sigh, Noah collapsed beside her on the bed, placed his hands behind his head and stared at the ceiling, suddenly deep in thought.

'You've gone all quiet on me.' Eloise didn't know what to say, but wanted some kind of response from him at least.

He turned onto his side, facing her, and started playing with her hair, their bodies almost touching but not quite, though their feet comfortably rubbed against each other.

'I'm not quite sure what to say. I thought ...'

'Noah, it's not you. I'd love to – honestly. It's just ... so complicated.' She couldn't help but tense at the words.

'Let me guess: complicated in a way you can't explain.' He couldn't hide the disappointment in his voice, and it upset her deeply.

'I'd give anything for my situation to be different, but it is what it is and I have to honour the agreement I've made.'

'Are you with Ivan? Is it more than just ballet?'

'No. I only dance for him, but ...' She was at a loss as to how to explain it to him without disclosing the details. Details she was not at liberty to discuss.

'I've never met anyone like you before. You're so beautiful, vivacious, graceful, oh so incredibly hot, and – what's the word I'm looking for? – oh yeah, pure at the same time. How could I forget that? It's a lethal mix for any guy.' His shook his head in dismay.

'Noah, I think the same about you, but I just can't do anything about it at the moment. I promise you, I would if I could.'

'Honestly?' His eyes were hopeful and his mischievous grin returned when he added, 'You think I'm pure?'

She laughed, punching him lightly on the arm, and he pretended to roll over injured.

'Very funny!' she responded. 'No, I'm not as pure as you think I am, just because I've never smoked – and by the way, as an athlete you should never smoke, *ever*! Particularly not if you want to be Number One.'

'All I do know is that I've never felt this way about anyone before, *ever*!'

He made sure he emphasised the word in the same way as she had. Neither of them could hide their smiles. 'Anyway, what gives you the impression I want to be Number One?'

'Why do you play if you don't want to be the best?'

'I'm young, I happen to be good at tennis – which is lucky because I love playing. I get to travel the world – which I also love. I have great friends on the circuit. So life's good, much better than I ever expected. Until playing against Ivan I suppose I've never really believed I could make it into the top ten and now that might occur.' He shook his head in disbelief and looked directly into her eyes. 'Why, do you think I should take it more seriously?'

'It sounds as if you haven't really had to work too hard to get to this position.'

'Don't get me wrong, I love winning and I work hard when I need to but I suppose I haven't had the desire to take it too seriously. There is a lot of losing involved in tennis you know!'

'I just can't imagine not wanting to be the top of your field.'

'Well, maybe you are the motivation I've been lacking until now, Miss Lawrance.'

'And maybe you are what I need to relax and enjoy life a little more, not take things so seriously ...' she reflected.

'See, we could be a match made in heaven if only you would give us a chance.' He laughed before he tenderly tucked a loose lock of hair behind her ear. 'So are you going to tell me how *you* feel or are you avoiding the topic?'

'Even if I did, what good would it do? It wouldn't change anything ...' She sighed, disheartened by this turn of events. Her heart and body were yearning for his touch but her mind was resolute.

She tried to sit up but he held on tight to her hand, ensuring she stayed lying next to him on the bed.

'Let me ask a different way, then. If you didn't have this "complication", would you want to be with me?'

Eloise looked away. She honestly didn't know what to say. Of course she wanted to be with him, she was attracted to him in every way. It felt like forever since she'd been with a man. And now, before her very eyes, within her grasp but beyond her reach, was the unimaginable oasis of Noah. He was like milk chocolate and sunshine morphed into one delectable package – and the most fun-loving, easygoing, playful, warm-hearted guy she had ever met. His body was as sculpted and toned as that of any male ballet dancer, and she couldn't deny that the thought of being intimate with him was exciting beyond her wildest dreams. He was everything she'd ever hoped for and more. She yearned to say yes, but Caesar's rules were abundantly clear, and what if he found out? She'd be left with no contract and no ballet. She couldn't decide whether to answer with her head or her heart, and was ultimately afraid of being betrayed by both. Telling him the truth just wasn't an option and the last thing she wanted to do was to hurt Noah.

'Elle?'

She stroked his cheek with her hand, letting her fingertips rest on his delectable lips, which proved frustrating for both of them that she couldn't take things further. 'Believe me, I would love to be with you, Noah, but only when the time was right.' Heart then head felt like the right answer.

'And that would be when?' He pushed for an answer while holding her fingers and kissing them gently.

'Just not now, Noah. I can't … I'm so sorry I wish it could be different.' Tears began to well in her eyes such was her disappointment in having to say no to this precious man.

'OK, OK. You just don't know how hard it's been for me to keep my hands off you since the moment we first met in the pub.'

'So far you haven't!' She lifted her hand, still being squeezed by his, to prove her point and lighten the mood.

'Well, other parts of you.' He chuckled in an attempt to cover his own disappointment.

'I would love for us to be more than friends, Noah, I've never felt like this before either. It's just that for the next eighteen months … well, the commitment I've made needs to take precedence …'

'But I shouldn't give up, I should just wait a while?'

'Quite a while, but yes, I'd be devastated if you gave up on me.'

'Then I won't – ever!' He rolled her over and playfully slapped her butt. 'Let's go for a run.'

'I hear you.'

With sexual tension still oozing but knowing the air was clear between them, Eloise was more than happy to join him for a jog and release some of the pent-up frustration between her legs.

Chaste

There was only one bed on the narrow boat, and each night they shared it, but only for sleeping. Most evenings they talked way into the night, eventually falling asleep holding hands, their bodies barely touching – thwarted but still preferring to be close. Eloise was continually torn between admiring Noah's chivalry and heroic restraint at her insistence on not taking their relationship further, and desperately wishing he'd have his wild way with her – were it not for Caesar. Her feelings could fluctuate between the two in any given moment, but in the end she was grateful that he respected her wishes with fortitude, even though they were both denying themselves the sexual release they fervently desired.

Lying on the bed in her summer pyjamas – a singlet and boxer shorts – Eloise would enjoy watching Noah as he stripped off his shirt before settling in next to her. She still got a thrill from having him so near her each night, and took every opportunity to gaze at his sculpted torso, knowing anything more than that was strictly forbidden. Though she'd had sex a few times before, this small degree of intimacy she shared with Noah felt so much more meaningful – albeit physically infuriating.

'Your eyes are glazing over, Elle, you look a million miles away,' he said to her one night.

'I was distracted by you,' she replied as he jumped in beside her.

'I'm more than happy to distract you a bit more; just say when.' His hand slid over to her knee.

'Noah, you know how hard this is for me already!' She grudgingly removed his hand and instead gently touched the tattoo on his shoulder, a four-sided shape that looked a bit like a knot. 'Have you had that for long?' she asked.

'About five years, I suppose. I got it when I was nineteen.'

'I like its symmetry. Does it have any specific meaning?'

'It's called Mpatapo, a West African symbol of peacemaking and reconciliation.' He grinned at her curious eyes as she lightly touched it once more. 'I had it done after my parents got over themselves and became friends again. I'd always wanted a tattoo and it's a useful reminder to them whenever they start squabbling like kids; all I do is flash my shoulder and they stop. Having them both on the same side has had a huge impact on my tennis, so now they behave – for the greater good.'

'It's weird, I've never had parents but I always imagined the fairytale kind. You know – a mother and father who will love each other until the day they die. Never ones who hate each other.'

'Well, I'd rather have my mum and dad than not, that's for sure. It must be so hard for you …'

'It's difficult to explain, but you don't know what you're missing if you've never experienced it. Sometimes I just feel really alone and empty; other times I don't think about it until something triggers the feeling of never really belonging to anyone or anything. The ballet is the closest thing I've ever had to family, and I walked away from it. But then again, if I hadn't, I wouldn't have met you …' She smiled, then yawned, resting her head near his chest so she could fall asleep to the beat of his heart.

He smiled a heartfelt smile, twisting her long, voluminous hair between his fingers, and marvelling at her beauty inside and out as she drifted off to sleep beside him. He wondered just how long they would have to wait before they could be together. But of one thing he was sure: it would be *when*, not *if* they were together. For he knew deep down that he had found his soulmate.

This thought provided him with great comfort, as the warmth of her body and the canal boat's ever so gentle rhythm eventually lulled him into slumber.

On their last stop before returning to London they visited Oxford, and Noah surprised Eloise with the gift of a snow dome. Ensconced within the glass was a canal boat, featuring a boy and a girl and a dog sitting on the rooftop.

'Just like us!'

'I know, that's why I couldn't resist.'

'Now all we need is a dog.'

'One day ... Who knows?'

'Thank you, Noah. I'll treasure it always.'

'As I do you.'

Eloise was so touched by the unexpected gift from Noah that she couldn't prevent a stray tear from escaping her eye. She flung her arms around his strong neck and buried her face in his chest, never wanting to let go. Gifts had been few and far between in Eloise's life; each passing birthday had only reinforced how alone she was in the world.

Though slightly taken aback by the strength of her reaction, Noah held her tight against the warmth of his body. Their hug was long-lasting and meaningful, as their time together touring the canals came to an end.

Eloise had felt happier than she had ever been over this past week, and the vision in the snow dome gave her hope for the future – one they might share together. She knew that every time she looked at it, she would remember how precious her relationship with Noah was. He brought sunshine to her life. That night, she drifted off into a dreamless sleep, grateful for the good fortune of having had this time with him.

She had always wondered what it might be like to feel cherished, and with Noah she felt more special and accepted than she ever had before. It was a feeling she hoped would live with her for a long time.

At the end of their chaste yet flirtatious time together, both of them knew that, had circumstances been different, they could have become so much more than friends. Having to be content with their shared camaraderie – for the time being at least – they said their goodbyes, knowing their paths would indeed cross again on the other side of the Atlantic, sooner rather than later.

During their long and meaningful conversations throughout the course of the week, Noah had detected a strange undercurrent in relation to Eloise's arrangement with Ivan and her involvement in tennis, but he'd respected her need for privacy and hadn't pressed her too hard for details. Instead, he'd encouraged her to be true to her passions and to pursue her dreams as soon as she was ready. Something he promised himself to help her achieve.

Even though she had never had a best friend before, Eloise knew that there were some secrets that shouldn't be shared until the time was right, and sensed that giving away any more details about her relationship with Ivan fell into that category.

What she hadn't sensed during her perfect week with Noah was the photographer who had been discreetly tracking and photographing their every move together.

US OPEN I
August–September

Dichotomy

When Eloise met up with Ivan again in the US, it was clear that he had all but lost his spark for tennis and niggling strains in his hamstring and Achilles had become cause for concern. Although she still danced for him before each game, he watched her perform as a distant bystander rather than with his previous rapture at her skill and precision. She felt sorry for him, sensing that his loss at Wimbledon was still raw, which was confirmed by Caesar, who explained that this malaise caused him to miss the Australian Open earlier in the year. It seemed Ivan's motivation was at rock bottom and everyone was questioning whether this tournament might indeed mark the end of his tennis career.

It was within this apathetic atmosphere that the US Open began with little gusto for either of them. Ivan didn't ask her to attend any matches at Flushing Meadows, so she busied herself around New York City's incredible museums. SoHo had always been a firm favourite and one of the few places she liked to do some boutique shopping. One afternoon she took a tour of the Lincoln Center for Performing Arts to go 'behind the scenes' of the New York City Ballet. Needless to say it felt very strange being on the other side of the fence as a tourist rather than as a dancer! However, more often than not – other than her early morning jog around Central Park before it became too busy and hot – she stayed within the confines of the iconic Caesar Towers Hotel, keeping her body toned with swimming and working out at the gym. The sporadic messages she shared with Noah were without doubt the highlight of her day.

Eloise didn't pay much attention to Ivan's matches, vaguely aware that he was struggling through the tournament on a wing and a prayer. She was concentrating on some intermittent sprint training on the running machine in the hotel's gym when the sports news caught her eye – causing her to misjudge her steps, topple off the conveyer belt and land awkwardly on her weak left ankle. She sat on the carpet, momentarily befuddled, as she absorbed the reality that Noah had just been awarded the match over Ivan – who had forfeited the match in the fourth set, unable to continue due to a hamstring injury.

She couldn't believe what she was seeing. Ivan limping up to the net to shake Noah's hand, Noah placing his arm around Ivan's shoulder in genuine sympathy for such a misfortune. Noah was through to the finals of the US Open! Her new 'best friend', the twenty-four-year-old slightly French Aussie who drank martinis and pints and who was quite partial to smoking on the odd occasion! She was forced to admit to herself that she hadn't honestly believed it was possible for someone so laid-back to ever reach the pinnacle of his sport; from her perspective, he just didn't seem to take it seriously enough. Although she had to concede, he was steadily climbing up the ranks with each match he played, which must be exciting for him.

All of a sudden, the final of the US Open held far greater significance to her than it had mere moments before. Not only would Noah be playing in his first grand-slam final, but Ivan's status as Number One was also potentially at risk.

Throwing a towel around her neck and ignoring the pain in her ankle, she quickly returned to her suite to shower. Afterwards, she flicked the TV to the channel dedicated to the US Open. A reporter was interviewing Stephan Nordstrom, who had made it through in straight sets to the final against Noah.

His face and his deep authoritative voice immediately captivated Eloise, and her belly pulled tight at the sight of him.

The only thing that distracted her was the buzz at the door as the concierge delivered a message to her room. The gold-embossed envelope announced that it was from the one and only Caesar.

Dear Eloise,

This message is to inform you that should Stephan Nordstrom win the US Open, he will immediately become Number One in the ATP men's rankings. Arrangements will be made for your transfer to him within twenty-four hours of the end of the match, should he agree to this. Should Noah Levique win the final, there will be no change in ranking and you will remain assigned to Ivan Borisov until otherwise notified.

You may wish to acquaint yourself with the copy of your contract that I have included with this letter. My solicitor has highlighted the specific clauses you would be expected to uphold should such a transfer of Mastership occur.

My driver will pick you up from reception at 3pm tomorrow to escort you to my private suite at Arthur Ashe Stadium so we can enjoy this momentous match together.

May the best man win.

Caesar

As Eloise placed the note from Caesar on the desk in her suite, sounds of the interview with Stephan echoed in the background.

She had signed up to Caesar's game of human chess, and now he was making his next move. The thought that she was merely his pawn sent shudders down her spine, though she couldn't decide whether they were from excitement or fear.

She wondered whether Noah had any hope at all against the formidable Stephan Nordstrom. She sent her friend a text message, congratulating him on reaching the finals and wishing him the very best of luck.

On the spur of the moment, she decided to quickly dress and go out to source a snow dome from one of the tourist shops to commemorate the occasion. She chose a dome featuring New York's skyline, with King Kong holding a large tennis racquet on top of the Empire State Building. The ever-helpful concierge kindly organised its express delivery to Noah's hotel and she once again cherished the memories of the special week they'd shared.

The next afternoon Eloise ensured she was impeccably attired for meeting with Caesar. She prepared with the same fastidious care as she had always done for the stage, and felt suitably glamorous as she was escorted into the enormous luxury limousine waiting for her.

Looking out at the stadium from Caesar's private suite, she felt like she was in a bubble, not really part of the commotion of the crowd but still able to sense its raw energy. It was a far cry from the polite decorum on display at Wimbledon – the spectators nowhere near as homogenised, most of them flamboyantly showing off their uniqueness. Music was blaring from the speakers; some people were smoking joints, entwined in each other's arms; others were jiving to the sounds on their headphones. You could literally feel the vibrant pulse of New York City pumping through your body. On her way to join Caesar she'd even passed a couple of brawling men who were in the process of being escorted out of the stadium by security.

Despite feeling a little removed from the action, she was glad to be witnessing the commotion from safely behind tinted glass panels, in air-conditioned comfort. Otherwise she could easily have believed she was in a modern-day Colosseum, awaiting the arrival of lions and gladiators.

This thought made her immediately aware of what was at stake, the dichotomy of her feelings causing her muscles to tense in anticipation of what the result might be. Though she would love for Noah to win, she couldn't deny her personal desire for a change in her own circumstances; after the coldness of Ivan a new Number One would be more than welcome.

The reality was that her life could be vastly different in a matter of hours, depending on who won this match, and it finally hit her with such force that she inadvertently lost her grip on the crystal glass of Krug. A waiter arrived swiftly at her side, offering another before cleaning up the expensive mess she had made.

Caesar watched her every move from the corner of the room like a hawk sitting on a perch. She truly was a beauty to behold; there was no denying her attractiveness to every male in her midst, even those more than double her age, like himself. But Eloise was far too innocent a creature for him; these days, his relationships with women meant only sex, never love. Besides he despised the look of older men with much younger women hanging off their arms. He thought them pathetic and believed such relationships merely provided an entrée to financial grief.

There had only ever been one true love in Caesar's life, and that had been many, many years ago. Even though the relationship had been brief, his heart had been crushed so completely he had never recovered enough to trust or love another woman again.

However, it didn't stop him from admiring the graceful curves beneath Eloise's pale pink wrap-around dress. One could never deny she was a ballerina; it was just that today she wore a more elegant outfit, appropriate to the circumstances.

Caesar found himself reflecting that it was a shame his father wasn't here; he'd always appreciated beauty, even though he'd never really respected women. (This remained a sore point between father and son – though Caesar had to admit he was growing more cynical about relationships himself these days.)

The relentless onset of Alzheimer's ensured that Antonio King was now essentially a prisoner within the grounds of his Sussex mansion, under the constant care of Nurse Victoria. Caesar tried to mask the constant worry he carried for his father, his ever-present poker face allowing him to effectively shield his true feelings from others. Winning substantial amounts of money always proved an excellent distraction for Caesar, so whenever his emotions threatened him, he deliberately increased the stakes, hoping the euphoria of winning would provide the ultimate high and deaden the feeling of loneliness that sometimes seeped through.

More than his many other business dealings, his intriguing Number One Strategy was proving an excellent tonic for his emotional state. The smile returned to his face as he considered the money he had made already, knowing that was only a pittance compared with what was to come, particularly after today's match was won.

And Eloise was just where he wanted her for this momentous match. She was ever discreet and softly spoken in conversation – features he always appreciated in a woman yet rarely found – but he was fascinated that she had mentioned nothing to him of her week in London with Noah. He wondered if she honestly believed he wasn't aware of her every move on any given day.

He sighed inwardly. She might be beautiful, but she was still so young and unworldly. Even so, as long as she honoured her end of the deal, he would always honour his.

In the meantime, however, there was far too much at stake for her to be roaming around aimlessly as she had been with Noah Levique – of all people – when Ivan disappeared into an emotional hole after his loss at Wimbledon. Caesar's sources had mentioned nothing of a relationship between Noah and Eloise before she was offered the contract. Only time would tell if she was being secretive or merely naive in her actions; he didn't know her well enough yet to say. But either way, if she honestly believed her contract with him allowed her that much freedom – with a tennis player he didn't represent, no less – she was sorely mistaken. This was the sort of inside information he depended on – indeed, was betting on, and not insignificantly! It was time to stalk his prey a little more closely ...

'Lovely to see you again, Eloise. How are you?'

'Very well, thanks, Caesar. And you?'

'Couldn't be better. Nothing more exciting than the potential changing of the guard, don't you think?' There was a twinkle in his eyes as he said the words and nodded to the waiter to refill her glass.

Talking to Caesar when her life could be about to change was making Eloise nervous, so she made a deliberate attempt to remain as polite and calm as possible, carefully considering her answers before she spoke.

'How have things been with Ivan?' he asked.

'Well, as you'd be aware, he hasn't quite been himself since the loss at Wimbledon, and now with his injury and all ...'

'I know. Poor chap, things haven't gone his way recently. So what's been keeping you occupied?'

Eloise's nerves shifted a gear but fortunately her voice remained steady.

'Taking in the sights; there's always plenty to do in New York.'

She offered nothing more, and he decided to let the matter rest, for now. 'Indeed there is. So tell me, what are your thoughts on these two players?'

'I'm no expert on tennis, Caesar; you'd know far better than I would.'

He silently congratulated her on her answer: sticking to generalities rather than getting personal. Perhaps she had more intelligence than he'd given her credit for.

'Yes, yes, quite right.' He chuckled. 'Then let me phrase my question more succinctly. Would you prefer a change, or for your circumstances to remain as they are?'

She paused before answering, unsure of what he was hoping to hear. 'My preference is irrelevant, Caesar. I will accept whatever happens; that's the commitment I've made.'

'I'm very pleased to hear that you're taking the contract as seriously as I am. I'm not one for deviations once something has been agreed. Enjoy the game, Eloise; heaven knows I shall.'

With a clink of his glass and a cheerful wink that belied the veiled threat in his words, he excused himself to go and chat with his other guests as the pre-match tension rose steadily around them.

The knots in Eloise's stomach tightened as the two players entered the stadium and applause instantly erupted. Noah came out first, and the crowd enthusiastically welcomed the new kid on the block. Though he was smiling and waving, everyone could sense his nervousness at being in his first grand-slam final. Eloise beamed with pride, hoping he'd received her message and small gift. Caesar didn't miss a single twitch of her expressive face from the other side of the room.

The cheering changed when Stephan Nordstrom appeared on the court, sporting his sponsored Maui Jim sunglasses. The newly appointed tennis superstar acknowledged the crowd with a brief nod before immediately getting down to the business of ensuring the brands of his clothes, racquets and even his drink bottles were facing the right way for maximum exposure. It took three attempts for him to find the racquet with the perfect string tension, then he carefully placed the other two back in his sponsored sports bag, ensuring they were in the exact position he wanted them. Some might have called him obsessive–compulsive – and many had, often – but the sponsors Caesar had secured on his behalf would handsomely reward such meticulousness.

Once these actions were performed, he sat perfectly still, more focused than a neurosurgeon about to make his first incision. It was as if the crowd no longer existed in his mind. The look on his face made it clear that Nordstrom was here for one reason only.

To dominate and to win.

Eloise's nerves electrified as she was torn between her excitement at the prospect of a new Number One particularly a Swedish god like Stephan – and wanting to protect her gorgeous Noah from such a tour de force. Though beaming at Noah, she found herself drawn to Stephan, wondering if he was as domineering in person as he was on court. She watched in awe along with thousands of other fans as he sat trance-like in his seat before the announcer summoned the players onto the court for their warm-up.

Eloise desperately hoped the knot in her stomach would ease when play commenced.

Nothing could have been further from the truth.

Transition

The entire match lasted a little over an hour – much to the disappointment of the crowd, some of whom had paid a small fortune just to witness a wipeout.

There was no opportunity for Eloise to find Noah and offer her condolences on losing so catastrophically in straight sets. Realistically, she had no idea how she could even have attempted to locate him, given the security around the stadium. Since her brief conversation with Caesar she had sensed he was watching her every move, so she didn't even dare send a message to Noah in case he showed up and aroused Caesar's suspicions further.

Caesar's people ensured she was escorted directly back to the hotel to await further instructions. Once again, she felt like an object in Caesar's world – a world where he oversaw her every move until the transition was complete. She was sure that, had she attempted to leave the premises, she would have been prevented.

She tried to call Noah when she was finally alone but went straight through to his voicemail. She left a message telling him she was sorry but reassuring him that it was only the first of many grand-slam finals to come. She couldn't help but think that perhaps eliminating smoking from his lifestyle might guarantee better success, but she didn't dare say it!

After meeting up with Ivan for a platonic yet warm goodbye, she was informed of the request for her to be in the hotel boardroom at 9pm to meet Stephan Nordstrom.

Eloise felt like she was in limbo. So to keep her thoughts and emotions at bay, she went for a long swim in the hotel pool. After which, she prepared herself, dressing simply and elegantly in a black cocktail dress and heels, her hair pulled into a low chignon.

At 8.50pm there was a sharp knock on the door of her suite. A suited man, no doubt one of Caesar's entourage, silently escorted her to the boardroom. The butterflies in her stomach were as violent as they'd been before her first performance as Principal.

She sat demurely with her eyes lowered while Caesar's lawyers negotiated with Stephan's. As the paperwork was signed and exchanged, every fibre of her being could sense Stephan's wild excitement as he courteously pulled back her chair from the boardroom table. As she stood, she looked up to meet his intense gaze as his steely-blue eyes feasted on her petite form and the dynamic between them intensified. Stephan's dominance on the court was nothing compared to meeting the man himself – and it took her breath away, literally – as the electricity between them was undeniable to everyone in the room.

'So, tomorrow morning, then, I shall see you at the Waldorf?' His eyebrows rose in question, as if not quite believing this extraordinary situation to be real.

'Yes, sir,' she responded quietly, knowing even as she uttered the words that her relationship with this Number One would be entirely different from her distant relations with Ivan.

'I shall await your arrival with pleasure.'

A delicious shiver ricocheted to the core of her belly at the prospect of what was to come. If his words had that effect on her, then who knew what impact his touch might have …

As if sensing her body's response, he guided her out the door with a sudden smile.

It was rare for Stephan to agree to a meeting straight after a match – particularly one involving his lawyers – but when Caesar's letter had arrived requesting a private audience at Stephan's earliest convenience, he'd accepted immediately. Since signing with The Edge, his success both on and off the court had grown exponentially. So Caesar was the last person he'd decline to meet; after all, Caesar was to tennis what the Pope was to Catholicism. However, to say Stephan was anything less than dumbfounded at the private discussion he'd had with the great man right before meeting Eloise would be a lie.

Stephan's celebrations that evening after his third grand-slam victory were tinged with unexpected visions of what his future might hold given Caesar's 'bequest' of Eloise Lawrance. Stephan had never been with a professional ballet dancer, but had he met one as exquisite as Eloise, he'd have rectified that situation immediately.

After he'd laid eyes on the enigmatic Eloise, the bevy of inane beauties who accompanied him for drinks at the hip Ling Ling Bar at Hakkasan Restaurant didn't quite have the desired effect on his usually virile libido. Not that it seemed to bother the leggy blondes and brunettes, as long as the zesty martinis kept flowing between their ready lips and the eager photographers captured their image as they partied with the man who would adorn the front pages in the morning.

Two of them accompanied him back to his suite just beyond midnight. But instead of enjoying the *ménage à trois* as he usually would, Stephan found himself distracted by the sight of the milky limbs and innocent aquamarine eyes gazing at him from the portfolio Caesar had left with him. As soon as the girls had finished blowing him – a perfunctory experience at best – he called for Garry, who managed his security and his life, to escort them out. He and Garry exchanged a look that suggested Stephan would have no problem should Garry want to enjoy the sexual delights the ladies had to offer.

To the best of his understanding of Caesar's proposition, Eloise would be on loan to him, for his personal use, so long as he retained the ATP ranking of Number One. Her role in his life was to be discussed and mutually agreed between them. A bizarre arrangement, but he had no wish to argue after their introduction last night.

For the first time in a very long time, he was excited about something other than tennis. It was no surprise that sleep came to him like a steam train after such an eventful day.

Perfect

The next morning Stephan dismissed his staff from his suite at the Waldorf, to ensure the privacy he wanted with this stunning ballet dancer. He needed to understand more intimately the machinations of this highly unusual relationship.

'Eloise! Come in, please,' he called as her polite knock was heard at the door.

As soon as pleasantries were exchanged, they both settled onto the lounge, looking out at the most impressive cityscape in the world. Eloise sat demurely in a pale blue jersey dress and beige peeptoe court shoes. Stephan spread his arms wide across the lounge, looking exactly like the Scandinavian sports god his publicists liked to suggest he was. His striped blue and white shirt seemed startlingly bright against his tanned skin, and sat taut across his broad chest and shoulders. For Eloise, his presence in the room was even more dominating than on either the court or the screen as he took up at least three times the space she did.

Stephan was not one for small talk, so he wasted no time in getting to the point.

'So, let me get this straight: you are apparently mine, as long as I retain the Number One position.'

'That is correct, sir.'

'And we are to mutually agree on the role you will play in my life?'

She nodded.

'Please answer me directly.'

She raised her eyes to look directly into his from beneath her lids; he was a completely different species from Ivan, and Noah for that matter …

'Yes, sir,' she responded. 'It is important that I understand your expectations and boundaries in order for our relationship to work.'

'I see. Then I suppose you should know my life is about two things, Eloise: perfection and control.' He paused to gauge her reaction. 'Let me be clear. Domination is my life. Winning is my world.'

Shivers raced through Eloise from head to toe as his words resonated deep within her, and although she made a concerted effort to hide her reaction, it was without success.

A satisfied smile stretched across his lips as he noticed her muscles quiver at his words; her eyes remaining steadfastly fixed to one spot on the floor. His groin instantly reacted to the sexual tension between them.

It had caught him off guard that she was even more appealing in person than her photos had suggested. He loved her prim English accent, with the merest hint of Australian casualness to it. Her lithe body with her toned curves seemed to be begging to be stroked. The discipline she maintained over herself as she tried to rein in her reaction to him caused him no end of arousal.

She was perfect. And he worshipped perfection.

'Do you think you can handle that?'

'I hope I can always rise to a challenge, sir.'

'Do you understand what I am saying?'

'Yes, sir.'

'I sensed as much.' He paused thoughtfully, rubbing his chin between his thumb and forefinger. It was a rare experience for him to be so entranced by a woman. 'I would expect your total honesty in all aspects of our relationship. Can you agree to that?'

'I can, sir.

'Excellent. Tell me about the relationship you had with Ivan, your previous Master.'

'I danced for him, sir. Before every match he played, and sometimes afterwards.'

'That's it? Nothing else?'

'Nothing else, sir, no.'

Stephan was astonished by this revelation. He found it almost impossible to believe any man could keep his hands off such a sexual delicacy. Perhaps the rumours floating round about Borisov's sexuality were true …

'And you were content with that, given the other conditions outlined in your contract?'

Stephan noticed the slight shift in her body language and the rose colour that flushed her cheeks before she answered.

'Meeting his wishes made me content, sir.'

'Answer me honestly, Eloise. What if he had wanted more?'

'I would have given him more, sir,' she replied simply and honestly.

Stephan ran his fingers through his thick, sculpted blond hair. He wasn't used to the array of emotions his body was experiencing, wild and confused. He needed to take control of himself immediately.

'Stand up for me.'

Eloise immediately stood from her seated position, her eyes still cast downwards.

'Did you bring your ballet slippers today?'

'They are always with me, sir.' She pointed to her bag.

Stephan swore this woman's actions had the potential to break him. Her submissive nature wound around his cock like a vice.

'Good. I'd like you to dance for me, like you did for Ivan; I want to see what he saw. You can prepare in the bedroom.'

With a flick of his hand, he quickly dismissed her, lest she see the undeniable physical effect she had on him. He was pleased that he had organised for the furniture in the dining room to be shifted prior to her arrival so she could dance on the parquet flooring. He always liked to be prepared.

It was as though the music awakened his senses like never before as her disciplined and finely honed body moved gracefully in front of him. Stephan couldn't take his eyes off her; she was mesmerising as she danced. He became as lost in her world as she was, a space that seemed far removed from reality, as though it existed in an entirely new stratosphere. After the last flutter of her pale arms had played out in the tips of her fingers, in perfect timing with the final note of Chopin, both of them were lost for words.

The female before Stephan blew his mind. So frail yet so strong, so fragile yet so athletic. Eloise remained in her demure position, face towards her pointed, slippered toes and eyes lowered, awaiting his next move. He gathered himself quickly, forcing his mind back into the here and now.

'I can see why Ivan had you dance for him. Such beauty, such serenity ...'

He gently stroked the line of her long neck as she remained in position, not having moved a muscle since completing her dance. She was entirely still except for her beating heart and the delicate rise and fall of her chest: something much easier said than done.

He allowed his fingers to follow the line of her shoulder and trace the length of her arm to her fingertips. She didn't utter a word, nor did she encourage or dismiss his touch. Boldly, he lifted her fingers to his lips, slowly kissing their tips, his curiosity at her reaction to him ensuring that his eyes never left her face. The sharp intake of her breath was barely audible, but certainly noticed.

The slightest of smiles that reached both their lips confirmed that their relationship with each other would certainly be much more than ballet, and both silently acknowledged it would be far from chaste.

Eloise burnt in places that she had previously been able to subdue, to deny the existence of in her body. Her glow was as much internal as it was external, and her muscles pulsed with excitement as she thought of how her relationship with this tennis god might unfold.

He pulled her body against his muscled torso and she felt every inch of his six foot four inches of height. Her petite frame felt even smaller as she rested against his bulk and inhaled his crisp, fresh scent. He wrapped his arms around her, encasing her body, and bent down to feather light kisses on her long neck. The simultaneous dominance and softness of his action threatened her upright position.

'You are simply exquisite,' he whispered into her ear, his words far less commanding than when she'd arrived. 'Where have you been all my life? I'm sure I must be dreaming. Tell me I'm not dreaming, Eloise. Please, put me out of my misery.'

'You are not dreaming, sir.' She sounded as breathless as she felt light-headed.

'What am I to you?'

'You are my Master.'

'And you choose this, of your own free will?'

'I do, sir.'

He paused for a moment, allowing her words to fully sink in to his consciousness.

'Why?' he asked.

Unbelievable

For the first time, Stephan felt her tense beneath his touch. He observed her hesitation as he guided her back to the lounge and wrapped a throw around her shoulders, understanding the need for her to stay warm after such physical exertion.

'Just like you, I need to understand what makes you tick if this is to work,' he explained. 'Talk to me …'

'I need boundaries. I like discipline. I love to please.' She didn't make eye contact as she said the words.

'I can understand that.' He idly played with a strand of her hair that had fallen free from her tight bun. 'Tell me more.'

'You have my file, just as I have yours, sir.'

'I want to hear it from your mouth.' The words rolled off his tongue so sensually that she couldn't imagine denying him anything.

'The ballet gave me all of those things. All the details of my life were organised for me – what I ate, what I wore, where I went, what

I did. I had focus, I had ability, they had control and I loved what I did. I had no social life, no life at all other than the ballet. When that stopped …' She inadvertently rubbed her ankle … 'I felt like I was in freefall. My life lost all its meaning and purpose.'

She raised her eyes to meet his and they locked for some time.

'And your family?'

'I have no family – only the ballet, since I was twelve, sir.'

'I see. By the way, you don't need to keep calling me sir,' he said before continuing his inquisition. 'Boyfriends?'

'Not really, sir – oh, sorry,' she corrected herself.

'I can't believe there was never any interest.'

'There *has* been interest, yes, but I considered it all a distraction, as I was dedicated to the ballet. Dance always came first by a long way, so nothing ever developed.'

'And now? Friends?'

'Not really – some of the other dancers, perhaps, but I don't keep in touch with them now. I suppose we were close in some ways, but we were also in constant competition with each other so it didn't foster strong relationships. The constant bitchiness left me worn out so I tended not to socialise more than I had to. I've never been comfortable around a lot of people.' She looked into his eyes, trying to read his face before continuing. 'This role has given me the opportunity to enjoy a better lifestyle, continue my dancing and see the world from a different perspective. *And* to be of service, I hope.'

She felt a slight twinge of betrayal for not mentioning her relationship with Noah, but given that Stephan had just annihilated him at Arthur Ashe Stadium she thought it best to say nothing. It was all a little too close to home.

'I find you utterly intriguing … perplexing, but intriguing.'

Stephan's mind was racing. The entire premise of a relationship like this presented endless possibilities. The constant arguments he had with Ava, his current girlfriend, were monotonous and exhausting. Stunning as she was, her jealousy added a dimension to his life he didn't need, and over the last few months she had become like a noose around his neck. Complaining about all the travel and never being able to see each other, telling him he wasn't being sensitive to her needs and didn't respect her career as a model. He still couldn't believe she could even compare her job with his, but never even bothered getting into that argument, so futile would it be. He rolled his eyes in frustration just thinking about it.

Ava hadn't even managed to make it back from her exotic photo shoot in the Maldives to witness his grand-slam victory yesterday. It was the US Open, for Christ's sake, but she'd somehow managed to miss her connecting flight. Did she honestly expect him to sit idly around waiting for her when his career had just placed him on top of the world? What was he supposed to do when women threw themselves at him at the glamorous events he attended? Their persuasiveness could be intense, and he couldn't help it if his eyes, and libido, led him astray on occasion. And now that he was Number One, he certainly had no intention of settling down with just one person. The world was his oyster, and it seemed as if he had just discovered the perfect pearl!

Here in front of him sat this delicate peach of such serene beauty, who was willing for him to be her Master – in all ways – and who wanted nothing but to be of service to him as he continued his all-important journey towards grand-slam domination.

It was unbelievable! Nothing excited him more than ultimate control; he thrived on it. And she was giving herself to him on a platter – and then some!

'I suppose the main thing you have to decide is whether you want me and in what capacity,' she said.

'There is no doubt that I want you, Eloise. That decision has already been made.'

She was surprised at how his words roused deep feelings within her. To be wanted by someone meant more to her than anything else. It touched her to the core. It felt different from being wanted by Noah, who respected and accepted the friendship she'd enforced. She felt Stephan would never accept such a compromise; he was such a powerful force he would always demand more, and this realisation stirred strong and unexpected emotions within her psyche.

Stephan, meanwhile, could barely believe that a woman like Eloise existed. He made a mental note to check with his lawyers that the contract between them was rock-solid. He knew what doing business with Caesar could be like and he didn't want her slipping between the cracks.

'If that is your wish –'

He interrupted her at once. 'It most certainly is my wish – and then some.' His grin broadened to a full-blown smile at the thought that from this moment on, she was his.

She continued, 'Then within the terms of the contract and the role we agree together, I am yours.' She returned his smile with shy yet mischievous eyes.

'But if I don't retain the Number One ranking?' He could never bring himself to say 'lose'; it just wasn't part of his mindset.

'Then I am no longer yours. My contract with you would terminate and my involvement would be negotiated with the new Number One, just as it was with you yesterday.'

It dawned on Stephan that this was where she held some of the power.

'Luckily for me I don't have any desire to change my status.'

He looked down at the notes he'd scribbled when he reviewed the contract before she arrived. 'It says in the contract that I may give you a new name, to protect your identity, given my profile.'

'Yes, sir – oh, sorry – yes, that's correct.'

He thought for a moment before deciding.

'I would like to call you, Nadia. Just being near you, watching your movements, the way you carry yourself with such composure, such grace. *Nåd* means "grace" in Swedish.'

'To be called Nadia would be my pleasure.'

'Do you like it?'

'I do, sir. More importantly, I'm pleased it has meaning for *you*.'

Stephan had to pinch himself to be sure this was really happening.

'So ...' He leant forward, with his legs spread wide, his elbows on his knees and his knuckles nestled against his chin. He paused for a moment, adjusting to the idea that he had just renamed this precious, petite beauty sitting before him 'Nadia'. In his mind this signified just how much control over her he had been given. 'It appears that if I want to keep you, I have no choice but to remain at the top of my game?'

Stephan couldn't deny that Caesar was even more clever than he'd thought. Being Number One meant everything to him, but this arrangement took things to an entirely new level. His motivation to win would be even more intense, to ensure that Nadia remained his possession, and his only. She would be at his beck and call, without the emotional collateral of having a girlfriend. Sex would be at his discretion, and couldn't be denied him unless he acted outside the boundaries of the contract. If such a discrepancy should occur and couldn't be resolved between both parties, Caesar's lawyers would step in to arbitrate – not that Stephan ever had any intention of letting things go that far.

'Yes, sir, it sounds like you understand perfectly. The second you are not consistently on top of your game, you lose me.' The cheekiness in her voice belied the underlying seriousness of her answer. The tension between them immediately shifted gear to 'game on', which excited Stephan no end.

'Well, it just so happens that my personal goals are spectacularly aligned with such a scenario.' He chuckled, and noticed a dimple appear on her cheek as she attempted to stifle a grin.

He rose from the lounge, towering above her. 'I want to finalise the details of your role in my life today so we can begin as soon as possible. Are you ready to do that now?'

'Nothing would please me more, sir.'

He looked directly at her as he reached for her hand. Obviously her old habits died hard.

Commitment

'Would you like a coffee?

'I don't drink caffeine.'

'Really? Do you drink alcohol?'

'Only rarely, sir, but admittedly a bit more often since meeting Caesar.'

'Ah, yes, he does love a celebration.'

'It seems he has had a lot to celebrate recently.' She smiled. 'I would love a green tea if you have any.'

'Apparently you are as pure as you look. And I notice a guide to your diet has been included as an appendix to the contract.' He waved towards the paperwork on the kitchen bench. 'You are sure you would prefer me to control your food?'

'As long as I don't put on too much weight and you don't starve me, yes, I am comfortable with that, sir.'

'I can assure you – *Nadia* – I have no intention of starving you; it would not be in my best interests. And as for putting on weight, let's just say I have many ideas that will ensure your physical activity is kept at an appropriate level.'

The salacious grin that accompanied his words caused Nadia to shift in her seat as her groin responded directly to his words.

Her sexual body was awakening with a vibrancy she hadn't experienced since forcing it to remain frustratingly dormant since her time with Noah.

His piercing blue eyes finally released her from his gaze as he turned to prepare the drinks.

'One issue we need to get sorted out quickly is this whole "sir" thing. You seem far more comfortable using it than my name, which you haven't uttered once. Why?'

'My training. My instructors were always referred to as "Madame", "Mistress", "Master" or "sir". It comes naturally to me after so many years.'

'I see – and is this the way you would prefer to address me?'

'I will try to adapt to whatever you decide.'

Stephan deftly made her green tea, passing it over the bench and gently trapping her hand as she reached for it. Once again, he looked intently into her eyes as if attempting to decipher her thoughts. He had certainly never met anyone like her.

What was his decision? He had to admit that although he had never considered it, he quite liked the idea of her so naturally addressing him as 'sir'. It was embedded with respect. 'Master' seemed a bit much, but who knew what he could get used to in the foreseeable future …

'You can call me "sir" when we are alone or with my staff, and "Stephan" or "Mr Nordstrom" when we are with others, depending on the situation. I'll let you know what's appropriate.'

With that, he began to painstakingly make his own coffee with his immaculate new Clover coffee machine. Stephan loved the way it allowed him to control every aspect of the coffee-making process – which made him ponder just how much control he might have over the beautiful creature with pale milky skin and aquamarine eyes sitting at his kitchen bench.

He couldn't help but test the boundaries. 'I'd like to see you with your hair out.'

'Of course.'

'Now.'

'Oh, I must warn you, I have very unruly hair, sir; it's much more manageable left like this.'

Stephan collected his perfect coffee, placing it on the bench before moving to stand behind her barstool. His proximity put her on high alert, her body reacting instinctively to his raw masculinity.

He lowered his mouth to her ear. 'Thanks for the advice, but I'd like to touch it, if I may.'

He felt her body tremble at his words as she agreed to his request. He released her hair from the tight confines of the low bun. Long auburn locks immediately cascaded past her shoulders and settled just above her waist, like a magnificent mane blanketing her upper body.

'You have astonishingly beautiful hair. I would never have guessed, the way you wear it – so tight, so controlled.' He couldn't keep the surprise out of his voice.

'Unfortunately, it is not the most ideal hair for a ballerina.' Her hair had always exasperated her during preparations for performances, given the time it took to secure in place; other dancers would have theirs done in a quarter of the time.

Stephan ran his fingers over her silken locks, stroking, lightly tugging and playing with them. 'Your natural colour?'

'Yes, sir.'

'And your pubic hair, is it the same?'

She blushed deeply at his words and he tilted her chin up with his finger, sensing her embarrassment but silently demanding her to make eye contact. 'As I mentioned before, to make this relationship work I need your complete honesty. I need it at all times and without delay. Do I have this commitment from you?'

Eloise knew she would cross an invisible boundary with Stephan as soon as she answered both questions. Nervous energy consumed her thoughts; she couldn't deny her attraction to the Adonis standing before her.

She thought of Noah, and how she hadn't been upfront with him about the contract with Caesar, even though it would have explained why she couldn't be with him. In fact, the contract explicitly prevented her from being completely honest with him – with anyone outside the agreement. What would it do to their friendship if he ever found out?

Yet she didn't have much time to focus on any of this, as Stephan, the man she was contracted to please, the man whose mere proximity made her weak at the knees, was towering above her, waiting for her response.

'Yes, sir.'

'Yes to what?'

'Yes to both.'

'Say it.' He cupped her face between the palms of his hands, enforcing his dominance. 'And look at me while you do.'

Eloise had the sense that she was on the edge of an abyss, knowing her life would change irrevocably from this moment on. Her fate was in his hands. She inhaled before responding, knowing that deep within her psyche she was longing to obey this man, to farewell her old identity and become fully immersed in his world – as Nadia.

'Yes, my pubic hair is the same colour. Yes, I will be completely honest with you.'

He raised his eyebrows, awaiting more.

'At all times and without delay, sir.'

'Thank you, Nadia. This is non-negotiable from my perspective, and I can't express how much your commitment means to me.'

Energy

As soon as Eloise's new role as 'Nadia' had been agreed with Stephan and sent to the lawyers as an addendum to the contract, Stephan wasted no time in whisking her away from New York to his luxury house on one of the canals of Grand Cayman. Sweden had not made the semifinals of the next big tournament, the Davis Cup – other than Stephan there were no Swedish players ranked in the top fifty – so the timing couldn't have been better for him to get to know and understand Nadia in complete detail. No one could dispute that his current form was exceptional; the US Open had proved that beyond any doubt. And as long as he kept to his training regime with his coach, he considered he should have no trouble competing in the Shanghai Rolex Masters in a month's time.

The first week Nadia and Stephan shared together was like walking on sexual eggshells. As each day passed, their attraction to each other intensified. Her dancing was an undeniable aphrodisiac and his dose needed to increase daily. The more she danced for him, the more physical release he required.

His coach couldn't put his finger on what was driving the energy and stamina in Stephan's training particularly so soon after having won a grand slam. All he knew was that during the first week or so at Cayman, it was impossible to keep up with Stephan's physical demands, either on the court or in the gym.

Ava was away on yet another photo shoot in Tahiti and knew nothing of Nadia's sudden entrance into Stephan's life. This was a stroke of luck from Stephan's perspective, as he would have been hard pressed to come up with an acceptable explanation. Ava hated spending time in the Cayman Islands, even though it was where Stephan relaxed the most. Her preference was to be surrounded by the hives of activity the world's great cities had to offer, which made more sense for her career, so she tended to spend time with Stephan only when it coincided with her work and social schedules.

Stephan's ego had rationalised that it was more than fair to enjoy the odd one-night stand should the opportunity present itself (and it did more often than not), particularly if Ava was unavailable to sate his sexual needs. So it was peculiar for him to want to take his time with his new acquisition. But what an exquisite acquisition she was. As he had every intention of being Number One for some time, he wanted the perfect plan in place to introduce her to his compelling world of desire.

As Stephan released his pent-up energy on the court, acing his coach for the eighth time in a row, he finally gave the man some relief by easing into a baseline rally. He let his mind wander again to Ava. Under the terms of his contract with Nadia, there was no obligation for him to disclose anything to her of his relationship with Ava. And the last thing he wanted was for Nadia to be exposed by Ava – for both his and Caesar's sake. The sooner Ava was officially out of his life the better. Ava's proclivity for drama would keep the social pages buzzing for weeks; Stephan knew how much the tabloids loved the scent of a rift in a high-profile relationship and how they typically blew it out of all proportion. He would finish things with Ava before the one scheduled event they would both attend – their friend's art exhibition – before taking the next step with his secret possession.

Just as he'd arrived at that thought, his coach waved his arms in surrender. 'Enough, Stephan, I give up! It's time for a break. I am officially giving you some time off; you need to focus on something else for a while and save this sort of play for a tournament.'

Stephan laughed and walked off the court, throwing a towel at his coach. Then he grabbed one for himself, using it to wipe down his glistening, ripped torso.

He knew *exactly* what he wanted to focus on as the seeds of a plan sprouted in his mind. And they brought a smile to his face and tension to his groin.

* * *

Although Nadia was free to leave the house, she was content to stay within its confines, keen to learn Stephan's habits and preferences in order to perfect her role of servitude. She had taken some time off from dancing so she could secretly watch Stephan training with his coach from the bay window of her room. His body looked magnificent and her eyes were drawn to his tanned torso and toned six-pack, visible right beneath her window, unfortunately just beyond her reach.

The fluidity of his movements reminded her that there was indeed artistry in athleticism. He played a more masculine, rawer game than Ivan and was undeniably absorbing to watch. She loved having such a bird's-eye view all to herself.

She wondered what Noah's true style was on the court, and was disappointed that she had only had the opportunity to watch him play against Stephan, which certainly hadn't shown him at his best. Although she had tried calling him a few times since then and he'd returned her calls, they'd always managed to miss each other, so their communication took place via text messages. At least it made it easier not having to explain her new life to him, but she felt really bad about not having spoken to him since New York. And if she was honest, even though life with Stephan was all-consuming, she missed his voice.

So when she knew Stephan was in the downstairs shower, she called again.

'Noah, finally! How are you?'

'Hi, Elle! Great. Sorry we keep missing each other. Where are you, still in the States?'

'No, not exactly … I'm so sorry about your loss.'

'There's still plenty of tennis to win, but thanks. It was good experience, and at least I know what I'm up against next time.' His comment sent shivers down her spine.

'Listen, I'd love to see you, when can we catch up? It feels like forever ago that we were lazing around on the canals of London.'

'You're telling me!' She reflected on just how much her life had changed in the last fortnight; it was incredible. 'But I'm not exactly sure what my plans are at this stage.'

'How's Ivan going? I hear he's pulled out of the circuit.'

'Yeah, he has, but he's OK …'

She heard Stephan's voice calling out, 'Nadia!' from downstairs.

'I've got to go, sorry. I'll call you again soon.'

'Oh, OK. I miss you!'

'Miss you too. Bye!'

As she pressed 'End' she wondered again what Noah would think about her new 'arrangement' with Stephan. In one sense she told herself she was merely fulfilling the business terms of her contract with Caesar. She was now well acquainted with each and every term, and knew that as long as she abided by the rules, her financial independence would be guaranteed at the conclusion of the eighth grand slam. Her life would finally be her own. So her sole focus during this time should be to meet the needs and expectations of her Master, her Number One, 24/7. It was clear and mutually agreed on, and she was as determined as she had ever been to ensure she succeeded.

Even so, she couldn't help but ponder what Noah would have to say about the sexual implications of her contract. And though she tried not to, she often found herself contemplating what might have happened if she had fallen for Noah *before* allowing

Caesar to uproot her life. Unfortunately now she would never know …

As far as she was concerned, Noah was her only issue with this entire situation. He didn't even know her as Nadia, which was another aspect of her relationship with Stephan that would take some explaining should the moment present itself. She reflected on the special, carefree time they'd shared travelling the canals, a treasured period of fun, friendship and mutual attraction. Yet it seemed like a delightful walk in the park compared to spending time with such an all-encompassing force of nature as Stephan.

It was like comparing a playful kitten with a cunning lion.

Nadia was unable to dislodge the lingering feeling that Stephan would never approve of her friendship with Noah, no matter how she might try to persuade him. So she decided it would be best to keep both worlds apart for as long as possible and attempt to push her conundrum to the back of her mind. No mean feat, given both of them were involved in the competitive world of tennis, but she would do what she could.

Unwilling to risk receiving a phone call from Noah while Stephan was around, she turned her phone off and instead kissed the snow dome he'd given her, which sat on her bedside table. She still missed him immensely but just couldn't see how their friendship would ever work in her new world.

She checked her appearance in the mirror and ran downstairs, eager to respond to her Master's call. His voice and his presence were intoxicating to her – just as they were to most people he came into contact with, which ensured she was in a continual state of giddying arousal when they were together. She had never felt such tension, and she was on tenterhooks waiting to discover when their intimate relationship would flow into becoming a sexual one.

Tension

When Stephan returned to Miami to fulfil his obligations with US sponsors having won the US Open, his absence created a hollow within Nadia she hadn't anticipated. So she coped with her feelings the only way she knew how: she danced. Stephan had kindly converted part of the gymnasium in his basement to a dance studio, so during the days he spent away from her, she threw herself into dance. The more physically demanding it was, the better.

During his absence, she studied more challenging dances, learnt new ballets from less recognised choreographers and found herself being drawn to dances embodying more sexually explicit themes, something she had never explored before. She was surprised at the depth of satisfaction she felt as she focused her mind and forced her body to master the demanding new routines, hour after relentless hour. There was one dance in particular that resonated with her more than the others, its raw tribal rhythm thrust her body to lusty heights in the privacy of the studio as she raised the bar of her own already high personal standards, forcing herself further and harder towards mastery … until the strain on her weakened ankle caused it to crumble under the pressure.

'Damn it!' she yelled into the room, her voice reverberating against the bare walls. Collapsed on the floor in pain and angry with her ankle for preventing her from continuing, she thumped the floor in exasperation as tears slid down her cheeks.

'You have been pushing yourself too far, Nadia, working too hard.'

She was startled by the voice coming from the shadows of the room, though surprise didn't prevent her belly from igniting.

'I'm sorry, sir, I didn't realise you were home,' she said, embarrassed that he had seen her frustration and vulnerability, her weakness, when she thought she was alone. She attempted to pick herself up, but her ankle buckled beneath her the minute she tried to put pressure on it.

Stephan moved so fast that he had her in his arms before she landed back on the floor. Lowering her gently back down, he rested her back against his chest, his arms encircling her light frame as it lay between his strong, toned legs.

As they rested against the wall, they could see each other's reflection in the mirror across the room. Stephan deeply inhaled the scent of her sweaty femininity, a surprisingly strong aphrodisiac for his senses. He imagined her in this state after a session in bed, or elsewhere, with him. He was forced to adjust her frame away from him momentarily until he could regain control of his groin.

He encased her entirely as he strengthened the grip of his body around hers, feeling powerful and protective towards her. It was as though she were a delicate, injured bird that he needed to prevent from flying so she could heal. He held her in silence, waiting patiently, until she finally gave in, exhaling and allowing her muscles to relax against his sheer strength.

'I have been watching you for twenty minutes. I've never seen you dance that before; it's new?'

'Yes, sir.'

'Such passion, such force for someone so delicate.'

'I'm not as delicate as you think I am … and I haven't mastered it yet; it will take some time.'

He laughed gently. 'I have no doubt you *will* master it, Nadia; it's in your nature.' He tenderly stroked the ringlets that had escaped during her dance, and his next words were like steel encased in velvet.

'You are not to dance again until Greta assesses your ankle and provides me with a detailed report.'

'Greta? Your physiotherapist? But, it's not bad –'

'Nadia!' His voice echoed around the studio. 'Do I have your word?'

'Please, sir, I'll rest this afternoon. It will be fine by tomorrow, really ...'

'Not until I have the report. You can't go on like this, your ankle needs time to heal.'

For the first time, Nadia looked utterly dejected at his words. Not allowing her to dance was like asking her not to breathe. While he'd been away it was all she'd had to occupy herself with.

He gently tilted her chin up towards his face until she was looking at him directly, rather than at the mirror.

'Who am I, Nadia?'

'My Master.'

'You know I am only doing this because I care about you and your future. And is it not my responsibility to look after you?'

He awaited her answer.

'Yes,' she said petulantly.

He raised his eyebrows, indicating he wasn't happy with her tone.

'OK. I don't like it, but I suppose I understand.' Her voice was quiet, as though darkness had eclipsed her heart.

'I will organise for Greta to see you this afternoon. In the meantime, you are not to be on your ankle. That is an order, Nadia. I hope I am making myself clear.'

An order? she thought. This was the first time he had used those words, and although they surprised her, she also found them unusually titillating.

'Abundantly, *Master*.' She said the word with emphasis, and the slightest of smiles simultaneously appeared on both their faces.

'And besides, we are going out tonight – and with what I have in mind, your ankle will get just the rest it needs.'

'Really? How?' She raised her eyebrows in anticipation, hoping for further explanation.

'Enough said.'

With that, he scooped her up from the floor, carried her to her quarters upstairs and organised a hot bath with Epsom salts in which to soak her tired body. Crutches arrived not long afterwards, alongside a lunch that included seafood bisque, a turkey and salad pide, homemade vegetable juice and a note.

Do not leave your room until you have eaten everything on this tray. Greta will see you at 2pm.

Dutifully, Nadia followed his instructions without complaint, knowing that disappointing Stephan would cause her much more concern than the trepidation she was feeling about her appointment with Greta. She'd had minor ailments before, but she knew deep down her ankle wasn't in great shape, and it certainly wasn't the first time it had given her problems. She vividly remembered her fall on the morning of the fateful day she left the ballet. The gruelling twelve-hour days took their toll on a dancer's body, with no downtime for minor injuries to fully heal. This had ensured the ballet's full-time physiotherapists were kept exceptionally busy, with dancers having to squeeze in appointments around classes, rehearsals and performances. With only one day off per week, Nadia had never taken a holiday other than the enforced summer breaks she spent further honing her skills.

She had been lucky enough to avoid a serious injury to date, but since her fall that day she had noticed the additional strain on her ankle each time she'd danced, particularly *en pointe*. She had doggedly chosen to ignore it. Yet just as her ballet masters could halt an entire class in the middle of their *grands battements* to send a dancer for treatment, she realised her new Master, her *tennis* master, now wielded the same power over her.

She had to admit she found some comfort in this idea, feeling suddenly more at home with him than she had ever felt with Ivan. At least she knew Stephan cared.

Attention

Meanwhile, Stephan was revelling in the control Nadia's injury had granted him, and enjoyed the fact that the emphasis was not on his own physique and injuries for once. Surprisingly, for one usually so focused on himself, he was actually enjoying the responsibility of looking after someone else: something he had never done before. And the fact that his orders (although not *always* happily received) were complied with precisely and without reprisal made him feel even more powerful in her life. So when Greta's report arrived for his perusal, he cancelled his weight session in the gym to give it his full attention.

Nadia had a Grade II ankle sprain with a partial tear of the ligament, and would only be permitted to walk lightly on her ankle if absolutely necessary. Crutches would be used for extended periods of movement. The clincher was that there was to be no dancing whatsoever for at least a month – otherwise the ligament could become completely torn, which would be a far more serious injury that could affect her dancing capability long term.

He understood how she would feel about this, but it was for the best. He would just need to be strict and keep her occupied with other things while she rested … This idea placed his trademark smile on his face. The same smile that provided him with more cash and product endorsements than any other player on the circuit. And the best part about all of this was that his plans for the evening would not need to change whatsoever.

'Perfect!' he muttered to himself as he sprinted off to inform Nadia of her physical state of play – in the short term at least.

Awaiting her fate, Nadia went to call Noah; she needed to hear his soothing voice. Much to her disappointment it went through to voicemail, and she couldn't bring herself to leave a message.

'Nadia?' Stephan gave a quick tap on the door before opening it and seeing her lying on the bed. Her slender leg was raised on two pillows, with an ice pack resting on her ankle.

This arrangement met with his instant approval.

'Good, I'm glad to see that Greta is doing her job. I've just received her report.'

Nadia thanked her lucky stars Noah hadn't answered just then. She didn't want to think about Stephan's reaction if he'd caught her talking on the phone to a friend she wasn't meant to have, particularly one who was his tennis rival.

She waited to hear Greta's verdict, but Stephan picked up the snow dome on her bedside table instead, giving it a shake and watching the colourful glitter land on the scene inside.

'You like snow domes?'

'I suppose so.' She tried to keep her tone casual.

'Have you been on a canal boat before?' he asked, inspecting the inside of it.

'Oh, a long time ago ...' The last thing she wanted to do was discuss that with Stephan, so she held out her hand for him to return it and put it away in the top drawer of the bedside table. It was only a snow dome, but it was precious to her.

'So ... what does Greta say in her report?' she asked warily, nonetheless eager to change the subject.

Stephan was in his element as he delivered a factual summary.

Nadia retaliated vehemently. 'No dancing for a month? You can't be serious!'

'Wow, you're certainly feisty when it comes to dancing – or not, as the case may be. I've never seen you like this!' He was genuinely taken aback by her response. '*At least* a month, and no more dancing *en pointe* until you are given the all-clear by Greta.'

She couldn't hold back a frustrated tear. If she couldn't dance, what would she do when he was training, or off on business trips?

Stephan sat on the bed next to her, feeling for her but in no way relenting. He remembered how a similar thing had happened to him when he was twenty-one. He'd believed his calf injury marked the end of his professional career, but with hindsight, he could see the overreaction of youth, and in the longer term it had actually made him a stronger, more powerful player.

'It's not for long. I'll look after you, and you'll be better than ever in no time, I promise. You know this happens in physical professions such as ours.' He tried to wipe away her tears but she shifted her face away from his hand. He had never seen her behave this way, and wasn't sure whether to admonish or comfort her.

'I know it's for my own good, but I feel like I'm being punished ...' The words came out before she could catch them.

'Nadia!' The stern look on Stephan's face made her retract her words immediately.

'I'm sorry, sir. I shouldn't have said that.' She sighed with relief as she saw the gruffness vanish, so that he relaxed a little.

'Never mind,' he replied. Then he added somewhat flippantly, 'Besides, if there are any punishments to dish out, I am more than happy to oblige.'

This time it was Nadia's turn to be shocked, which amused him greatly.

'You should be aware that I am quite partial to punishments; in fact, I derive much pleasure from administering them. Your being unable to dance doesn't fall into that category.' He raised an eyebrow and looked directly into her eyes as he continued. 'But it's good to know what buttons I can push if you do something to really piss me off, so I'll certainly keep that in mind.'

Although he grinned, Nadia couldn't decipher whether he was serious or not, though she had no doubt about interpreting his next comment as a stern finger pointed towards her face.

'Let me be clear. As long as you obey my command to stay off your ankle, there will be no reason for punishments per se.'

Just before he left the room, he turned back towards her. 'However, I can't promise you there won't be punishments for other misdemeanours as they occur – and I can't tell you how much I'm looking forward to that.'

The astonished look on her face was priceless and he couldn't hide his smugness.

'I suggest you have another look at the addendum we sent to the lawyers; you may see it in an entirely different light after this conversation.' His piercing blue eyes sparkled with amusement. 'We'll be leaving in an hour, so make sure you are well acquainted with the gift next to your bed.'

With that, he promptly shut the door and left her.

Nadia stared at the door blankly, forcing her mind to recollect the details of the addendum. If her memory served her correctly, he had every right to punish her should she not follow through on what they had agreed. Since she'd never considered disobeying him, she had believed the clause was fair enough but essentially irrelevant.

The concept of his deriving pleasure from punishing her was perplexing. If he was enjoying it, how could it be considered a punishment? Her innocence ensured she couldn't remotely fathom what he meant.

As her mind grappled with the unknown, her grief over her ankle was steadily being replaced with the heady anticipation of whatever would be happening tonight …

Trust

Stephan's friend and neighbour, Jose Velez, was an attractive middle-aged Catalonian. Though he owned art galleries in Europe and America, he was partial to having smaller private exhibitions on Cayman, to which he could invite various acquaintances for the weekend. Tonight he was launching his 'Nouveau Egyptian' exhibition at his small but stylish gallery. It was only a portion of a larger exhibition that would be shown in Miami later that week, but he was pleased that the 'local' residents had shown so much support, and quite a few of his clients had organised to fly in and enjoy the experiences an island such as Grand Cayman had to offer.

Jose had been planning this exhibition for some time. His aim was to combine both historical and modern artifacts with living art forms. One such exhibit was 'Living Mummies', in which real people would be wrapped in bandages, their eyes shown in full Egyptian make-up. As soon as Stephan had seen Nadia's eyes in all their aquamarine glory the day they first met, he had toyed with the idea of volunteering her services, and making this exhibition her first secret foray into his public life. Given that he had no intention of ever sharing her with anyone else, her being enshrouded would provide the perfect alibi.

There was also a distant possibility that Ava would be there – even though she hated the Caymans – as Jose was a close friend of both of theirs. Stephan had already dedicated many hours to ensuring their relationship had ended as smoothly as possible. After screaming at him relentlessly about his sadistic tendencies and abusive traits, she had eventually accepted that it was over. He didn't want to inflame her further by openly appearing at the exhibition with Nadia. Knowing Ava was a firm believer in the adage that all publicity was good publicity, he had no desire to entangle his new life (and his new possession) in her drama.

Tonight, he wanted his focus to be solely on Nadia. In his mind, this was her first big hurdle, the first test to see how far she would go to comply with his commands. He needed to know if she trusted him enough to do this for him. Only then could she truly be his.

Stephan was as excited as a child on Christmas Eve as he revved the engine of his sleek blue Ferrari F430, before turning out of the driveway and setting off. With money came luxury cars, and he was more than pleased with the specialised shade of blue that he had chosen to resemble the colour of the Swedish flag. He was fiercely patriotic when it suited him to be. 'Are you ready?' he asked.

'How can I answer when you haven't told me what I need to be ready for?' she replied.

Stephan hadn't given her the slightest indication of what she should wear, telling her: 'Anything will be fine, it's not important. Just bring your flesh-coloured leotard with you.' Nadia was more than a little apprehensive about their first outing, but was thrilled that it was finally happening, even more so after the misery of this afternoon's news. Other than being told they were going to his friend's art gallery, she had no idea what the evening would involve, except that she would still be his secret.

'Do you have your gift?' he asked.

'Yes, it's in my bag.'

'Do you like it?'

'I've never used one like that before, but I'm looking forward to trying it.' Her cheeks immediately flushed at her bold reply, but she was becoming more used to his need for direct and detailed responses from her.

'I'm pleased to hear that, Nadia. The Tiani is designed in Sweden, just like me.' His smile broadened as he placed his hand just above her knee after a slick gear change. 'I am hoping tonight will be a first on many fronts for both of us.'

Her upper thighs automatically tensed at his touch, and the prospect his words presented.

'I would like you to wear it tonight. Can you do that for me?'

'What – now?'

His icy stare momentarily fixed on her, indicating his displeasure at her response, before he returned his attention to the road.

'I'm sorry, sir. Of course I can,' she immediately replied.

'Better. Did you bring your leotard with you as I asked?'

'Yes, I did, but I must admit I'm not sure whether it is appropriate attire considering I'm not allowed to dance.'

'I want you in both items this evening. You will be one of the star attractions tonight, Nadia, but I promise that you will be completely covered and your ankle will be well rested. Oh, and make sure you use the bathroom when we arrive. You won't have another chance for some time.'

'You're not going to tell me anything else about tonight are you, sir?'

He smiled, shaking his head. 'I just need you to follow my instructions and trust that I will keep you safe.'

The mischief in his eyes was undeniable as he pulled into a car space and helped her out of the car.

'Here, let me hold you. I want you to keep as much weight off your foot as possible.'

She couldn't help but roll her eyes, but knew better than to argue with him after their tense discussion following Greta's assessment.

Instructions

Stephan's excitement was at fever pitch as they arrived at the back entrance of the gallery. Art had never had this effect on him before.

Jose met them in the storeroom at the back of the gallery and introduced them to Irene, who would be looking after Nadia.

Nadia was taken into a small room and told to sit down for her make-up to be done. The rich, vibrant colours on the make-up tray included sparkling golds, Aztec blues and forest greens. Irene wasted no time in applying them, then adding thick black liquid eyeliner, and finished off with long false eyelashes. Nadia's already large, round eyes were highlighted to such an extent that it was as if the rest of her face didn't exist. She thought it strange that only her eyes had been made up and not the rest of her face, but didn't utter a word.

'Excellent, we're done here. You may change into your leotard.'

Once in the small bathroom, Nadia opened the discreet black pouch that held the small, rose-coloured SenseMotion massager. He had asked her to place the smooth silicone object so it nestled snuggly against her clitoris; she could instantly feel her own arousal.

Nadia's limited sex life had never been overly exploratory and she had certainly never shared a sex toy with a man before. So tonight she was highly nervous about what Stephan might have in store, though excited that their relationship might finally be crossing a sexual threshold.

'Is everything OK in there, Nadia?' Stephan's deep, penetrating voice interrupted her reverie. Clearly that was her cue to get a move-on. After ensuring the device was both well hidden and securely in place, she pulled her flesh-coloured leotard up over her shoulders. She opened the door and stood tentatively, awaiting further instructions.

The small group nodded their approval. 'She's perfect, Stephan, the exact size.'

'I know,' answered Stephan, his eyes aglow as though he'd personally created her. 'Where would you like her?'

'Just up on this bench will be fine. She's light enough to move into position from there.'

Stephan couldn't help but notice the many questions in Nadia's eyes, and loved the fact that she nevertheless remained silent and compliant as he picked her up and carefully laid her body out on the black bench in front of them.

'You followed my instructions precisely?' he whispered in her ear.

'Yes, sir.'

'Excellent. Lie still.' He turned to Jose. 'I'm assuming it's fine for me to stay here and watch?'

'Knowing you, Stephan, I would expect nothing less. Please, make yourself comfortable.'

Stephan settled into a lounge chair and took a moment to fully absorb the sight of this exotic creature with heavily made up eyes, so vulnerable yet so trusting in the hands of others – and all for him.

Jose and Irene methodically began the process of transforming Nadia into an ancient mummy with moving eyes, beginning with the tips of her toes.

'Be careful with her left ankle, she has a torn ligament.'

'Of course.'

Stephan was enthralled as Nadia's legs were bound together. He was surprised how aroused this process was making him, and couldn't stop himself from issuing instructions, knowing what he had in mind for Nadia later on.

'Make sure she is bound tightly, I don't want anything to unravel during the exhibition.

'I'd prefer another layer of bandages to ensure she is secure, particularly around her thighs and hips.

'I'd like to see the reaction of her nipples when the bandages touch them.'

Nadia didn't dare utter a word, knowing after his last request that her shallow breathing and rapid heart rate would ensure her nipples spoke volumes on her behalf. No one was disappointed.

Jose and Irene continued to work, silently obeying Stephan's many commands. Finally Nadia's arms were bent into position across the top of her body then tightly bound, before more wrappings were bound around her entire torso as they manoeuvred her from side to side.

Stephan's eyes never once left her body during the entire process. The more they wrapped her up, the more ownership and possession he felt over her. Ava would never have done anything like this for him.

When they reached her neck Stephan interrupted again. 'Nadia, would you like some water? Once they cover your face you will be unable to speak for the rest of the evening.'

'Yes, thank you.' Her voice was quiet, submissive. She had been in a trance-like state throughout the entire process as she contemplated what was happening to her.

He awkwardly angled a straw into her mouth and she sipped up the cool liquid.

'Are you OK? You're doing so well, I'm so proud of you.'

She nodded. She couldn't do anything but comply, now she had allowed them to go this far.

'I'd like her to wear these earphones so I can communicate with her, given she will be stationary for so long.'

'Of course, great idea,' Jose agreed.

'That way you can hear my voice, or the music I'll play for you.'

Nadia was sure her body shuddered but there was apparently no sign of movement externally; she had been so securely bound. The silicone device was pressed firmly against her already swollen clitoris, trapped in place for the foreseeable future.

She had never done anything like this in her entire life. Stephan had promised her a night of firsts, but she would never have envisaged this.

He gently placed the small earphones into each of her ears, checking again that she was OK with what was about to happen.

She whispered back so only he could hear. 'Yes, I am. If this pleases you.'

'Oh, more than you can imagine, Nadia.' He stroked the loose hair away from her forehead before moving away and signalling that he was ready for them to continue.

Her mouth was clamped shut as the bandages were wound over her chin and across her lips, then around her face and head. She experienced the strange sensation of feeling her mouth disappear, and along with it, her right to speech.

Irene and Jose carefully avoided her nostrils and her eyes, the only parts of her body that would remain opened to the elements. Once the wrapping process was completed, they painted a light resin over the bandages, then left it to set and harden.

Nadia was giving Stephan control of her senses; her emotions were as tightly bound as her body. He was good at this: playing a slow, sophisticated game of control, one where he had all the power and where she had no choice but to submit. It seemed to defy all logic, but she had to admit she had never experienced such anticipation, nor been so highly aroused – and he wasn't even touching her.

Discipline

The entire process had been as meticulously planned as all the other aspects of Stephan's life. *He* would decide what Nadia heard, what she saw, and now, in this position where she had lost all movement in her body, he had complete control of every nerve, including in her clitoris.

It was as though Nadia had been frozen in time, entombed with her own private thoughts, removed from the world, objectified. She closed her eyes and attempted to calm her rising nerves, knowing that Stephan was right beside her and that she was with professionals who had clearly done this type of thing before. She forced herself to temper her breath, which seemed an impossible feat, since her chest could only rise and fall within a limited space.

Just as panic was about to set in, it came to her.

Discipline!

Discipline was what she needed to calm down, to accept her current reality. So she tapped into that core part of herself: a trait she had honed to perfection over the past decade. It was a ballerina's role to make standing still *en pointe* look effortless, flawless, ensuring the audience was never aware of the tiny adjustments required by each muscle group to maintain the pose.

If she couldn't dance, she could still do this. Her skills and training would enable her to calm her nerves enough to cope with whatever her Master expected of her. If it pleased him – and it seemed to very much, judging by the look in his eyes – she would force herself to trust that it would most certainly please her. Even if it meant she was forbidden to touch, or move for that matter.

When she opened her eyes again, Stephan was standing directly above her, staring into them; his deep voice reverberated in her eardrums. Only his voice could she hear, only his face could she see. As if he were reading her thoughts, she found his words pacified her, his intonation providing a hypnotic rhythm to calm her racing pulse.

'I can't tell you what this means to me, Nadia – doing this for me, facing the fear of the unknown that I can see in your eyes. I am learning so much about you, seeing you like this. I promise I will treasure you and awaken you in ways you have never dreamt of before. I have never experienced anyone like you, Nadia. To me, you are perfection personified.

'Tonight is the beginning of you fully succumbing to my demands. You have caused a level of yearning within me that I never knew existed before I laid eyes on you. I want to own you, possess you, like I have never wanted another woman in my life. This is what you have done to me. Your submission inspires my domination. I want to be the Master you truly desire. Keeping you as mine means I *must* be Number One. The stakes have never been higher. Winning has never meant more.'

He paused for a moment, their eyes locked in a silent, lingering gaze. 'I plan on looking after you, caring for you and protecting you from the outside world for the entire term of our contract, if not beyond.'

Irene interrupted Stephan briefly to let him know it was almost time. The slight nod of his head acknowledged her words while his eyes remained fixed on Nadia.

'You look beautiful. Seeing you here tonight, the process of having you bound, has all made me hard. As you can't feel for yourself, you will have to take my word for it, but believe me, being given the opportunity to study your reactions in detail throughout this evening, through your eyes – and only your eyes – will provide me with unimaginable insights. This evening your body will have no choice but to absorb the pleasure that I alone will bestow upon it. You will be living art, to be shared and viewed by all, but owned and controlled by one. Your Master. From tonight, Nadia, I shall have the sweet pleasure of initiating you fully into my world.'

With those words, Stephan pressed the small, rose-coloured remote control. Nadia immediately felt the low vibration between her captured thighs. It warmed her from the inside out as the heated flush spread from her core and radiated beneath her hidden limbs. Although for now the feeling was exceptionally pleasant, she had to wonder how on earth she was going to get through the next few hours should it continue to ratchet up.

'Make me proud that you're mine.' Stephan turned to walk towards the door, calling to Jose, 'OK, she's now ready and waiting to please the crowd.'

Nadia's heavily encased body was hoisted into an intricately designed and colourfully painted Egyptian coffin. The lid was closed and darkness enveloped her as the wheels, and vibrations, were set in motion for her entrance into the gallery, where life would truly imitate art.

Submission

The complete darkness was disorientating, Nadia's cocooned body unable either to pre-empt or to prevent its next movement. It allowed her to focus on Stephan's voice alone.

'Close your eyes.

'Concentrate on your breath.

'Immerse yourself in the music.'

When the music commenced Nadia felt her tomb being hoisted into an almost upright position. If she could have smiled at his choice of music she would have, as the operatic strains of an aria from *Madame Butterfly* floated into her brain.

'When the music stops, open your eyes immediately.'

His words were her only contact with the outside world. She found herself depending on them for her mental stability.

The vibrations were mildly caressing her inner sanctum, ensuring she was tingling all over, knowing the Tiani was trapped in position, tight and snug within her. She began to breathe into the sensations, knowing that this was what Stephan wanted her to experience. For him, she allowed her body to become immersed in the consistency and privacy of the pleasurable waves.

So lost was Nadia in her secluded world that when the music suddenly stopped she barely registered that the top half of her tomb had been opened.

'Now!' Stephan's voice boomed into her ears breaking her reverie, and she was so shocked that she immediately opened her eyes. The sudden light was blinding; she couldn't help but blink repeatedly before her pupils adjusted. It took a few moments for her to register the crowd of people gathered around her, and a few more to grasp the reality that she was indeed the 'exhibition' they were staring at.

To the audience it honestly looked as though a mummy had suddenly come back to life. A few muffled screams and gasps escaped from the small but delighted crowd, followed by a few laughs at the surprise that this particular 'mummy' had real, blinking, human eyes that returned their gaze. Spontaneous applause broke out around the room, with cries of: 'Bravo! Congratulations! So unexpected! Just superb!'

Nadia could barely make out Jose's muffled voice from the far corner of the room as he explained the process of mummification and the genesis of the replicated tomb. Her sheer objectification left her completely startled. Her eyes scanned the room, eliciting more 'Ooohs' and 'Ahhhs' from the audience, but she could not see Stephan even though she could sense he was watching her every blink.

After Jose's brief presentation people stepped even closer to her – so close she could almost feel their breath against her skin, and was grateful that the bandages and the wooden coffin protected her.

Their conversations meandered around her as though she didn't exist, while they waved their fingers in front of her face, pointing at the intricacies of her make-up, causing her to blink furiously in case someone poked her in the eye. Blinking was her only line of defence, given that she couldn't speak or shoo their intrusive fingers away from her face. There was not a thing she could do to stop them and they didn't seem to care one bit.

Many a husband stood gawking at her, chuckling and wondering out loud whether they could organise the same thing for their wives, so they could have some peace and quiet around the home. There was even a suggestion, amongst many guffaws, that Jose could patent the process and make a fortune – restoring the rightful balance of power in the world so that women would be seen but not heard. Nadia's previous state of shadowed serenity abated as she seethed with fury beneath her linen cloth at these misogynistic men, and the disregard they had for the women in their lives.

She wondered whether this was what some men honestly thought, what they really wanted. It was as though she were being given a secret insight into a world she'd thought no longer existed. She was screaming at them on the inside, but could do nothing other than be seen and not heard – and she had brought it all on herself. As much as she attempted to furrow her brow at their words, to show her disapproval through her eyes and let them know how insulted she was, her gestures went completely unnoticed and the group of men moved blithely along to the next exhibit.

Just as she began questioning why Stephan had wanted to put her through this, just when she thought she could take no more, his face appeared directly in front of her, blocking all sight of the rest of the room and the chauvinist males she had overheard. Nadia couldn't tell if he was protecting her from them or asserting his power over her. She was desperate to say something, to ask him to release her, not make her go through this a second longer, to tell him that she couldn't bear people scrutinising her as though she didn't exist, to beg him to please take her home. Her eyes pleaded these unspoken words. But he said nothing, just continued to gaze at her as though she were indeed a historical wonder of the world.

Though she was fully covered she felt like she was naked before him, and as she continued to look into his icy blue eyes they penetrated her mind, wiping her thoughts of anger away and making her remember his hypnotic words from earlier.

I promise I will treasure you and awaken you in ways you have never dreamt of before.

Your submission inspires my domination. I want to be the Master you truly desire.

You are my secret possession. I shall have the sweet pleasure of initiating you fully into my world.

Nadia's mind forced her to acknowledge there was a part of her that needed him to be her Master, and that to deny him would be to deny herself. She would submit to Stephan's will, pleasure or pain, as long as he was Number One.

Stephan's eyes captured hers, monitoring the dilation of her pupils in detail, knowing her eyes were the windows to her true feelings, feelings she was otherwise unable to articulate this evening. Each moment they held each other's silent stare she felt the pull of his dominance over her strengthen, demanding her to concede her will to him and to do it now. She could feel the sexual magnetism between them tugging at her inner being. It was as though he were breathing the first intoxicating, sexual breath into her previously closed and sheltered world. In that moment, she felt like her ballet career had merely been a training ground to give her the discipline she would need to submit to him.

Stephan didn't utter a word, just stared deeply into her eyes as the vibrations of the Tiani intensified deep within her. The remnants of her frustration dissipated as the sensations took over her body and diluted her mind. He had initiated the process of control when they first met, and now he was taking the first step towards complete mastery of her body.

She was forced to absorb the cascading waves of pleasure he dictated, without movement, trapped within herself as he ensured she remained on the cusp of release. He was willing her to accept that the journey he had mapped out would be his journey and not her own, commanding her to let go, to trust and give herself freely to him, and in doing so, relinquish everything and everyone else.

The drama of the last week or so with Stephan washed over her – the emotion, the submission, the unfulfilled sexual tension ... She had never experienced anything like it; it was overwhelming, yet it was just beginning. She could do nothing to prevent the tears from welling up as he continued to assess every emotion reflected in her eyes.

Though entombed, her pulse raced and her groin throbbed with desire as every part of her being dared her to give herself wholly over to him. His penetrating eyes forced her to recognise the part of her sexual psyche that had lain dormant during her immersion in the world of ballet. Her tears cascaded into the cloth as she conceded that she craved to be dominated by a man like Stephan.

As if reading her mind, he understood her tears represented her absolute commitment to him. He covered her eyes with his palm, liberating her from the intensity he demanded.

At last she could block out the exhibition and the people who had been given permission to examine her in intricate detail. Calmer, gentler music wafted into her ears, replacing the dramatic chords of *Madame Butterfly*.

A final thought fluttered away into the back of her mind. In order for their partnership to be successful, her assertive self had to die – or at least hibernate – to enable her complete transition into the world he would carefully craft for her.

A world where she would willingly sacrifice her sexual fate to the Swedish god of tennis.

Hidden

After the initial viewing period Nadia's tomb was moved, so that for the rest of the evening she was no longer upright but lying flat on a podium. She remained encased in the bottom half of the tomb, with its lid lying beside her. That way people could admire the detail of the paintings on the outer casing as well as the handiwork of the mummification process. They took delight in touching the resin-covered linen cloth that bound her body as they flitted and chatted around her with their continual refills of champagne.

The delightful steady buzz emanating from between Nadia's loins relaxed her to such an extent that she drifted off into a light, blissful state of semiconsciousness, grateful that Stephan had allowed her to keep her eyes closed. Unfortunately this restful state was disturbed when she heard him speaking in terse tones directly above her head.

'Ava! You made it after all.' It sounded like someone he knew had arrived.

'Yes, Stephan. Does that disappoint you?'

'Why should it?'

'I'm here with someone else. He's a merchant banker, has his own private jet.'

Stephan laughed hollowly. 'I see money and status haven't lost their special place in your heart.'

'And you? Did *you* bring anyone?'

'Not that it is any of your business, but no.'

'Oh, now why doesn't that surprise me? It may be more difficult than you think trying to find someone to suit your – how should I say it politely in public? – more unusual tendencies?'

'There's no need to be spiteful, Ava. Let's just drop this.'

'What? Drop this conversation, just like you dropped me, you self-serving bastard? Your arrogance is astounding. Did you honestly expect me to give up something as important as my career to be with someone like you?'

'I asked you to drop the subject.'

'You can't control me now, Stephan. You have no right to tell me what I do or how I dress, or when I can come. Do you honestly think you will find someone who is willing to be at your beck and call 24/7 to do all of the kinky shit you want them to but remain idly mute?'

'Ava, enough! Keep your voice down.'

'Don't you tell me what to fucking do! Everything is fine when it's going your way, but when it doesn't, God help the rest of the world! You depraved control freak!'

Nadia, coincidently lying idly mute, was left to assume that Ava must be a disgruntled ex-lover of Stephan's and desperately wished she could hear the rest of the conversation. But Stephan had swiftly switched her earphones back to music and increased the strength of vibrations as Ava became more hysterical, so Nadia was back trapped in her own private world of auditory and internal stimulation.

The commotion around her tomb receded as these other sensations took over. Attempting to pant through the direct stimulation to her clitoris as best she could, she wondered if Stephan was still in control of the vibrations or had forgotten about her altogether due to the altercation with Ava. She was heating up due to the rising demands of the buzzing below, and the frustration of not being able to move an inch to diminish its impact. Her shallow breaths were trying in vain to keep pace with her heartbeat, when she suddenly saw a glass of champagne hurled across her line of vision. She would have covered her face with her hands, but could only close her eyes to protect herself from the flying drink, before opening them again to see arms flailing above her.

Eventually, everything returned to its previous state of calm. People drank their champagne and continued their discussions.

136

Nadia now had no idea where Stephan or Ava was, and began to find the music more frustrating than soothing given her particularly heightened state of arousal. She had never been this stimulated for so long without detonation, having always had the control at her own fingertips. She tried to wiggle, to no avail, instead attempting Kegel exercises as a last resort, which only served to increase the friction, making her need for release dire. If the sensations lasted much longer she feared her body would literally implode within the confines of the resin, such was the build-up of energy within her. She fleetingly wondered what effect the sweat on her brow was having on her make-up, fearing she would soon look like a melting figurine from Madame Tussauds.

Much to her relief, a moment later the music stopped, signalling that Stephan was back in control.

'Open your eyes,' came the soft command of his voice. 'You may blink, but you will keep your eyes open from now on.'

Nadia had no idea where he was but she opened her eyes just as he'd asked. There was a strange man looming over her. His face was hidden behind a large telescopic camera lens pointing directly at her eyes, and there was a strong light behind him.

Just as he began to snap photos of her, Stephan pressed his remote control and the heady vibrations within her changed their tempo. She would have given anything to squirm, to move, to shift even slightly to avoid the penetrating ambush. The tempo continued to increase until staccato pulses pumped into her clitoris and her entire body inflamed with the sustained stimulation. Her eyelids became heavy as her mind gave way to her body's pumping rhythm. Her feelings could no longer be contained, with her thighs and legs squeezed and bound together more tightly than they had ever been.

The intensity reached fever pitch, and the relentless pulses merged into one energetic force as the urgent command of 'Now!'

made her eyes open wider and forced an explosion into the abyss, where time and space didn't exist.

Her immobilised body spasmed uncontrollably against the bounds that entombed her. Her internal thrusting, unseen by those who observed her, ensured she had no choice but to absorb every major and minor sensation, until the last cascading ricochet had left her body.

All the while, the cameraman's relentless shutter speed captured each fraction of a second, to record the hidden journey she had made through to the controlled release of her orgasm.

Stephan couldn't wait to study the photographs. That way he would see every sensation reflected in her eyes, and in future would take great delight in eliciting her pleasure and pain with reference to this treasured record. The first orgasm he had ever controlled for her would be forever immortalised.

'Welcome to my world, Nadia. You now belong completely to me.'

Commands

Nadia was so exhausted that she fell asleep in the car on the way home, and was astonished to find herself neatly tucked up in bed when she woke the next morning. Much to her disappointment, she was alone in her own room. Even though her body tingled from the shenanigans of the previous evening, Stephan still hadn't touched her – and she hungered for his touch more than anything else in the world.

She had never experienced anything like this. Despite last night's release, her pent-up desire was reaching volcanic proportions. The more Stephan denied her, the greater her need for him became. After the intensity of last night she was desperate for their bodies to connect, for the undeniable friction that had been building between them since their first meeting to escape.

Such was her frustration that it took her a moment to notice the breakfast tray on her bedside table, and next to it a note.

Eat your breakfast. Use your crutches to walk to the
bathroom. You will be spending the day in bed.

Although she had followed terse instructions her entire dancing life without any physical response from her body, she couldn't deny the tightening sensation in her groin whenever Stephan commanded her to do anything, even if it was something that she might have preferred to ignore. Though his instructions were in written form, it was as though she could hear his deep voice penetrating her eardrums, making it impossible to refuse him anything.

In ballet, her desire was to perfect her every move. Regarding Stephan, it was to follow his every command and never disappoint him.

Remembering Stephan's words last night at the gallery, she felt hyper-aware of her sexuality and intimately connected with her Master in a way she had never been with another man – even Noah. It was an overwhelmingly powerful force, and she wholeheartedly welcomed this new sensation of belonging only to him.

So it was because of her deep-seated need to please him that, after her breakfast, she reluctantly used the crutches to visit the bathroom, swallowing her vexation at being told to stay in bed for the day with stoic pride.

When she returned in her silk robe, Stephan's bronzed body was lying across her bed, looking unbearably seductive in blue briefs and nothing else. If this image were posted on a billboard in Times

Square, it would no doubt cause traffic accidents for pedestrians and vehicles alike!

Nadia was grateful she had her crutches to grasp for support as her eyes feasted on the epitome of masculinity lounging before her. When she managed to regain her composure, she wished she'd done something with her mane of unruly hair before stepping back into the bedroom.

'Good morning, Nadia. You slept well.' It wasn't a question but she thought she'd take the opportunity to respond nonetheless.

'I did, unfortunately.'

'Unfortunately?'

'I would have preferred to stay up with you after we came home.'

'Is that so? It would have been cruel to keep you up when you were so clearly exhausted. Did you enjoy last night?'

What could she say? She felt a blush creep over her face before admitting shyly but truthfully: 'Yes, sir. I did.'

'I'm pleased. So did I – very much – except for the intrusion of Ava, which is all now fortunately in the past.' He murmured the last part to himself as much as to her. Nadia briefly wondered what Stephan could have said or done to ignite this woman's fury but didn't dare ask, she was just grateful it was in the past. 'Now, I was serious about your spending the day in bed.'

She attempted to hide her bitter disappointment as her mind raced to find a polite way to protest against his instruction. But before she could formulate any words, he swung his long muscled legs over the side of the bed and easily scooped her up in his arms, sending her crutches crashing to the floor. Opening her bedroom door wide with his foot, he headed straight down the hall and into his enormous bedroom suite. Sun was shining in through the huge window, highlighting the mocha and beige tones of his luxurious bedroom. This was the first time she had been in his quarters, and she soaked in the sight of the anything-but-feminine furnishings as he gently eased her down into the centre of his king-sized bed.

'You are not to leave this bed today without my express permission.' The cheeky smile told Nadia that he was having fun with this, so she played along.

'Yes, Master, your wish is my command.' It was hard to pretend she was anything but elated at this news; she doubted there would be a straight woman in the world who would say no to him right now.

'That's exactly what I want to hear.'

'Are you training today, sir?'

'No, not in the traditional sense. I'm spending the day exploring.'

She pouted.

'Don't look so sad!' He lifted her chin. 'I'm exploring you.'

'Oh!' But her delight in these words was short-lived as his expression became immediately business-like.

'You have been celibate since signing the contract with Ivan, is that correct?'

'Yes, sir.' She silently congratulated herself for not having slept with Noah in London, as she couldn't imagine having to explain that to him right now.

'Good. Have you ever been restrained before, Nadia?'

'No, sir – well, not until last night.'

'I would like to restrain you now, so I can study your reactions to my touch in detail.'

'You don't want *me* to touch *you*?' Thoughts of this moment had been building in her mind for so long; her visions always featured her hands all over his taut muscles, discovering and delving into every inch of his ripped body. Inhaling his scent, swallowing his seed ... So many images collided in her mind that she clasped her hands together beneath her knees in case she found herself acting on them without his approval to do so.

'No, not yet. I need full control.' She sensed he didn't want to explain himself further, and that he was in the mood for things other than discussion. 'Have you heard of the five Ts?'

She was thrown by this question at first, but then remembered one of the dancers had a book about them and raved about these five Ts, saying they had really improved her relationship with her partner.

'Touch, token, time, task, and I can't remember the last one ... talking, maybe? I think that's it but I'm not sure.'

'Very good. They're the five Ts known to the general public, but there'll be no need for you to remember those – though it *would* be helpful for you to remember mine.'

'Are they very different?'

'They are taste, tickle, torment, torture and titillate. All of which I'm hoping to do with you today.' He chuckled as he said these words, leaving her none the wiser as to whether he was serious or not. 'Just something I read somewhere that tickled my fancy, so to speak.'

Then all sense of frivolity left his face and his voice became serious again. 'So, may I? I won't proceed unless you agree, you know that.'

Nadia only hesitated an instant before giving her permission. 'Yes, sir, you may restrain me.'

Regardless of her desire to touch him, excitement immediately pulsed through her body.

'Thank you, Nadia. Please don't speak again unless I specifically ask.'

She nodded, becoming highly attuned to the intricacies of his need to dominate in all things.

Exploration

So long had Stephan denied himself this moment that he cautiously removed her silk robe as if unwrapping a precious gift, sliding it off her shoulders to expose her nakedness beneath.

He had imagined her lithe body naked many times over, beneath the protection of her dance attire, but had never imagined the flawlessness of her alabaster skin. He was in awe of the sight she presented to him.

The shallow rise and fall of her chest caused her small milky breasts, with their pale rosebud tips, to do the same as he eased her gently back onto the bed. The giant four-poster had already been prepared for her restraint and he slowly bound each wrist with a plush cushioned cuff, followed by her right ankle, leaving her injured left ankle tenderly elevated on a cushion. He followed each intricate response of her body with the intensity he would use in analysing one of his opponents on court. The silence mounting between them was intense for both.

Stephan had been looking forward to this day since they first met. He had given all his staff the day off and told them that under no circumstances was he to be disturbed. His focus was akin to what it would be before a grand-slam final. Nadia was going nowhere until he knew her body better than she did, and denying her permission to touch him ensured he could establish complete control from the outset. Of course he would allow her to touch him eventually, but he wanted to be able to use that strategy to reward her when she pleased him.

He could already see in her eyes how motivated she was to do so. She was a natural submissive, just as he had been born to dominate. The perfect match. He would relish her traineeship under his masterful direction. The fact that she had signed a contract to guarantee their roles just made the entire situation even more incredible from his perspective.

Only after he had fastidiously placed her in the exact position he wanted did he allow his fingers and tongue to explore every crevice of her delectable body. He smelt, tasted, nipped and touched, exploring this sacred terrain for the very first time, watching her reactions, understanding the sounds she made. She had no way to hide from his sexual inquisition and he was in no rush. He tested her pressure points, the intensity of his touch ranging from feather-light to firm and probing, assessing her capacity for both pleasure and pain. It was as though her body amplified its reactions for his benefit, in unison with the sighs he elicited from deep within her.

Nadia found herself floating into deeply relaxing, blissful states as his strong hands massaged and intimately caressed her body. At other times she gasped from the sensations he created – tickling pleasure and tormenting pain. She was aching with frustration, her body quivering with desire for more as he continued his all-consuming marathon. No words were spoken – adhering to her Master's rules was a critical part of her training and discipline, and fortunately had always been intrinsic to her success in her career. So she was pleased that he provided her with such boundaries, knowing it illustrated their respect for one another. More importantly in this instance, it ensured she became fully immersed in his sensate world.

Being a professional ballerina, Nadia assumed she knew her body's responses to most things – the aches, twinges, pains, pressures ... Yet Stephan proved he was more than capable of exposing her to previously undiscovered sensations. Her glazed eyes and involuntary sounds informed him precisely how she felt, how far he could go. At times she found herself gasping for air or screaming into the room as she worked through the intensity he evoked, desperate to maintain eye contact with him lest she lose herself completely, only to then find herself wallowing in a dreamy state of delirium that cascaded over her body when he converted the pain so skilfully to pleasure. She had no choice but to acknowledge that before today she had known nothing of her sexual self, compared with the information Stephan was able to extract without a single word in the hours that followed.

'You are even more exquisite in bed than you are *en pointe*, Nadia.' He nipped each nipple between his teeth, causing her to yelp, before gently kissing between her breasts then removing himself from her body.

'We will take a break. Then I will learn more about how you orgasm. It is something I like to perfect early on in any intimate relationship.'

Nadia could barely raise her head to look into his eyes, but she finally did so through heavy lids, only to see that his face was one hundred per cent serious. Unwavering in his plans for the day.

'I'll be back soon with some food. You will need stamina for this afternoon.'

She shook her head and thought back to the times when she had had sex with guys who had clumsily navigated their way around her body until they were ready for their own release, only to be left to masturbate herself to orgasm after they had gone. Perhaps male dancers would have been different but she had never allowed herself to be with them in case it became complicated and interfered with her performance. And now she had been given Stephan, a dominating Scandinavian god who was dedicating an entire day to understanding her body more intimately than anyone ever had, including herself.

Was it too much? Too extreme? She had no idea. But she knew that however peculiar it seemed, she loved every exhilarating moment of it. All thoughts receded from her mind other than how on earth she was going to get through the afternoon session – but this was interrupted by her stomach, rumbling very loudly for nourishment.

Exhaustion

Stephan loosened Nadia's binds so she could sit up, but did not remove them completely.

'I'd prefer you not to speak, but if you have something to say, now is the time.'

She could think of nothing she wanted to say, so decided to follow his wishes and remain silent. He seemed to be as immersed in this intense, unique environment he had created as she was.

She reached for her soup but he shook his head. Instead, he raised the spoon to her mouth so he could feed her.

Nadia struggled with the emotions she felt at this one gesture. No one had ever fed her like this, when she was ill or otherwise. Being treated this way felt awkward and foreign to her, since she had never experienced the cherished love of real parents. It was even more unexpected coming from someone like Stephan, who could have anyone he wanted the world over, with or without a contract.

Though confused, she was delighted in the extreme. For the first time she could remember, she felt alive *sans* ballet.

She had always needed dance to protect her from her life's emptiness, and it had served her well in the past. But it meant that she had never developed an identity other than as a ballerina. In her dark moments, she knew that she wouldn't really exist in the world if it weren't for dance; there would be no place for her, and she would disappear into a black hole along with all the other people no one cared about. But right now, at this very moment, she was the epicentre of Stephan's intense world, and she loved it. She was enjoying herself more than she'd ever dreamt possible, and she couldn't wipe the smile from her face – that was, unless Stephan asked her to.

Her thoughts were forcefully interrupted as the afternoon session commenced. If she had thought the morning was intense, the afternoon was a wipeout. Stephan could have competed with the most demanding ballet masters and have left them for dead in his desire for perfection, which he achieved many times over. Nadia had no idea any man was capable of such sexual stamina and self-discipline. If she had had any desire earlier to get out of bed that day, she didn't now. It was highly unlikely that she would have the energy to move even by tomorrow. It was her first experience of being psychologically and physically spent, more than making up for so much sexual absenteeism.

Stephan languidly stroked her pale skin, secretly stunned and amazed by what her flexible body was capable of. In his mind, she was simply superb, a canvas of contradictions: strong, supple; steely, soft; passive, reactive. He couldn't wait for the opportunity to mark her body more completely, but for now he was content to take small steps. There was plenty of time, and he sensed a strategy of 'slowly but surely' would prove most beneficial in the long run.

Even though he had released her bonds, he had not given her permission to touch him yet. So far it was only *he* who knew *her* body inside out.

'I'd like you to sleep in here tonight with me, Nadia.'

'You're unfair, sir.'

'Why?' He laughed, not having expected that response.

'You know I'm too exhausted to lift a finger.'

'Then it's lucky you don't have to.'

He grasped both her wrists firmly and spooned his body against hers. Though she couldn't see his face, she was content to feel his hot, hard body against her back.

Then, for the first time, he slid his rock-solid length into her, and although she was raw and swollen she was also more than ready to accept him, opening her legs to accommodate his length and girth. He filled her up with every inch of him, slowly and rhythmically finding his pace inside her as he firmly massaged her breasts. His breath was hot as his lips kissed, his tongue played and his teeth bit into her neck and shoulders. As his pace became more urgent and his grunts more primal, he hoisted her uninjured leg high and held her body firmly against him, his hands almost bruising her skin.

She screamed harder than she ever had, unleashing the tension of many weeks as he pounded her depths, thrusting ever harder and faster before exploding, at long last, deep inside her. Shattering her, physically and emotionally.

Neither of them had any memory of going to sleep that night, only of waking up the next morning entwined in each other's arms, her small torso enveloped in his long, muscled limbs. Which was exactly where she wanted to be.

Over the next few weeks, while Stephan trained, Nadia conscientiously completed the physiotherapy and hydrotherapy required to heal her ankle, and did not dance at all – as requested, or more precisely ordered.

Stephan loved to dive, and Nadia discovered it was the main reason he had bought this property. She had never had any hobbies or learnt much outside her schooling at the White Lodge, so she was both nervous and excited to spend time each day with Dan, the local dive master, in Stephan's pool. Stephan wanted her accredited in the shortest possible timeframe, and she had no intention of failing him. Apprehensive at first, as she wasn't an overly confident swimmer, with his encouragement she threw herself into this new underwater world and it proved the perfect distraction from dance. Between exploring the depths of the ocean and the sexual depths of each other – including a wonderful day playing with friendly stingrays – the time flew by, and soon October was upon them. With the Shanghai Rolex Masters looming, followed by the BNP Paribas Masters in Paris, the last demands of the tennis calendar penetrated into their blissful tropical world.

Although Stephan still kept her presence in his life a secret in public, in private they became inseparable. Neither had ever experienced such intense feelings of arousal for another human being. They were utterly absorbed in their sexual passion for one another.

The more time Stephan spent with Nadia, the more he wanted to control every aspect of her life, day and night. Though others might have found such behaviour constricting, perhaps even suffocating, Nadia had never received such attention before, and felt truly alive and treasured. The thought of not being in Stephan's world literally brought tears to her eyes, as did the intensity of her orgasms – regularly. She became a slave to his touch and adoration. Which was exactly how he wanted her to be.

Legacy

The hand-carved wooden box of Black Dragon cigars was delivered to Caesar's desk in his London office late in the day. Although he had many friends and acquaintances, it was rare that he received spontaneous personal gifts of thanks. So he was chuffed that Stephan Nordstrom had sent the cigars, with an accompanying note of sincere thanks to Caesar for orchestrating the intriguing arrangement with 'Nadia'. He declared his intention to retain his Number One ATP ranking for the long haul and secure Nadia's continued presence in his life along with it – something he felt was definitely worth fighting for.

Caesar was impressed; Stephan was certainly a force to be reckoned with and Caesar was more than reaping the benefits financially. In fact, Stephan's win in the US Open had enabled Caesar to 'acquire' the majority shareholding in another casino in Cancun, Mexico via his Club Zero syndicate, which he was thrilled about as such an asset would only ever become available on the open market under extraordinary circumstances. Nordstrom had the spirit that separated the winners from the losers in life, particularly when victory would only ever belong to one man. Such were the demands of the game. Which was why Caesar loved it so much!

He wasted no time in opening the box and cutting open one of the fat cigars, an indulgence he always appreciated, either socially or alone. It was excellent timing on the part of the world's Number One, as today happened to be Caesar's father's birthday. This was the first year he wouldn't be celebrating it with him as Tony was currently in a specialised Alzheimer's clinic having extensive tests to establish the severity of his condition.

Caesar lit the cigar, savouring its rich, woody scent as he puffed several times to get it started. He rested his feet on the solid mahogany desk and gazed out towards the crane-infested skyline of London as he remembered all the birthdays he and his father had celebrated together.

Caesar wished his father were still of sound enough mind for another of his legendary speeches, but he knew those times had passed. Instead, he remembered all his Papà had achieved from nothing, and vowed to make the rest of his days as comfortable as possible. After all, he owed his Papà his life.

Caesar returned his focus to the cigar he was puffing. He allowed himself a quiet moment to reflect on how his Number One Strategy might play out over the next year. The entire proposition became more interesting with every grand slam.

Borisov was out for next year at least, if not forever. Levique, having made it to the finals of the US and the semifinals of

Wimbledon was now ranked sixth so it still left the current Numbers Three, Four and Five – all of whom Caesar managed. He flicked on his computer to confirm the rolling points of each of the top five players and their current odds for winning the next slam. Amazingly, if Nordstrom's Number One status faltered, it was anyone's game. This meant it was more than plausible for 'Nadia' to become 'Eloise' again and be contracted to a new Number One – all depending on who won the Australian Open …

It was fascinating to think about what could happen and just how far his Number One Strategy could go with such potential uncertainty in men's tennis. Caesar's lips curved into a sly smile as a variety of scenarios danced through his sharp mind. He had all the information he needed on Nordstrom, who was currently one of The Edge's best assets, given his proclivity for product promotion. But he really didn't know much about Levique, who, much to Caesar's disdain, didn't currently have an agent – something Caesar would do his best to rectify, personally if need be, by the end of the year.

It was obvious that Nordstrom was nothing less than besotted with the arrival of Nadia in his life, and according to Nordstrom his interest in her was more than reciprocated. But what of her relationship with Levique? Nadia hadn't disclosed anything to him at the US Open – merely deflected his query by confirming her commitment to the contract, which was commendable. But what if she was hiding something? Something that could cause his strategy to come unstuck?

This thought bothered him as he unlocked a drawer to scrutinise the photos of them both together more closely. As he looked at the playful gestures they shared and the sparkle in their eyes, he could see her close connection with Noah was irrefutable.

Caesar remembered the only time he had felt like that, more than two decades ago, and how wonderful it was to be in the presence of the woman he thought he'd spend the rest of his life with … until it all went horribly wrong. He gazed towards his beloved Saint-Germain painting hanging pride of place in his office – mesmerised by the eyes of the only woman he had felt true love for and turned regretfully away. It was the one event in his life that had left a dull, remnant pain in his heart.

Caesar forced the bitter memory from his mind and returned to the question of what Eloise was trying to achieve behind his back. Maybe she wasn't as innocent as he'd thought. Perhaps both men were ignorant of the role the other played in her life, and she was keeping the truth hidden from them just as she was from him – or at least, thought she was.

He put the photos away in frustration. As his Papà often declared, 'Never trust a woman, it will only cause you grief!' He was starting to think his Papà might be right. And if he didn't act decisively, his potential Number Ones might all be thinking the same way too by the end of the contract … and that was completely unacceptable!

If there was one thing Caesar hated above all else when it came to business, it was not having enough information to make an informed decision. It weakened his position of power, and there was no way he was going to let this situation get out of control.

This conclusion spurred him to seize the moment and regain control. He placed a call to Nordstrom, both to thank him for his gift and to check in on how things were progressing with Nadia: something he vowed to do more regularly from now on.

'She is your responsibility as Number One, Stephan. You must keep her close; I don't want any loose ends.'

'There is nothing that would give me greater pleasure, Caesar. Consider it done.'

Caesar felt confident that Stephan was the right man for the job. He was on top of the world – for now, at least …

He would see to it that from this moment on, Eloise would obey every condition of the contract she had signed with him, come hell or high water. Judging by the photos, her liaison with Levique had the potential to violate the rules, and if it did, she would pay a hefty price. Anyone who risked deceiving Caesar once never had the opportunity to do it a second time. He controlled her life for eight grand slams and she would learn to behave like a puppet on a string, not a runaway train. A point he would reinforce without a shadow of a doubt when he met with her personally in Melbourne.

Clouded in billows of smoke and feeling a little more composed, he picked up his phone and made some more calls to hedge his bets for the coming year. After all, he'd hate to ever be a disappointment to his precious Papà, irrespective of his health.

The King legacy must go on …

AUSTRALIAN OPEN I
January

Fanfare

The tension was palpable and the atmosphere electric as the travelling circus of the tennis world arrived in Melbourne town for the first grand slam of the calendar year. Media fanfare surrounded the arrival of the Number One male tennis superstar and his growing entourage. At six foot four, the blond-haired, blue-eyed Scandinavian commanded the attention of everyone around him. An aura of egocentricity surrounded him like a cloud. Some people admiringly called him a perfectionist; others despised his control-freak arrogance ... But there was no doubting that either way, the masses wanted to see him and hear him and read about his activities, both on and off the court.

Stephan loved the Australian Open, because it had been the scene of his first ever grand-slam victory a year ago. Therefore he had a soft spot for the Aussie crowd and in return, they mostly adored him. Even those who didn't could not deny his supremacy in this exceptionally lucrative global game. Somewhat surprisingly to those not close to him, his game had improved significantly over the past six months, his previous volatility having all but vanished. Many commentators tried to pinpoint the reason. Their theories included his new coach; removing his previous manager; and breaking up with Ava, his girlfriend of more than three years. Even his personal stringer, Ron, who had recently been added to his list of employees had been credited with his solidified success over the past six months. However, only Stephan, Caesar and a handful of lawyers and staff knew the truth.

This year, at the commencement of the new grand-slam season, Nordstrom had come to win, and heaven help anyone who stood in his way.

As Stephan stood at full height and acknowledged the waiting crowd from behind his Dolce & Gabbana gold edition sunglasses (part of a new sponsorship deal), he was wearing a pale blue collared shirt – with the first three buttons undone, highlighting his bronzed chest – as well as a fitted navy blazer, designer jeans and Giuseppe Zanotti high-top shoes. A generous wave and trademark grin ensured all could see that he lived and breathed the life of the sponsored international sports star.

He was the quintessential playboy of the tennis world. Branded and endorsed the world over, he was smooth, suave, sophisticated and utterly lethal to every one of his opponents. They all wanted to emulate him, play like him, be like him. But at this moment in history, he was a world apart from all of them, and planned to happily watch as the next top three players scrambled for the runner-up position. Try as they might, Stephan had no intention of ever letting them come close.

He loved the status and the many additional benefits that his super-athleticism afforded. But being Number One, as he had discovered much to his surprise last year, had brought an even greater prize. A prize that he would never willingly relinquish.

Stephan's entourage guided him into the reception area of Caesar's Crown Casino and Entertainment Complex, where he was greeted warmly by Caesar himself. They exchanged a heartfelt hug, gripping one another's hands and posing confidently for the cameras flashing wildly about them. Caesar lived for publicity such as this, and given that Stephan was genuinely grateful for what Caesar had done for him, now more than ever the tennis god was happy to comment on the excellence of his good friend's world-class facilities here in Melbourne.

While all the celebrity commotion was occurring out the front, security guards opened the door of a second van that had driven directly around to the back entrance. Although there were a few keen photographers loitering near this door, all they saw were two men escorting a young woman wearing a wrap-around coat, a silk headscarf and over-large sunglasses. There was little fanfare from the press before she hurriedly vanished from view. One of the photographers noted she was of small to average height with a petite frame; he couldn't place her as anyone famous, but he tried to capture a few shots.

With her head lowered and her hand raised to shield herself from any potential prying eyes, she was taken through the alleyways of the kitchen and straight into the goods lift. The doors opened at the top floor, and she was escorted directly to the luxurious penthouse suite and left alone inside. As the door closed behind her, she was not offered the security key.

Caesar made a brief speech to the crowd gathered before him, waxing lyrical about Stephan's tennis superstardom and noting their close friendship, before handing the microphone back to Stephan and opening up to the press for questions.

'Stephan, welcome back to Melbourne. Will you be attending tonight's players' party?'

'I would never miss one of Caesar's legendary events, so yes, I will.'

'Are you attending with anyone special?'

'Ah, you waste no time in getting to the point. I have many special people in my life, and as you know, I'm always open to having many more.' (Trademark wink followed by shrieks from the females in the crowd.) 'But no, no one in particular tonight. My focus here in Melbourne is on the game. I'm looking forward to catching up with the other players for the first time this year, then I'll be off to bed early, I'm afraid. Unless, of course, circumstances change ... I'll keep you posted!' (Laughs all round.)

'How do you feel about being here this year?'

'Fantastic. I love the Australian Open – it is where I won my first grand slam. I'm thrilled to be defending my title here this year.'

'How is your form at the moment?'

'Superb.' The way Stephan managed to say the word with aplomb, and without too much conceit, was astounding to all present.

'Are you concerned about any of the other players coming up through the ranks this year?'

'Not particularly; do you know of someone I might not be aware of?' (Laughs again.)

'Do you foresee any problems in making it to the final this year?'

He paused to look the reporter directly in the eye before answering: 'None whatsoever. Let me be clear: *I am here to win this title.*'

With that, the members of the press were asked to finish up and Stephan graciously signed some autographs for lingering fans with special access.

It was only when his personal bodyguards handed him the security key to his suite, which he placed safely in his top pocket next to his heart, that his face visibly relaxed into a genuine smile. He turned to acknowledge his fans and thank Caesar for his exceptional hospitality before excusing himself to meet with his coach and manager.

Under no circumstances could he afford to lose this tournament if he wanted to keep what was his, and he had no problem keeping his secret and most precious possession under lock and key if need be.

Impeccable

Nadia removed her accessories and coat, taking care to place them neatly in the wardrobe. Only now could she feel the thrill of having had nothing on under her coat other than her powder-blue bra, barely covering her taut breasts, and her sheer 'barely there' lace panties. Other than her ballet slippers that she had changed into upon her arrival, it was all she was wearing.

Stephan had requested she remove her skirt and blouse on the plane, leaving her to go through Customs in just her coat. Given that it was the height of the Australian summer, both of them knew that she would look at best ridiculous, and at worst suspicious, as though she were hiding something. Her pleas to try to change his mind only served both to amuse him and to make him even more adamant that she obey his instructions, threatening that he would insist she remove her underwear as well if she kept arguing. Needless to say, though deeply embarrassed, Nadia tried to remain as calm and stoic as possible when she passed through Immigration.

Other than a possible split-second glimpse of her thigh as she stepped out of the van, she was thankful that her lack of clothing had gone unnoticed. She reflected on how Stephan liked to test her boundaries more often these days, and seemed to love the challenge of pushing her further and further. She had experienced many emotions in complying with his demands, but so far had not managed to let him down. For to her, that would be failure.

Nadia looked in the mirror to ensure her skin was clear and unblemished, and freed her bountiful long hair from its low bun.

Stephan only liked it out when they were alone, never with others. He considered the release of her hair a private matter – only ever between them.

She had no idea how long he would be at the press conference and wanted to be in exactly the right position for him, ensuring she always moved with slow, considered care, just as Stephan wished. The last thing she wanted to do was disappoint her Master.

She cautiously eyed the bountiful fruit basket that had been delivered to the suite and was sorely tempted to burst one of the plump grapes between her teeth, but she knew better – most of the time, anyhow. He controlled her food just as he did every other aspect of her life, and she willingly conceded this responsibility to him. After all, he was her Number One so she belonged entirely to him. In return, he took excellent care of her every need, albeit on his own terms.

Poised on the stool expressly provided at Stephan's request in the centre of the suite, she calmed her breath and remained seated, with her eyes lowered. Her tailor-made lingerie shimmered against her skin in the sunlight that filtered through the sheer blinds. Her legs were spread wide and her feet barely touched the ground, her toes perfectly pointed in her ballet slippers.

As she rested the palms of her hands lightly on her knees she allowed her mind to wander, and began to reflect on how her life had evolved since she had abandoned the ballet. What an unexpected detour – all thanks to Caesar. She could never have anticipated the path she had travelled ...

She allowed herself a slight smile at recent memories of her submissive sexual awakening with Stephan, and how their relationship continued to deepen and intensify each day. But as soon as she heard the muted sound of the security key in the door, her face became completely free of emotion and her body stilled. Her years of dancing had proved impeccable training for this surprising new career, and although her dream in life was and always would be ballet, she couldn't believe her luck in landing such a position. She was looked after and secure and wanted for nothing, as long as she played by the rules – increasingly, Stephan's rules. She slowed her breathing and closed her eyes, content to await the arrival of her Master and his next command.

The door opened and closed quietly. Nadia could sense Stephan's presence but kept her eyes lowered towards the floor, relishing the arousal already oscillating between them. He walked up to her and immediately dropped to his knees, deeply inhaling her delectable scent.

'Don't move,' his voice whispered into her opening as he nuzzled his nose against her panties. He could feel the shivers run through her body at his words, loving the power he wielded over her. Nothing in his life had ever been so intoxicating; the only thing that bettered this feeling was holding up the winner's trophy in front of an adoring grand-slam crowd. And he was determined to have both, many times over.

Nadia remained steadfastly still and silent on the edge of the stool. Two of his fingers shifted the sheer lace to the side, exposing her. Automatically, she inhaled, sensitive to his touch. 'Wider,' came his command as his large hands held her knees in a horizontal position and his tongue found the entrance it so keenly sought. Her breath caught sharply in her lungs as he kissed her inner folds, and gently teased her sweet spot with the tip of his tongue and a nip of his teeth. It took all of her concentration not to let her head fall back to fully absorb the delicious pleasure he bestowed upon her.

With much determination, Nadia remained in her upright position, allowing her Master full access to what was his, without words or obstruction. The pressure built within her as his tongue expertly explored her depths. Her body trembled in response but she did not give in to its audacious demands. She understood all too well the importance of discipline and control in these situations, and her Master had trained her well to meet his strict requirements.

She was on the cusp of losing herself completely when Stephan fortunately uttered the word 'Now!' to signal her permission to come. It was then, and only then, that her mind gave in and allowed her body to take over. Her groans filled the room as her climax released the pent-up spasms of her ecstasy into his willing mouth, and he ravenously claimed his secret possession. He had never felt more potent.

Everything about her enabled him to believe he could conquer the world.

Nadia's body collapsed over his shoulder as the orgasm consumed her: an art he had perfected from the first time they were together. He held her tight before carrying her to the nearby lounge overlooking the Melbourne skyline and the milky chocolate torrent of the Yarra River, and waited patiently until she returned to full consciousness. Although his cock throbbed in his trousers at the sight of her like this, he would control his sexual appetite during the term of the tournament, and instead channel the testosterone into his game. It was excellent discipline and one of his steadfast rules, keeping him on an aggressive edge with his opponents. Ultimately, such self-denial motivated him to win.

The trophy presented at the end of the tournament would only mark the beginning of his celebrations, and he needed Nadia's body supple and prepared. But most importantly, he thought knowingly, his abstinence ensured she remained desperately in need of him and his touch – which he could choose to bestow upon her or deny her at any given time. Such power was his ultimate weapon in controlling his delectable submissive, and therefore his ability to direct her life was in the palm of his hand. So far, he'd never had to deny her anything; her behaviour had been consistently impeccable.

He picked up a handful of grapes and fed them to her, one by one. He loved the way her perfect lips wouldn't argue, wouldn't tell him she wasn't hungry, just opened and accepted whatever he put between them. He appreciated the way she wouldn't speak to him until she was spoken to, the way she was responsive to his moods and his emotions. She never argued with him if he stayed out late, or complained if he didn't come home. For these reasons, she had become increasingly invaluable to him, deeply enmeshed in his life and something he would protect at all costs.

With a silent smile, she accepted the grapes he languidly offered as she lay on the lounge and he sat on the floor beside her, worshipping her, as she did him. As he watched the pout of her lips enfold each voluptuous grape, his thoughts meandered back to the wonder of the time he saw the first orgasm captured within her eyes, remembering how desperately she'd wanted to close them, to lose herself in the sensations her body was experiencing. But she hadn't because he had asked her not to, and his every wish was her command. She had proved that to him time and again.

She was perfection itself, and as such he placed her on an ever higher pedestal, towering above all others. Such standards were demanded of him on court, and he expected nothing less of her. In his mind, this was what guaranteed their joint success.

Focus

'Welcome to Melbourne, my little minx.'

'Why, thank you, kind sir! I'm thrilled to be here.'

'As am I. Our first of many grand slams together.'

Whenever he said things like that she felt warmth flush through her body from the inside out.

'I've organised tickets for you to watch each of my matches, Nadia. It's important that you don't miss a moment of my play during this tournament.' He caressed her inner thighs with his lips as he spoke.

'Oh, really? Then I do hope you will win each of your matches as quickly as possible.'

'Is that so? Are you suggesting that you find my tennis boring?'

'Well, not boring exactly, but sometimes ...'

In one swift move Stephan was sitting on the lounge and Nadia found herself pinned across his lap, her face pushed against one of the plush cushions.

'But sometimes?' he questioned. 'You may want to think carefully about your next words before you speak again, Nadia, and I strongly suggest you consider your manners as well.' He entangled the fingers of one hand through her boundless hair, curling it into his fist at the nape of her neck as his other hand caressed the twin mounds of her buttocks. It was this mix of force and tenderness that Nadia found undeniably erotic. Every second stroke he allowed his middle finger to stray between her moistened legs to confirm she was as excited about this as he was. Nadia still found it astounding that she was so titillated when he dominated her, her sated loins swelling again in seconds with the anticipation of more.

He turned her head to the side so he could see her eyes when she answered. 'Well?'

'Well, you know I don't mind watching you –'

Swat! The sound of his palm slapping the cheek of her buttocks sliced through the room before the slight sting registered, and he simultaneously pushed her face further into the pillow, muffling her scream at the shock.

As he lifted her head she was quick to offer an apology. 'I'm sorry, sir. Thank you for the reminder.'

He had become so taken with her addressing him as 'sir' that he rejoiced when she forgot, so he had the opportunity to spank whatever part of her body was most accessible to him. At this precise moment, Stephan was delighted that it was her almost-bare, silky-soft, heart-shaped arse that his palm had happened upon, his personal favourite.

It was a game that had started just after their first marathon session together when he realised just how aroused she became when his palm slapped her skin. Which was lucky for her, as it was an important part of play and punishment from his perspective – both erotic and otherwise. He had taken to swatting parts of her body for any misdemeanour and waiting patiently (or impatiently depending on his mood) until she uttered the words she had just spoken – an apology and a thank you. Sometimes the slaps would land in quick succession, leaving her breathless and unable to communicate clearly, and he would then ask her to remove an item of her clothing and would repeat the process on her bare skin to ensure the lesson was more effectively learnt. It reinforced their respective roles *and* kept the sexual tension between them ever present.

'Better. Now, tell me.'

'May I sit up please, sir?'

'You may sit between my legs.' She sat facing him, letting her teasing hands rest on his bulging crotch. He shook his head, unable to keep the grin from his face at her overt intention.

'Not facing me, you cheeky minx. Turn around with your back to me and sit on your hands, otherwise I'll tie them up.'

She pouted before following his instructions, having no doubt that she would be bound in less than a minute if she didn't, given his appetite for restraining her.

There was no denying the frustrating tension, which bordered on desperation at times, building within her at the seemingly endless discipline he had over his body during tournaments, when she was denied all access to his body. Though the same rules didn't apply to him. Deftly undoing her bra, he let it slowly slide down her shoulders, giving his hands free access to her breasts. As his palms massaged and played, her back nestled into his chest and her eyes lost focus of the room as sensation replaced conversation.

A sudden tweak of her nipple brought her immediately back to the present. 'Well?'

'I'm sorry, sir, but you have distracted me from what we were talking about.'

'I have distracted you? Or you have forgotten?'

'Er, well both, sir, I think.'

'Is that so? Since my arrival, Nadia, you seem to be having quite a bit of trouble focusing on anything, wouldn't you agree?'

She sensed a change of tone in his voice but couldn't see his face to decipher whether he was still playful or becoming annoyed at her inattention. She didn't dare turn around to check.

With experienced dexterity he rolled and pinched each of her nipples between his thumb and forefinger. The sensations caused her mind to lapse once again into a befuddled state and lose all focus on his words as her world became his touch, her previous orgasm still responsible for the heightened state of arousal infiltrating her body.

'Oh sir, please ...'

'Or is something else distracting you?'

He pulled one of her nipples hard while continuing to fondle the other. She couldn't manage more than a few desperate groans, which echoed around the suite.

'Nadia, focus! You can do better than this.' His voice was low and deep in her ear as his teeth bit into her lobe, causing her to yelp while she attempted to stay still with her hands placed securely beneath her butt. This was sensual torture.

'Tennis is what we were talking about. At least attempting to. You know, the sport in which I am Number One in the world?' He added with pride as he re-clasped her bra with record efficiency, 'Seeing as though you are incoherent, I have an idea that will assist in ensuring my tennis is not "boring" for you to watch. It is exceptionally important to me that your focus remains entirely on me, that it will never deviate from my game. Do I have your attention?'

Nadia nodded against his chest, which earned her a swift, stinging slap on her thigh.

'Yes, yes, sir, you have my attention. I apologise.'

'Your manners are slipping badly today, Nadia, and you know my thoughts on that. I will not warn you again.' Another swift slap landed on her other thigh.

She sat up straight, sensing his agitation. 'They are, sir. I'm sorry, honestly. It won't happen again.'

His tense palm relaxed and began gently rubbing the strawberry-coloured marks left behind.

'You will count every ace and fault I serve during each match I play in the tournament. For each ace, you will receive my pleasure; for each fault, you will accept my pain. This plan should help focus your attention and maintain your interest in the game.'

'I have no doubt it will, sir. Definitely.'

Nadia thought back over the last few months and how Stephan had steadily introduced her to his concepts of pleasure and pain. Or fortunately, more precisely, pain followed by pleasure. Never before had she imagined that such an intense, sensate world could exist within a relationship, and she slowly but surely found her body eagerly awaiting each learning experience on offer.

After each session, Stephan went to great lengths to ensure he understood her reactions to everything he did to her. Even though at first she had felt incredibly awkward having to provide such detailed descriptions of her feelings in answer to his probing questions, she began to love the way he took this time to so completely understand her – as no one ever had before. Nothing had ever made her feel so special, and she willingly offered up her body and mind to serve and please him. She adored the power he had over her and relished his attention.

Stephan was immensely pleased when her tolerance to pain steadily improved during their time together. She was more than willing to continue with his so-called 'conditioning sessions', as the sensual gratification he bestowed on her afterwards never failed to blow her mind – and the pain never occurred without the pleasure.

'Do you think you are capable of keeping track of the statistics in each game?'

Nadia chastised herself for letting her mind wander again, Stephan's deep voice once more grounding her in reality.

'I will certainly try my best, sir.'

'Let's hope your best is one hundred per cent accurate, Nadia. Should you get either score wrong, you will be punished. Do you understand?'

'I understand the pleasure and pain, sir, but I'm not so sure about …' She hesitated, as she couldn't see his face to judge his reaction.

'Say it, Nadia.'

'Well, punished … how exactly?'

'I have developed a list.'

'Oh, I see. You sound quite prepared for this.'

'Where you are involved, my sweet possession, there is nothing I leave to chance.'

Although his words could be taken a number of ways, she was content to bask in the glory of just how much she meant to him.

'I want you to highlight the ones you feel are acceptable – or not – which I will use as reference moving forward. This is important, Nadia, and will become part of our agreement with each other. You will complete this task this afternoon.'

'Yes, Master.' Nadia, although acutely aware of his fingers playing inside her like a harp, instinctively knew that he was completely serious, so answered him with deference. She also hoped like hell she could concentrate better when she was watching him play tennis than when he was playing with her as he was now. At least that way, she could potentially avoid punishments altogether, should she not take a liking to his list.

'One more question, if I may, sir?' She commended herself on remembering her manners, as she glanced towards the now fading print of his palm on her thighs.

'Yes, of course.'

'Am I able to use anything to record the statistics during the match?'

'Oh, Nadia, I thought you knew me better than that.'

His legs stretched her wide on the edge of the lounge. His expert fingers took her to the cusp and left her wanting, leaving her body a quivering mess of frustrated nerve endings, apart from her hands, becoming numb under the weight of her body.

'That would be cheating and take your punishment to a whole new level.' His experienced fingers held her in a constant state of arousal, so much so that she thought she might soon shatter into pieces.

'Besides, how else can I be sure you are paying attention to something that is so important to me?'

For a fleeting moment she wished she could slap him, such was her frustration at his incomplete ministrations.

He tilted her chin back up towards his face as if sensing her errant thought, so she could see the highly amused yet determined look in his eyes as he waited for her acknowledgment.

'That is certainly one way to ensure you have my attention, Master.' Her panted response was aligned to the rhythm of his touch, and both of them seemed to please him no end.

'Naturally, I will aim to maximise my aces. After all, it's the ultimate prize I'm after.'

Nadia hadn't anticipated the nip on her neck to coincide with his fingertips pressing her swollen clitoris through the flimsy lace, and then tapping firmly, rhythmically against it. Thank goodness she hadn't slapped him – not that she ever would, or could, given the dexterity of his reflexes.

By about the fourth or fifth tap, she had no option but to temporarily lose all focus – her mind once again entering the subspace he controlled via that part of her body.

Yet again he revelled in his patiently acquired expertise, knowing only too well that his sexual prowess regarding Nadia was now as finely honed as his tennis skills on court. He couldn't wipe the smile from his face. He honestly couldn't decide whether he hoped she would fail or succeed …

Invitation

Nadia was shocked to find Stephan had already left the room when she became fully conscious. And her panties had vanished – again! She hated to think how much he spent on lingerie that either disappeared or was destroyed after the first time she wore it.

The crunch of paper as she rolled over brought her attention to Stephan's list of punishments, which had been conveniently tucked between her breasts, held firmly in place by her bra. Impossible to ignore!

Though she didn't think she was partial to punishments per se, she spent some time considering the list as requested and believed she could tolerate most of the options he had proposed. Confinement, being forbidden to dance, restraint, humiliation … Even though he had been slowly but surely introducing her to all of these things during their time together, she couldn't honestly say that she wanted any of them to occur, and certainly hoped to avoid all of them. As much as she thought she should cross out 'Varying degrees of corporal punishment' she couldn't deny she was becoming used to the perplexing pain associated with such proceedings, particularly as it had always been a precursor to extreme, sometimes intoxicating pleasure.

Somehow the idea of being denied his touch and her orgasms – also included on the list – had a far more terrifying impact on her psyche, sending cold shivers down her spine. He had indulged her body to such an extent that she was conditioned to – dependent on, really – being pleasured many times a day.

Reducing her orgasms to one per day would be punishment enough. But denial for a specified timeframe, to be determined by him … that would constitute pure hell from her perspective!

Sighing loudly into the empty room, she supposed that punishment wasn't meant to be pleasant. Indeed, a reminder of this was included in his notes. From the outset he had always made it clear that punishments were a necessary part of their relationship and would only ever occur following *her* violation of one of their *agreed* rules. It was stated in black and white in the addendum sent through to the lawyers, and had therefore become a condition of her contract with Caesar.

All in all, it was only the annotation at the bottom of Stephan's list that concerned her a little. 'Any variation and/or combination of any of the above may occur.' She could only wonder what he meant by that! Hopefully she would never have the opportunity to find out – but then again, she reflected, maybe she would …

She certainly had no regrets so far. Besides, the last thing she wanted was to disappoint her Master. So she decided she could live with his list and signed and dated the document unchanged.

Startled by a knock on the door, Nadia wrapped a robe around her body and looked through the peephole.

'I have a delivery for Nadia from Mr Nordstrom.'

She opened the door for the concierge, who wished her good afternoon and placed the delivery on the table. Just as she was feeling incredibly awkward for not having any money for a tip – there had been no need for her to even carry a purse since becoming cocooned in Stephan's world – the man himself strode back into the room.

'Ah, Richard, excellent service. I'm only just back myself.'

'Thank you, sir. Don't hesitate to ask if you require anything else at all. I'm at your service.'

'Thanks, will do.'

Richard nodded towards Stephan and promptly left the room. *Apparently no tip required,* Nadia thought, relieved, as Stephan opened the box and held out a dress, checking its size.

Nadia was desperate to say something but remained silent as Stephan grinned at her.

'You're not going to ask?'

'I'm sure you will tell me in your own time.' He raised his eyebrows. She quickly added 'sir' to the end of her statement and was rewarded with a kiss on the lips.

'I've decided you will attend the function tonight, wearing this dress.'

He presented her with a sleeveless cocktail dress with a racer-cut neckline and a fitted bodice. It was made of silk and featured a pleated peplum flounce. It was a gorgeous aquamarine colour – the colour Stephan chose more often than not for Nadia to wear, as it matched her eyes, though this was a little lighter than his usual shade. As always, there was lingerie to match.

'Well … thank you very much, sir.'

She stopped herself before asking the obvious question. He sensed as much, and encouraged her to go on.

'It's OK, you can ask.'

She didn't need to be told a second time. 'I didn't think you ever wanted me to be seen with you in public, sir.'

'You won't exactly be seen with me, but it doesn't mean I don't want to look at you when I'm out. I like to know you are in my line of sight. If anyone asks, you can tell them you were invited by Caesar – an old family friend. My team will escort you in and inform you when to leave. Try not to talk to any one person for too long; I don't want you drawing unnecessary attention to yourself, or, more likely, others being drawn to you. As you know, you belong to me.'

His smile was smooth, his words iron-clad. Nadia had never met anyone who had the ability to warm her from the inside out and send chills through her bones simultaneously. He certainly had perfected the art of such an oxymoron.

'Of course, sir. I won't let you down.'

'You know there'll be consequences if you do. Here, try it on right now; I want to make sure it's a perfect fit.'

Nadia took the dress and began walking towards the bedroom.

'Right here will be fine, Nadia. I can assure you, there is nothing I haven't seen before that I don't want to see again.'

Her cheeks instantly flushed, while Stephan settled himself into an armchair, sipping a Perrier and watching her every move. She carefully dressed in her new outfit, his eyes glazing over at the perfect shape of her body and the grace of her movements.

Finally she stood before him, awaiting his inspection, knowing approval was never guaranteed until he was happy with every detail.

'Almost, but not quite.' He reached for the phone.

'I'll just look in the mirror, sir.' She took a step towards it.

He covered the handset before answering.

'Is that your decision or mine, Nadia?'

'Yours, sir.'

'Correct. Stand right where you are.' He returned to the phone.

'Hello? Yes, I need a seamstress to come to my suite immediately.'

He hung up and began unbuttoning his shirt. 'Don't move an inch. I'm going to get ready.'

She was grateful he didn't close the bathroom door, so she could appreciate the view of his magnificent, freshly showered body. Although she knew he wouldn't be inside her again until the end of the tournament, she couldn't deny the arousal his naked form provoked within her. Many hours could be whittled away gazing at such a sight; it was like watching a poster of your favourite pin-up come to life. Her voyeuristic opportunities made her role that much more of a privilege. She found herself literally weak at the knees when his taut white backside and tanned, muscled back and shoulders were in full view. And every time she saw the tattoo of the Swedish flag on his right butt cheek she couldn't help but smile.

Her Stephan. Made in Sweden. He turned around to see her tongue slide unconsciously along her full lower lip and her eyes fill with lust as he caught her looking.

'Enjoying the view?'

'Oh, more than you can imagine, sir.'

Another knock at the door interrupted her reverie and he quickly got dressed and let the seamstress in.

Nadia felt like a mannequin as she was hitched and stitched according to Stephan's instructions. He wanted the bodice tighter to emphasise her tiny waist and a little more length in the skirt.

When the seamstress left he explained that he had no intention of her legs being ogled by any lecherous males – or females, given the invitees. The roll of her eyes at this earned her a quick slap on the wrist.

Decoration

Stephan had never felt so possessive of anything in his entire life. It was as though Nadia were made of intricate, fragile glass, requiring round-the-clock protection that only he could provide. Believing that she could only truly shine when she basked in the glow of his presence. He couldn't bear the thought of anyone else touching her – accidentally or otherwise – and was becoming increasingly frustrated that people were unaware that he owned such a priceless treasure. It was becoming a nagging loophole that required closure as soon as practicable.

An only child who had been adored from his first breath of life, he had been brought up as the apple of his parents' eye. Those outside his family unit might have said he was lavishly spoilt, and his friends at school knew he was disposed to be selfish, calculating and at times downright cruel in his actions towards others. Unfortunately many people only discovered his ability to manipulate and intimidate after the damage had been done.

His sporting prowess and natural intellect had enabled his confident and dominant personality to persuade and impress the adults in his life, seeing him secure leadership roles from a young age. This only served to reinforce to his parents the sheer genius of their only son. The path was clear for him to achieve whatever he wanted in life, and they supported him in every endeavour he undertook, given the financial resources at their disposal.

He had informed them a few years ago that he'd prefer they stay at home rather than travelling to tournaments with him, saying that their presence made him more nervous and he wanted to focus on winning – an explanation they graciously accepted, wholeheartedly supporting his decision. In his mind they were a means to an end and they had more than served their purpose. These days he rarely spoke to them, though he always called after he won a major tournament; he knew they would listen unconditionally as he described the intricate details of his victories, which he greatly enjoyed doing. At least this way he could live his own life, on his own terms and without complications or distractions.

So although he appreciated his good fortune in securing Nadia, he wasn't overly surprised something like this had happened to him. It was only to be expected, if he really thought about it – and it certainly didn't sound like Ivan had made the most of such an opportunity. *What a waste*, he thought as he stepped out of the lift on his way to Caesar's reception. He was aglow with hubris, delighted that he had made the decision for Nadia to attend tonight. His perfect decoration – like a beautiful angel delicately placed on top of a Christmas tree.

To be admired by many but touched only by one.

Until he decided to place her carefully away again.

Stephan squared his shoulders and walked through the doors, not needing a ticket for such an event and certainly not needing to show identification. They all knew who he was and he loved that they did. To ask for identification would be an insult to his status. He was surrounded by whispers about how happy and confident he appeared this year, all of which was recorded for the Australian newspapers and took even less time to appear online. Stephan chatted to those in attendance with ease, as if he didn't have a care in the world, graciously signing autographs and making a deliberate effort to converse with the other players and, most importantly, all of his sponsors.

All the while the cameras were flashing. Everyone wanted to be seen talking to the world's Number One, and he wanted everyone to know just how relaxed he was about the coming tournament. He even posed with every one of the native Australian animals, understanding this type of photo was loved on social media and sold copious women's magazines. It was an all-important public relations exercise that made good business sense, though the seasoned professionals on the tennis circuit knew that his personality would change 180 degrees when competing on the court over the coming fortnight.

As he glanced around the room after checking his watch, he was surprised Nadia hadn't arrived. She was supposed to be escorted down at precisely 8pm as per his instructions. Cameras flashed wildly as Marlene, the women's champion from Switzerland, walked towards him, distracting him from his rising agitation. They had known each other since they were juniors, so they greeted each other warmly and engaged in friendly conversation, capturing the avid attention of the press. Towards the back of the room Nadia entered without fanfare, feeling slightly anxious yet thrilled that Stephan had made the significant step of inviting her into his public world.

In fact Nadia had arrived on schedule, but had taken one of the rare moments afforded her to observe Stephan without his knowledge, appraising his universal magnetic appeal as he held sway over all those around him. Seeing his smiling lips, which had just tenderly kissed her goodbye, and watching his hands gesture in conversation, knowing his fingers had expertly ignited her loins mere hours ago. She tried to drag her eyes from his presence and steady herself against a pylon to calm the swelling arousal of her most recent, decadent memories. That he could have this impact on her from afar was a little disconcerting to say the least, when she had once been so self-contained.

She reflected that this event wasn't completely dissimilar to a ballet reception after a gala performance, though there was definitely a more energetic vibe here than at those subdued gatherings of philanthropists and dancers. She grinned to herself as she realised that many of the people there looked exactly like what they were: athletes in cocktail attire. It sort of worked, but for the most part the women looked as if they would be far more comfortable in their Nike trainers and sweatbands than in stilettos and sequins. Nadia found she was enjoying being the outsider in this competitive world rather than the centre of attention, which never came naturally to her in social settings; only ever when she was onstage.

Stephan, on the other hand, seemed to love basking in the glory of being Number One, with everyone clamouring for his attention. He looked as though it was the most natural thing in the world for people to be loitering around waiting to meet and greet him.

Catching her breath, she realised his alluring presence caught many off guard – men and women alike – but unlike the masses, she knew that he could do things to her that he would never do with them. She felt abundantly special as she smiled at this secret knowledge.

Disruption

With her gaze lingering on the delectable sight of her Number One, Nadia was not paying complete attention as she stepped back behind the pylon. She stumbled directly into another man.

'Oh my goodness, I'm so sorry!' Her apology was spoken before her eyes even made contact with his.

'Well, well … Look who it is! No need for apologies, as *I'm* not sorry at all!'

Nadia recognised the voice immediately, along with the enticing warmth of his body. She looked up to be greeted by a gorgeous face and a warm embrace.

'Noah! Wow, you're here! Look at you!' She exclaimed, excited to see him again and unable to cast her eyes away from the muscled form of his chest and arms. There was no doubt he had been training a lot more seriously than when she had last seen him.

His genuine smile as their eyes connected touched her heart. 'Of course I'm here, Elle. It's great to finally see you again, it's been forever. You look amazing yourself.'

His hand grasped hers and held her arm high so he could spin her around for a 360-degree viewing. Her face blushed red as she giggled in response. Within seconds she was within his embrace and returned his hug with conviction, allowing herself to relax in his familiar presence and soak up the sunshine that was Noah. Her smile was wide and heartfelt as she inhaled his masculine scent then deeply exhaled – as if it had been her first true breath for some time. She closed her eyes with her head nestled against his broad chest as thoughts of their time together in London flooded her mind.

Such memories were brought to a sudden standstill when she remembered exactly where she was. Her eyes immediately sprang open and she forced her body to disentangle itself from his embrace.

'Hey, what's wrong? What's happened?'

'Nothing's happened, nothing at all – it's just, well, there are so many people here, you know, it's so public ...' Her eyes shifted uneasily around the room. She was desperate to change the subject and not draw any further attention to herself. 'So how are you? Your training has obviously been getting more intense by the day.'

Noah looked baffled as he wondered what on earth was wrong with her. He noticed the concern, almost fear in her eyes, and paused, before deciding to let it go – for the moment. 'That's the aim, but we have more important things to talk about than tennis. How have you been? You barely return my calls any more. What's news?'

'I've been great, really well. No news. You know, just the usual, nothing much, same old ...' As her voice trailed off she knew she had stuttered out the words and sounded flustered and unconvincing. She felt like a child, unsure of what to say or do in a new environment.

Noah could see her discomfort. 'Hey, it's OK. Listen, do you have time to catch up now? We can duck out if you'd prefer a bit more privacy. I've been dying to see you again.' He placed his hand around her waist to guide her towards the door.

She swiftly removed it. 'I'd love to, but I can't, not now. I need to stay here.'

Stephan finally caught her eye. His steely gaze made her feel as though there were an iron grip around her throat, and she subconsciously raised her hands to her neck and coughed.

'What's wrong, Eloise? You're trembling.'

'Am I? Must be the air conditioning or something. I'm sorry, Noah, but I can't really talk now.' She then felt guilty for not having been in touch with him for so long, noting the concerned look in his eyes. 'I'll be around the whole tournament, though. Maybe we can catch up some other time.'

She glanced warily in Stephan's direction, only to see him excuse himself from his conversation before making his way over towards them with smooth determination.

'Tell me, who are you here with? Ivan is not playing.'

Before she could answer, Stephan was by her side, with a smile plastered on his face and his hand outstretched.

'Noah, good to see you again. Congratulations on a great season last year.' They grasped each other's hands firmly as Nadia stood nervously between the two men in her life.

'Hey, Stephan. Likewise, though it would have been better to have a US Open title under my belt.' Noah winked good-naturedly. Considering the catastrophic loss he'd had to Stephan during the finals, the way he seemed to take it all in his stride was impressive.

'There's always this year – but I don't plan on making it easy for anyone to take that title away from me now that I have it.' Stephan returned his wink. 'So you two know each other?'

Though Stephan asked casually, Nadia felt the tension underlying his apparently innocent question. Suddenly she felt the compulsion to speak first, sensing the urge to protect both herself and Noah.

'We met briefly at Wimbledon last year.'

Noah gave her another strange look before asking the same question in return. 'And the two of you?'

She didn't have a good feeling about any of this.

'After the US Open. Seems that tennis has a way of bringing people together.' Stephan laughed insincerely. 'Anyway, nice seeing you again, Noah.'

He was effectively dismissing him as he placed his arm possessively around Nadia's shoulders. 'Come, Nadia, Caesar has been asking after you.' She nervously glanced towards Noah, seeing confusion written all over his face as she was guided away into the throng of people by the man who had asked her to remain incognito throughout this event. So much for *that* strategy!

Noah stood staring after Eloise – who was now apparently 'Nadia' as far as Stephan was concerned – utterly perplexed and wondering what had just happened.

Was she with Stephan now? It certainly appeared that way. Maybe that was why he hadn't seen her or heard from her recently other than a few scant messages here and there. He couldn't imagine someone as domineering as Stephan letting her out of his sight, and he obviously didn't for very long. For the first time in his life, Noah felt what could be described as his blood boiling at the situation at hand. It was a strange, unpleasant sensation. One he didn't care for at all …

Now he was even more determined to talk to Eloise about what was going on. Not least because she looked positively radiant, even more beautiful than he remembered, but something was masked. She wasn't quite herself – or at least the self that he had fallen in love with on the canal boat. There was an underlying tension he couldn't get to the bottom of without talking to her first-hand.

Just when he thought he might have a chance with Eloise now Ivan was off the scene, it seemed she had fallen into the dominating clutches of Nordstrom. Of all the men to choose – or had she chosen at all? He needed to talk to her about what was going on, to make sure this was something she wanted of her own free will. If it was, there was not too much he could do about it, he supposed, but if it wasn't …

The feeling of his blood boiling rattled his veins for the second time that night and he immediately knew that he'd do anything to make sure she was safe.

He exhaled deeply in the hope of tempering his rampant emotions, and glanced towards Eloise again – surrounded by Stephan, his manager, Caesar and another woman Noah recognised from Tennis Australia. It all looked normal enough, but she was edgy, and she kept glancing in his direction. As he caught her eye, he gestured for her to call him and she gave him the slightest nod. In response he blew her a kiss, causing her lips to curve into a gentle, reassuring smile.

Stephan noticed immediately and a stern expression crossed his brow as he positioned himself to block her from Noah's view. Noah decided that he would leave her be for now and call it an early night. He obviously wouldn't have another opportunity to speak with her again this evening.

It was abundantly clear to Nadia that her interaction had ruined Stephan's plans, and she reprimanded herself for letting her guard down with Noah – it was undisciplined and Stephan didn't deserve to be treated that way. And Noah certainly didn't deserve the wrath of Stephan either! As much as she had tried to forget about Noah these past months, seeing him again in person stirred up strong feelings she hadn't expected. But at this precise moment, in such a public forum, she needed to do something to make amends for her behaviour, so she forced all thoughts of Noah from her mind, clasped her hands in front of her and lowered her eyes to the floor to indicate her subservience to her Number One.

Fortunately, her actions were received by Stephan with a nod of approval, and he handed her a glass of wine picked up from a passing waiter. Much to the surprise of both of them, she drank every drop, adding to the heat already on her face from the fierce emotions inhabiting her body.

As soon as Nadia had finished her wine, Stephan nodded to Garry to escort her back to their suite, signalling the end of her evening in the public domain. An hour or so later, after ensuring he had been photographed talking to a number of models attending the event, Stephan excused himself, knowing that he needed to be prepared and well rested for his first match.

He decided to say nothing to Nadia for the moment about her conversation with Noah, as he had no desire for such distractions over the next fortnight. However, now that he was aware that they knew each other, he would certainly be keeping a close eye on Noah.

Nadia slept restlessly, tossing and turning on the crisp Egyptian cotton sheets. Her unconscious mind struggled with the events of the evening and her dreams spiralled into a physical and mental blur which more often than not found her restrained by Stephan's wrought-iron grip, her crossed arms pinned against her slender waist. In every dream, Noah was so close, almost by her side, but although she could see him and sense his warmth, he was frustratingly beyond her reach. The shock and concern haunting his eyes even though he was smiling caused an ache in her heart. She shouted for his attention, only to discover Stephan's palm clamped against her mouth, denying her freedom to speak.

Needless to say, she awoke many times in a sweat, grateful that her unconscious dreams were not her conscious reality.

Attitude

For most people, the intriguing interaction that had occurred earlier in the evening between the threesome would have gone unnoticed. But Caesar never considered himself to be like 'most people', and the incident went far from unnoticed by him. Commending himself on his brilliance as he observed how his Number One Strategy was playing out, he couldn't deny that this entire proposition was becoming far more interesting than he had ever thought possible.

Having closed a deal to represent Noah Levique earlier in the day, he felt confident he had his bases covered, and had already lined up a few Australian sponsors for the rising star. Speaking of which ... given the look on Nadia's face when Stephan snatched her away from Noah's grasp, Caesar was tickled pink that his own stars seemed to be aligning and that Stephan was keeping up his end of the deal. For the time being, Caesar had all the information he needed, so there would be no reason for adjustments to his strategy or his extensive betting arrangements. Which pleased him no end.

* * *

Ever since his trouncing in the US Open final, Noah had become much more determined to win. He hadn't forgotten Eloise's words on the canal boat about giving up smoking if he wanted to be Number One. And he realised he *did* want to be Number One.

He was coming to recognise that if he really wanted something, he had to fight to make it happen, rather than simply waiting for it. Achieving great results wasn't possible without a lot of hard work and a little bit of luck – and up until now he had simply gone with the flow of life, letting his talent in tennis take shape in its own casual way.

This year would be different. He was ready, he was focused, and he wanted to win more than ever before. All of which had caused him to make a number of changes in his career.

Not only had his coach begun an intensive new training regimen to instil the characteristics of a winner into his psyche, but he had also accepted the offer of Caesar King to be managed by The Edge. In the process he had discovered first-hand just how persuasive Caesar could be. He'd heard rumours from all and sundry about Caesar's larger-than-life personality, but he'd never expected the man to exceed his reputation. Caesar was a whole lot more than a colourful personality. He was more professional, informed, determined, unflappable, intelligent, perceptive and passionate in person than even the media had portrayed him. And ultimately his agency made Noah an offer that it would have been ludicrous to refuse – so he didn't. After all, if it worked for the top five players it would work for him too.

Noah had well and truly made the big league, and that was exactly where he intended to stay. Being passionate about the game had enabled him to get this far, but he realised he had to put much more effort in to ensure he had the continued drive to win each and every match he played. His motivation had just reached new heights and he was hoping it caught all of his opponents off guard – even if some of them were his friends!

It was with this attitude in his mind that he was intent on performing better at the Australian Open than he ever had before. And after seeing the look on Nordstrom's face tonight after he dragged Eloise away, he was determined to make it through to the final so he could wipe the smugness off that arrogant face.

Aces

The next morning Nadia lingered beneath the cold water from the strong jets of the shower to awaken her tired body and frazzled mind. She needed to ensure she was alert for Stephan's first match of the Australian Open. Navy shorts and a pale blue Ralph Lauren polo shirt had been laid out for her by Stephan: an obvious signal that she should try to blend in with the rest of the casual Aussie crowd. The cap and sunglasses silently dictated that not a single strand of her somewhat unruly hair should be loose.

She smiled to herself, loving the intimacy between them that meant he could communicate to her effectively without so much as a word. Part of her role was to ensure she remained Stephan's secret and therefore should never be recognised or associated with him in public. Last night had been a regrettable exception – and as she dressed she promised herself she would never compromise him like that again. Fearing the worst when he returned to their suite last night – or at the very least some form of inquisition about her relationship with Noah – she'd been relieved when Stephan hadn't mentioned a word as they said their goodnights.

She couldn't decide whether she feared or hoped to cross paths with Noah some time during the next fortnight. But either way, she reasoned that when dealing with a force such as Stephan, she must put last night's distraction behind her and prove to her Master that her focus was entirely on him. She conceded that it was much easier to manage her feelings for Noah when they were on separate continents, with technology facilitating their much-needed discretion.

As she entered Rod Laver Arena for the first time, she was taken aback by the liveliness of the crowd. People's faces had been coloured to match the countries they supported, and outlandish wigs made people's heads the same size as their shoulders, giving them the look of cartoon characters. Children and grandmothers alike were just as boisterous as the bellowing males in the arena. It was as though each member of the audience around her believed they were a fundamental part of the game. The support for Stephan was obvious, with substantial pockets of the arena inundated with blue and yellow. It wasn't exactly the festival atmosphere of the US Open, but it wasn't far from it. The noise was deafening as it was announced that the players would soon be arriving on court. Footage was televised on giant screens showing their progress along the Walk of Champions, lined with portraits of the tennis greats of past and present.

Captivated by the images of her Number One, Nadia was acutely aware of the tension that would be seeding within Stephan at the beginning of such an important tournament, just as it always had in her before the first performance of a new ballet. She had become so tightly bound to him these past few months that it was as if the adrenaline provoking his nervous system were being replicated in her own body. She didn't want to do anything to upset his rhythm, knowing the slightest mishap could swiftly change his attitude from playful to aggressive during tournaments, and at such times it was her job to accommodate his every mood swing. She loved her role in his life, although she continued to deny she loved it more than ballet, for that would be to deny knowing herself.

There was no doubt in Nadia's mind that Stephan was deadly serious about her remembering the statistics of each match he played, so she would need to be super-alert the whole time. She rationalised that if she could memorise the choreography for entire ballets, it couldn't be too difficult. It was only aces and faults, after all.

As she settled into her seat, she wondered whether she could get away with keeping tabs on a piece of paper, just in case. She didn't want to be dealing with punishments on day one of the tournament. It only took a moment for her to reach into her bag and realise Stephan was already a step ahead of her. As much as she was sure she had had a pen and notepad in her bag yesterday, they were gone today. Instead she found a small pair of binoculars, presumably to watch him play at closer range, given that her seat was located high up in the stadium, so she could blend in with the rest of the avid fans. Her phone had been turned off, with a Post-it note attached to it.

Don't even think about it! You know I will know.

She was surprised when she felt a fleeting temptation to rip it off and say that it must have fallen off in her bag. But she found it impossible to lie to Stephan; even being vague with the truth was becoming an agonising process. It was as if he had direct access to her mind; it would only take a quick glance at her face for him to know she had cheated. Besides, if she was honest with herself, she had no desire to disappoint him – ever.

Like a drug, his approval had become her addiction.

She smiled and put the phone straight back into her handbag. Adjusting the lenses of the binoculars, she focused on her Number One, standing as composed as ever on the service line. Except for a strip of yellow on his shirt and shorts, it was as though he and the blue court were one. He was checking the balls he'd been given, and as he turned around he appeared to look directly up at her seat. His eyes instantly penetrated what little privacy she had in the stands.

Stephan knew exactly where Nadia was sitting, and as he looked at her, for a fleeting moment he allowed himself a memory of the look on her face just before she came. A face so angelic that the depths of her eyes were permanently etched into his brain. He considered it one of his triumphs that at that given moment he had absolute power to either fulfil or deny her pleasure. She was always wholly dependent on his next move. Such dominance over her body and mind proved an endless aphrodisiac to his ego.

The scent of her panties was forefront in his mind, as he had discreetly inhaled the remnants of her loins while prepping in the locker room prior to walking onto centre court less than fifteen minutes ago. This ensured his senses were inundated by all things Nadia and focused his mind on exactly what was at stake. There was no question that with her in his life, he felt completely invincible. So it was with that mindset that he walked onto the court and owned the tennis stage, allowing his fans to adore him as they cheered and screamed their homage.

Stephan forced the image of Nadia to recede in his mind and replaced it with the image of serving the first of many aces. Such control ensured his focus was now on the game and nothing else. All of his best matches were played one point at a time, and he knew this one would be no different.

Nadia's hands were shaking as she attempted to maintain focus on Stephan through the binoculars. How could he have such an impact on her, just seconds before his match began? She could have sworn she detected the slightest curve of his lips and a wink of his eye, causing her to cross her legs to quell the reignited desire pulsing between them, before his face morphed into an intense mask of sheer concentration.

'Play.' The umpire's word reverberated in Nadia's ears as she sat up straight, paying absolute attention to the game before her and the supreme athlete who was here for one reason only.

To win.

And that he did. Convincingly.

Nadia need not have worried about her scorekeeping abilities. Sixteen aces and no faults against an unseeded Russian player were easy enough to keep track of – particularly when the three-set match lasted only forty-two minutes. Stephan raised more of a sweat during one of their 'conditioning sessions' than he did throughout the entire match under the heat of the summer sun. He was smooth, suave and perfect. After a few words and laughs with the courtside commentator, he left the court as triumphantly as he had entered, waving to the crowd, and bowing his head towards the female groupies who seemingly adored him worldwide.

It had been quite some time since tennis had had a Number One with model good looks, the presence of a Scandinavian god and an ability that put him in a league of his own. Nadia felt like the luckiest person on the planet, because although Stephan had eyes for many, she knew he had proprietary rights to her body, and for now, at least, he belonged only to her. Excited shivers rippled through her as she basked in the private knowledge of being his.

It took no more than a second to decide it was best not to contact Noah again, for that would open a door she wasn't sure she could close, and she certainly didn't want Stephan having to close it for her. Though she could anticipate Noah's disappointment, she was sure it was better for everyone this way.

She lingered in her seat well after her Number One had left the court, amazed at just how much she had come to love this game.

Cornered

It was a perfect day; the sky was blue, and a gentle breeze took the heat out of the January sun. After media interviews, Stephan would be having his post-match physiotherapy session with Greta and a discussion with his coach, so Nadia decided to walk back to the hotel via the promenade along the Yarra and enjoy some people-watching.

She couldn't find Stephan's security team, and didn't want to draw unnecessary attention by trying to contact him directly, so she left Rod Laver Arena just like any other fan making their way back to the heart of the city.

Pausing at the gates, she turned her phone back on and saw three messages from Noah. At the same instant her phone started ringing; it was him. Butterflies commenced flight in her stomach, although she assured herself that they were more from nerves

190

than anything else. She hesitated before answering, but knowing Stephan was preoccupied for the foreseeable future, she wanted to take the opportunity to get the message across to Noah about not contacting her for a while.

'Noah, hi.'

'Finally! Where are you?'

'At the main gate,' she responded without thinking. Then she remembered herself. 'Listen, Noah, you need to stop –'

'Don't move, I'll be there in just a minute!' he interrupted, before the line went dead.

She quickly turned her phone off so he couldn't call her again, and thinking that Stephan had probably expected her to leave it off. Not knowing what to do, she looked around in a frenzy, wondering whether she should stay to meet him, or make a run for it through the gates. Her indecision temporarily froze her sneakered feet to the ground.

Before she knew it, Noah was bounding towards her with his gorgeous smile. This time he hesitated before hugging her, instead giving her a swift kiss on the cheek.

'You're difficult to catch!'

She couldn't help but smile. 'I know, I'm sorry. But I really can't stay, I have to get going.'

'Where to?'

'Back to the hotel.'

'I'm heading the other way, into the city. Walk you to the Southbank Footbridge?'

She nodded as a group of teenagers came up to him asking for his autograph. It was a strange sensation for her to be around Noah as a famous and easily recognised tennis star; it just didn't seem real.

As he started signing Nadia silently slipped away from the small crowd that had gathered around him and out through the gates, feeling guilty about leaving but knowing it was for the best. If one of Stephan's people saw them together she sensed it wouldn't go as smoothly as it had the night before.

As she hurried out the gates, she heard him call after her.

'Wait up, Elle! Why do you keep ignoring my messages? And now you're running away from me!' He grabbed her hand, stopping her progress and making his point. 'It's OK, I only want to talk – we can do that, can't we?'

His face was a mix of frustration and sadness as her eyes darted around anxiously.

'Please don't do this, Elle – there's no crime in talking, is there, as friends?'

He refused to budge as he pleaded with her, and the longing in his eyes finally made her give in. He was right: since when was she not allowed to talk to people, particularly her one and only friend? She suddenly felt ashamed of the way she had been treating him.

'I'm sorry. Of course we can talk. But can we get out of here? It's just too close to everything tennis.'

'Sure.' He smiled gently.

They walked in silence for a bit until he sensed she was a little more relaxed.

'Elle, I need to know you're all right, particularly after seeing you again last night. You know how much I care about you.'

She sighed, and relented.

'And of course I care about you too, Noah. Please don't ever doubt that. It's just that a lot has changed since we last met, which makes things even more … well, awkward.'

'I sensed as much. Like you being with Stephan?'

'I can't talk about it.'

'Why not?'

'I just can't.' She paused before adding, 'He wouldn't like it.'

'So what if he wouldn't? Elle, stop. Look at me for a minute.' He placed his hands on her shoulders and turned her so she was facing him. Her eyes were reluctant to meet his, and when they finally did he couldn't decipher her thoughts.

'What's happened to you? Something's changed, you just don't seem yourself. It's like you're constantly on edge, and it's worrying me. Tell me. What's going on?'

'Noah, please understand, I honestly can't talk about it, but I'm fine. There's nothing for you to worry about and there's really no more to say. If you want to talk, can you please choose another subject? But either way, I need to keep walking.' She ducked from beneath his hands and strode off along the Yarra. She couldn't put her finger on what she was feeling. She knew Stephan could almost read her thoughts, but with Noah, it was much deeper. As though he could tap directly into her heart opening a range of emotions she was unaccustomed to feeling and didn't understand, causing tears to well up in her eyes.

She refused to give in to their surprise appearance and continued her steady pace.

'OK, if that's how it has to be, I'll respect your wishes for now.' He jogged a few steps to catch up. 'But just so you know, I'm not going to give up on this until I know what's going on and that you're all right.'

She was desperate for him to give up, but she thought silence was the safest option and obstinately kept up the even rhythm of her strides.

She visibly relaxed a little when he eventually changed the topic. He talked about catching up with his family before the Open, spending time at El Questro in Western Australia with his extended family and visiting all the fabulous spots the locals were aware of but the tourists weren't. He even went so far as to say that he'd love to take her there some day – when she was ready – to meet his nan, whom he adored. As long as he didn't veer anywhere near the topic of Stephan, the conversation flowed easily between them.

Noah made no attempt to hide the fact that he had never met anyone like her. Surprisingly, this knowledge soothed her, and she admitted that their time together in London would always be special. This was the first occasion since meeting Stephan when he hadn't consumed her thoughts, and she felt the easing of tension that she hadn't even realised she was carrying. He asked about her dancing and she told him about her ankle injury and how she was now in better condition physically than she had ever been, but yes, she still missed performing.

'Here we are,' she said, as they reached the footbridge.

'Always at a crossroads, it seems.'

'On one side of the world or the other!' They both laughed.

'It's nice to hear you laugh again, Elle. You seem much more serious these days, intense.'

She reflected on this for a moment and couldn't deny that around Stephan she was filled with nervous energy, always trying to anticipate his next move. As she'd realised as far back as the night at the exhibition where she had been mummified, it was far more intense than the Royal Ballet – particularly from a psychological perspective. Chatting with Noah had completely the opposite effect on her; she felt light, carefree, young.

'Still as pure as ever, though.'

She went to lightly punch his arm, knowing he was teasing her, and he caught her fist mid-swing.

'You know I've missed you.' He raised her chin with his fingers so they were facing each other again, not letting go of her hand.

'Likewise – but we never really had a chance to get anything started.'

'One day?'

'Who knows? Maybe.' She retracted her hand from his. 'But not for a while.'

'You know I meant what I said the first time I met you?'

'You said many things that afternoon.'

'I'll be there if you need saving.'

She smiled warmly, and they looked deeply into each other's eyes again before coming together in a friendly hug.

'There is nothing you need to worry about, Noah. I promise.'

Suddenly his demeanour changed, as though something had just clicked in his brain.

'This is all still about being Number One, isn't it?'

'Noah …' she began.

'You must know the reputation he has, Elle …'

'Please don't … I'm happy. I can't deny our relationship is intense, but I wouldn't change it, honestly.'

'OK, OK.' He raised his hands in the air in mock surrender, still concerned but accepting her words.

'Thank you.'

'There's just one thing I want to do before you go.'

She anxiously looked around, wondering how long they'd been.

'It will only take a minute. I promise.' He reached into his pocket and presented her with a small lock.

'What's it for?'

'It's for here and now, and maybe the future.'

She turned it over and noticed it was engraved.

Eloise & Noah
Forever

She tried to stifle her emotions and find words, but couldn't, and was relieved she didn't need to as he gently took the lock from her hands and fastened it onto the rail of the footbridge.

It was only then that she noticed just how many other locks were attached to the bridge. Noah watched her adoringly as she began to read some of the other locks engraved with promises and proclamations of love, discreetly wiping tears from her eyes.

'I've seen this in Europe before, but didn't realise the Aussies would be into it ...' She paused and looked up into his eyes. 'Noah, I don't know what to say ...'

'Then don't say anything.' He wrapped his arms around her and kissed her lips softly, briefly. Not wanting to force her into anything, but not wanting to say goodbye without letting her know how deeply he felt for her.

'Let me know when you're ready to be released, I'll have the key waiting.' He patted the pocket on his chest where he'd put it.

She was touched by his actions and taken aback by the strength of her feelings as she took one last moment to touch the lock, which was now a permanent fixture on the bridge. The sight of it pulled at the depths of her heart.

'Thank you ... I'm sorry the timing is so bad ...'

'Our time will come.'

With those words, coupled with a wink, the mood between them lightened: one of Noah's many strengths.

'I suppose this is goodbye, until I can corner you into seeing me again.'

She nodded, though her grin couldn't hide the regret tainting her eyes.

He kissed both her cheeks like he had in London and turned to walk away.

'Noah?' she called after him. Their eyes met as people wove around them. 'Good luck in the Open.'

'Thanks! With any luck you'll be seeing both of us in the final. You can tell him from me to make the most of being Number One, as I now have that position in my sights.'

'Hmm, I might leave that for you, I'm not that brave!'

'We'll see.'

Grinning and waving, Noah returned across the bridge with a bounce in his step as she glanced after him with a full but regretful heart.

She found it difficult to tell from his tone whether his final words had been frivolous or solemn, and honestly couldn't decide which she'd prefer.

* * *

The photographer had discreetly followed them for the entire walk. He was particularly pleased he had decided to carry his long-range lens in his camera case this morning. A decision that was sure to pay off handsomely. Being retained by Caesar to monitor the girl's every move in Melbourne was lucrative in itself, but after seeing Nordstrom with her the other night at the players' party, and now snapping her with Levique could mean an even bigger bonus than he'd expected. Perfect timing to pay off his credit card, after higher than anticipated spending on the kids' Christmas presents. He looked forward to getting back to his studio to develop the photos, so they could be on Caesar's desk by tonight.

Shame

Nadia was surprised to discover Stephan was already there when she opened the door to their suite. She knew it had taken her a while to get back from the arena, but didn't think it had been long enough for him to get there before her.

'Where have you been? Your phone was off. Security couldn't find you anywhere and you weren't here when I got back. Has something happened? Did you get lost?'

He bombarded her with questions as soon as she entered the suite, slamming the door shut behind her and inhaling her sweet scent as he wrapped his arms possessively around her. He was both angry and relieved at her reappearance, just as a parent might be when a lost child is found.

She was taken aback by the intensity of his reaction. 'I'm sorry, sir,' she said quickly, and with sheer determination, forced her mind into the present. Away from Noah and back to Stephan. Any warm feelings that remained from being with Noah completely evaporated, transforming into guilt as she wondered how she had allowed herself to be lulled into spending so much time with him. 'I didn't mean to worry you, I just decided to walk back on such a beautiful day.'

'You *decided*, did you?'

There was no mistaking the storm brewing behind his steely blue eyes. Nadia knew she was in deep trouble.

'Yes ... well, I ... I couldn't find anyone from security and I didn't want, well, knew I shouldn't bother you, bring attention to myself ...' She found herself completely flustered, and it was difficult to articulate anything with him towering above her, his hands painfully gripping her upper arms.

'Who makes your decisions, Nadia?'

She felt her face drain of all blood at her error in judgment as his hand flipped her cap from her head and grabbed hold of her thick braid. He strengthened his grip on her hair and led her to a chair, forcing her to sit down.

'Answer me!' His voice pierced the room as he knelt before her, yanking off her shoes and socks as though she were a child, throwing them with a loud bang against the door.

'You do, sir.' Her voice quivered.

'And did you mention to me at any time that you would like to walk back after my match?'

'No, sir.'

'Or to security?'

'No, sir, I didn't. I thought –'

'That is exactly the problem here, Nadia, isn't it? You *thought*! And you thought wrong. Now, stand up and take off your clothes.'

She felt tears stinging her eyes but couldn't tell if they were from shame, fear or regret at having disappointed him so much. No doubt it was a mixture of all three.

He glared at her with anger as she fumbled with her shorts and polo top, which fell to the ground, leaving her trembling in her underwear.

'Do I treat you badly, Nadia?' he demanded as he led her into the bathroom.

'No, sir.'

'Do I respect you?'

'Yes, sir.'

'Then why is it that you show such disrespect for me?'

'I'm sorry, sir, I never meant … I had no idea … I *do* respect you …' By this stage tears were streaming down her face and her words were interspersed with sobbing.

'Quiet! I don't want to hear your mumbling excuses. Step into the bath.'

Nadia was conscious that he hadn't asked her to remove her underwear, but didn't dare raise such a concern given the circumstances. She stepped tentatively into the lukewarm bathwater, keeping her eyes lowered and resisting any urge to do anything other than what he explicitly asked.

'Lie down and put your head back.' He roughly untied her braid and pulled her hair into the water, ensuring it was wet before lathering his palms with shampoo. He scrubbed her scalp and washed her hair before turning on the cold jet and rinsing off the foam as she shivered.

'It's a shame you weren't here when the water was steaming hot; I'm sure it would have been a far more pleasant experience for both of us.' He reached for the conditioner to continue the process but this time his fingers massaged her head slowly and methodically, his emotions reduced from a boiling rage to a simmering anger.

The silence between them lengthened, both of them lost in their own thoughts. Nadia was deeply sorry for what she had put Stephan through, knowing how important the Open was to him. Although she'd loved spending time with Noah, she had known something like this might occur, sensing the risk even as she said yes to him. Silent tears continued to slide down her face and she sighed as Stephan's massaging fingers established a more sensual rhythm. The last thing she ever wanted to do was to disappoint him, and much to her regret, that was exactly what she had achieved.

Stephan, on the other hand, was taken aback by his own response to not knowing where she was at any given moment; the depth of his aggression had shocked him to the core, only to be replaced by the blurred emotion of relief when she walked through the door. He was used to having the world revolve around *him*, not the other way round, and he was forced to consider whether he was becoming too reliant on having Nadia at his beck and call. When he had discovered Nadia was not waiting for him in the suite, adrenaline had spiked through his body at the same rate as it would have before he served for match point. He had long ago mastered his emotions during a game; they were to be expected. But this … he just didn't comprehend.

Forcing the analysis of this unknown emotion from his mind, he conceded that when it came to one aspect of their relationship at least, he was abundantly clear. Given their arrangement, and her agreed submission, it was his duty to ensure Nadia understood without a shadow of a doubt that under no circumstances would he tolerate such a deviation from her again.

'I'm deeply sorry for what I have done, Master. I never meant to disappoint you. I promise it won't ever happen again.'

And just like that, her perfect words soothed his concerns – for the moment at least – as he knew from her tone and the despair reflected in her face that her use of the term 'Master' had been utterly sincere.

'Apology accepted, Nadia. But not forgiven or forgotten – yet. Until now, I hadn't realised how important it is for me to know where you are and what you are doing at all times. You should be aware that your behaviour this afternoon was unacceptable.'

This time he heated the water before gently rinsing the conditioner from her hair, for which she thanked him in a whispered voice.

The tension eased between them as he helped her out of the bath.

'You may take off your underwear.'

Demurely, she removed her soaked bra and panties, with her eyes cast towards the floor, and handed them to Stephan. He promptly wrung them out before tossing them in the bin, clearly indicating they weren't to be worn again.

He thoroughly towel-dried her hair and wrapped a warm fluffy bathrobe around her shivering, naked body. Strong arms pulled her towards his chest, embracing her tightly as their eyes met in the steam-rimmed mirror.

'So tell me, did you enjoy your walk?'

Her body involuntarily shuddered at his question, which gave him cause to raise his eyebrows.

She took a deep breath to steady her voice before answering him. 'Yes, sir, it was a beautiful day and you won your first match.'

'That I did, very convincingly. And the stats?'

'Sixteen aces, sir.'

'At least you got *something* right today.'

'I was concentrating entirely on you, just as you asked. But sir?'

'Yes?'

'Under the circumstances, knowing how much angst I have caused you, I would willingly accept your punishment should you believe it necessary.'

Nadia was hoping this would appease him, and was more than a little intrigued as to what his response would be.

'I'm pleased to hear you say that. In my experience a suitable punishment always ensures a lesson is well learnt. And remembered.'

'Oh,' was all she could manage in reply. She wasn't sure exactly what answer she'd expected from him but it wasn't that.

'So now that you have raised it, we may as well deal with it immediately. Follow me.'

Stephan strode into the bedroom and opened the wardrobe door.

'I have ten belts hanging up in there. Choose one.'

Nadia looked into the wardrobe and back into Stephan's eyes. There was no humour there, no playfulness. He merely waited for her response.

She had no idea which belt would hurt more or less – or even whether Stephan wanted to hit her with it, though she assumed that would be the case. He had used other instruments such as wooden spoons, rulers, hairbrushes and tea towels to promptly remind her of her misdemeanours. She had even enjoyed the paddling she'd received after they played table tennis the first time. After he won the game, he'd wanted to 'beat' her again, ensuring her butt cheeks were plump and rosy as he splayed her body across the table. Though it had left her hot and flustered, that had been for all the right reasons.

This situation was completely different, and she was certainly not expecting any pleasure this time. Her fingers nervously fondled the hard leather, then the soft, finally resting on the canvas belts. Then she let her hands fall back to her side.

'I would prefer you to choose, sir.'

'Very well. Wait for me in the lounge room.'

Pain

Stephan selected a dark brown leather belt that he hadn't worn for years but which would serve today's purpose. It had quite a bit of give but was still firm enough to control, and he liked its thickness. It would hurt and leave a mark, but not as much as some of his others.

He strode into the lounge room, pausing to look at Nadia's reflection in the glass as she gazed out towards the lights of the city sparkling across the river. Twilight was slowly descending on the day. She watched the trains and trams busily moving the bustling crowd around one of the world's most livable cities as he slowly untied her robe, leaving the front of her body exposed.

'I am going to use this belt to strike you from behind, Nadia.' He paused for a moment to absorb the rising colour in her cheeks, knowing that both fear and excitement would be pulsing within her loins at his words. '"Under the circumstances" – to use your words – I will use it initially for your punishment and, depending on how well you accept it, then your pleasure.'

He took a step closer and his index finger lifted her face up towards his, ensuring their eyes met. He could sense her surprise and knew instinctively that she hadn't been expecting pleasure, only pain given this was a punishment. This was a good sign: catching her off guard gave him the upper hand and kept her on her toes – so to speak.

He quickly removed the smile at the corners of his lips that was caused by the anticipation pulsing through his veins. He needed to maintain control of his mind before other areas of his body attempted a physical ambush.

'Do you accept this, Nadia?'

Nadia knew that she must. This was not a test she could afford to fail, nor did she want to.

'Yes, I do, sir.'

He gently removed the robe from her shoulders, letting it fall onto the floor at her feet. The sight of her naked body – demure yet somehow overtly pert – and the wild, deep auburn locks cascading over her milky breasts against the backdrop of the Melbourne skyline ensured the lurch of his groin. He withheld a sigh as he guided her away from him and towards the table.

'Bend over with your breasts resting against the table and hold on to either side with your hands.'

Nadia followed his instructions, the cold surface making her shiver, her nipples hardening against the glass as she flattened her body. Her face rested sideways towards the view.

'Now, spread your legs. I need access to your thighs as well as your arse.'

His precise instructions indicated that this was not going to be a light-hearted, spur-of-the-moment session. There was no doubt in Nadia's mind that she was about to be taught a lesson, Stephan style.

Fear of the unknown constricted her throat, but even as she widened her legs she could sense the heat between them, and the cool air-conditioned air whispering against her loins. Her whole being was full of contradictions: hot and cold, fearful and excited, hoping for pain and pleasure. She didn't want this but she did. Either way, she knew she could not turn back now, and on some deep level she accepted that this punishment would somehow do her good, cleanse her from her deep connection with Noah – or so she hoped.

Stephan languidly slid his palm over her silky-smooth, alabaster buttocks and lingered on her inner thigh, eventually encouraging her with a subtle push to open a little wider. 'That's better. Perfect.'

Her breath quickened at his words and his touch. All she could think was that this was the calm before the storm. She had no doubt about the depth of his anger when she had arrived late, and though he had managed to control it, she sensed he wouldn't hold back on unleashing his feelings on her bared backside – which would be in stark contrast to the soft, caressing touch of his fingers against her skin at this precise moment. She was hyper-alert – as though she were centre stage under blinding lights, paused in position waiting for the music to commence, but not knowing the dance she was required to perform. Her heart was beating faster by the second as she tried to relax her muscles enough to melt into the table – to no avail. Her discipline was the only thing that ensured her body remained anchored in position rather than taking flight.

Aware of every intake and exhalation of his breath, every slight movement or adjustment he made, she convinced herself that she was ready, that she could do this. Once again her mind confirmed that she both desired and deserved this punishment.

Sensing her nervous energy, Stephan swept the hair away from her face, leaving it flowing across the table and her eyes clear to focus on the view. He lightly ran his fingertips along her outstretched arm, causing her to shiver in response.

'I am happy to tie your wrists if it will make it easier for you to stay in position.' His face was level with hers as he knelt beside her, taking a moment to absorb her body from above and below the glazed glass.

'I won't move, sir. I accept this.' Although her voice trembled, there was an underlying determination in her words.

Stephan had to distract himself from the amazing sight of her so willingly before him. It took him to a place he might never want to leave. So he moved away from the dining-room table to pour himself a glass of icy-cold water, though swallowing it did nothing to subdue his throbbing balls.

'You will receive one strike for every minute you kept me waiting. My intention is to mark your skin but not draw blood. Every time you sit down for the next few days, you will be reminded of your misconduct and how it made me feel, so it should never occur again. Do you understand?'

'Yes, Master.'

That was all he needed to hear.

Nadia temporarily welcomed the distraction of trying to calculate how long it had taken for her and Noah to walk back, knowing that would be the maximum time he could have been waiting. But her mind screamed to a halt as the first lash of the belt met her tender flesh. Suddenly she was forced to focus solely on accepting the pain Stephan was administering. No longer could she see the glittering lights of the city, only the flashes of light behind her tightly closed eyes. Desperately, she pressed her upper body into the glass table, palms grasping the sides as tightly as possible to help absorb the impact and to prevent her from shifting away from the next strike, which was exactly what every muscle wanted to do.

Her mind became fully focused on accepting each expertly delivered strike of the belt. She was surprised the glass hadn't shattered under the pressure! It hurt like hell, but she could do this, she *must* do this. She knew she had suffered through worse pain, albeit under completely different circumstances. If only she had let him tie her hands – it had to have been easier than this.

Another crack, then another, shattered her mind, and she broke her silence in a shriek that almost pierced her eardrums.

When she could no longer withhold her guttural screams at her continuing punishment, Stephan paused briefly to stuff the tie of her robe into her mouth, while tenderly and reassuringly stroking her tear-stained cheek.

'No one can hear you now, Nadia, so let go and scream as loudly as you need to. I'm not finished with you yet.'

Unleashing his anger and disappointment on her body like this proved a strong aphrodisiac, and his erection grew more forcefully with each strike as he became carried away with the power he wielded over her. Only when he sensed her entire body was racked with pain did he force himself to stop, lest he went too far, too soon. He was momentarily chastened by the perverse joy he received seeing Nadia's white flesh reacting to his belt, forming embedded welts. He needed control, fast, so he eased the harsh bite of the leather and it grew smoother against her inflamed flesh, giving her some reprieve. He systematically returned to her thighs, then the tops of her legs, until he reached just above her knees, the lashings sharp and swift.

Nadia understood by this time that he could have been using far more force than he was, and she was adjusting to the pain and his rhythm. It was more than bearable. She allowed her muffled screams to escape from deep within her, knowing that each strike was driving Noah further and further away, beating back his influence on her to a tiny corner of her mind, and her heart.

Much to her astonishment, she found the physical pain obscurely cathartic. Not once did she think of asking Stephan to stop, nor of releasing her grip on the table, so determined was she to show him the depth of her regret at disappointing him. Just as he'd said, it was a lesson she would never forget, and one she had every intention of remembering.

Even though there were no words left to utter, he left the gag in her mouth. All of her remaining nervous tension and energy had evaporated as he rolled her limp body over on the table to meet his lustful gaze. She whimpered as her scalded buttocks and thighs met with the cold chill of the glass table, though once she had adjusted to the feeling it helped calm the angry pain of the swollen welts.

'Thank you for accepting my punishment, Nadia. You never cease to amaze me.' His whisper seduced her ear as he gently placed her hands above her head and held her wrists together.

Once she had focused her eyes, she looked in horror at the tip of the belt as it flicked down towards her breasts. A succession of quick, light blows to her nipples sent her depleted body into sensory overdrive, the direct hit of pleasure connecting with her now tingling groin. Before she could gather her thoughts the lashes landed directly on her clitoris, and in less than a few seconds, she found herself screaming harder from the fiery pleasure he was inflicting than she had from the pain.

She was spent. She was broken. She was utterly his.

Without a word, Stephan carried her into bed as he might a floppy doll. He insisted she drink some water and wasted no time in gently massaging some cooling ointment into her tormented thighs and buttocks. He wrapped her exhausted body up in the duvet, knowing she needed warmth and rest before she became fully conscious again. He would order room service tonight; there would be no need for either of them to go anywhere.

Desperate as he was to masturbate so as to liberate what was about to explode, he knew he needed to subdue his urgent need to maintain his edge for the matches ahead. So instead he set the running machine at high speed and hoped exercise and a cold shower would provide the necessary distraction and quell the pent-up energy keeping him hostage to his sexual needs.

Tonight he had broken through a barrier, pushed the boundaries of their relationship to the next level, and Nadia had more than risen to the challenge. Using the belt against her sensitive alabaster skin and seeing the marks he inflicted had created such intense arousal in Stephan it had taken him by surprise. He had never felt this way in his life – and it wasn't as though he didn't have a plethora of experiences to draw upon.

The more obsequious she became, the more he craved her in every way. The problem was, he had never known someone to submit themselves to receiving pain as much as he enjoyed inflicting it – and he enjoyed it almost too much, more with Nadia than anyone else. Most of the time he had managed to keep such urges contained on court, within specified rules and guidelines. Inflicting pain on his opponents was what made him so competitive. The experience of delivering such orchestrated pain to Nadia was beyond his imagination, providing a sexual high he'd never dared to hope for.

Until tonight.

For the first time, Stephan had released the dark, dangerous seeds of his desire, seeds that until now had been buried deep within his psyche and never been permitted to see the light of day.

Tamed

Throughout the first ten days of the Australian Open, Nadia was inundated with flowers, perfume, baths, massages and facials to keep her focused and occupied as Stephan continued his impressive progression towards the finals. He had been so pleased with her behaviour since her indiscretion that he had even given her a pair of unique aquamarine earrings with petite embedded diamonds, to reflect the sparkle and colour of her eyes. Not only was Nadia becoming captivated by the world he created for her with his material gifts, but she had also become more dependent than ever on the physical release he provided her with. One of Stephan's favourite things to do after the 'business' side of each match – interviews, massage, debrief with coach, catch-up with manager etc – was to wind down by playing with her body. In essence, she became the hobby he'd never had.

Ever since the first time they were together in the Cayman Islands, when he had bound her to the bed for the afternoon, he had become obsessed with the reaction of her body to anything he did to it. Restraining her in various positions entertained his mind when he wanted to switch off from tennis, and this need for distraction was ever present during the tournament. He found that seeing her flesh turn from alabaster white to blushing pink when he used the crop or belt on her breasts, stomach, buttocks and thighs aroused him sufficiently to enable him to abstain from sexual release – for that needed to wait until the trophy was his. So instead, his pleasure was derived from causing Nadia pain, using just enough force to ensure that the marks from her 'punishment' remained a constant reminder. And if she satisfied him enough, it would result in her eventual pleasure. There was no doubt in his mind that she enjoyed this game of cat-and-mouse as immensely as he did.

As Nadia sat in the stands in awe of her Master on court, she could feel her body tense in anticipation with each ace he served, causing her to double-cross her legs and stifle moans with her hand during every match he played. He had trained her well.

She was grateful, though always a little nervous, when Stephan arrived back at their suite afterwards, never quite knowing what was in store for her. She found that her body tensed at the mere sight of an instrument in his hand, wondering what he might do with it. Her body often ached for release, and if it was denied she noticed she yearned for her next orgasm like a drug addict might crave their next hit.

So when Stephan didn't arrive back within reasonable time after winning his fourth-round match, she was like a rat in a cage. She hadn't asked permission to go out and therefore nothing had been arranged with Garry and his security team; the last thing she wanted to do was suffer the wrath of Stephan should she not be here when he eventually returned.

She was intensely frustrated at being forbidden to masturbate in his absence, and she almost wished she could tie her own hands together to make sure she kept this promise. She distractedly ordered some room service, but left it uneaten, watched TV that didn't interest her, had a bath, which only served to accentuate her longing, jogged on the running machine to exhaust her urges, even turned music on loud and danced around the enormous lounge room in her lilac lingerie. But still she felt the pulsing urge in her groin, demanding detonation.

It was then that she heard her phone vibrate on the coffee table. Thinking it was Stephan, she picked it up to find another message from Noah. Guilt flooded her mind and her heart as she ignored yet another plea from him, asking if they could see each other again. She turned the music up even louder, letting her body take over, and danced with a forced freedom she had never allowed before.

When Stephan finally walked through the door, she threw her arms around him and dropped to her knees, unzipping his trousers as though her life depended on it.

'Whoa! Wait up. What are you doing?' His hands immediately clasped her wrists, preventing her from going any further.

'I can't do this any more. *Please* let me touch you! I need you!'

'You know the rules, minx! Not yet.' He effectively dismissed her as he walked over to the dining table to inspect the cold, untouched food beneath the domed silver lid. 'Haven't you eaten any of this?' he asked. 'It's late, Nadia; you should have had dinner by now, with or without me here.' He reached for the phone and ordered food for both of them. She hadn't noticed anything he ordered on the standard menu, but that was life with Stephan.

'Come and we'll have a quick shower before it arrives.'

She had no desire to give up an opportunity to get wet and naked with Stephan, even though she'd already bathed, so she raced him into the bathroom and stripped off her bra and knickers.

'You're cheeky tonight. What's got into you?'

Nadia's wandering hands caused her a number of slaps on her wet behind. She didn't want to beg, but she would if she had to; she'd reached the point of no return, slipping and sliding against the tennis god of the world. She just couldn't take any more.

'Please sir, I need to come. I've tried to wait and follow your rules –'

He interrupted. 'Did you come while I was gone, Nadia?'

'No, sir, I've been trying to distract myself for hours.'

He turned her face towards his to assess whether she was telling the truth. Satisfied, he pinned her hands behind her back.

'Who decides when you come, Nadia?'

'You do, sir.'

'Anyone else?'

'Never.'

'How long has it been since you last came?'

'This morning.'

'And you honestly can't wait any longer?'

'No, sir, I'd prefer not to wait another second.'

'Then it will have to be quick; our food will be here soon.'

With that he thrust his fingers directly between her legs and he merely flicked her clitoris twice before she erupted, all too hard, fast and unfulfilled.

'In future, don't bother asking.'

She let out a frustrated groan as he washed the suds off her body. He wasted no time in towelling her dry, then they donned their robes just in time for the arrival of dinner.

Stephan had no desire to sleep without Nadia by his side,

but each night it became more difficult for him to sustain his abstinence when her wandering hands found their way to his body. And tonight she was worse than ever, like a cat on heat. He knew he'd been harsh in the shower, but she'd asked for it and he must maintain control.

'Nadia, this must stop. You know I need to remain celibate until the end of the Open, and you're not helping.'

'You know you're going to win! Please, just once – I need to feel you inside me, it's been so long!'

'How can you complain? I service you several times a day!'

'I know, and I don't mean to complain, sir. But you won't even let me touch your body. I'm dying here! I miss you!'

She sounded desperate even to herself. She was indeed well and truly 'serviced' on a regular basis, but it had been over ten days since she'd touched his cock. Even responding to his embrace she was forced to keep her hands by her side.

'What you need to understand is that the moment I let you touch me, I will want you to keep going. As long as I don't, I know I have the discipline to win.'

'You sound completely superstitious. It's ridiculous.'

'Did you just call me ridiculous?'

Nadia mumbled something into her pillow.

He had to maintain order. Rising from the bed, he walked over to the walk-in robe and returned with a bag. He had wanted to avoid this, but she had given him no choice. It was difficult enough sleeping next to her when she wore a slinky negligée, even worse when she was naked. The finals were approaching and he could no longer afford the distraction of all things Nadia, particularly when she was being so deliberately disobedient.

'Put this on.' He pulled a black and white striped jumpsuit out and tossed it in her direction.

'Now? Why?'

213

'So you look less appealing to me.'

'You're serious?'

'Deadly.'

'Would you prefer I slept in the other room?' She looked at the jumpsuit as though he'd retrieved it from the garbage.

'Not at all. I want you exactly where you are – so I *know* where you are.'

'But I'll look like a zebra ...'

'Nadia! You are trying my patience. Put it on now, or I'll happily do it for you.'

She went to the bathroom in a strop and came out still complaining. 'What were you saying about ridiculous?'

He couldn't hide his amusement.

'I'll sleep in the other room; it will be easier for both of us.' Petulance screamed from every pore of her body.

'Once again, not your decision to make.' His fast hands grabbed hold of the outfit's tail as she tried to pass, and dragged her back into the bed.

'You *do* look like a zebra, but it's having the desired effect.'

'Very funny! I'm completely inaccessible to you and to myself.'

'Exactly, that's the point. Do you normally touch yourself in bed, Nadia?' His interest piqued as colour painted her cheeks.

'This doesn't sound like a conversation you should be having when you want to *control* yourself,' she retorted with disdain.

'You have quite the attitude tonight, I must say.'

Nadia couldn't believe she was getting away with it, but her frustration was overflowing and she couldn't contain it any longer, particularly when she had to sleep in this atrocity. She glared at him but managed to hold her tongue as she turned away.

'Give me your hands.' He waited patiently, still grinning at her while she processed his request.

Eventually, stubbornly, she presented them to him.

'Thank you.' He grabbed hold of her wrists and swiftly bound them together using the tie from her bathrobe.

'Stephan, no! Please don't do this!'

He glared at her, his face now furious, with every trace of amusement gone.

Suddenly she was backtracking as quickly as she could. 'I'm sorry, sir, I didn't –'

'How would you rate your manners tonight, Nadia?' he interrupted, while he tested that her wrists weren't too loose or too tight.

She felt exactly like the zebra she was dressed as: a wild animal that had just been cleverly trapped and was about to be tamed.

'Poor.'

'Would you like me to tie your feet also?'

'No, sir, that won't be necessary.' Suddenly, her manners were at the forefront of her mind.

'Your attitude?'

'Probably worse than my manners – sir.'

'Exactly. Who am I doing this for, Nadia?'

'For you, sir.'

'Who else?'

'For me, sir.'

'Does anything more need to be said?'

'No, sir. Nothing.'

'Goodnight, Nadia.' He switched off the light.

'Goodnight, sir.'

'Oh, I forgot to mention: I have a leopard jumpsuit for tomorrow night.'

She rolled away from him with her wrists bound, and groaned loudly into the pillow as he silently smiled beside his impudent, beautiful and finally tamed beast.

Plaything

It was only during the final round before the quarter-finals that more faults crept into Stephan's game due to the length of the matches and calibre of the other players. Though Stephan comprehensively won against a player from the United States, to proceed to the quarter-finals not having lost a set, he served his first double fault of the tournament in the second set, followed by another during the final set. Nadia knew that to him this was akin to failure, regardless of whether he achieved the desired result.

She notified Garry that she was going to the gym after the match to get rid of the anxiety coursing through her system about what might happen that night, understanding all too well that his faults meant her pain – as agreed at the beginning of the tournament. With that thought in her mind, working herself into a sweat proved good therapy, and she rewarded herself by spending some time in the spa and the steam room before showering. By the time she returned to the suite she was refreshed and in a better frame of mind to accept whatever might come her way.

As she put the kettle on to make herself a peppermint tea, she noticed an envelope with her name on it. Sensing it was from Stephan, she opened it quickly.

Be naked when I arrive wearing only your pointe ballet shoes. Your hair should be out, with a braid plaited either side of your face. Do not disappoint me!

She cursed loudly into the room for having spent so long at the gym. He could walk through the door any minute! She sprinted through the lounge room into the master bedroom, frantically discarding her clothes as she went. She remembered her pointe ballet shoes were still in her suitcase, placed high in the wardrobe, just beyond her reach. She couldn't believe she hadn't danced in them for weeks and had barely noticed – something that would have been unheard of with Ivan.

Trying to drag the large velvet lounge chair from the corner of the room was impossible due to its weight, and suddenly she felt like she was in one of those awful dreams where all her actions were in slow motion and everything she attempted was impossible. She raced back through to the dining table to drag a lighter chair into the bedroom, which finally gave her access to the suitcase. In her haste she yanked at it too hard, and it toppled down over her head and fell open on the floor – empty.

'Ouch!' she exclaimed, rubbing at her head. If the pointe ballet shoes weren't in there, where could they be? Stephan's note had put her into a state of frenzy and she knew he could be there any second. *Do not disappoint me* were the only words that echoed in her head.

She took a deep breath, trying to calm down and think more rationally. On some level she understood that her behaviour was erratic, but she also knew there was little she could do about it – that was the effect Stephan had on her.

Then she noticed she was still in her underwear. It was at that precise moment that she heard the door of the suite being unlocked. Her heart skipped a beat and perspiration beaded on her forehead.

She tiptoed into the palatial bathroom and quietly closed the door, giving herself some much-needed privacy to compose herself before they were face to face. As she turned around she saw her pointe ballet shoes, a brush and comb and three hair bands awaiting her arrival.

How could I have been so stupid? she reprimanded herself silently. Of course he would have had it all planned.

She wasted no time in flinging her underwear into the bath and sitting on the edge to tie her shoes with fumbling fingers, by which time Stephan's giant frame loomed in the doorway.

'Tsk, tsk, tsk. A simple task, so poorly executed.'

He walked over to her as she was about to tie the final ribbons in place.

He grabbed her ponytail, forcing her to stand, and walked her over to the mirror as she winced in pain, trying to keep pace with his movements.

'How hard can it be, Nadia? Everything in place; you didn't even need to think. My match finished hours ago, yet your clothes are scattered everywhere, your suitcase open on the ground. And worst of all, you are not even prepared.'

'I'm so sorry, sir. I only just saw your note –'

'Don't speak. I don't want to hear your pathetic explanations. This is inexcusable. You have until I get out of the shower to follow my instructions precisely.'

Stephan stripped off his shorts and polo shirt and stepped into the steaming shower as Nadia stood naked and shivering, carefully braiding her hair, silently cursing her decision to shower at the gym instead of here.

He stepped out, naked and glistening, as Nadia waited anxiously with her eyes lowered while he inspected her hair. Without a word, he walked out of the bathroom, returning wearing a pair of black jeans with his fly open, showing her beyond doubt that he was commando style, and carrying a bucket of ice and a suspicious-looking black bag – at least, one that didn't belong in the bathroom.

Nadia didn't dare move. Stephan wasted no time in cuffing her wrists together in front of her, raising her arms and attaching her wrists to the highest hook on the wall, the one usually reserved for hanging a luxurious hotel bathrobe. He retied the ribbons on her shoes so that her feet were bound together, causing her to balance *en pointe*, to avoid dangling freely from the wall.

He went back to his bag and carefully laid out ropes of varying lengths, two clamps with rings attached, a number of bull clips and a bag of steel pegs, with the precision of a surgeon arranging his instruments prior to an operation. He emptied the pegs into the bucket, shuffling them around in the ice to ensure they were covered, and replaced the lid.

Nadia's brain froze as she watched him. She was part of the scene but she wasn't. It wasn't until he came towards her, with one of the clamps in his hand and the other in his pocket, that she suddenly became directly associated with the proceedings.

He lowered his head to her nipple, sucking it forcefully and grazing it with his teeth. He slowly released the now elongated nipple from his lips and clamped it, causing her to yelp at the sharp pain. For the first time, he smiled, but she sensed it was more cruel than kind.

His eyes glazed over and he repeated the process with her other nipple. Just as a scream escaped her throat he kissed her deeply to silence it, with a force and possessiveness that left her unable to breathe until he released her mouth. Panting oxygen into her deprived lungs, she wondered whether she could endure this, but was too afraid to break her silence with any words of protest.

He gave both nipples a small tug to ensure they were secure, and, try as she might to contain herself, Nadia cursed loudly into the bathroom. As apologies came flying out from between her lips, Stephan simply looked at her with mild amusement.

'I asked you not to speak and the first thing out of your mouth is an obscenity, followed by a string of insincere apologies! You are making this so much worse for yourself.' He tormented her bottom lip with his finger as he spoke. 'Your disrespect has turned this exercise in managing pain into a punishment as well – which is such a shame, as I would have preferred your mouth accessible.' He placed a ball gag in her mouth, tying the straps around the back of her head.

Nadia remained silent and did not struggle, watching with caution as he threaded her long front braids through the rings attached to the clamps on her nipples, and fastened the braids together at a specific tension using the bull clips. If she moved her head up, the clamps would pull; if she lowered her head, she was fine. Her heart rate was increasing rapidly as each step was carefully carried out.

Drawing the rest of her hair into a tight ponytail, Stephan intertwined it with rope to form a thick braid, which he secured with the third hair band. He deftly tied a large knot further along the rope and placed the knot at the apex of her thighs. Then he secured the end of the rope to the hook on the wall to which he had tied her bound hands – essentially ensuring she was held captive by her own hair.

Having painstakingly tested the tension, he was eventually satisfied that everything was exactly how he'd planned to create the level of friction he desired. He felt her body quiver as the knot settled firmly against her loins, only to be teased away by the need to lower her front braids to ease the sharp pull on her nipples.

With pride, he stepped back to admire his handiwork, having achieved the perfect balance between pain and pleasure, which she could control with her own movements. Something that he would very much enjoy watching.

It was only then that he spoke to her with any trace of kindness. 'You know why I am doing this, Nadia? I'd like you to answer as best you can.'

She mumbled an inaudible sound through the gag. 'You'll have to nod or shake your head. Unfortunately, I can't understand you.'

Nadia nodded carefully, with a determined effort to not cause too much movement.

'Was that a yes? Show me. I need to see clearly.'

She groaned with frustration into the gag and rolled her eyes before she could help it. Then she slowly moved her head up and down, relishing the tension in her moist loins but feeling a simultaneous sting as her nipples pulled upwards.

'It seems you are adjusting a little too well. You like the tension between your legs; I can see it in your eyes. Just blink if you'd like some more.'

Nadia's eyes blinked madly. She'd give anything to come, if only she could get the knot in the right place.

He tightened the rope around the hook on the wall, which was like a pulley system, immediately causing the knotted rope to grind into her moist slit. She wasn't sure which was more humiliating, being strung up like this or wanting to get off on it. Yet she moaned through the gag at the delicious pressure cutting into her core.

'But as we are both acutely aware, Nadia, today isn't about your pleasure.' With nimble fingers, he tightened the nipple clamps, causing a stifled scream to escape from her mouth and tears to well up in her eyes as she desperately attempted to process the pain and find the position of perfect balance. If she didn't concentrate, she caused herself immediate grief.

'Better. Now for the decorations.' He brought the ice bucket closer to where Nadia was hanging. '*So* many options.'

He was watching her intently, assessing the reactions of various parts of her body.

'Your nipples and tongue are already occupied. Your earlobes are an obvious choice, so let's start there.' He retrieved two pegs from the ice bucket and attached one to each of her lobes. The freezing cold of the steel was a bizarre sensation, but fortunately she managed to maintain the precarious position of her head.

'I'm tempted to …' He looked thoughtful. 'Your dirty mouth has been appalling ever since my arrival. I think I'll try something and watch what happens …'

With that, he clipped a peg to her nose, leaving her to breathe solely through the ball gag in her mouth. She immediately panicked, unable to inhale because she was trying to scream. She was desperate to tell him it was too much, she couldn't take any more of this, it was scaring her.

She had lost focus on the amused yet intense blue eyes cataloguing every reaction, when his deep voice penetrated her brain. 'Just nod vigorously, Nadia, if you'd like me to remove it.' She nodded cautiously, still wary of how the knot and clamps could bite into her flesh yet knowing she needed more oxygen.

'That isn't vigorous! Show me you're serious.'

She thought she might black out before she had the chance, so she braced herself for the pain and nodded with all her might, pulling her head back and forward, until finally he removed the nose peg so air could rush back into her brain. Her head was spinning and her arms ached in their sockets, and she momentarily lost her footing causing the knot between her legs to embed itself deeper into her.

'You truly are the ultimate plaything!'

She was angry, shocked and grateful all at the same time when he finally removed the ball gag and offered her some water, which she gulped down as if it would save her very life.

'Don't speak.'

She didn't dare utter a word. She hated the gag and didn't doubt he'd replace it if any sound escaped her mouth.

'I take it you don't like the gag, or oxygen play for that matter?'

She shook her head from side to side, which only caused her to wince.

'Well, then, I do hope you have learnt your lesson, yes?'

He was still teasing nods out of her, but after the shock of what had just happened, the pain and tension were becoming more bearable, so she nodded to both please and appease him.

'Good little minx. Poke your tongue out.'

She hesitated and his expression turned into a scowl.

'Do as I say without second-guessing me, Nadia, otherwise I will leave you hanging here all night.'

She immediately stuck out her tongue, to which he attached two more pegs, which were freezing and metallic and bit into her, causing her to whimper in defeat.

'Just in case you're tempted to speak, they should prove an appropriate reminder.'

He methodically went about fastening the rest of the pegs to various parts of her body. If she reacted even slightly, they stayed in place; if not, he removed them to find a more sensitive area.

Once the process was complete, he went to fetch his camera and took a series of photos of his delectable ballerina, all tied up, clamped and pegged, and hanging against the cold bathroom tiles on the wall. Even like this, she was magnificent, lusting after his fully erect cock with hunger in her eyes. He was sorely tempted to let her have it, for both their sakes, but that would diffuse his power and his goals were clear.

As he packed the camera away, he knew he would treasure these photos for the rest of his life.

'I have a meeting now, so I'll be back later. Don't fret, my sweet, I know you'll get through this for me.'

As he switched off the light and closed the door behind him, he gave himself a stern reminder that he could no longer afford to 'accidentally' double-fault in order to entertain his pain fantasies with her. He was at the pointy end of the slam.

All in all, though, he considered this afternoon's session an extremely worthwhile experience. If Nadia survived this – and it was clear from the desperation in her eyes that she was more than willing to take the pain so as to achieve the pleasure she craved – he wouldn't need to play games to do whatever he wanted with her in future.

Once again, he silently thanked Caesar for providing him with his ultimate plaything. He honestly didn't believe life could get any better than this!

Sensations

Nadia couldn't believe Stephan had left her like this in darkness, with the temptation of securing her pleasure but only at the risk of pain, giving her no option but to distract her mind and breathe through the various sensations occurring within her body. Finally her nipples adjusted to the tightness and became numb from lack of bloodflow, as did her earlobes. However, her breasts, underarms, belly button, ankles and fingers still pinched from the pegs. She could have forced the pegs from her tongue with her lips, but knew there would be serious repercussions if Stephan came back and found them on the floor – and there was no way she wanted to spend the night in here like this! So she made an effort to keep them in place as saliva dribbled from her mouth.

Her arms ached from being stretched above her and the cuffs cut into her wrists whenever she tried to ease the tension in her legs. But it was the knot, the damned knot, that caused her more anguish than anything else, and she had no doubt he had known it would. The pain she could process and deal with, but the potential to give herself pleasure – but having it just out of reach – was infuriating. She tried wiggling her lower body this way and that, aching for the raw, exquisite tension, but it was never quite enough, and she shuddered with the frustration of it.

She had signed up to his punishments and it appeared that this one was introducing her to a combination of items on his list – pain, humiliation, confinement, restraint and, worst of all, denial! She was so tantalisingly close to release but so agonisingly far.

Strangely enough, there was not one moment when she blamed or hated Stephan for doing this to her. In her mind her imperfections and lack of preparedness had caused his displeasure and this punishment was justified. She would learn from his lessons on her road to perfection for him. Anything less was failure, something she didn't plan to experience again any time soon. So deep into his darkness had she journeyed with him that she never thought to question his motives more deeply, and instead focused on his commands as though her pleasure, and life, depended on it – which most days they did.

It wasn't too long before Stephan returned, blinding her as he flicked on the lights. 'My little minx! I'm so very proud of you for doing this for me, for understanding that this is what I need. You know me like no other.'

Warmth flooded through her aching limbs at his words of praise – followed by disappointment when her eyes had adjusted enough to notice his erection had all but vanished. He untied her ankles and removed the pegs slowly and methodically, one at a time, leaving the ones on her tongue until last. The pain was searing as blood came flooding back into each pinched part of her body.

He untied her braids from the nipple rings. 'This will hurt.'

Nadia closed her eyes in anticipation.

He undid one clamp and paused, knowing the rush of blood would be momentarily excruciating before the feeling subsided. His mouth suckled her nipple as she processed the pain with a short, sharp scream tapering off to a whimper, and he mirrored the process on the other. Besides her restrained arms, the only thing remaining was the rope between her legs.

'You like this?'

She nodded, still unsure as to whether she was permitted to speak.

He loosened the pulley system slightly, giving her more leverage on the position of the knot.

'You may come.'

Stephan stood back and watched as his not-so-sweet possession began to grind her writhing body against the knot, creating raw friction against her needy clitoris until she came ferociously, slamming into the wall.

'You are too perfect for words, Nadia. Just incredible.' He released her from the hook, leaving the cuffs on her wrists, took her battered body in his arms and carried her to the softness of the king-sized bed. He then slowly and fastidiously pleasured her until she was whimpering into the room – first with his fingers, then with his mouth – taking her to heights.

'Thank you for being mine, Nadia.' He took care releasing her raw wrists from the cuffs.

'My pleasure, sir.' She lay spread out on the duvet, too spent for anything but to accept his pleasure, his adoration of her marked body, as he replaced the pain he'd caused in the bathroom with tender kisses in the bedroom, until she drifted off into a blissful, exhausted sleep.

* * *

Although she always initially feared such experiences, not knowing whether she could withstand the pain, what would happen next or what Stephan expected of her, over the next few days she grew to crave the sensations he allowed her and loved the proud gleam in his eye when she successfully endured whatever he had planned. He was the supreme maestro, orchestrating her every move and emotion, skilfully and systematically whetting her masochistic tendencies and eagerness to try more. Which was exactly his intention.

Every day she basked in the afterglow of her orgasms and tended to any left-over pain. She couldn't imagine a day without his

226

fingers, palms, tongue, crop, belt and rope dominating her body, continually providing her with new and more extreme sensations. But still she longed to have him deep inside her – to truly connect with his body – and she found herself counting down the days and hours to the Australian Open final, when finally he could forgo all abstinence and make long, slow love to her, filling her completely with the essence of his manhood. Where she could touch him freely – unrestrained – and they could share their orgasms as their bodies united.

Seek

It was no surprise to anyone in the sport that Stephan sailed with ease into the semifinals of the Australian Open. He was in formidable form and his confidence seemed to grow with each successive win. During one press conference after securing his place in the second semifinal he was quoted as saying:

> 'There's no stopping me from winning this slam. That's
> what I came here to do. I am in exceptional form. There are
> no weaknesses in my game, only strengths, and that makes
> me very dangerous to my opponents. Invincible, really.'

The Australian press tended to admonish this sort of outspoken egotism, but much to their frustration, there wasn't too much they could disagree with other than his self-aggrandisement. His results spoke for themselves. He was a supreme athlete at the top of his game. Full stop. And there was nobody who honestly believed that anyone other than Nordstrom would be standing holding the winner's trophy above his head on the night of the final.

So the endorsement and sponsorship offers had continued to roll in – everything from designer clothes and sunglasses, to watches and cars, to champagne and whisky. It seemed the corporate world couldn't get enough of 'Brand Nordstrom'. The Swedish icons of Volvo and IKEA couldn't resist getting in on the action, which, thanks to Caesar's negotiations, landed Stephan record-breaking deals with both companies.

* * *

It was only in the shadows of Noah's mind that he allowed himself to believe that one day he would see Stephan come crashing off his ever-so-high sporting pedestal.

He was increasingly shocked by these malicious thoughts – they weren't a natural part of his personality – but the more times he failed to contact Eloise, the more he blamed Stephan, and worried for her safety. It wasn't like he could tell anyone of his suspicions; after all, what was there really to say? That she had chosen Stephan – his greatest on-court rival – over him? They'd just accuse him of being jealous – personally and professionally. But he was sure there was more to it than that.

Meditation helped temper his emotions and focus his mind. This had served him well in the past, particularly when he lost big matches such as the Wimbledon semifinal and the US Open final.

This time round – much to the delight of the local press, and indeed the whole country – he was on track to make it through to the final against his nemesis, Nordstrom. The media was hungry for more exposure of their home-grown star – they tended to forget his French ancestry and claimed him as fully Australian – and were quietly more than pleased that he was so much more grounded and gracious, and far less arrogant, than the Scandinavian demigod. (The Australian media had deliberately downgraded him from 'god' – just because they could!)

Noah's Aboriginal heritage invited comparisons with the much loved Evonne Goolagong Cawley, former world Number One. His success at the Open had even heralded a government- and corporate-funded program, Hotshots in Hot Spots, specifically targeting the advancement of Aboriginal and Torres Strait Islander kids in tennis.

But all the buzz and media frenzy couldn't make up for the fact that the person he cared for most wouldn't return a single one of his messages. Somehow Eloise seemed perpetually beyond his reach. It was as though he no longer existed in her life whatsoever – and this was not something he was prepared to accept.

So after winning his semifinal he was determined to find her. He assumed she would be watching Stephan play in the second semi, so it was only a matter of scanning the crowd to locate her. No mean feat in a stadium containing almost fifteen thousand people. But he'd engaged the help of some mates, and, sitting in a box armed with binoculars, he and his friends scanned the arena row by row. If only she'd worn her hair out, they would have identified her in minutes. But no doubt so would the cameras – continually panning around the stadium, always on the lookout for a beautiful woman – and she was never one to draw attention to herself.

Finally they were successful. Noah handed his mate Shane the note he'd written to her. If she refused his calls, he was sure she wouldn't want to be seen with him in public, and it didn't help that he was more than recognisable these days as well. But he hoped she'd accept a note delivered by a friend.

He watched with anticipation through the binoculars as Shane made his way around the arena with an all-access pass and ensured the note was delivered in person without arousing too much suspicion. Noah couldn't determine her response due to her cap and sunglasses, but she nodded towards Shane, which he considered an excellent sign.

Shock

After the match, when he knew Stephan would be at least an hour, Noah waited impatiently in the box he'd organised to give them some privacy.

She slipped in through the door with barely a sound.

'Elle! Finally!' It was a relief just to see her in person.

'Noah, this *must* stop. I honestly can't see you or talk to you any more. *Please* don't put me in this position.'

'What position? You sound like you're going to get into trouble. I'm worried about you, Elle. I just can't get it off my mind.'

'Well, you need to. It won't be good for either of us.'

'Five minutes is all I ask. No one knows you're here, I've been really discreet, and we both know Stephan is occupied. Please, just sit down and talk to me.'

He indicated a chair and smiled hopefully. She glanced between the chair and the door, looking anxious and unsettled, before finally relenting. 'Five minutes, that's it. I *can't* be late.'

As she sat down she winced visibly from the dull pain on her butt and legs. Stephan had decided before he left in the morning that a few additional lashes would ensure her focus on today's game, as she had miscalculated by one ace in his previous match.

'My God – are you hurt?'

'No, no, it's nothing. I'm fine.' Though the subdued pain was an excellent reminder that she should be nowhere near Noah. 'This is a bad idea. You need to trust me on this, Noah: I really shouldn't be here. I'm begging you to stop contacting me. *Please* just concentrate on your tennis.'

As she stood up to leave, a random stranger opened the door then apologised that he'd come to the wrong place. As the door closed it created a light breeze that lifted her knee-length skirt, momentarily displaying the faded welts on her upper legs. She quickly pulled it down and stepped towards the door, but Noah was way too quick and stood against it, blocking her escape and looking utterly aghast. As he examined her more closely he noticed the red marks around her wrists and faded bruises on her arms.

'What the hell has he been doing to you?' His face was as pale as it could be with fury and disgust.

'Noah, I need to go, let me pass. I shouldn't have come, it was wrong.'

'You are not going anywhere until I have some answers, Elle. Did *he* do this to you?' He gently picked up her fragile wrist to indicate the deep red marks on her skin. He turned her around and lifted her skirt slightly. 'Is this why you can't sit down? My God, he's an animal! I feel like calling the police!'

'God, Noah, no! It's nothing! I'm not hurt. Honestly, it's OK.'

'*Nothing* is OK! Can't you see? *Everything* about this is wrong. You're not yourself any more and you can't even see it!' His voice was desperate. 'You're being abused – don't you *see*?'

'No! It's not like that. I choose it most of the time, and the other times I deserve it.'

'*What?!*' he shrieked, not believing what he was hearing. 'Eloise, please, I'm now begging you: listen to me, this is NOT normal. You don't deserve to be treated this way – *ever*! No one does.'

'I have to go, *please* let me out.' She tried to keep her voice down as it trembled with fear, urgency. Her attempts at opening the door comprehensively failed as he continued to block her.

'What happens if I don't?' He stood there defiantly with his arms crossed.

She broke down. 'Please, Noah, you are all I have in the world, besides Stephan. You are the only one who understands me, my only true friend. If I can't count on you, I have nothing. All I can tell you is that if I am not with Stephan's security team in ten minutes, all hell will break loose. You don't want that and neither do I.

Now, please believe me, I *have* to be with him. It's different from what I expected but I like it. Honestly.'

She willed herself to speak her words with conviction. Why was it that every time she met Noah she became unstuck? It was like he unlocked a secret part of her that she'd stored safely away to protect herself.

She pushed her face into his chest, loving his warmth but knowing it was not where she belonged. She was Stephan's until Caesar told her otherwise, and she repeated this mantra over and over in her mind as she pounded Noah's chest with her fists.

Tears flowed freely, wetting his shirt. She tried to pull away but Noah hugged her tight, her pummelling not causing the slightest impact on his broad chest.

He desperately wished he could whisk her away, keep her safe, but from what – herself? It was deeply distressing seeing her like this, but he also couldn't be sure how much grief he was causing by wanting to see her. The welts on her thighs made him feel sick. How could Stephan treat her that way? And how could she say she liked it? His mind was a maelstrom of contradictory emotions.

'I belong to Stephan, end of story.'

Suddenly anger got the upper hand over Noah's other emotions. 'What, like some kind of possession? Relationships aren't meant to be like that, Eloise. They should be full of love, respect, trust, kindness, encouragement, support, fun … Do you have those things with him?'

'Noah, please, don't do this. I am OK, he looks after me. I don't have any other friends except for you and I don't want to lose either of you. I need you to understand: you're all I have aside from him.' There was desperation in her voice and fear in her eyes. 'But I mean it: I need to leave this very second.'

'All right, but so help me, Eloise, if he hurts you against your will …' He thumped his fist against the door, trying to rein in his uncharacteristically wild and angry thoughts, and took a deep breath. 'You know I'm only a phone call away.' He hugged her tight, kissed her on the forehead and reluctantly let go of the highly strung jitterbug his beautiful, battered Elle had become.

'Thank you, Noah. Never forget you mean the world to me. All of this will be over one day and I will be fine, you don't need to worry.' With great relief, she scurried out the door.

'Famous last words,' was the only thing Noah mumbled as he tried to assimilate what had just happened. Not a bone in his body felt everything was 'fine', and he had just confirmed all of his worst nightmares about the type of man Nordstrom was: an arrogant, self-serving, abusive monster.

If Eloise was so desperate for him not to intervene, he would respect her wishes for the time being – not that he wanted to but what other choice did he have? Nonetheless, he couldn't wait to annihilate Nordstrom on court for having treated Eloise this way.

He vowed that if it didn't happen in this final, it would definitely happen during one of the other grand slams this year. He would win for his own sanity as much as hers. He knew that to be the best, you had to beat the best. And that was exactly what he intended to do!

* * *

Nadia raced towards Stephan's security team, immediately apologising for being late by explaining she had been held up in the ladies' toilet. She was shocked to see one of Garry's team note the time and explanation in a notebook before she was ushered into a car and whisked away from Melbourne Park.

On the drive back to Caesar's hotel she realised she was shaken to the core. It sounded so strange now when Noah used her 'old' name. Her entire life she had never been called anything but Eloise, yet now, it was as though that person no longer existed; she had been transformed into Nadia – completely beholden to Stephan. All she could hope for was that Noah wouldn't do anything stupid to jeopardise things with Stephan and therefore, ultimately, Caesar.

Why did Noah have that effect on her? Why was he so worried when she loved being so needed by Stephan? Why did he make her feel as though what she was doing was wrong in some way? It never felt wrong when she was with Stephan, but somehow, when she was outside the cocoon he had created for her, she sensed she needed to hide what went on behind closed doors.

The look on Noah's face at the sight of her body haunted her thoughts. He'd seemed repulsed by the bruises and welts that she had taken to caring for with such dedication. She had never had a relationship with another man, so she couldn't judge what was normal or not. Besides, it wasn't for her to question.

She wondered whether her relationship with Stephan had any of those qualities Noah had listed. Would Stephan still want to be with her if she said no to the things he asked of her? She didn't know the answer, and was frustrated at Noah for making her ask this question in the first place.

It was at times like this that she wished she had a mother and father to confide in. She had always envied the ballerinas who had close relationships with their parents; they always seemed more grounded in their emotions. She stopped the thought from pervading her mind. All she had was herself, no family, no other friends – she could not have anything to do with Noah from this point on – so all she had to focus on was Stephan. He was her life right now.

After the final he would be able to touch her again and she needed that bond far more than being his playful minx. Though she loved being teased, tormented and tantalised, she longed for his seed inside her, fulfilling her. To touch him, feel his warmth, without obstruction.

So she reassured herself that it was this lack of intimacy and sexual bonding that was causing these errant thoughts and insidious feelings about their relationship. Though sexually sated every night and day, she was desperate for so much more intimacy with her Master. And fortunately there was not long to wait ...

Evidence

Today marks the conclusion of the 'Happy Slam' in the Great Southern Land. With over 1.5 million fans through the gates over the course of the tournament, the blue-ribbon ticket remains tonight's men's singles final, when Rod Laver Arena will be packed to the rafters. This year's final is a particularly exciting one for local fans, as Noah Levique is the first Australian to reach the final in over a decade. Though he is the underdog in this match, Australians will barrack for him fiercely until the last point is played.

Noah spent the last twenty-four hours before the final attempting to wipe Eloise from his mind, sensing that his clandestine meeting with her had been a huge mistake – that was, until he received a brief text message from her, wishing him all the best for the final. He was thrilled, regardless of the fact that he had received the exact same message from many fans the world over. A message from her was special and proved she was thinking of him after all, which added an extra bounce to his step.

Under the eagle eye of his coach, he focused on analysing and dissecting every aspect of Nordstrom's so-called 'perfect' game, point by point. The last thing he wanted was a repeat of the slaughterhouse result at the US Open, but this time he felt more prepared – mentally and physically – to meet his opponent head-on.

Even securing a set from the world's Number One would indicate he was making significant progress.

Bounding around the locker room, darting this way and that and punching the air to the beat of the music pounding through his red headphones, it was as though his feet were made of springs as he allowed his mind a moment's peace from the pressure building all around him.

* * *

Nadia looked the quintessence of youthful elegance in the outfit Stephan had carefully selected for her: a figure-hugging cornflower-blue short-sleeved dress embroidered with delicate pale lemon flowers. This was indeed a dress that left no doubt as to who she would be cheering for today – or to whom she belonged.

'No mishaps today, Nadia; no disappearing. I expect *perfect* behaviour from you. Know that I am winning today for both of us.' He caressed her satin behind with both palms as an abundantly clear reminder.

'I understand, sir. You have nothing to worry about.'

'Good. Be polite and receptive to Caesar. That is an order. He's important to both of us.'

He kissed her deeply, claiming her with his tongue while securing her arms behind her back. She responded immediately, impatient for more but knowing her attempts would be unsuccessful – as they had been for the last fortnight.

He disentangled himself from their kiss with a grin.

'Settle down, you cheeky minx. I need you to be prepared for all sorts of celebrations when I have that trophy in my hands again. I feel like I'm about to explode.'

She felt exactly the same way.

'Have no doubt that when I'm finished with you, you'll be aching for the next few days, and then some.'

With that he slapped her taut buttocks, smiled his killer smile and left her so he could finish what he'd come here to achieve. Victory.

As at the US Open final, Caesar had invited Nadia – with Stephan's approval – to join him in his executive box with his other guests to view the game in a cooler, more civilised setting than the boisterous ranks of the kaleidoscopic crowd. Nadia was fidgeting and uncomfortable, knowing that at any other slam, she would have worn the outfit Stephan had chosen with pride. However, at the Australian Open, in the country where she grew up, with an Australian in the final who was also her best friend, she felt hemmed in by the dress's somewhat restricting design and uncomfortable in her extra high heeled sandals. Every move she made forced her to focus on her posture and make minor adjustments to accommodate the figure-hugging dress and potentially ankle-breaking shoes. Even the simple act of sitting was a conscious movement – as though Stephan were there beside her, testing her, reminding her of just how important her actions were to him at all times.

Nestled in the confines of Caesar's box at Rod Laver Arena, instead of feeling liberated by his attention to detail, she felt unsettled, unpatriotic and definitely outside her comfort zone.

Why did Stephan have to be playing Noah in the final? She was thrilled for both of them individually, but seeing them compete against each other tied her stomach up in knots.

As both players were invited to the court for their warm-up, she felt faint and wished she could curl up into a ball, only to wake up when it was all over. She understood the impossibility of that as Caesar offered her a mandatory glass of champagne, which she accepted with impeccable manners – just as her Master had ordered.

Then the match began. Stephan claimed the first set with ease as Noah seemed to struggle with the nerves of playing in a final in front of his home crowd. But by the second set he had found his rhythm against the world Number One, and the rallies became breathtaking as each point was fiercely fought, the set taken to a tiebreaker. The Australians in the crowd could barely sit in their seats, their excitement for their countryman was so extreme. At set point, they were forced into silence by the umpire and held their collective breath as Stephan challenged Noah's backhand passing shot. It was called in, only to be confirmed as out on Hawk-Eye (the official computer system), giving Stephan the second set – much to the disappointment of the groaning Aussie spectators.

Stephan's confidence went through the open roof at the beginning of the third set – until Noah broke his serve, managing to return what would have been aces to most other players. Suddenly Stephan seemed to lose his rhythm, and Noah wasted no time in capitalising on it. Much to everyone's surprise – and to the sheer delight of the Aussie contingent – Noah snatched the third set from the world Number One.

This was the upset everyone had been hoping for, but not actually expecting – after all, it was the first set that the great Nordstrom had dropped since Wimbledon last year. And it had been won by an Aussie. More beers all round!

Nadia found herself breaking into a sweat as though she herself were playing, not watching the drama unfold from the comfort of the corporate box.

'Is everything all right, Nadia? You look quite pale. Here, take a seat.' Caesar indicated towards the lounge and motioned for some Perrier.

She accepted both graciously. 'Thank you, I'm fine, really. I just think it has been a hectic couple of weeks, and of course, you know, this means so much to Stephan.'

'And to Noah, I imagine,' he said with a gleam in his eye, sitting down next to her.

'Oh, yes, of course, to them both,' she stammered.

'Do you have any doubts that Stephan will be Number One for the rest of the year?'

If she was honest, she hadn't even considered the notion that he wouldn't be, so she was taken aback by the question.

'Do you?' she blurted out without thinking – to hear Stephan's voice in her ear, reprimanding her harshly.

Fortunately, Caesar laughed.

'Well, anything can happen. Noah has significantly improved his game over the past six months, but whether it's enough to take a title from Stephan ... who knows? Depends how motivated he is to win, I suppose. You need to have a killer instinct to take titles.'

The twinkle in his eye brightened as he spoke, and Nadia turned to analyse his face more carefully before she responded. It was as though he was playing with her, trying to coax something out of her – though she couldn't be sure of this.

What did he know, exactly? And how could she find out without rousing his suspicions?

'Noah appears more motivated to win here than at the US Open, probably because of his home-crowd advantage.' She decided to play it safe; this was Caesar, after all.

'I agree with you, Nadia. Motivation, preparation, commitment ... it's good to see these qualities in Noah. He has so much potential, don't you think?'

'Of course.'

'You know him well?'

She sensed this conversation was heading in a potentially dangerous direction.

'I know him, yes.'

'Better than Stephan believes you do, perhaps?'

Caesar's face remained a congenial mask, while Nadia's instantly drained of all colour.

She had no idea how to answer this question, or where it would lead.

'No matter, you don't need to answer that.'

He handed her a plain manila envelope, encouraging her to open it. She did so with trepidation.

'Have a look. They say a picture is worth a thousand words.'

Her hands began to shake as she saw the photos of herself and Noah walking back to the hotel together the first afternoon of the tournament. However, she had an out-of-body experience as she recognised the special time they had shared in London captured in a series of candid images. Their intimacy and attraction to each other were undeniable, their supposedly private moments anything but. There was no doubting from this evidence that she knew Noah far better than she had led both Caesar and Stephan to believe.

She was breathless. She was speechless.

Caesar went on, 'But please tell me – I'm interested – how are things with Stephan from your perspective?'

Flags and danger signs continued to swirl in her head.

'Fine.' She could barely whisper the word, her mouth had gone so dry.

'Really? You will continue to abide by the conditions of the contract?'

'Of course, Caesar. I have no intention of letting either of you down.'

'Good, let's keep it that way, shall we? And as per our contract, I strongly encourage you to concentrate on your Number One – and *only* your Number One. Any distractions won't end well for anyone. I take the protection of my assets extremely seriously.'

He patted her hand with authority and retrieved the envelope from her still trembling fingers.

'Enjoy the rest of the match, Nadia. I do believe it will be Stephan who is victorious at the end of the day.' With that he got up and strode away.

Trophy

Nadia watched Caesar walk away from her with suspicion and dread, having no idea whether Stephan had seen the photos or not. In a haze of uncertainty, she tried to assimilate the nuances of the conversation she had just been part of, unable to decipher whether Caesar was playing the role of benefactor or saboteur in relation to her future.

Was it really so wrong that she was friends with Noah? If she was honest, the answer was no, but the photographs made them look like so much more than that, not to mention the blurry, long-distance photo of them lying in bed together on the canal boat. Her main concern was not having been entirely truthful with Stephan when he first questioned her about the people in her life.

Since she had originally denied her relationship with Noah early in their time together, the situation had grown into a muddled mess, which had only escalated when the three of them met at the players' party. If Stephan ever saw those photos, she couldn't bear to think of the consequences. One thing she now knew with certainty was that Caesar had her followed whenever she wasn't with her Number One, and had the evidence of his photographer's watchful lens to prove it. He had managed to remind her of her absolute subservience to him and to Stephan – that her life was far from her own. Something she'd never be in a position to explain to Noah.

And as for protecting his assets, what had Caesar meant by that exactly? Was *she* considered an asset, or was it Stephan? She had no idea. All she knew was that she must continue to play their game by obeying their rules, for to go against either would be to risk everything. Both men had the right to destroy her contract and throw her out into the world alone, with nothing – which was what she feared more than anything. She vowed that from this point on she would behave flawlessly, giving them no reason to question her commitment to the contract again.

'Double fault.' The words echoed around the stadium and shattered her thoughts, bringing her back to the court and the fact that she had no idea of the statistics of the game. 'Damn it!' She accidentally let the words escape, reprimanding herself that this was certainly not a good start to enacting her new resolution.

The evening was unfolding in a way she had never anticipated. She didn't dare ask Caesar for an update on the number of aces and faults; Stephan had probably mentioned this 'test' to him in their casual meetings, and it would only serve to get her into more trouble.

She was now fretting about meeting Stephan after the match, because firstly, she had no doubt she would be punished for her ignorance of the statistics, and secondly – and far more seriously – she didn't even want to think about what would happen if Stephan had seen the photos. She had no doubt that any form of punishment she had received to date would seem like a walk in the park by comparison. She shivered from head to toe, as though Antarctic winds had just rushed across Bass Strait, reaching the city of Melbourne at a rate of knots.

'Championship point, Mr Nordstrom.'

Nadia stood up. Her figure-hugging Swedish-coloured dress felt so tight around her body it was as though a python could have been constricting her as Stephan's final ace pounded down the centre of the court. The hushed crowd roared into life as Stephan won his second Australian Open and third consecutive grand-slam title. Stephan Nordstrom was the undisputed Number One tennis player in the world.

Nadia felt faint again and needed to sit back down as she watched the two men shake hands at the net. Though they looked amicable towards each other as Stephan patted Noah's shoulder, those who knew them best could detect the hostility in their eyes.

Stephan held the trophy with pride, passion and a hint of defiance, as if to say that defeating him was an insurmountable feat for anyone who tried – which on this occasion (and so many others before it) was completely true. He looked every inch the greatest tennis player on earth as the world's press snapped the photos that would adorn the front page of most major papers around the globe tomorrow morning – or at the very least, the front of the sports pages.

Nadia only had a few brief moments to take in the scene of triumph and loss being played out in the middle of Rod Laver Arena before being escorted out of Caesar's box by security – under the instructions of Mr Nordstrom. She found herself alone in a private offshoot of the men's locker room, experiencing heart palpitations as she awaited Stephan's arrival.

A few moments later, as fear ran wild through her body, Stephan bounded in with a triumphant smile that couldn't be wiped from his face. For the second time that day, she was speechless. Luckily he didn't require her to talk. He stripped off his tennis shorts and Andrew Christian boxer briefs, letting them fall down around his ankles. He hitched up her tight little dress, easily snapping her flimsy thong between his fingers. Grasping both her wrists and holding them firmly above her head against the lockers, he wasted no time in impaling her on his throbbing manhood. With a few strong, determined thrusts, he exploded into her, releasing a long, deep growl into the hollow of her neck.

'My God – it took me one set too long to do that to you.'

She buried her face in his sweaty shirt, stifling her groans and salty tears against his chest. The revelations of this evening had all been too much, and now this ... It was overwhelming. She told herself to be grateful that he was inside her, though a small voice suggested it had been a little too quick and not quite as she had envisaged. Her body flushed with relief that he was smiling, and she didn't dare utter a single word lest she ruin the moment for him.

He kissed her lips passionately, forcefully; the need to dominate her seemed as important as his performance on court. It was as though he needed her to taste his victory, needed to claim her powerfully, confirming that he was Number One beyond any doubt. Without the need for words, he was telling her that she belonged entirely to him. It was the only way it could be. It was Caesar's way.

His forceful mouth ravaged her neck and face. 'I had to have you now. Needed to claim you as mine. My hands on the trophy and my hands on you ten minutes later – life doesn't get any better than this.' One hand was still firmly holding her hands above her head, the other grasping her cheeks and forcing her tear-filled eyes to meet his.

He looked deeply into them before continuing: 'I want you by my side, Nadia. From tonight, you are no longer my secret possession; you are mine in public and in private, in body and in mind. You belong to me – one hundred per cent.' And then he removed himself from inside her.

His words resonated deep within her psyche. This was what she had been desperate to hear to banish any doubts from her mind. She belonged to him! Not just behind closed doors, but everywhere he went! She would no longer be a shadow in his world. She had an anchor in her life that ensured she wasn't adrift.

She knew she should feel elated, thrilled – and in a way she was. But she couldn't understand, for the life of her, why she still felt an unfathomable emptiness deep within her heart.

Neither of them had ever used the word 'love' to describe the intensity of their feelings for each other. Stephan claimed what he wanted and gave Nadia what she needed. In a broken way, they complemented one another, and perhaps, at this moment in time, that was all that mattered.

Stephan quickly changed shirts, pulled up his pants, ensured that his shirt, socks, trainers, sweatbands, watch and water bottle were all correctly positioned to highlight the name of his sponsors clearly for the cameras, and left an astonished and emotionally shattered Nadia to gather herself in private, his semen steadily trickling down her inner thigh. The powerful and triumphant athlete closed the door behind him to greet the adoring world in public, with words that would be played tomorrow on every TV channel, and printed in every newspaper.

'I love being Number One. I'd recommend it to anyone!' (Trademark smile.)

'The feeling of winning is something I'll never give up without a fight.

'My life is incredible, my tennis is unbelievable.

'I'm euphoric. Winning has never meant more to me.

'I've never felt more invincible, truly at the top of my game.

'Thank you, Australia, for making my dreams come true.'

Yang

After five-star Japanese dining at Nobu, the celebrations continued well into the night, with far too many glasses of Veuve Clicquot (one of Stephan's many sponsors) being consumed by all. Stephan was in his element, at the centre of the world's attention: a place he loved to be.

Nadia was fluttering discreetly close by, in a long-sleeved dress like the one she'd worn to the players' party. Stephan didn't want her body on display to others, not least because of the bruising from their celebratory bondage session between the final and the party. Before they left for the evening a stylist had arrived to apply the finishing touches to her outfit and do her make-up, and a hairdresser had straightened her hair for the first time ever. Without curls, it reached to her hipbones.

Fortunately Stephan was so busy with his entourage that he didn't notice her apprehension over dinner as she sat between him and Caesar, nor when they were invited back to the private party in Stephan's honour at Caesar's casino. Nadia felt as though she had just completed a five-hour ballet performance, she was so drained from the day. Every time she approached Stephan to ask permission to go back up to their suite, he would wrap his arm possessively around her shoulders and introduce her to yet another person she had no hope of remembering in the morning.

He was on such an adrenaline high that once the party had finished, he invited the remaining partygoers back to their suite for yet more champagne. Nadia thought the night would never end, but kept a smile plastered on her face and acted with grace and poise, just as Stephan – and Caesar – expected her to.

Stephan's coach and manager were the last to leave, exclaiming their tipsy congratulations and reminiscing about Stephan's moment of glory before finally calling it a night. Stephan's stamina far outdid Nadia's, and at around four in the morning her eyes could no longer stay open, the emotional highs and lows of the long day taking their toll, even though she would have loved to have Stephan inside her again now that they were at last alone.

'I was so proud of you tonight, Nadia. You looked stunning and your behaviour was impeccable. Thank you for representing me so well.'

She just nodded, too tired for words.

'Looks like you need some sleep, little minx.'

He kissed her goodnight – good morning, really – and directed her to bed. Much to her relief, her negligées had been returned and all evidence of the hideous animal jumpsuits had disappeared.

Still too wired from the euphoria of winning his fourth grand slam, Stephan decided to stay up and make some calls to Sweden, including to his parents, wanting to recount the glory of his win in detail, before heading down to the casino to see what was happening.

Just as he was heading out the door he heard Nadia's phone beep. It had fallen out of her handbag by the side of the lounge, and as he picked it up, he saw that the message was from Noah.

Thanks for your wishes, Elle. They mean so much to me.
    Unfortunately today wasn't my day but I know I'm getting closer.
    I'm still worried about you and need to know you are OK.
    The sooner you are away from that monster the better!
    Keep in touch.
    Forever, Noah xo

Stephan froze. With rising panic, he read through every one of the messages Noah and Nadia had exchanged. They proved beyond a doubt that the two were more than casual acquaintances, and that they had been in contact during the entire time Nadia had been with him.

He stared for a long time at Nadia's most recent message to Noah, wishing him luck for the final. It was inconceivable to him that she would wish his opponent luck in a match against him!

This discovery shook him to the core – for two reasons.

The first was that Nadia had effectively lied to him when they first met – something she would definitely come to regret. There was no doubt in his mind that she would pay dearly for such deceit.

Secondly, Noah had now consolidated his position as Number Two in the world after being runner-up at both the US and the Australian Open, the other top seeds having only made it through to the third round. Though Stephan never doubted his own abilities, this was a little too close for comfort, given what he had just discovered about Noah's relationship with Nadia.

He had too many questions and not enough answers. Was it serious? Had they ever been intimate? Did he love her or she him? If so, Noah was a much greater risk to his and Nadia's future together. And what if they had been conspiring against him?

And he was forced to consider the possibility that Noah might be aware of his own arrangement with Caesar, making him an even greater threat. It meant that he himself had much to lose and Noah had everything to gain.

The blood in his veins felt like it had turned to ice as he smashed his glass of vodka so hard onto the coffee table that the tumbler smashed to smithereens.

Like most spoilt children, Stephan had never learnt to share his toys – least of all his most precious one. Resisting the temptation to smash Nadia's phone against the wall, this time he managed to control his anger and merely switch it off and place it in his tennis bag. He had no intention of letting Noah contact her again unless it was on *his* terms. Nadia belonged to him and him alone, and anyone who stood in his way would be annihilated – on or off the court, preferably both. Something they would both soon understand with far greater clarity.

The next morning, after the obligatory media photo session, with Stephan holding the trophy on the bank of the Yarra River, he returned to the suite to find Nadia still asleep. He stood transfixed, watching her shallow breaths and full of wonder at her serene beauty. He shifted the sheet to uncover the pure alabaster skin of her limbs, gently allowing the tips of his fingers to stroke the marks tarnishing her flesh.

He was immediately torn between making slow, sweet love to her and taking the crop to her body to punish her as he had never punished her before, and indelibly imprint her to ward off all other predators. The two extreme emotions blurred, sitting side by side in his psyche – just as yin didn't exist without yang. His desire to possess her was both violent and thrilling, and he knew that over time, he would give her both pleasure and pain in equal measures. Although he couldn't help but think that the precarious balance of the scales had now well and truly tipped to the latter ...

But right now, patience was paramount to his plans. Only fools rushed in where angels feared to tread. He must exercise control over his intense need to dominate every aspect of her life, including her body. And be content instead, for the time being at least, with taking some photos of his Sleeping Beauty to add to his ever-growing private collection.

* * *

Noah was more than a little sceptical when he received an invitation from Stephan that morning for a brief catch-up before he left the country. But given that he hadn't heard back from Eloise after the final, he was not going to miss an opportunity to try to protect her from further harm – no matter how slim the chance or how mysterious the location.

Yin

When Nadia eventually woke up, Stephan asked her to dance for him. She was elated. She had perfected the dance that had put so much strain on her ankle in the Cayman Islands, and had been waiting for an opportunity to perform it for him without distracting him from his tennis.

Caesar had provided Stephan with access to an oval room lined with mirrors, which had a parquet floor and an elaborate chandelier hanging from its centre. It would be perfect for their private performance. Nadia wanted this dance to be her special gift to Stephan, a heartfelt congratulations on his win, so she was fastidious in her preparations.

Given the dark, seductive elements of her performance, she chose dramatic black make-up for her eyes, with a matching low-cut leotard and fishnet stockings. The deep red ribbons of her black ballet shoes complemented the luscious, glossy shade on her lips. Knowing she and Stephan would be alone, she thought it would be acceptable to wear her hair loosely half up, fastened with a thick black velvet ribbon, allowing the rest of her long locks to cascade freely towards her waist.

After tying up her ballet shoes she stood up from the bench – the room's only piece of furniture – to survey her appearance in one of the many mirrors. As she gazed at her reflection she barely recognised her new provocative self, though she couldn't deny she liked what she saw. A real woman, experiencing deep sexual arousal and an ever-increasing desire to please her man. She shivered lasciviously at the thought of just how far she had come with Stephan, and wondered how much further they still had to go.

Hearing his firm steps approaching, she took one last look in the mirror and turned to greet him.

His eyes widened in surprise as he silently absorbed the seductive vision before him, and his lips curled into a mischievous grin. His response was exactly what she had hoped for.

'I'd like you to wear this as well.' He offered her a black tutu featuring layer upon layer of soft tulle that shimmered a deep burgundy red in the light.

Nadia smiled. 'Really? I'm not sure this particular dance requires a tutu, sir.'

'I insist.' He wrapped it around her slim waist and fastened it in place. It added a feminine element to the outfit, softening her appearance and tantalising him with the mystery of what treasures lay beneath – even though he was intimately acquainted with them – the tutu would serve another purpose today.

'If it pleases you,' she said teasingly, with a slight curtsy for added effect.

'Oh, believe me, it does.' He tapped her nose with his finger and moved towards the edge of the room to start the music, while Nadia positioned herself in the centre to begin.

The music took over Stephan's auditory senses and he realised it had been quite a while since he'd seen her perform, given his recent focus on tennis. He was once more completely taken aback. She was overtly seductive and utterly exquisite, particularly in this dance routine. Her raw sexual energy permeated the room, affecting both of them in equal measure. It was as though she were actually experiencing the violent love she was portraying, such was her gift. Her dancing had matured, and Stephan congratulated himself on exposing her to the darker side of her psyche, knowing there was still so much more they could discover together – depending on what happened next.

When she finished, the room was filled with silence before his slow, rhythmic clap entered the space. 'Bravo, my little minx. A flawless performance.'

She maintained her position, attempting to calm her breathing as quickly as possible after such exertion. A small part of her desperately wished she were back onstage, experiencing a standing ovation, but she was still needy for Stephan's admiration.

'You are truly breathtaking.' He stood close, his hand against the softness of her face.

'Thank you, sir. I have been mastering this dance especially for you.'

'And believe me, I appreciate every ounce of your effort.'

He held her leg towards him and massaged her thigh for some time before speaking, as if weighing up the pros and cons of his next move.

'Do you trust me, Nadia?' he asked, searching the depth of her eyes.

'Yes, of course. You know I do.' She was flummoxed by his question as she returned his gaze, wondering at the darkness glazing over his normally bright eyes.

'You know I would never let anything or anyone come between us, what we have.'

Apprehension cascaded over her entire body, her eyes suddenly wide with fear, her breath quickening. If Caesar had shown him the photos ...

Stephan didn't miss any of her reactions. 'I would prefer you to address me as "Master" until we leave this room.'

The heaviness between them intensified as the sweat that had settled from her performance began to chill her skin.

'Of course, Master.' She immediately lowered her eyes, knowing it would not be wise to look at him any longer for a multitude of reasons. Even so, she couldn't help the question escaping before she could capture its release.

'Have I done something to upset you Master? If I have, I –'

'Tell me, Nadia: what were my stats for the final? I neglected to ask you during the celebrations last night.'

Both relief and anguish flooded her body.

'I'm sorry, I don't know. I was distracted by Caesar and, well, the whole atmosphere. Forgive me ...'

He let a disappointed sigh escape his lips.

'You know the rules, Nadia.'

'I do, Master.'

'You will accept your punishment?'

'Yes, of course. It was my mistake.'

She was so relieved this had nothing to do with the photos that she was willing to do anything he asked of her.

'Place your leg on my shoulder.'

She straightened the leg he had been caressing, leaving her body in a position of almost vertical splits against his torso, her tutu opening like a magnificent rose as she stabilised her body with her other foot on the floor.

'Hold on to me for support.'

He took a Swiss Army knife out of his pocket and flipped open the sharp blade. Nadia inhaled sharply, forcing herself to stifle a scream.

'This will not hurt as long as you stay very still.'

His words did little to diminish her fear as he positioned the knife between her legs. She shut her eyes tightly and held her breath. She didn't dare move a muscle as he carefully sliced into the material of her leotard, then her tights, to create an opening. Satisfied it had done its job, he closed the knife and returned it to his pocket.

He watched her face intently as he slipped his middle and index fingers into her and moved them in a circling motion, intrigued as her expression was transformed from fear to relief. A third finger entered her, also massaging against her moist, inner walls as relief gave way to arousal. She sighed, relaxing into the stimulation.

He removed his fingers and slid a dildo into her, watching intently as she sighed, easily accepting the new pressure settling inside her, without question or complaint. He placed his glistening fingers between her lips, pushing through them onto her tongue so she could taste herself: something he had never done before.

Nadia couldn't discern his thoughts; his face was a mask. He lingered there, playing with her tongue, pushing his fingers deep into her mouth as his eyes grew hazy.

'You are too exquisite for words.' He supported her body as he gently lowered her onto the floor, merely transferring her vertical position to a horizontal one. Given Nadia's inherent flexibility she smoothly adjusted her body against the floor. Her training automatically ensured that the toes of both feet were elegantly pointed towards either end of the oval room.

'Raise your arms into fifth position.'

Nadia did so with grace and without hesitation. Stephan was pleased that he'd researched this; he liked to be well prepared.

He sat down on the floor beside her with his legs crossed. He looked both gorgeous and formidable in black, the top buttons of his shirt undone to expose his smooth chest.

'Are you comfortable in this position?'

'Yes, Master. It is called a *grand jeté*, though I should be in the air.'

'I'd like you to maintain it until I say otherwise, but I'm happy to provide support for your arms, should you need it.'

'It won't be a problem,' she said with determination, keeping her eyes lowered.

'I appreciate your effort, but even so, if it gets too much, just nod.'

'Thank you, sir.' He raised his eyebrows. 'Sorry. Master.' She had never had to address him this way so consistently before.

'This exercise is about so many things, Nadia – pleasure and pain, stamina, rules, obedience, trust …'

His voice trailed off as he caressed her breasts, and took her by surprise when he lowered his mouth to her nipple and suckled through the material of her leotard. As the suction of his tongue intensified, she felt a direct connection to her groin, causing her to moisten even further below. When he replicated the sensation on the other nipple, tugging and teasing her bud with his teeth, she felt swelling against her vaginal wall. She shifted slightly in an attempt to gauge what was happening.

'The sensation you feel is the dildo reacting to your body temperature. It will continue to stretch until it physically cannot; this will cause you immense pleasure if you stay still, or a bout of pain, should you move. Naturally, I am hoping you have enough discipline to enjoy the experience, Nadia.'

He smiled. She knew he was testing her in a way he hadn't before. He was always coming up with creative ways of keeping her on edge.

He raised her arms a little higher above her head to maintain her position in fifth as he kissed her lightly on the lips. They were face to face, eye to eye, when he uttered words that had the potential to shatter her world.

'As you know better than anyone, Nadia, perfection is my world. Very early on in our relationship you promised me honesty – at all times. Did you not?'

Her body trembled in response before she could reply. On the outside she looked magnificent – confident, seductive, perfectly positioned: the quintessential ballerina. On the inside she was fragile, inexperienced, ashamed and terrified as to how she would get through what might happen next. She bowed her head, believing she was a person who kept her word yet knowing that she hadn't.

'I did, Master.' Her words escaped as a whisper while the swelling inside her continued. She had never experienced a dildo quite like this before.

He raised her chin with his finger so their eyes met.

'So perfect on the outside; is it too much to ask for perfection on the inside as well?' He sighed. 'It is critical for me to understand you better than you understand yourself.' He paused, breathing deeply into the intensity of the moment. 'I need to know what is going on in *here* for us to work, Nadia.' He lightly tapped the side of her head.

'Mentally ...' His finger slid down from the top of her head past her nose, lips and chin.

'Physically ...' He pressed his hand against her throat, momentarily constricting the flow of oxygen.

'Emotionally ...' He massaged her left breast, symbolically cupping her heart.

'And, last but certainly not least, sexually ...' His hand worked its way down past her belly, disappearing beneath the soft folds of tulle that hid the rising tension in between her legs, and he slid his fingers along the length of the opening he had sliced into her clothes, tormenting her clitoris.

Nadia's breaths were shallow and fast as she struggled to maintain her position in fifth. His rhythmic touch ensured that the swelling inside her continued, and it was all she could do to concentrate on keeping still.

'You know as well as I do that you have disappointed me, betrayed me.'

His words sliced through the intensity between them and coincided with his fingers' pushing the expanding dildo deeply into her, causing her to gasp.

'I want you to think about that while you are in this position. How much I really mean to you, Nadia.' He looked searchingly into her eyes. 'Unfortunately you have given me no choice but to put you in a situation where you will need to prove it to me, once and for all. You say you trust me, but can I trust *you*? I'm not so sure any more ...'

So many emotions collided within her; it was too much for her to bear, and a sole tear slipped through her emotional armour. She was lost for words ...

A tap on the door startled her, causing her to jump and ensuring she felt the dildo embed deep inside her. It wasn't uncomfortable at this stage, but she felt its potential to become so. It filled the empty void that his words had left in her heart. Its presence helped to protect her from being abandoned, anchored her to him, to his world, lest he choose to cast her away. Being abandoned would destroy her.

It was as though Stephan's manhood were deep inside her, challenging her from the inside out while he stood watching every detail from the outside in. He was truly omnipresent; he was every breath she breathed. She had never experienced anything so intense, so erotic, so frightening.

'I'm sorry …' was all she could manage as he captured her tear and placed it on her lips to silence her with his finger.

He whispered low and deep into her ear. 'Every word you speak will tell me whether you are truly sorry or not. If you move from this position without my instruction, or your answers are unacceptable to me, I will inform Caesar immediately that our agreement is over, and there will be nothing more between us. Your bags have been packed to either stay here or fly with me at midday. The choice is yours.'

Déjà Vu

Stephan picked himself up off the floor and walked over to the door. He opened it with contempt and ushered Noah into the room.

Nadia screamed inwardly when she saw him enter. Every muscle in her body was torn between running to him and warning him to leave as quickly as possible. Yet the swelling dildo inside her meant she remained a frozen fixture, securely anchored to the floor.

She experienced an overwhelming sense of déjà vu as her mind placed her back into the nightmarish dream that had propelled her to accept Caesar's offer in the first place. The dream where she was thrown high into the air before shattering into tiny pieces as she crashed violently onto the stage floor, only to be unceremoniously swept away forever into the trash outside.

'Noah, I appreciate your coming at such short notice.' Stephan sounded smooth and dangerous as Noah ignored his outstretched hand and tentatively stepped towards the centre of the room.

'Eloise, is that you?' It was hard for him to be sure under all the make-up.

'It's a shame you weren't here a little earlier. *Nadia*,' he said her name with emphasis, 'just performed the most magical routine as a special gift to congratulate me on winning the Open. Isn't that true, my sweet?'

She nodded stiffly in response.

'What's going on here? Eloise, are you OK? Why are you in that uncomfortable position? You look like you're in pain!'

He knelt by Eloise, noticing the black tears staining her face. He was about to touch her when Stephan's deep voice thundered into the room.

'Don't you *dare* touch what isn't yours! She is in this position because this is who she is. And this is how you should remember her.'

Noah stayed beside Eloise, searching her eyes in silence for the real answers.

'It appears you two are good friends.'

Stephan waved Nadia's phone in the air, causing her a sharp intake of breath. She forced her arms to stay in fifth position even though they faltered at Noah's proximity. Like in her dreams, he was just beyond her reach, and she didn't dare move. She wondered how long Stephan had been accessing her phone, recalling the many messages Noah had sent her throughout the Open.

'Your relationship with each other is not acceptable to me.'

This was exactly what she had feared for months and she couldn't believe it was happening like this. She knew there was no hope of it ending well.

'So there will be no contact between you whatsoever after today.'

He removed the SIM card from the phone and slipped it into his trouser pocket, then hurled the phone onto the floor, crushing it beneath his foot, showing both of them who had the real power in the room.

'I am merely offering you the opportunity to say goodbye, once and for all.'

'I think that's up to Eloise to decide, not you.'

'Yes. I believe it *is* her decision.'

'Well, really, is it? Then why isn't she speaking for herself, you arrogant bastard?'

It was unusual for Noah to speak like this to anyone, but there was something about Stephan that curled his stomach in fury.

'Is this true, Elle? Is it really what you want?'

As he said the words, Eloise flinched, and the dildo stretched further inside her, as if on cue: a physical reminder that she belonged only to her Master.

'Answer him truthfully, Nadia, so we both know, once and for all.'

His deep voice boomed within the confines of the oval room.

Nadia took a deep breath, and the words came from her in a low murmur. 'It's true, Noah. I want to be with Stephan. I choose to be with him.'

She hated saying them, but had no choice; everything in her life was at stake. But she couldn't explain this to Noah, not now and not until all of this was over, and her life was finally her own. She desperately hoped he still remembered her previous words about how much he meant to her.

259

Noah was aghast. 'I don't believe you, Elle. What have you done to her?! I've seen the marks and bruises you've left! You're sick and you need help.'

Nadia's body convulsed at Noah's words, dreading how Stephan would react. She attempted to adjust her body, but just as Stephan had warned would happen, she was full to the brim. It was as though his anger were building inside her as she grimaced and whimpered at the discomfort it was causing. Her arms quivered above her head and her calves began to cramp, a chill settling into her muscles after her earlier exertion.

'How interesting that you feel it's your place to make such judgments about me and about my relationship with Nadia. She knows *exactly* how much she means to me. It seems you don't know nearly as much about her as I thought – which is probably just as well.'

His voice was ice, and Nadia sensed his patience had reached its limit. He walked over to her and lifted her torso from the floor. She had no choice but to wrap her arms around his neck for support, given the pins and needles in her legs. She pressed her face into his chest to stifle the pain she felt now that her legs had changed position and were pressed together. Stephan possessively returned her embrace, secretly pleased at how touching their interaction must appear to a seething Noah.

He went on, with venom in his voice. 'I thought I was doing the right thing by giving you the opportunity to say goodbye. But it just sounds like you're a poor loser – in tennis and in life.'

It took all of Noah's self-control not to take the bait that Stephan was dangling in front of him. Instead, he returned his focus to Eloise.

'It is clear that he's making you choose, Elle, but never forget what I said the first time we met: I'll always be there when you need me.'

'She doesn't want or need *you* when she has *me*. For God's sake, enough is enough. Tell him once more, my sweet, so the message finally gets through that thick skull of his.'

She winced at his insult, knowing he was deliberately rubbing salt into an already raw wound, which made the words she was being forced to say that much harder.

'Please, Noah, you need to leave me alone. I can't see you any more. Stephan is my life now; I need to be with him. I *choose* to be with him.'

'Can't you see what he's done to you, Elle? What he's doing to you? This is *your* life, not his! It breaks my heart to see you being treated like this.' He ran his fingers through his thick curly hair in anguish. 'But fine, if this is how it is, then so be it.' He made direct eye contact with Stephan, his hands balled into fists by his side. 'But so help me, if something happens to her, *you will pay*.'

He took one last look at Eloise, the black tears streaking her face, unsure whether he should pity her or protect her. Shaking his head, he strode to the door, needing to distract himself from thoughts of punching the smirk off the Scandinavian's smug face.

As he turned to close the door behind him, inspiration hit. 'Enjoy being Number One, Nordstrom, because I promise you: you won't be by the end of the year.'

It took those words for Stephan to flinch ever so slightly as Noah slammed the door.

Although Nadia's heart was pleading with her to run after Noah, her mind kept her firmly anchored to the ground. Regardless, it would have proved difficult to move from this position, with her legs cramping, her vagina aching and her emotions in overdrive. If Stephan walked away she would literally crash to the floor.

'Oh, my God!' Nadia exclaimed into the room, racked by pain as Stephan removed the dildo with a perfunctory nod; obviously it had served its purpose. The emptiness it left behind was absolute.

He scooped her effortlessly into his arms. 'Not a word, Nadia, not a single word.'

He sat her on the same bench where she had so carefully prepared for her performance as a different person. Her body and emotions were numb as she stared listlessly at the image in the opposite mirror. He removed the streaked make-up from her face and pulled her hair into a tight, high ponytail that strained her scalp. He stripped off her ballet clothes and dressed her in skin-tight black jeans that left little to the imagination, a crisp white tailored shirt and red knee-high boots that laced all the way up. Bright red lipstick completed the look. She allowed the process of her transformation to occur without protest, as though she were a mannequin being dressed for a shop window.

He walked away from her briefly, returning with a pair of scissors. He grabbed her ponytail and held it high above her head, with the scissors poised near its base. It took every ounce of her will not to start screaming as he menacingly threatened to butcher her hair.

He stared at her contorted face reflected in the mirror. Her eyes were huge with alarm at what he was about to do. He watched intently as they flooded with tears and her body convulsed, overcome by all she had just gone through. He yanked her hair harder, his grip tightening, pulling at her scalp, almost lifting her body off the chair.

She had never had short hair in her life, and she couldn't bear to watch what he was about to do to her. She scrunched her eyes closed and forced her hand across her mouth to prevent any screams from escaping.

'It's fortunate that you can still follow my commands, Nadia. One word from you was all I would have needed.'

He placed the scissors on the bench and she realised her silence was the only thing that had saved her magnificent mane. Her body shook with relief that he hadn't followed through. It took all of her discipline to force herself to remain perfectly still; he hadn't given her permission to move.

She was a living trophy that he could admire, threaten, punish and play with at his whim.

For a brief moment she tried to find a trace of Eloise in the darkened reflection before her – but all she could see was Nadia. Stephan's Nadia. She realised with horror that there was nothing left of her former self.

Turmoil

At midday, true to Stephan's word, all of Nadia's belongings from the suite had been packed and were waiting in the foyer: a visual reminder of her potential to be cast away. She still didn't know whether he would fulfil her worst possible fear and abandon her or whether she would be accompanying Stephan; he had given nothing away. Her body shook with the thought of just how easily she could be discarded from his life.

The foyer was buzzing with media and Stephan's arrival ensured an immediate frenzy. He nodded to Garry, who, dressed in his standard black 'uniform', instantly appeared by Nadia's side. She anxiously searched Stephan's features for any hint of what her future held, but his champion's face was securely in place, masking any emotion, as Garry's hand firmly clamped itself onto her arm and guided her away towards a line of waiting limousines. He reached the first vehicle in the line and opened the back door for her. She cautiously settled into the seat, tears welling in her eyes. Her stomach was in turmoil as she watched him load her luggage into the boot, every muscle tensed with anxiety as to what would happen next.

The locks engaged and she was trapped within the subdued silence of the limousine. No one could see in through the heavily tinted windows; no one except the driver would hear her should she speak. Panic began to consume her as she watched Stephan graciously engage with his fans and the media, smoothly signing some final autographs prior to his departure.

Caesar arrived to bid Stephan farewell. As they chatted amicably they looked like old friends who eagerly anticipated catching up again. They shook hands as if they had just reached some form of agreement and both glanced towards the car in which she was trapped.

Watching the scene unfold, Nadia was left in no doubt that she was merely a pawn in Caesar's high-stakes game. With no handbag, no phone, no wallet, no identity, the realisation that she only existed in the world on the say-so of these two men came slamming home. All she could do was helplessly await their next move.

At Stephan's behest, she had just slaughtered her relationship with Noah, and her only hope of extricating herself from this bizarre world she was imprisoned in. If Stephan decided that her behaviour earlier hadn't been good enough, she could be cast out of his life within minutes.

Finally Stephan extracted himself from the remaining crowd, donned his sponsored sunglasses as he headed into the sunlight ... and made his way to her limo. Nadia's body convulsed with tears of relief as he joined her on the back seat. She had never experienced such a rollercoaster of emotions in one twenty-four-hour period.

The car smoothly eased from the kerb and out into the traffic, heading towards the airport. As the Melbourne skyline streamed behind them, Stephan reflected with pride on how the events of this morning had unfolded. It was critical that Nadia understood that she was utterly dependent on him, and that any external influences – particularly Levique – would not be tolerated. Suitably satisfied by how shaken she was – threatening to cut her hair had been a stroke of genius – he conceded that the message he'd needed to send had been received. So he stretched his arm out towards her and scooped her up onto his lap, wrapping her quivering body in his embrace.

'I'm so sorry, so very sorry. *Please* forgive me. I'll do anything for you …' she stuttered between heavy sobs.

'I know, my sweet – and sometimes I must reinforce that point. You still have many lessons to learn …'

She clung to his chest, not wanting him to let her go. 'I do, Master. I'm so very sorry.'

He squeezed her knee. 'There'll be plenty of time for you to make it up to me. You belong to me, Nadia, and only me, until I decide I don't want you any more. It's important you remember that.'

She continued to sob into his chest, overwhelmed by her intense remorse, until the limo pulled up close to a private jet on the tarmac. Though massively relieved that she hadn't been cast out of his life, and silently vowing to be whatever he wished her to be, she couldn't shake the feeling that her world had just shrunk to miniature proportions – as though she were trapped in a genie's bottle that only Stephan could open, close or discard at will.

Her heart ached as she thought of how she had hurt Noah back at Caesar's hotel. What must he think of her now? She knew that what she had done was unforgivable, and in the process she had lost the only true friend she'd ever had in the world. Visions of the lock he'd left on the footbridge flashed through her mind as the plane ascended into the sky. Although her heart wondered at what might have happened between them had she taken a different path, her rational brain told her that now she had essentially thrown away that key forever.

When the plane levelled out, Stephan removed their seat belts and wasted no time in undoing his fly. 'I know you've been waiting a long time for this, and frankly, so have I. Kneel before me and clasp your hands behind your back. I only want your mouth.'

Nadia dropped to her knees, facing his exposed crotch, and did what she told herself she'd been longing to do all week, though it was with tears in her eyes and remorse in her heart. He grabbed hold of her ponytail and forced himself deeper into her throat.

As Stephan basked in the sensation of Nadia's mouth as it worked his cock, he wished Levique could see her like this – his subservient little plaything, so eager to please. Then his eyes darkened as he reflected on Levique's incomprehensible threat that Stephan would no longer be Number One by the end of the year. Stephan's ego immediately reassured him that this would never happen; Levique had nowhere near his mastery or stamina on court.

So, having confirmed this in his mind, he returned his focus to his petite possession and her unacceptable breach of the rules of their agreement.

He reflected on Caesar's reminder before they left to keep a close eye on the valuable asset from which they both benefited. Stephan had assured Caesar he would personally ensure she was kept under lock and key. Which had seemed to be music to Caesar's ears as they said their farewells. Stephan had every intention of keeping his word; indeed, he planned to keep Nadia on a permanently tight leash from now on.

Such distracting thoughts meant that Nadia had to work long and hard to earn him his climax. Fortunately the thought of her on a leash did the trick.

'Don't waste a drop,' he commanded as he pumped into her mouth and she obligingly swallowed.

She understood perfectly that although he might have accepted her apology, he hadn't truly forgiven her and would certainly never forget. She wondered how long she would be paying for her mistake.

After the exceptionally satisfying blowjob, he dismissed Nadia to the bedroom, asking her to wait for him face down, naked and spreadeagled on the bed. He needed a few minutes to himself to do something he'd been contemplating ever since finding Nadia's mobile.

He picked up the phone and called his mother for the number of one of her best friends, Karin Klarsson, a professor of psychology specialising in facial micro-expressions. Deciding to strike while the iron was hot, he called the professor's mobile. She told him she would be thrilled to meet with him whenever it was convenient, and her research team would be more than happy to assist him in any way they could.

Content that he would get the answers he needed one way or another, he was more than in the mood to join Nadia in the bedroom and have his wicked way with her once more. After all, she belonged to him – and she needed to be taught some important lessons about exactly what being on a tight leash felt like in his world. Which provided him with no end of twisted pleasure.

Fire

A flame ignited in Noah's belly as he ran alongside the endless murky flow of the Yarra, trying to assimilate the events of the morning. Although he'd heard the words from Eloise's mouth, everything about their interaction had been fundamentally wrong. It was as though Nordstrom were a ventriloquist who controlled every word she said.

Usually Noah was the type of person who brought positivity to those around him, his warm heart reflected in his sunny personality. He was close to his friends and his family, and none of them ever doubted he'd be there if they needed him, helping, supporting, consoling, cheering. He had always worked hard at his sport – particularly over the last six months – but it was because he loved what he did. Many of his opponents were his close friends, and though he'd become much more driven since the US Open, winning would never come at the cost of someone else's misfortune.

But this was different. Stephan Nordstrom was different. Noah despised his winner-take-all arrogance. There was something about him that riled Noah no end.

As his feet pounded the pavement harder and faster with each step, Noah decided there was definitely more to this than his feelings for Eloise and his on-court rivalry with Nordstrom. He had a very bad feeling about the entire situation. He upped his pace, freeing his mind to concentrate on the situation at hand.

Noah had another twenty-four hours before he boarded the plane that would transfer him to Europe's cold, harsh winter for the first round of the Davis Cup in France. Though it had shaken him, the interaction with Stephan and Eloise had given him just the impetus he needed to formulate his own winning strategy for the next twelve months.

Eloise's stricken face and the haunted look in her eyes would remain etched in his mind as he imagined the self-serving Swedish monster imprisoning her in his suffocating embrace. It was enough to cause his protective instincts to skyrocket. The more he thought about it, the more he was convinced that the reason she was with Stephan was something to do with his status as Number One. So if Noah himself became Number One, things would have to change.

If that was what was needed to ensure she was out of harm's way, he would do whatever it took to achieve it. For the first time he refused to let anything stand in his way. The fire in his belly was poised to engulf everything in its path – just like the devastating bushfires of the Australian summer. Tennis had always been his passion, then it had become his business, and now it fuelled his urgent desire to save Eloise from Stephan – and, even more importantly, from herself. He had never wanted anything so badly in his life.

The stars seemed to be aligning even as he arrived back from his run. Before he had made it to the shower, the hotel receptionist informed him that Toby Brooks – one of the greatest tennis coaches of all time – was on the line. Dripping with sweat, Noah accepted the call and was surprised to hear Toby offer his services for the next six months on a subsidised basis. Arrangements were made to meet up, and just hours later, the two men sat down together and discussed an ambitious plan that would focus on the speed and placement of his serve, improve his performance at the net, and intensify his strength and agility training. In addition to this, Noah would continue his meditation regime and attend psychology coaching specifically designed to optimise his winning mindset both on and off the court.

Noah's exposure to competition would increase dramatically on his path to Wimbledon. In addition to playing the eight mandatory ATP World Tour Masters 1000 tournaments, he would compete in all of the ATP World Tour 500 tournaments (where possible), to maximise his potential points in the ATP world rankings, which couldn't have suited him more. Once everything had been agreed, his revised schedule was sent to The Edge for their reference.

Toby called his good friend Caesar to thank him for suggesting he make contact with Levique, and let him know how well the meeting had gone. He conceded that although he had spent the past twenty years coaching some of the best players in the world, there was something unique about Noah and he was willing to devote as much of his time and energy as he could to the ongoing success of this young man's career. It was rare to find a player at this level whose focus wasn't ego-driven, and equally refreshing to work with someone whose arrogance didn't cripple their ability to learn.

Caesar agreed wholeheartedly and wished him every success with his newly contracted player. There was nothing Caesar loved more than a good, close competition – particularly when he managed both players. It was good for business, and he always agreed that the best man should win. He didn't care who it was, but he certainly did care whether he backed the right one on the day.

* * *

The positive press from the Australian Open had reached saturation point and ensured that Liam Noah Levique – the underdog – was now a household name in his home country. He was the sporting hope of a nation – and sport was Australia's religion. The tennis world was watching with bated breath to see whether he had it in him to knock the Scandinavian demigod from his ever-so-high perch!

THE GRAND SLAMS
Round Two

There can be a very fine line between
pleasure and pain;
winning and losing;
life and death ...
It just depends on whether
the pendulum of fate
swings your way – or not.

FRENCH OPEN II
May–June

Darkness

Stephan and Nadia headed back towards Europe, stopping off in Hong Kong and Shanghai for a few exhibition matches. Though these matches didn't count towards Stephan's world ranking points, they certainly made a hefty contribution to his bank balance via lucrative sponsorships in China.

Nadia waited patiently at the sidelines under Garry's watchful eye as Stephan attended photo shoots for product endorsements. She hung off his arm when he attended functions, always demure and always following his explicit instructions as to how she should behave.

The fateful day she had forced Noah from her life had never been mentioned between them again, and she tried to convince herself that she had made the right decision by proving her complete allegiance to Stephan. There was no disputing who held the reins in their relationship, and whenever she slipped, they were held all the more tightly within Stephan's unrelenting grasp.

She had no choice but to watch, with conflicting emotions, as Noah and Stephan both progressed through to every final of the mandatory ATP World Tour Masters 1000. It was as if the rest of the players on the circuit were irrelevant. Under the expert guidance of Toby Brooks, Noah's tennis had matured even further over recent months, as he steadily eliminated the imperfections from his game and strategically honed his strengths. While he played as many tournaments as humanly possible, Stephan focused more on accumulating the financial wealth that his Number One status enabled. But most of all, he channelled his energy into training his prized possession to become the ultimate submissive.

The ATP Tour Masters events were breathtaking, edge-of-your seat spectacles for the crowds and attendance records were smashed. Everyone wanted to witness the laid-back Aussie and the Swedish supremo belt it out on court, and it always proved excellent value for money. Every spectator watching could feel the antagonism between the two players. Nadia would have benefited from a substantial dose of Valium each time they played, such were her nerves.

Noah caused the tennis upset of the year by finally overpowering Stephan in the fifth set in Miami. The match was so close that the difference in the scores was due to one break of serve. Most put it down to luck – Noah had a few net cords go his way at vital moments – but when he claimed his second victory over Stephan in Madrid, suddenly everyone was paying attention and Noah's followers on social media quadrupled overnight. Sports reporters worldwide were caught off guard by how quickly Noah Levique's game had developed, from his catastrophic loss in the US Open last year to his phenomenal form leading into the French Open. They'd known he was a rising star, and it seemed his star had indeed risen, making the upcoming grand slams anything but a foregone conclusion.

Stephan despised being in the position of having to congratulate Noah and explain his own inferior performance to the press. Needless to say, his interviews were short and sharp: a far cry from his glowing monologues at the Australian Open.

Although Stephan proved he was still Number One by beating Noah at Indian Wells, he had been so disturbed by his previous losses that he pulled out of the Monte Carlo Rolex Masters, citing a strained thumb, which enabled Noah to cruise through the rounds with ease and claim the trophy in the finals.

Not surprisingly, the unspoken tension between Stephan and Nadia during these tournaments escalated to new heights. But Stephan told himself – and the press – repeatedly that the slams were an entirely different ballgame from the masters.

Stephan restricted Nadia's freedom more and more each day, as the fear of losing her consumed him. There was nothing Nadia could say or do to reassure him that he would win again, that he was still Number One and that she still belonged to him. From the moment he'd walked off the court in Miami as runner-up to Noah, the possibility of losing his coveted status – and Nadia – was constantly on his mind.

Her life rapidly changed from one of being by his side attending glamorous events to one of being left alone, locked in hotel suites. She was only ever allowed to go anywhere if Garry was by her side, and only when she had Stephan's explicit permission.

Sexually, the state of play between them had also changed for the worse. Stephan's punishments became more frequent and her forced orgasms were less than desirable. His power was based on fear, driving his need for domination to ever darker places, and the playful, fun side of their relationship steadily evaporated.

Nadia had become so conditioned to constantly seeking the approval of her Master that she had lost all sense of self. Every moment was occupied with trying either to please him or to appease him – but to her bitter disappointment, nothing ever seemed to be enough. Somehow she always managed to upset him instead of placate him, so she readily accepted whatever he dished out, believing it would help her improve. What she hadn't grasped was that the more perfect she tried to be for him, the greater his fear of losing her became – let alone losing her to Noah.

Stephan tried desperately to prevent such thoughts from sabotaging his mind – without success. The only thing that seemed to work for him was to take it out on her body. Each time he took the strap to her, he hoped to overcome the demons threatening to consume him. He convinced himself that the more he punished her psychologically and marked her physically, the more he would prove that she still belonged to him. It was a miserable existence for both of them. And they no longer shared words that could rectify the hopelessness overshadowing their relationship.

Much to Nadia's relief, it was eventually Stephan's coach, who coerced him into focusing back on his game. He returned almost to his previous supernatural self, annihilating Noah with a vengeance in Rome just two weeks before Roland Garros.

Though his confidence soared on the night of the win, he still held Nadia on a tight leash – literally. After a few celebratory drinks with his coach and manager, he arrived back at their hotel suite to announce that they were dining at Il Convivio Troiani with a family friend from Sweden. Nadia was thrilled to be allowed out with him for the first time in weeks, and made sure she was impeccably groomed as she waited the endless hours for Stephan's return. She couldn't be found looking unkempt when he did eventually arrive.

Without words, he stripped her clothes from her body, including her underwear, and stared at her naked form. Nadia knew better than to speak or make eye contact during such intimate inspections, so she calmed her breathing and cast her eyes towards the floor, knowing this process could be over in twenty seconds or last as painstakingly long as half an hour. If she moved or even flinched he would either fetch his crop or tie her up, sometimes both, ensuring she had to ask for his assistance with her most basic needs.

He absorbed her beauty and poise as he glided his fingers along her tainted skin and gently pressed her bruises as though she were a uniquely crafted trophy for him alone to adore. Eventually he encouraged her to bend over and place her hands on the edge of the bed. His calloused hands followed the curve of her waist and massaged her buttocks and thighs as his eyes admired the remnants of his most recent lashing. Wounds he needed to see tormenting her alabaster skin as proof that she was his. He swiftly raised his palm hard and fast to each cheek as she stifled a yelp behind her lips.

'You please me, Nadia.'

'Thank you, sir.'

'You may turn around.'

He walked out of the room and returned with a dress that looked almost black but shone aubergine when it caught the light.

'Arms up.'

He placed it over her head and pulled it down until it settled smoothly on her hips. The top of the garment was an elaborate corset, attached to a silk skirt that came to her thighs and was covered by layers of chiffon falling a few inches above her knees. Although the dress was beautiful in its detail, as Stephan laced the corset, forcing the breath from her lungs, she realised it was certainly more than a fashion garment. Her petite waist was cinched to minuscule proportions, causing her usually small breasts to plump above the top of the corset. Two pieces of chiffon covered the top of her breasts and were tied up around the back of her neck. As Stephan fluffed the skirt around her lower body, it was so light she could barely feel it against her skin. The outfit was doubtless intended as a visual reflection of the hold he had on her, and his ability to control what she could and couldn't do at any time. Even her breathing was restricted.

It reminded her of ballet, of needing to become the character via an array of constricting costumes, and that in turn reminded her of how long it had been since she had performed onstage – something she longed to do again. She'd convinced herself that Stephan's busy schedule hadn't allowed her the opportunity to dance for him, and of course she hadn't dared to raise her concern directly with him. The memories of her last performance for Stephan still haunted her dreams – or nightmares!

Next Stephan presented her with the highest stilettos she had ever seen. The heel was transparent, giving the impression that she was standing on tiptoes, and aubergine ribbons spiralled up her legs. She thought it would be easier for her to wear her pointe ballet shoes out than these – at least she was in control being on her toes – the enormous heels merely served to put her ridiculously off-balance.

He completed her look with decorative silk wristbands that intertwined and were attached to the bottom of the V-shaped corset. It looked like she was casually overlapping her hands, as one might see in many a royal photo, but in reality she was incapable of moving them from this position.

Nadia looked like an elaborate bondage ballerina. She was completely dependent on Stephan for support, and should he leave her side, she'd be stranded. If she attempted to walk in the shoes alone, she could break her ankle. On the rare occasions when they were out in public together, he ensured that there were obstacles should she want to do anything independently. However, this outfit took her submission, and his dominance, to an entirely different level.

'Do you like this outfit, Nadia? Be honest.'

Nadia had come to realise that honesty with Stephan was about finding the right words to soothe his ego: something she had become more adept at with each passing day. She had learnt to keep her answers simple, direct and, most importantly, free of complaint.

'I do like it, Master. It's a beautiful colour.'

He stepped closer, dropping his head so his lips settled on the nape of her neck as he whispered his words against her flesh. 'And the corset? Can you breathe?'

'With each breath, I think of you.'

'And your shoes? Can you walk?'

'With each step, I depend on you.'

'And your wrists?'

'My movements will be with your permission.'

He purposefully lowered his hand beneath her dress, between her legs.

'And here, you have nothing protecting you ...'

'I am yours.'

Stephan wrapped his arm around her waist to hold her steady as his skilled and precise fingers commanded her orgasm.

He then settled his panting bondage ballerina on the edge of the bed and walked over to the phone.

'We're ready. Bring the car to the front.'

Lies

As far as Stephan was concerned, the dinner that followed was sublime – not least because, as usual, he was the centre of attention. Nadia had been hoping it would be just the two of them, and felt deeply awkward at being restrained in front of others – though at least after his win Stephan was in a jovial, social mood.

It was a private party, with only his direct entourage in attendance, in addition to Professor Karin Klarsson, who was an attractive woman in her fifties, and her associate, Dr Matthias Freidman. Karin and her team were developing software to recognise facial micro-expressions that had the potential to be linked to security systems the world over, most significantly at airports, in order to detect criminal behaviour, including potential terrorist attacks. The software was used during interviews to determine whether people were covering something up.

Stephan appeared fascinated by her work, asking many questions to garner more information. At the same time, he diligently fed Nadia half-portions of exotic Italian delicacies such as fungi porcini and boneless oxtail with celeriac.

His coach and manager were so well acquainted with Stephan's control of all things Nadia that they no longer registered anything as unusual. They knew Nadia did as Stephan commanded – at all times, in private and public – whereas Karin and her colleague could barely draw their eyes away from the interaction between the two of them, not to mention Nadia's extraordinary outfit.

'Of course, there are always *degrees* of lying,' the professor explained, trying to stay focused on the conversation. 'It is unusual for things to be completely black and white – even though many people want them to be. It would certainly be easier for the authorities if they were.'

'What do you mean, exactly?' Stephan asked.

'There is really no such thing as objective truth. So although we can interpret facial micro-expressions and correlate them with certain emotions, only the individual can provide the context.'

'Please, continue … I'm intrigued.'

Karin was taken aback by Stephan's behaviour, though she politely said nothing. Nadia silently attempted to overcome the acute embarrassment she felt by demurely accepting each mouthful of food Stephan placed between her lips. She ate when he fed her just as she spoke when he asked her to. The corset ensured her posture was perfectly upright during the entire meal, but also constricted her stomach to the extent that it was difficult to continue eating.

'Well, normally lies are used deliberately, to deceive another person. People may also lie to avoid consequences of some kind.'

'Yes, I'm certainly aware of that.' Stephan squeezed Nadia's thigh hard under the table as Karin continued.

'Of course, there are probably times when a person *should* lie – for example, to protect people from harm, or to avoid pain …'

Stephan was so engaged in the conversation that he didn't notice Nadia shaking her head vigorously when the next forkful arrived in front of her firmly closed mouth. She knew better than to ever interrupt him, so the steaming spaghetti alle vongole fell down her décolletage and onto her lap as she stifled a scream.

A waiter immediately appeared by her side and attempted to remove the spaghetti from her lap. Stephan raised his hand, preventing the waiter from going anywhere near Nadia. 'Just bring me another serviette.' He rolled up the soiled one from Nadia's lap, replaced it with the new one and continued his conversation as if nothing had happened. He didn't see or register the aghast looks on the faces of his guests as the remaining sauce was left to dribble down her chin. Nadia was so ashamed that her face looked as if she'd had an allergic reaction – leaving Karin no option but to say something.

'Excuse me, Stephan, I'd be happy to take Nadia to the ladies' room to help her clean up.'

'That won't be necessary; besides, the dish would be cold by the time she returned.'

He picked up his fork to stab a clam, twirling it through the spaghetti and raising it to Nadia's mouth. Those around the table fell utterly silent, unsure of what to focus on but transfixed nonetheless.

This time Nadia's mouth dutifully opened and accepted what was offered. It was only then that Stephan used his napkin to dab some of the sauce from her face and offered her a sip of wine to help the food slide down her constricted throat into her overfull stomach.

Any attempt Karin made to include Nadia in the conversation was met by Stephan's answering on her behalf, or her responding with as few words as possible. When Karin rose to use the ladies' room, she asked Nadia if she'd like to go with her. Nadia raised her eyes towards Stephan for approval and he merely shook his head.

'No, thank you, I'm fine,' she answered quietly.

Karin was utterly thrown by their relationship; she had no doubt people might choose to behave this way in private, but it was like nothing she'd ever experienced in public. She had studied abusive relationships but she couldn't detect any fear in Nadia's facial expressions, just an unusual degree of acceptance. She was certain that the spaghetti incident had embarrassed Nadia deeply, yet she had detected only shame on her face, as though it had been her fault, not any fear of Stephan. As far as Karin's expertise could suggest, for all intents and purposes Nadia revered the man she sat next to, and he did her – so she just couldn't put her finger on the exact dynamic between them.

As their unusual dinner came to an end Stephan suggested that Nadia would be a suitable female candidate to further test the software being developed by Karin's research team. Karin shared a dumbfounded look with Matthias that revealed they were both at a loss as to what to make of such an offer.

Karin cleared her throat awkwardly. 'Unfortunately we leave for Berlin tomorrow morning and most of our equipment is still in Paris, but perhaps when you are next back in Uppsala –'

'That's great news. We're on our way to Paris for the French Open; I'm sure we'd be able to make something work. You mentioned earlier that you needed more access to females in the twenty to twenty-five age bracket, so Nadia would be perfect.'

Stephan was obviously not the type of man to accept no for an answer. Eventually his charisma worked its usual charm and Karin's curiosity got the better of her – it was unusual for her to be so perplexed – so she agreed, implicitly understanding that asking for Nadia's opinion was an unnecessary step in the approval process. Even so, she made a silent commitment to herself that she would aim to get to the bottom of their relationship one way or another, and should she uncover anything sinister she would deal with it then.

Although Nadia had listened to their conversation during dinner, she was still unsure as to exactly what would be expected of her. But, as always where Stephan was concerned, she focused minute by minute – so their next meeting with the professor seemed a long way off and she was determined not to stress about it. She had enough on her mind with the potential outcome of the French Open.

Stephan assisted Nadia into the car after they said their goodbyes and settled next to her on the back seat, caressing the inside of her exposed thigh with his palm.

'One way or another, my sweet, I will find out what is going on in that head of yours, and I hope for your sake it is what it should be.'

'Please, sir, you have nothing to worry about.'

'You say that, but how do I really know?'

He wrapped his arm protectively around her shoulders and drew her in close, making her feel small against him. 'I know your body from the inside out, Nadia, but now I will also have the information I need to study what's going on in your mind. I'll finally know whether you have been lying to me all along about Levique.'

Nadia involuntarily shuddered against his body. These days, she wasn't sure whether her mind was her own anyway.

'So it was a very worthwhile dinner, don't you think?'

She meekly nodded her head, sensing the shift in his mood. 'I suppose … but how exactly do Professor Klarsson's team detect lies?'

'Have you ever seen the American TV show *Lie to Me*?'

She shook her head as he watched her intently in the shadows.

'Well, I'll make sure you watch an episode. What Karin and her team study is along the same lines. Basically, they detect minute involuntary movements in our facial expressions with the help of technology, in order to interpret the underlying emotions.'

The car pulled into a darkened alleyway, away from the steady flow of traffic.

'And now you have the opportunity to be a part of their research, to which I'll be privy!' He squeezed her bare knee, looking positively delighted. 'But for now, we have far more important things to attend to.'

'We're not going back to the suite, sir?' she asked tentatively.

'Certainly not! We're in Rome, and I intend to thoroughly celebrate my win having smashed Levique into the ground. Let's just say we have a long night ahead of us.'

And that was as much information as she was given, though feelings of foreboding settled into the edges of her bones like a cankerous rot.

Property

Stephan led Nadia through heavy double wooden doors with enormous latches, and down a marble staircase. If he hadn't physically supported her there was no doubt she'd have toppled to the bottom, collapsing in a heap. Instead, she felt like a featherweight as he carried her with ease down the dimly lit steps.

Another set of doors saw them greeted by a woman dressed in a tight-fitting tuxedo and top hat, who handed each of them an elaborate mask as she ushered them into a change room. Stephan removed his shirt, which still always proved an aphrodisiac for Nadia, and she sighed in silent frustration that her hands were still tethered. Not that it made much difference these days whether she was bound or not, as she was forbidden to touch him freely, only by explicit request; such was the emotional distance that had developed between them since the Australian Open. It saddened her more than anything, but she accepted his wishes, knowing that any argument she mounted would only have caused her more grief. So she looked but didn't touch as he turned her around to loosen the taut corset. Finally she could breathe more freely, and she inhaled deeply.

'Don't relax too much, I'm only adjusting it,' his words warned her, and with surprising ease he removed the material covering her breasts and dispensed with her skirt, which she discovered was only fastened to the corset via hooks and eyes. Nadia gazed at her reflection in the mirror, Stephan's enormous presence shadowing hers as he yanked the corset even more tightly around her stomach and ribcage, causing her to automatically steady herself against the mirror. She feared he might crack a rib if he cinched it any tighter.

Her breasts were now fully exposed above the corset, rapidly rising and falling with each short, shallow breath. Her slim hips, smooth derrière and lithe legs were also fully displayed. He was naked on top, she naked from the corset down.

He removed a lipstick from his pocket that was as dark as her outfit, with only a hint of plum. Squeezing her cheeks between his fingers, he covered her puckered lips, giving her a gothic look against her pale face. Then, to her horror, he bent her over and proceeded to write with the lipstick across her thighs and buttocks.

Property of #1

He replicated a smaller version of the bold letters across her chest and breasts.

Property of #1

And then he went over his words again and again, reinforcing his ownership of her body.

A wave of nausea wrenched her gut as she was turned towards the mirror to absorb what he had made her. Though words flooded her mind, she couldn't put her finger on exactly what she had become – a product, a pet, a plaything? Whatever the answer was, there was not an inkling of 'Eloise' reflected back into her haunted eyes and only the mere shell of the body that used to be her own.

Would the Eloise of the past have defiantly smeared the written words across her skin until they looked like bad bruising, and point-blank refused to be treated this way? Where once she'd been so proud that she belonged to him, the sight before her now was sickening and humiliating. That he had diminished her existence and her identity so that she was no more than his property – human property – made her ill. The vision before her truly said all this and more.

'I like you looking like this, so everyone knows you belong to me.' His eyes scanned her body as she reacted involuntarily to his words. 'I think I'd like something more permanent, though. Would you like that too?'

She nodded her head, desperate to keep her stomach and words under control. A deep part of her knew that she looked hideous, ugly. Another part told her that if he liked it, nothing else mattered.

'Perhaps if you're good, a Swedish flag with my initials on your delectable derrière would do the trick. Otherwise, I'd be very comfortable with this.'

She said nothing, as it wasn't a question.

'I need to mark you like this tonight, Nadia, because I'm going to share you.'

Had he punched her in the stomach it would have had the same physical impact. She doubled over in pain and her ears were filled with loud ringing.

He stepped back to look at her, pleased with his handiwork.

'Please, sir, no, don't do this, I beg you!' Her body was trembling, her voice barely a whisper.

'Have I punished you properly for Levique yet?' He held her arms behind her back at the elbows, forcing her nipples out.

'No, sir, you haven't, but ...'

Her voice trailed off, knowing her words carried no weight in his world. Deep down in her gut she'd known that this was coming, that it was only a matter of time before Stephan ensured that she paid for what happened with Noah. With each passing day the tension inside her had been building; she'd known the punishment would come but not when or how. He'd held this power of the unknown over her for months, causing her to live with unexposed stress.

This was it. It had taken winning this tournament and thrashing Noah in straight sets for Stephan's supreme confidence to return so he could deliver his retribution.

'You know you deserve it? That you have given me no choice in this matter?'

He yanked her hair back so her face lifted towards his.

'Yes or no, Nadia?' She felt the anger boiling beneath his skin.

'Yes, Master. Yes, I do,' she answered quickly, desperate to placate him.

'Then you understand why I am forced to do this?'

Barely able to breathe, she forced out her last desperate plea to try to prevent what was about to happen.

'Yes I do, Master, but please, not with others, please not that, I beg you! I can handle anything with you, but not with others. I ... I ... I've never done anything like this with anyone else.' The thought nauseated her.

He hesitated, taking a moment to feel her heart beating rapidly in her chest. 'Do you trust me?' He secured the elaborate feathered mask over her eyes.

She hesitated. Her heart screamed 'No' as her head counselled against that answer. 'I think so ...' she stuttered, reprimanding herself for sounding so unsure.

'Do you give yourself to me, to do with as I see fit?'

An uneasy calmness steadied her frantic nerves, though her stomach screamed in revolt.

'Yes, Master.' This time her eyes lowered out of fear of what she might see if she glimpsed his.

'You will do as I order, without question.'

He buckled a thick black leather collar around her fragile, long neck, tightening it with just enough pressure to make every breath more conscious, and held the attached lead expectantly in the palm of his hand, tugging lightly to reinforce his control.

She closed her streaming eyes, her mind begging for her silence as resistance ripped through her.

Another tug. Another tweak. Hands bound, leaving her no choice but to accept his will.

Her stilettos stymied her steps as Stephan held her upright and led her into the candlelit dungeon, where the scent of sex was abundant, the sweet saltiness of it infusing her nostrils.

Nadia could sense the potent mood around her. She could hear moans and whimpers, screams of pleasure and of pain. He paraded her around with great pride, describing to her in hushed tones the various rooms and instruments as if giving a tour. She was exposed to what could have been seen as a supposedly erotic medieval torture chamber and was left in no doubt about the various implements available to ensure her surrender.

People gathered to watch or partake in activities in respectful silence, making the atmosphere that much more heady. Some gazed directly at Nadia and discreetly nodded their approval to Stephan. Her body, still restricted by the tight corset and the collar around her neck, trembled with fear at what might lie ahead.

A tall, voluptuous woman with vibrant red glossy lips and dressed head to toe in leather – resembling Catwoman with a bullwhip – held out her other hand towards Nadia.

Stephan's hot breath whispered loudly in her ear, biting into her lobe.

'I want to hear you scream. Make me proud.'

What followed was something neither of them expected.

The events of the evening revolted against her.

She felt the room spin as her eyes lost all focus.

Her stomach constricted to such an extent that her breath was trapped, unable to be released from her body.

And then it erupted. Violently. Uncontrollably.

Releasing. Until there was nothing left inside.

She was empty.

Time

The vomiting went on and on, as though every part of Nadia needed to be expelled. She threw up until she was heaving unconsciously on the floor – then finally the doctor's injections worked their magic, providing a reprieve from her stupor.

Stephan was convinced she had a virus, and didn't dare go near her for fear of falling ill for Roland Garros. He and his coach discussed their predicament and agreed that Stephan should focus solely on his next grand-slam victory, so Nadia was immediately flown to an all-female health spa in Switzerland to recover. The two-week stay would be the longest time she had ever been away from Stephan since they'd met.

A nurse checked her in and ran some preliminary tests to determine her physical and mental health. The nurse at once noticed the depleted state of Nadia's body, and it was impossible to ignore the bruises and lesions on her arms and legs – including the vague traces of the stubborn dark lipstick against her white skin – when she removed her clothing to change into the gown provided.

'We can provide you with a safe for your wallet and mobile phone during your stay, as we don't encourage contact with the outside world for the first few days.'

'I don't have either.'

'Oh, I see.' The nurse looked a little startled then made a note on one of her forms. 'Have they been lost?'

'No.' A distant vision of Stephan smashing her phone beneath his shoe in front of Noah flashed through her mind and she shivered in response.

'I'm deeply concerned about the state of your body. How long have you had these wounds and bruises?'

Nadia's huge aquamarine eyes stared listlessly out the window, gazing towards the magnificent Alps. The trip to the spa had zapped every last bit of energy she had.

'Please, I can help you. Your body is very weak and you need time to heal.'

'I will heal, I always do.' Nadia looked at her limbs as if they weren't her own, knowing they belonged to her Master to do with as he wished.

'Are you being abused?'

'Abuse' was a word Nadia had never associated with herself. She remembered Noah had used it and she'd been shocked that he saw her situation that way – but that had been when things were better between her and Stephan. 'Abuse' sounded like a harsh, dirty word, and certainly not a word she believed should be attributed to their relationship. She *allowed* him to do this to her because she belonged to him, and it was what he needed.

She reflected on the time when he first marked her, how proud she had been and how tenderly she had cared for her abrasions. She'd seen photos of abused women, hiding their black eyes behind sunglasses, their bodies battered and bruised beneath their long-sleeved clothes. She willingly submitted to Stephan, so she was different from them; they didn't represent her. He might hurt her, but she knew she deserved the pain. Pain he *needed* to administer to teach her about his exacting standards and expectations of her behaviour. This was an integral part of their relationship; it defined their importance to each other.

Finally she turned to the nurse.

'I chose this for myself. I am his.'

The nurse made some additional notes. 'I'll make an appointment for you with our psychologist when you are more rested and settled in.'

Nadia didn't respond, so the nurse continued her physical examination in silence, then efficiently bathed Nadia's bone-weary body. Nadia was almost asleep even before her aching head felt the soft comfort of the pillow.

It took days for her stomach to settle. Her body felt like it had been put through a wringer several times over; she was exhausted physically and emotionally. Even after twelve hours' sleep at night she could still manage an afternoon nap. But rather than being in her usual state of agitation that revolved around Stephan and his world, she was able to doze peacefully day and night, with no concern for how she looked or behaved, and the tension finally eased from her body.

Her bruises faded, her wounds began to heal, and eventually her appetite returned with gusto. Ordering spontaneously and plentifully from the room-service menu, and eating as she had never done during all her years as a ballerina, she noticed the skin around her bones begin to fill out.

It was only when she felt better both physically and mentally that she went along to her first appointment with psychologist Dr Jayne Ferrer. After the usual preliminaries, Jayne made it clear that Nadia was required to do the majority of the talking: not something she was normally comfortable with.

'Tell me about your childhood,' Jayne began.

'I don't know who my father is, and I believe my biological mother was declared unfit to look after me. The only thing I have of hers is a music box, which I treasure. I think she tried to kill herself, but I'm not sure … So I was put into foster care when I was a baby.'

'What was that like?'

'OK, I guess, but when my first foster parents had kids of their own I was given to another family. Then I was handed on to one family after another for various reasons – if they had to move or something. So I never felt really settled in any one place but I can't complain, most of them looked after me or at least did the best they could, even though I knew they never loved me. But life got a lot better after I discovered ballet. From then on, as long as they let me dance, I was fine.'

Jayne looked at her notes. 'I see. Go on.'

'I grew to love ballet more than anything else in the world, and was asked to compete in Sydney, which was a big thing when you lived in the country, like I did. A ballet scout had arranged it with my foster parents – the Lawrances – so I could go, which was scary but also wonderful to have such an opportunity.

'Much to everyone's shock – including my own – I ended up winning the competition, and was offered a scholarship to study with the Royal Ballet in London. So the rest of my schooling was at White Lodge, where ballet became my life.' She remembered her nervous, insecure twelve-year-old self walking into her first class and settling into her new home – having left the empty loneliness of her Australian childhood behind her. 'It had been that way for ten years ... up until the last year or so.'

Jayne noticed the change in Nadia's demeanour as she described her life at White Lodge, and then as a ballerina with the Royal Ballet. She became animated and alive, her cheeks blushed with colour and her pupils dilated as she relived her happier memories. The smallest of smiles even skirted her lips – but instantly disappeared at Jayne's next question.

'So tell me, how did you end up here?'

Nadia's discomfort was immediately evident. She shifted in her seat, her eyes looked away and her hands fidgeted on her lap.

'Everything you say to me remains within this room.' Jayne poured them both a cup of steaming green tea. 'Please, I encourage you to speak freely.'

Cocoon

Suddenly Nadia felt like the whole weight of her contract with Caesar had been lifted from her shoulders. Finally she could unburden herself to someone she could trust, and in an environment where she felt safe. And unburden herself she did, recounting the events of her life for the next hour and a half to a sympathetic and non-judgmental ear. She spoke of her devastation at losing the role of Principal, her loss of identity after leaving the ballet, her fear of never belonging and of always being alone in the world. She spoke of ballet and tennis and Caesar, Ivan, Stephan and Noah, and how at the end of eight grand slams she was hoping for an opportunity to develop her own life, on her own terms – whatever those might be.

'How does Stephan make you feel?'

'Small.' Nadia was taken aback by how spontaneously that word had popped out of her mouth.

'Anything else?'

She thought about it a bit longer this time. 'I feel edgy around him; it's a mixture of anticipation and anxiety. I never know what's coming next and whether he'll approve of my actions or not.'

'And does it matter?'

'Absolutely it does. It means everything to me. I mean, he is the world's Number One player – have you seen him? He's like a god.'

'Only in advertisements or on TV.' Jayne smiled. 'And what if he doesn't approve of you?'

'Then I have to try harder.'

'How? Do you discuss it together?'

'We used to. Not so much now – well, more often than not, he punishes me so I'll remember the lesson for next time.' Nadia cast her eyes towards the floor and started subconsciously rubbing her upper thighs. 'I agreed to it, though, at the start of my time with him.'

'Do you *enjoy* the punishments, Nadia?'

'No, not any more – but I usually deserve them.'

Jayne could tell she was losing Nadia to a dark space and decided to change the subject. 'Tell me more about Noah …'

Jayne observed that she instantly re-engaged at the mention of Noah's name. It was as though Jayne were speaking to an entirely different person.

Nadia described meeting him for the first time by chance and how much fun she'd had during their week together in London. She mentioned how touched she'd been when he placed the lock on the bridge in Melbourne – and then shadows were cast over her words as she related how Stephan had discovered her friendship with Noah and forced her to choose between them.

'I'd like to see you each day you're with us, Nadia. Is that OK with you?' Jayne asked, glancing at her watch.

'Oh, yes, of course. Sorry for taking up so much of your time. I didn't realise I had so much to say.'

'That's what I'm here for. How do you feel now?'

'Exhausted, actually, but lighter in a way …'

'Good. Drinks lots of water and herbal tea and rest well. I'll see you tomorrow at the same time.'

When Nadia closed the door behind her, Jayne made a call to reception to see if it was possible to have Nadia's stay extended. She needed much more time than had been allocated.

Nadia enjoyed daily massages and therapeutic treatments, which served to further restore her body and rejuvenate her psyche. Her sessions with Jayne continued on a daily basis and helped her unravel aspects of her life she hadn't paid any attention to before. Jayne encouraged her to keep a daily diary and come along with any topics she wanted to discuss during their sessions, which proved very beneficial. Each day Nadia felt stronger, healthier and more comfortable in her own skin. Her troubled thoughts could be more easily switched off during meditation and yoga, and she had the freedom to meander about the spa without pressure and without other tasks to attend to. The fresh alpine air did wonders for her psyche and when she felt up to it she enjoyed mountain walks amidst the stunning scenery. Her skin glowed and she felt better than she had in months, cocooned away from the world in the all-women's facility. It was novel for her to be with other women in a non-competitive environment and she enjoyed their company very much.

Thinking about Noah made her happy, but at the same time saddened her deeply as she recalled their last meeting in the oval room, so she pushed all memories of him away as best she could. But when her desire stirred deep in the night, although she knew she was betraying Stephan by facilitating her own release. She discovered that it was Noah's face and body that kindled her arousal.

Although she intermittently thought of Stephan and wondered what he was up to, she was surprised that she didn't miss him as desperately as she'd expected. In fact, it was Noah's warmth and kindness that she drew on to aid her recovery and restore her spirits. She found herself absently smiling and hugging herself when she thought of him – but stopped short of allowing her mind to wonder 'What if ...?' Her anxiety returned whenever she considered the outcomes of the next four grand slams. She didn't dare contact him as she had no doubt that Stephan would find out.

Stephan hadn't made any contact with her during her stay, which she found strange at first. But she assumed he would want to stay focused on his preparations; they were what made him Number One. So she gave herself permission to relish the time she had to herself, time she'd never had before. All thoughts of tennis and ballet were far from her mind, and she lived solely for herself, surrounded by the beauty of the Swiss Alps during the last days of spring.

So one afternoon, when she returned to her room after her acupuncture treatment to find none of her belongings there, there was no doubting her surprise. She went to reception to inquire whether her room had been changed without her knowledge, when through the window she saw Garry placing her packed bag into the boot of a car.

She froze, not having expected to see him so soon. He was like a foreign intrusion into her neutral, serene land. He stood, holding the back door open for her as he pointedly tapped his watch. His body language was loud and clear: *Get a move-on*.

It only took this one gesture for Nadia to instantly transform back into her submissive self. She needed to obey Garry, knowing his instructions were a direct extension of Stephan's orders.

As she turned to leave she heard Jayne's voice behind her.

'Nadia, you're not leaving, are you? I've been trying to arrange to have your stay with us extended.'

Nadia shook her head, watching Garry walk doggedly towards her. 'I'm afraid that's impossible.'

'I don't think you're ready to leave just yet. Please, can we talk about this?' Jayne gestured towards a lounge, her eyes silently pleading with Nadia.

Garry's gruff voice responded on Nadia's behalf. 'There's nothing to talk about. The account has been settled. Let's go, Nadia. We need to leave *now*.'

He guided an acquiescing Nadia towards the car as Jayne watched. Just as the back door was about to close she ran to stop them.

'Nadia! Tell me, honestly, is this what you want?'

Nadia turned and looked directly at the concerned psychologist. 'I need to go back to where I belong.' Her eyes were glazed, her voice unnaturally smooth.

Jayne raked her fingers through her dark hair in frustration as she scanned her mind for options. 'Listen: take this, and call me if you need to talk – about anything. I'm only a phone call away.'

She handed Nadia a business card, something she didn't usually do when clients left the spa, but there was something about Nadia – a tainted innocence, a forlorn sense of abandonment, an unrecognised cry for help – something that pulled at her heart, perhaps because she had a daughter of a similar age. 'Please, call me any time.'

'Thank you, that's very kind.' Nadia said the words without emotion, as though she were already lost in the dark zone of her old world, while Garry started the engine.

Jayne Ferrer watched helplessly as Nadia was driven away, deeply concerned about what might happen to the battered young woman she had needed more time to save.

Strategy

Tennis was hotter than it had been for more than a decade and the rapturous crowds could not get enough of the awesome battles these gladiators of the game fought on centre court. The red clay of Roland Garros was beckoning, and the temperature was hot and dry, so the court was faster than it had been in previous years and could be a game-changer for many of the players.

Caesar was as anxious as anyone about the outcome of this grand slam. Noah's form had been phenomenal since his defeat in the Australian Open, and many months of planning had gone into ensuring his success was linked to his personal profitability. Not many people knew that his recent straight-set loss to Nordstrom in Rome had occurred immediately after he was informed that his cherished grandmother had passed away in Western Australia. He liked to keep his private life private; it was his only sanctuary.

Caesar was furious that Noah had been given the news just moments before he went on court for the final, mostly because Caesar had lost a huge sum of money; it was the first time he'd decided to back Levique over Nordstrom. He'd discovered that an eager member of his own staff at The Edge had taken it upon himself to inform Noah as soon as the message was received from the Levique family, without thinking through the consequences. Needless to say, even though Caesar had never met this rookie, he was immediately sacked and would never work in Caesar's empire again. There were certain protocols he expected his staff to follow and there were no second chances; there was always too much at risk. He had been set to make a significant sum of money, not lose it – both from Club Zero and his automated betting program. Although he counted his lucky stars it wasn't a grand slam.

It was his insight into the mindset of the players that gave Caesar the competitive advantage he needed, and this was an expected glitch that should have been managed far more effectively. But even though the road had a few bumps here and there, he continued to congratulate himself on the brilliance of his Number One Strategy. He couldn't have been happier with how the first year had unfolded, exceeding even his own expectations.

He had high hopes for the outcomes of round two, having observed how 'the love triangle' (as he referred to it) had played out in Melbourne, but he knew this second year was a different prospect altogether. He had enough experience to know what fear did to a man as egocentric as Stephan, and unfortunately this insidious emotion had inflicted harm directly on his tennis. Meanwhile, Caesar had seen Noah's tennis go from playful to lethal in the first half of the year. Although some were still questioning whether his sudden rise was sustainable, Caesar knew that Noah had the fight in him to win – and it was for more than just a title.

It was uncanny that these two men were both besotted by his ballerina in a way Ivan hadn't been, ensuring that the stakes couldn't have been higher. The French Open was anyone's tournament, so much so that his bets covered all bases – though he was certainly willing to take a punt at which way the cards would fall.

Nerves

Nadia hadn't felt nerves like this in her entire life. When she'd arrived in Paris last night, she'd been shocked to discover that it was already the eve of the final of the French Open – between Stephan and Noah! Although she had felt well at the clinic, her swift removal, the travel and the lack of sleep last night had made her feel lethargic again. She still hadn't seen Stephan, but all of the calm tranquillity she had absorbed in Switzerland was evaporating from her body as each minute passed. He hadn't left instructions as to what she should wear or do, which meant she felt like a virtual wreck. She tried to draw upon some of the strength she had recently accumulated, but she was too flustered to focus. She was terrified that he'd still want to punish her after she had escaped whatever he'd intended at the hellish dungeon in Rome; however she would be forever grateful for her stomach's spontaneous eruption.

As she was pacing the living room of her hotel suite, there was a knock at the door. It was the concierge overseeing the delivery of all sorts of equipment into the suite. A camera, screen, chair and antenna suddenly made the room feel much smaller than before. No one spoke to her directly, merely nodded in her direction as they went about their business, and it was all she could do to keep out of their way. They departed as quickly as they had arrived once everything was in place, leaving her wondering what on earth was going on.

Then Stephan himself appeared, looking every bit the supreme Number One that he was. He didn't seem exactly happy as he stood there in his trademark blue tennis clothes, but certainly not angry either – just calm and controlled, as far as Nadia could ascertain from his stance and the look in his eyes.

'Nadia!' He beckoned for her to come to him. 'Look at you!'

She wasn't sure whether he was pleased or not; her body shivered nervously as she slowly walked towards him under the scrutiny of his stare.

'Are you happy to see me, or has the cat got your tongue, my sweet?'

'Hello, Master. Of course I'm happy to see you.' She stood perfectly still in front of him, her eyes cast modestly downwards.

'Better.' He ran his fingers along her sleeveless arms, lingering where previously bruises had been. 'You look well, certainly better than when I saw you last.'

'Thank you, sir. I do feel better.'

'Well, are you ready for the big match?'

'As ready as I'll ever be, sir.'

'Good. Come.' He held out his hand, which she accepted, thinking they were about to leave, but he merely accompanied her a few steps across the room and signalled for her to sit down in the chair that had just been delivered.

She sat tentatively on the edge and stared up at him, puzzled. He lifted her body easily so she sat fully in the seat.

'You will be watching my match from here today.'

'But why? I usually watch grand-slam finals with Caesar ... sir.'

She grew immediately anxious as he knelt beside the chair and removed some Velcro straps from his pockets.

'Don't worry, I've explained everything to Caesar, he knows you won't be there.'

He gently picked up her wrist and placed it on the arm of the chair, securing it with one of the straps.

'Please, Master, you don't need to do this ...' Tears sprang from her eyes and she automatically withdrew her other hand as he began to replicate the process. She felt his grip around her wrist as he strapped it in place. He secured her elbows in the same way, completely restricting the movement of both her arms. 'Please, sir, this isn't necessary!'

'But don't you see, Nadia? It is. You've left me no choice. This is the only way I will know for sure how you feel, the only way I can get inside your head. It's the first part of your research assignment for Professor Klarsson's team. Remember our dinner in Rome?'

He placed another longer strap around her lap, using it like a seat belt to fasten her body to the chair, then secured her ankles to the chair legs.

Tears now fell freely from her eyes and she began to sob audibly as panic set in.

'So much sadness …' He wiped her tears away tenderly with his thumb. 'Or are you scared that I'll discover the truth? At least after this match I'll know for certain one way or the other.'

She understood words would be futile at this point and remained silent as he aimed the camera towards her. Instantly the enormous screen came alive, displaying the televised coverage of Roland Garros, with just her face and neck appearing in the top corner. To anyone who saw this footage of her it would look like she had voluntarily agreed to it, rather than being strapped to the chair.

'You didn't need to do this, sir – not like this. You only had to ask …'

'I know I can ask, I even know I can demand. What I don't know is whether I can trust you when I'm not here. What if you change your mind, or decide to take a break? I can't control that, and I'm certainly not prepared to miss a single micro-expression on your sweet face that can be used for analysis. This way I can concentrate fully on winning, and know you are secure here for when I return.'

She sat desolate, dejected that he felt the need to do this to her, that their relationship had come to this. Ultimately, the trust between them had been destroyed.

'I need to know, Nadia. I can't live without knowing.' His words had become soft and his blue eyes were deep wells of emotion. Then they turned just as quickly to steel as he stood to leave.

'Wish me luck?'

'Good luck, Master.'

She couldn't keep up with his mood swings, so her response was automatic, though she couldn't stop the sadness from entering her voice. The weeks in Switzerland now felt like a lifetime ago. Already the nerves and tension of being with Stephan were making her feel like she'd run a marathon.

'For your sake, Nadia, let's hope this time you mean it.'

He looked down into her eyes and pinched her cheek – not too hard, but not softly either. Then he turned and strode out of the suite, leaving her to stare blankly at the giant screen as she was abandoned – again.

Past

For Caesar, the French Open was always bittersweet. For more than two decades, before every final, he had wandered through the colourful streets of Saint-Germain, past the elegant Art Nouveau buildings, where the sleepy sound of the saxophone meandered around each corner, to visit the artist who had once painted a portrait for him. It was of a beautiful young woman, smiling at the unseen person with whom she was sharing oysters and champagne at an outdoor table on a bustling Paris street. The woman's joie de vivre was captured perfectly in her emerald eyes and dazzling smile.

Her name was Ashleigh Cooper. She was the only woman Caesar had ever dared to love – though not for long. Once more he wondered why he put himself through this trip down memory lane each year, never sure if it would soothe his aching heart or fill him with fresh anguish. Regardless, he knew his legs would walk the same route each year just hours before the final of Roland Garros.

However, this year was different. This year, the artist who had painted this most treasured portrait was not there waiting for him in their usual meeting place, and it wasn't until Caesar spoke to a local that he discovered the man had moved to Malta, seeking a warmer climate in his declining years.

Without the artist there was no one to keep the precious memory alive in conversation. Any trace of Ashleigh now only existed in his own mind. So a bereft Caesar sat in a café with no oysters and no champagne, just a café noir, and remembered, all alone, the best week of his life.

It was the eve of Caesar's twenty-first birthday, the occasion when he would cross the threshold from boyhood into manhood. His Papà had hired out the Lido, the famous cabaret theatre on the Champs-Elysées, for an all-male celebration. Tony didn't place too high a value on women – aside from the obvious – and they were certainly never around when there was business to be done.

The champagne fountain burst into action as a waiter poured the first magnum of Louis Roederer Cristal into the tower of glasses assembled to catch the cascading bubbles. Surrounded by his friends, Caesar listened to the speeches of his godfathers, Clive and Gordon, as they spoke sagely of the responsibility of being born a King, and even more attentively to the speech of his Papà, whose words were all the more precious.

'My son, on this momentous occasion, the very cusp of your adult life, words cannot express the love I have for you within my heart,' Tony began, thumping the left-hand side of his chest, 'and how proud I am of your achievements at such a young age. You have exceeded all of my expectations, and I can assure you they were high.'

Even Caesar was a little astonished at the tear welling up in the corner of his father's eye, which was quickly wiped away. He had never witnessed his father in such an emotional state. Although he had never doubted for a moment just how much his father loved him, he had been raised believing that to show your feelings was to let your opponents see your weakness. He was truly humbled by his father's words, and seeing his Papà let his guard down made him cherish them all the more.

'Tonight, Paris awaits your every desire. Nothing will be denied to my only son. You will enjoy the evening, and at midnight, you will have access to the city of Paris like you never have before. For the next seven days and nights you will drink the best champagne, dine in the most expensive restaurants, sleep with the most beautiful women. The week is yours, Caesar – do what you will.'

Everyone could sense Caesar's excitement as glasses were raised in his honour.

He responded to his father simply and sincerely. 'Thank you, Papà, for my life.' Never had more fitting words been spoken.

Rarely was the Lido closed to the hordes of tourists who had occupied its seats for many decades, but tonight, the show was dedicated solely to the small group of men celebrating Caesar's coming of age. Tony invited his guests to find a seat as he and Caesar took their place in the centre booth: a proud, celebratory moment shared between father and son as the clock steadily ticked towards midnight.

Tony leant over to his son and whispered in his ear. 'Watch the show carefully, let me know which one you like best and she will be yours – for tonight, for the week, whatever you want.'

'But Papà, you can't –'

'Of course I can, and I will. It's all organised. I have chosen only the best dancers for you tonight, and believe me, my son, they are even better up close than they are onstage.'

Caesar had been acutely aware of his father's sexual bravado from a young age. Finally, he too was to become a man amongst men. He beamed with pride at the thought of pleasing his father in this way. He had been so focused on academic results, sport and making money that his experience with girls had been fairly insignificant to date – which made tonight even more special. He looked affectionately at his father and nodded.

'That's my boy.' Tony squeezed his son's shoulder and winked his approval. 'You choose first, then I'll see what I can do for your friends.'

As midnight struck, all ears were deafened by fireworks that saw the stage explode into celebration. The alluring dancers appeared from behind a wall of coloured smoke, capturing the men's attention so quickly that their jaws dropped in unison. Their

*eyes found it difficult to decide exactly where to settle – tits, arses,
legs … They, and their erections, sunk silently into the plush seats –
knowing this was going to be a very special private show.*

*The dancer just to the left of centre captivated Caesar
immediately. Though she was perfectly synchronised with the
other dancers, there was something distinctly less tacky about
her. Her legs were smooth and long, her breasts were perfectly
proportioned, and her waist accentuated her perfectly round
derrière. Yet after he had taken some time to memorise the curved
dimensions of her body, Caesar was surprised to discover that it
was her sparkling emerald eyes and warm engaging smile that held
him transfixed in his seat. It was as though the rest of the show
had disappeared from the stage, with the spotlight in his mind only
capable of shining light on this one exotic dancer before him.*

*Tony wasted no time after the show in organising for this
particular dancer to be escorted to a private room where she and
Caesar could be introduced. Caesar awaited her arrival restlessly,
pacing around the confines of the small room. He was anxious
about living up to his father's expectations of manhood, and could
do nothing to prevent the nervous tension churning in his stomach.*

*Finally the door opened, and when he saw her smile light up
the room, his heart beat loudly and his trousers stretched of their
own accord, the air momentarily sucked from his lungs. The door
closed discreetly behind her and all of the noise and festivities were
suddenly mute beyond it.*

*She told him her name was Ashleigh Cooper, she was nineteen
years old and she had been in Europe for seven months, having
left Australia to discover the world. She was vivacious, captivating,
and even more pleasing to Caesar's eye without all the stage make-
up on, just as his father had said. She acted as though she didn't
have a care in the world, enabling his nerves to melt away as the
conversation flowed freely between them. He wasn't exactly sure of*

the arrangements his father had made, but he shifted any concerns to the back of his mind. After all, it was his twenty-first birthday.

Tony had to unexpectedly fly back to London sooner than he'd planned, so he left Caesar to enjoy Paris without him. Serendipitously, Caesar was now free to spend all of his time with Ashleigh; she had conveniently been given the week off, which caused no end of friction with the other dancers. The two young lovers were inseparable in their explorations of each other and the delicious city of Paris. Spring was beckoning summer, and it was with great excitement that Caesar introduced Ashleigh to the world of tennis via Roland Garros. He was feeling every inch the powerful man his father had wanted him to become, with the most beautiful woman he had ever laid eyes on accompanying him to the sport of his dreams. It would be one of the most treasured moments of his life. He wondered what it would be like to share the rest of his life with such a warm-hearted woman: something he had never experienced in his childhood.

The week passed in a whirl of shopping, museums, art galleries, sporting events, dining, clubbing and such passionate lovemaking that they didn't care that there was no time left for sleep. They had the rest of their lives to catch up on that.

Ashleigh was awestruck by his lifestyle; for an ordinary girl from Australia, the sheer opulence of it was intoxicating.

'You live the same life as the people in those glossy magazines, Caesar. None of it seems real. It's like a fairytale.'

'Well let's make it our fairytale, and you can be my princess. I've never felt like this about anyone, Ashleigh.'

'But my world is so different from yours. My parents have never even travelled out of New South Wales, let alone to another country.'

'But look at you, Ashleigh – look at what you've accomplished on your own. I've never had to worry about feeding, clothing or housing myself. I wouldn't even know where to start.'

'You're too generous, Caesar. When you go back to London, I'm sure there'll be plenty of other women in your life.'

'No one will ever be as special as you. I'm certain of it.'

As their wonderful week together drew to a close, Caesar knew within his heart – even as a twenty-one year old who had fallen in love for the first time – that Ashleigh was the one for him.

So he made her a proposition. 'Why don't you come back to England with me so we can be together? I'll organise it with my Papà.'

She laughed at his eagerness. 'We'll see … I'm not sure how he'd respond to such a suggestion.'

'You don't know him like I do.'

'True – and certainly not like some of the other dancers …'

Caesar wondered why she doubted his words.

'We just come from different worlds, that's all.'

'It doesn't mean they can't come together. I love you, Ashleigh! We will make this happen!'

'I love you too, Caesar – and I hope and pray you're right.'

Their final embrace was long and heartfelt, his strong arms wrapped around her, never wanting to let her go. He tenderly wiped the tears from her eyes as they said their last goodbyes, and promised he'd come back for her as soon as he could. He watched as the girl of his dreams walked through the backstage entrance of the Lido and vowed to call his father as soon as he returned to his hotel.

Back in his hotel room, surrounded by the memories and scents of his activities with Ashleigh only hours earlier, he made the call to his father in London.

'Oh, no, no, no, my son. You've had your fun. I need you back here; there is much to be done.'

'But Papà, you don't understand! I'm in love with her! I need to be with her and she needs to be with me.'

'Is that so? Perhaps you should ask her what her fees might be if you were to extend your time with her another week, another month – no? Did you discuss that with her? You need to be more astute, Caesar – I expected more from you. This is not your future. She is a hooker for sale, nothing more than a transaction – and a distraction, by the sounds of things.'

His father's words were like bullets hitting his chest. Thick emotion clouded his thoughts, darkened his mind. 'I will never find anyone like her again.' He could barely whisper the words through the phone.

'Listen to me, Caesar. You're a man now, not a child. What you are saying is nonsense. Men of our kind don't let women dictate our lives and we never show weakness. To be weak is to fail. The only true love in life is that shared by the bond of blood. You for me and me for you. That is it; nothing else is important in this world, certainly not some cheap little slut who dances in a club. This is a fleeting feeling you have – what do they call it? Puppy love. That's all. It will fade, you will meet another girl next week and the week after that and so on. In a month's time you won't even remember her name. She will be forgotten, history.'

Caesar felt suffocated by his father's words, Tony's cruel dismissal of Ashleigh crushing his dreams for their future together.

'Caesar?'

'Yes, Papà?' he responded on autopilot.

'The last thing I need is for you to become infatuated with some young hussy who shares the same name as a 1950s Australian tennis player. It's over. I want you back in London tonight. Make sure you are.'

The line disconnected and Caesar was left staring vacantly out the window.

For the first and only time in his life, Caesar had experienced his father's wrath. He had heard it directed at others many times, but *never at him, Tony's adored son. He had been conditioned over the years to recognise his father's commands as final; it was the way his life worked. Though he was tormented by conflicting emotions, he dutifully packed the last of his clothes into his designer suitcase and called for a porter.*

Just as he was about to close the door behind him, he walked determinedly over to the desk and quickly scrawled a note to Ashleigh on the hotel stationery.

I must leave Paris tonight. I will never forget our week
together. I promise I will return for you, my first love, my
true love. You will be in my heart forever.

Caesar

The words he had written made his throat catch. He was not used to expressing his feelings in speech, let alone in written form. He sealed the envelope, addressed it to Ashleigh Cooper and asked the hotel concierge to have it delivered personally to the Lido. The substantial tip would ensure its priority over any other errand.

When Caesar returned to London and tried to convince his father about Ashleigh, it was the first time they didn't see eye to eye. Caesar was desperate to have Ashleigh in his life on a permanent basis and his father stubbornly refused to listen, citing the same reasons he had on the phone. Caesar became concerned when he hadn't heard from Ashleigh since returning to London so as soon as his Papà went to America on business, Caesar returned to Paris to see Ashleigh again and confirm his love for her – regardless of his Papà.

There was no sign of Ashleigh whatsoever, it was as though she didn't exist. No forwarding address, no contact details … He spoke to the other dancers and all he discovered was that she left suddenly not long after their week together and never returned. The manager was no help saying girls in this business come and go like passing ships and assured him there were plenty more fish in the sea. That was the last thing he wanted to hear! It was as though she had disappeared into thin air.

Caesar was beside himself and found himself wandering the streets of Paris for hours as though she might miraculously appear. All he had was one photograph of their time together and he asked random strangers whether they had seen her – to no avail. In his despair he found an artist to paint a portrait of his only photo in an attempt to keep her vibrant and alive in his mind. Reluctantly he returned to London – again – without his beloved Ashleigh, having no clue in the world what had happened to her. He felt like he was grieving for a love that was never fulfilled. For years he did what he could to find her, without any assistance from his Papà – who refused to discuss it any further – but it was like trying to find a needle in a global haystack.

Countless times he asked himself what he could have possibly done to make her not want to see him again, but he could never pinpoint anything. Eventually, he put it down to his own inexperience with women. And though he had had many experiences with women since, none of them ever compared with the way he'd felt when he was with Ashleigh. She was his one experience of true love and he never wanted to believe it was any different for her. But as the weeks turned into months and the months into years and the years passed, so did any hope of their future together …

Caesar pushed his now-cold coffee away, along with all thoughts of the past. How could he be disappointed with a degree in Mathematics from Oxford and the ever-expanding King empire? By all accounts, he had done exceptionally well for himself!

He left some change on the table, and walked away from the café and Saint-Germain, finally letting go of the cherished memories he'd harboured for so many years. Time had moved on, and so should he. Besides, he had love interests other than his own to keep him more than occupied over the coming months – with significant financial benefits.

With that, Caesar made his way to Roland Garros in a sombre mood, hoping the final would lift his spirits. Although he was disappointed that Nadia wouldn't be joining him to watch the epic final as he'd come to expect, he understood that she had just returned from a Swiss spa after taking ill, and was pleased Stephan was clearly looking after her well.

So with champagne aplenty, he welcomed his other guests to his suite for the final of his bittersweet slam, knowing he stood to gain handsomely whatever the result.

He knew better than anyone how much the next three grand slams meant to these two players – over and above the trophy. And the tension was at fever pitch!

Scream

Nadia woke to a static screen, her body stiff and aching from being tied to the chair for so long. She had no idea whether the French Open final was over and had to assume something had gone awry with the technology. Nor did she know how long she had dozed off for; it could have been just minutes, or many hours. The last thing she could remember was the match level at two sets each, and both men holding serve at the beginning of the fifth when the first raindrops of the tournament turned into an unexpected downpour. Both players were shuffled off court for what felt like an eternity. During the seemingly never-ending broadcast repeats of other games she had no interest in, she must have fallen asleep in the chair.

Had they recommenced play? Had it been deferred? She couldn't believe she was trapped here without knowing whether play had been resumed, and if it had, the final result.

What if Stephan had lost and never came back for her? What if he'd won but wasn't happy with her micro-expressions during the match? Panic took over as she attempted to shuffle the chair towards the phone. But her jagged movements only served to tip it sideways, and she hit her head on the edge of the table as she and the chair fell to the floor.

* * *

The lights flashed on, blinding her. As she came to, her chair was being righted and she found herself face to face with Stephan. He remained silent, his face unreadable as she also attempted to stare back impassively; neither wanted to give their thoughts away to the other. Her head ached.

Garry was racing around the bedroom, collecting her things as quickly as he could and shoving them into her suitcase, then exited the suite with the case in tow.

Eventually, Stephan just shook his head apathetically.

'What to do with you, my delicate, petite bird?' he asked rhetorically as he stood behind her, his fingers massaging her shoulders and neck as she remained strapped to the chair. 'I can't bear to be away from you – but you need your wings clipped, you still need to be taught a few lessons.'

His fingers pressed harder into her neck and her pulse quickened. They both knew he had the strength to break it with one quick twist and she couldn't do anything to prevent it, still strapped to the chair. Her breath became shallow; she didn't dare utter a sound.

'Such a shame. What we had was so near perfect.' He looked forlorn as he knelt down before her, his hands opening her legs and caressing her thighs, while he sniffed her scent loudly and deeply before exhaling. 'And you had to ruin it by allowing

313

Levique into your life like a toxic weed – making me weak with the fear of losing you.'

His grip tightened like a vice, his fingers digging even more forcefully into her tender flesh. '*You* did this to me! *You* created this conundrum.'

She bit into her lip to stifle a moan and tensed her legs to push the pain away.

'It hurts, doesn't it, my sweet? To be treated this way … But you know you deserve it, after what you've done to me.' His fingers sunk savagely into her inner thighs, knowing his imprint would turn her pale skin purple within hours.

'Aarghh!' She screamed into the room as he twisted and pinched her sensitive skin.

'That's right, Nadia, scream. Let it out, just as I wanted you to do in the dungeon. It excites me to hear you like this, whether from unbridled pain or pleasure – I don't mind which.' He shook his head in dismay. 'You know you need to be punished for what you did.' He retracted his grip and instead teased her opening with his expert fingers. Then he stopped momentarily. 'Or maybe I have it all wrong. Maybe it's *Levique* who needs to be punished … or just happen to have an unfortunate accident.'

He seemed to be seriously contemplating the possibilities this option presented. 'Our picture would be perfect without him to deface it … and that might just solve all our problems, mightn't it, my sweet?'

Nadia saw the violence in his eyes and despaired about where this line of thought might lead.

'No, sir, please!' she panted as he increased the speed of his tormenting fingers. 'Let's not make this about him!'

'Oh, but it *is* about him, we both know it is.'

For the first time Nadia wondered whether Noah had in fact won the match, which would more than explain Stephan's mood and behaviour. If Stephan had been defeated, he had everything to lose – including her, come Wimbledon.

As much as she tried to bury her arousal, he had such perfect control over her body that her mind had no say. She was putty in his hands as he manipulated and played, forcing her to give in to the pleasure.

'Ahh ...'

'A car accident ... no, a stabbing perhaps ... That would work; it's not as if obsessive fans haven't gone to those lengths before in this game.'

'No! You wouldn't! *Please* don't talk like that!' Nadia was desperately trying to regain control of her mind and ignore the imminent eruption between her legs by focusing on the fury in his eyes. Eyes that seemed to have left reality behind and were conjuring all sorts of dangerous scenarios. So much so that the smirk on his face looked positively evil, not of this world.

Fear and arousal spiked within her body and she was held hostage, awaiting his next move.

'That's it! It is *Levique* who will be punished, permanently removed from the game, and he will never know why. Then he can never become Number One. And you will be mine, again. No one else will go near you – ever! Threat obliterated.' His eyes were ferocious.

'God, no! Please, Master – sir – listen to me!' She was squirming to dislodge his hand but it was useless, and she couldn't help but moan as she stuttered out the words amid his sexual ambush. 'I will do anything, absolutely anything you ask of me. Treat me how you want. Punish me like I deserve to be punished. Like I should have been punished in the first place,' her whimpering voice pitifully pleaded. 'I am your possession, to do with as you choose. I am yours, in every way. I promise you, I promise you. I will do anything you ask of me, follow your every command. I belong to you ...'

Her voice was high-pitched and imploring as tears sprang from her eyes as from an untapped well.

He looked at her, devoid of all emotion.

'Then prove it to me, my sweet, once and for all.'

His fingers triggered her release on cue, causing her body to spasm violently against her constraints. In no time he had unbuttoned his trousers, to penetrate her mouth with his fully erect and throbbing cock. Tugging her nipple with one hand and twisting her mane of hair with the other – his preferred style these days – he pushed himself further into her throat, ensuring she took all of him, suppressing her paradoxical cries as her loins pulsed with lingering pleasure.

After the sounds of his own release had permeated the room, he freed Nadia from the chair and assisted her to the bathroom, pacing impatiently while she used the toilet and washed her hands. Her legs were so unsteady beneath her that Stephan supported her as they headed out of the suite to the goods lift, and out a discreet back entrance to an awaiting car. He hadn't spoken another word to her.

And she was regrettably none the wiser as to who had won the French Open. Though she could hazard a guess, she was certainly not brave enough to risk asking the question.

WIMBLEDON II
June–July

Confinement

When Stephan and his entourage arrived at the luxurious manor house at Wimbledon SW19, it was abundantly clear that Nadia's wings had been devastatingly severed. Her room was located in the attic and contained only a single bed and a bedside table topped with a lamp. She could only stand at the apex of the ceiling, and if she extended her arms she could touch both walls of the A-shaped room. The locked windows had no curtains or blinds and overlooked the grass tennis court on which Stephan would spend hours training. Other than a small bathroom containing a toilet and hand basin, nothing else was located on the third level of the manor house. There was no need for a wardrobe, since all of her belongings had been taken away, leaving her with only the items of clothing Stephan made available to her, if at all.

Nadia watched in silence as Stephan painstakingly went through every pocket in her clothes. 'So, what do we have here? Did you make a new friend while you were away?'

'No, Master. She just gave me her card before I left.'

'A psychologist, no less! Why would she do that, Nadia? Did she manage to help you with your compulsion to lie?'

Nadia shook her head, not liking where this was going at all.

'If I hear your voice speaking to a human being other than me, I will burn you, just like this card.'

He reached for a match from the mantelpiece and took great delight in watching Nadia wince as he burnt Jayne's business card before her eyes.

'I hope for your sake you didn't mention my name. Because that would cause you endless suffering. Have I made myself clear, my sweet?'

He flicked the last embers away from his fingers, leaving the stench of burning paper in the air, reinforcing that her entire world consisted of him – the rest had literally gone up in smoke.

'Abundantly, Master.' She could only pray that Jayne wouldn't try to contact her or disclose any details of their discussions. She couldn't bear to think of the repercussions.

Stephan pinned copies of her new schedule to her bedroom wall and bathroom door. It was to be followed precisely. Any deviation from the rules would result in her being swiftly punished and left confined in the darkened basement: something she had no desire to experience for a second. As she looked at her Master's stringent requirements a significant part of her died. She existed only because he allowed her to exist and his approval was now her lifeblood.

Rules & Daily Regime

✤ *Kneel in the presence of your Master at all times, arms behind back.*
✤ *No music or dancing at any time.*
✤ *Eat as commanded.*
✤ *Drink as commanded.*
✤ *Do not speak unless requested.*
✤ *Do not move unless requested.*

❖ No *verbal* or *non-verbal communication with others* –
  whatsoever!

4.30am
Wake up. Eat two slices of plain bread (left in room the
night before). Drink one glass of water.

5am
Basement. Pain.

6.30am
Confinement.

7.30am
Shower.

8am
Breakfast.

9am
Attend to tasks (assigned daily).

11am
Work out in gym. Laps in pool.

1pm
Lunch (kneeling).

2pm
Locked in attic room (good behaviour) or restrained in
basement (poor behaviour).

4pm
Humiliation.

5pm
Yoga.

7pm
Dinner.

8pm
Master's pleasure.

9.30pm
Sleep.

He wondered why he hadn't taken this approach with her before; it suited him so well. Her schedule coordinated perfectly with his training regime, and his list of rules allowed him absolute power over her life. Nothing mattered other than her meeting his demands and expectations – and as far as he was concerned, that was exactly as it should be.

Stephan's staff knew better than to raise an eyebrow, let alone an objection to his treatment of Nadia, aware that their jobs would be terminated in an instant if they did. A few had already experienced his wrath first-hand. Stephan was a firm believer in Mao's principle of 'Execute one, educate a thousand', and it seemed to have worked well for him. Those who remained justified his actions by reminding themselves they had heard Nadia consent to his depravities again and again. She seemed to willingly accept whatever he demanded of her – so it wasn't their business to make a moral judgment.

As the days and weeks passed Stephan took her how and when he wanted her, and locked her away in any number of inventive ways when he didn't. He had never been more creative or motivated, physically or psychologically. After her arrival, her bare room was decorated daily with more and more photos of car crashes, broken limbs, bloodshed and other accidents as a constant reminder of the promise she had made to him in Paris – and the fate that would befall Noah if she didn't submit to his every whim.

Although Noah was far away from her – physically and emotionally – his potential fate at Stephan's hands was all she had to focus on to survive the daily drill of her life. So she applied herself with stoic discipline, knowing that if Stephan was pleased with her behaviour, she and Noah would both survive.

As indicated on her list of rules, at 9am each day he set her a task that needed to be completed within a certain timeframe. If it wasn't done to his satisfaction – and some of them were near impossible –

it would affect the food she ate (or didn't), the clothes she wore (or didn't), and the time she spent in confinement in the basement or tied to the bed. It would most certainly detract from the time she spent in the gym or pool or doing yoga – which provided her only sources of solace.

A private tour of the Tower of London inspired the medieval regime Stephan had devised for his beloved Nadia. From his perspective, the pillory he'd had placed in the basement proved useful for so many activities each day – humiliation, pleasure, pain release – that he wondered why he hadn't used one before. So many opportunities could be explored with such a handy piece of equipment.

Nadia was never exposed to technology of any kind – Stephan had essentially ensured she was living in the dark ages – so there was no opportunity for her to ever see or hear mention of Noah Levique, who always seemed to be figuratively nipping at his ankles in the press like a persistent puppy.

For Nadia, it was relentless, shameful and humiliating, and almost sent her to the brink of hysteria. Her wounds reflected his anger and would often be as raw as her beaten heart. Stephan's mood swings now bordered on bipolar, with enormous highs and frightening lows, and she did the best she could to protect her heart from emotion and numb her mind against feeling pain. She could only hope that as long as she complied with Stephan's wishes, Noah was safe from harm.

Even through all this, her body was so finely attuned to his touch it rendered her mind irrelevant. Some days he was so gentle, kind and loving it left her in a puddle of tears, desperate to cling to his touch – her only connection to the world. Other days it sounded like demons were being expelled from her body, she screamed and cried so hard, leaving her depleted and drained. Stephan enjoyed those days the most and rewarded her for such cathartic release, ensuring her body succumbed to the pleasure he offered thereafter. Either way, it was exhausting and intense for Nadia – which was just how Stephan planned for it to be up until Wimbledon commenced.

He took many photos of her during their time together at the manor house, in various situations of pain, pleasure and humiliation. Then he would share them with her and stick them up on the wall so she could analyse them and write detailed descriptions about what she had been feeling and why, which he would then scrutinise – agreeing or disagreeing with her thought processes and advising her of any modifications required to her behaviour. It was on this basis that he rated her overall progress – or lack thereof.

To ensure she was listening attentively to his views, he made her write *them* down as well, which sometimes meant she didn't sleep so she could meet his demands and deadlines. Her hand ached and her head spun from the amount of writing required of her. It proved to him that she was becoming fully aligned to his way of thinking and finally losing her own sense of self – some would call it brainwashing – which was exactly his intention. He wanted her to become addicted to the pain so she would beg for pleasure, both of which only he could bestow on her, and only when she pleased him. This was his goal for her life, the sole reason she existed in the world.

Stephan firmly believed that by the time he won Wimbledon, she would be completely reborn to become exactly what he wanted her to be: a specifically designed masochistic submissive – his perfect possession. It was everything he'd ever wanted in the world, and under no circumstances would he be sharing his creation with anyone.

Each night Stephan slept soundly, more confident in his tennis supremacy, knowing that Nadia was under his complete control and being moulded day by day to his precise requirements. Each night Nadia slept restlessly, if at all – tied and trapped within his world, but desperately hoping Noah was safe from his clutches. She would live through this hell for him.

Death

The lead-up to Wimbledon was Caesar's favourite time of year. The London summer meant garden parties offering strawberries and cream, and Pimm's and lemonade. His friends and associates travelled from various corners of the world to attend his glamorous soirées, at which many business deals were brokered, providing an almost endless list of opportunities to investigate for the next year.

It was when he was hosting a champagne breakfast for the twelve members of Club Zero a week before Wimbledon commenced that Caesar received the devastating news that his Papà had just passed away. Tony had apparently woken in the dead of night, wandered around the house and stumbled down the stairs towards the cellar. Given the instability of his legs and his deteriorated mental state, he'd fallen and cracked his head after tripping on a wrought-iron ring protruding from jagged brickwork. The poor man hadn't been found by his nurse until the next morning. It was a shocking accident, even if it had taken his life only a little earlier than anticipated by the Alzheimer's. Caesar felt the full force of grief at his father's departure from this world, leaving him with no other living relative.

So on the day that should have seen him entertaining hundreds of guests at a garden party, Caesar instead found himself immersed in arrangements for the funeral of the great Antonio 'Tony' King. He was touched by the messages of condolence that came in from all over the globe, and intrigued by some that didn't – particularly from one of his godfathers.

When he still hadn't heard from Gordon by the next morning, he picked up the phone himself rather than outsourcing the task to his personal assistant, which was his usual habit.

He listened intently as Gordon explained that he and Tony had had an irrevocable falling-out many, many years ago, though he didn't go into specific details. Caesar was surprised he hadn't picked up on this before now, but given the pace of his life, the years seemed to tick by all too quickly, and he realised he hadn't actually seen Gordon in decades. He couldn't fathom what could possibly have caused the rift between the two once-great friends, but invited Gordon to the funeral regardless. He also let him know that under the provisions left with Tony's lawyers, both Caesar's godfathers were requested to be present at the reading of Tony's will. He told Gordon that he would appreciate catching up with him some time even if he didn't feel he could attend either event.

The funeral was elaborate and state-like, as one would expect from the King family. Dancers, tennis players, gamblers, businesspeople, and dignitaries and celebrities of all kinds attended to show their support for Caesar and be photographed by the tabloids. The number of people who came along to pay their respects to his great Papà overwhelmed even Caesar himself. The details of Antonio King's funeral had been deposited with the lawyers many years ago, from the requiem mass to the elaborate memorial beneath which he wished to be buried in the corner of his estate in Sussex. Unfortunately the law of today prohibited his burial on this land, which caused a few delays, but fortunately provisions in the event of such an issue enabled his body to be cremated instead, so his ashes could rest within the designated marble structure. Caesar felt settled within himself that he had followed his father's instructions to the letter, so that Tony could now rest in peace exactly as he would have wished.

It was after the interment of the ashes, attended only by Caesar, Clive and Tony's lawyer, that Tony's will was to be read out. After the men had made their slow way back to the house, Caesar noticed

Gordon arrive. He had aged considerably from the handsome man Caesar remembered from his twenties, which was to be expected, he supposed.

'I'm so very sorry for the loss of your Papà, Caesar.'

'Thank you for coming, Gordon. I appreciate it.'

The men shook hands respectfully and patted one another on the back.

'I'm not sure what you have to do with my father's will after so long, but I suppose we'll find out soon enough. The others are in here; let me get you a whisky. *I* certainly need one after the week I've had.'

The four men sat in the huge mahogany office situated in the corner of the mansion, overlooking the rolling hills of the estate and in full view of Antonio King's memorial. Caesar smiled at the thought of his father seated in such a magnificent study in his younger days, making money and controlling the world – and envisaging his own final resting place. He was never one to leave any stone unturned – and Caesar had tried to follow his lead. As Caesar reflected on his upbringing, great sadness descended on him at the fragility of life.

Caesar, Gordon and Clive seated themselves in stuffed leather armchairs with whisky in hand waiting for Tony's lawyer, who was seated behind the grand desk, spectacles resting on his nose, about to read the last will and testament of the late Antonio Alfredo King.

In essence, everything had been left to Caesar, so there were no surprises in the will – except for one letter that was left to Gordon. It was after the others had left, and Gordon was alone with Caesar, that the whole basis of Caesar's life was overturned.

Gordon read the letter outlining the agreement he had made with Tony more than two decades ago, and therefore knew that his first job was to pour Caesar another whisky: the first of many that would see this day turn into a long night. The letter exposed a side of Caesar's Papà he had never known existed, and one that had caused the irrevocable rift with his godfather.

The evidence was irrefutable. Tony had organised Ashleigh Cooper's deportation back to Australia the same night Caesar returned to London. Gordon explained to him that men had collected her from the Lido after her performance that night and she had been placed on the next flight back to Australia. Tony had made it abundantly clear to all involved that this woman should irretrievably disappear from their lives.

Ashleigh had sent letter after letter from Australia to Caesar at his London address – all of which had been intercepted and subsequently destroyed by Tony. This was what Gordon and Tony had fought about: his godfather had believed Caesar had a right to know; Tony hadn't.

'I begged your father to give them to you, but he wouldn't hear of it. He believed she was a distraction you didn't need in your life. He said she wasn't your destiny. And the more successful you became in business, the more he believed his convictions had been vindicated. You know what he was like: even if he doubted the decision he made, he'd never admit he got it wrong to anyone. Eventually the letters stopped arriving ...'

Immediately the blood drained from Caesar's face, words eluding him: a first for the great man of business.

Then he found his tongue again. '*How could you not tell me this?*' His fists balled with fury.

'Now, wait a minute – just hold on. You know what happened when someone disagreed with your father. I was his best friend, and look what happened between *us*! We argued for days about this. So much so, it destroyed our relationship. He wanted me out of your lives and we eventually agreed that only upon his death could I discuss it with you. I was instantly cut off from him and from you; he made sure of it. And he successfully made sure we never spoke another word – until after his death.'

Caesar collapsed into the deep burgundy leather chair, the love he had had for his father transformed into the rage of the scorned. He found it incomprehensible that his so-called beloved Papà – whom he had trusted more than anyone on earth – had organised for Ashleigh to be eradicated from his life. How could he have done that to his only son, and why?

Gordon took a sensitive approach in explaining the entire situation to an utterly devastated Caesar. 'You know your father was a proud man, Caesar, who seldom showed his weaknesses or vulnerabilities. We had many arguments over his decision to keep you away from your first love.'

'Not only my first; she was my *only* love. There has been no one else. There *will* be no one else ...' As he said the words out loud the pain of never seeing Ashleigh again was etched on his face. 'You know he called it "puppy love" at the time? Told me that I'd forget her name and face in a month and move on ... But I never did. I've often wondered if she ever thought of me afterwards ...' He laughed a cruel, hard laugh. 'Papà thought she was a whore, and I could never understand why he said that. But he didn't know her like I did. She was only working at the Lido because she loved to dance; she said she felt free when she was onstage.'

'You were so young at the time; Tony wanted you to focus on business, on the real world. And no one can deny how successful you've been, Caesar. You've gone way beyond even your father's expectations.'

'Only from a financial perspective. Gordon, you have a wife and four kids, you have a family that loves you. You wouldn't trade that, would you – for money? You would never have done something as cruel as this!'

327

Gordon shook his head slowly. 'No, I wouldn't – and don't get me wrong, family life can be hard at times, but when you have that bond between you, nothing in life is more important; you'd do anything to protect them. And maybe in his own way Tony thought he was protecting *you* …'

'Protecting me from what? A nineteen-year-old woman? Love? I was his family, his only family! *How could he?* I just don't understand …' Caesar wept. 'And now I don't even have *that*. I have nothing but material wealth on the outside, and emptiness on the inside.'

Gordon refilled his tumbler from the crystal decanter while Caesar absentmindedly flicked through the papers and files forming part of his father's will, as if searching for any additional pieces of the morbid puzzle.

'You know, I tried to make myself interested in other women, but it was always so forced, nothing compared with Ashleigh. Every time I travel to Australia I look her up, just in case I missed something all those years ago, some clue that might reveal her whereabouts. Between searching in Australia and reminiscing at the French Open, where we spent our one glorious week together, she is always in the back of my mind. It sounds silly, I know. It was so long ago it even sounds ridiculous to me. Imagine if my father could hear me now, in his own house!'

'Perhaps if your father could have heard you speak this way, he might have regretted his decision – but we can't change the past, I'm afraid. When I think back now with more wisdom in my years, I realise he was scared of losing you, threatened by the thought that you might fall in love with someone else. He'd never known a woman he trusted in his life – ever. He had you, and only you. And he only saw you willing to risk your future for someone you just met. And we both know he had grand plans for your future.'

As Caesar's fingers continued rifling through the files, he came upon the note he had left with the concierge to deliver to the Lido all those years ago. His father must have blocked all means of communication before Caesar had even left Paris! Holding the note he'd assumed she had received and chosen to ignore brought back all his intense feelings for the only woman he had ever loved – flooding him simultaneously with anger and remorse. He broke down, kneeling wretched on the floor as gargantuan sobs racked his body. He felt as though his Papà were crushing him with his bare hands.

Gordon stood next to him, feeling the enormity of regret at the decisions made more than two decades ago, and wondered whether Tony would have chosen the same path of obstinate intervention if he could have seen his powerful, wealthy and successful son right now, so desolate, alone and bereft.

Investigation

The three days after his father's funeral were a blur for Caesar. There had not been a single day when he hadn't worked in the last twenty years, but for the first time in his life he allowed himself to do nothing but wallow in misery. He hadn't left his father's estate since the reading of the will, just wandered around in his dressing gown, unshaven and dishevelled. He had no appetite for food, but needed more whisky every time he thought about Ashleigh and pined for what could have been had his father not been the tyrant he'd turned out to be. There were no summer parties, no placements of bets or transfers of funds, no business transactions and certainly no thought about, let alone excitement for, the commencement of Wimbledon.

But what finally triggered Caesar's restoration from the depths of despair was Gordon's arrival back at the house. Gordon suggested that if he was still so miserable about the turn of events, it might be worthwhile trying to locate Ashleigh one more time. Although Caesar stubbornly dismissed the idea, Gordon knew that the small spark he'd seen glisten in Caesar's eye would eventually spur him into action. If he had inherited one thing from his father, it was his unmitigated tenacity when an idea took hold.

Within twenty-four hours, Caesar had eaten, slept, showered, shaved, dressed and assembled a team of private investigators to scour the globe for the only woman on earth he had dared to love, more than half a lifetime ago. By the end of the briefing in Tony's study, everyone on the investigating team was perfectly clear about two things: there was to be no stone left unturned and there was to be no expense spared. Although most of them had worked for Caesar many times over the years, they had never seen him so determined to achieve the result he was after, to find his Ashleigh. He needed to put his mind, and heart, to rest once and for all.

So it was that he found himself on a long-haul flight to Sydney less than seventy-two hours later. To his absolute delight, Ashleigh was alive and well. His investigators had discovered that Ashleigh Cooper was now Ashleigh Ryan, and had recently relocated to Sydney's Northern Beaches with her two children, Jennifer, eleven, and David, eight, to accept a job as instructor at the local dance academy. She had been married, but her husband had died four years ago in a horrific mining accident in the Hunter Valley, when an internal wall collapsed deep within a mineshaft and he was crushed to death along with three workmates.

Caesar was so nervous about actually meeting Ashleigh again that it took him almost the entire plane journey to Australia to decide on the best way to approach her after more than twenty years. What if she didn't even remember who he was and he had flown halfway around the world to rekindle memories that only existed in his own mind? It took every ounce of his considerable confidence to convince himself that if he had come this far, he needed to see it through. So just before he touched down at Sydney International Airport, he made a decision to keep things simple.

Once he was through Customs he had his executive assistant organise a beautiful bunch of flowers – fleurs-de-lys – to be delivered to her after her last class, and attached the original note he'd sent to the Lido after the last time they laid eyes on each other – the same one his father had made sure she never received!

After watching the florist's van arrive to deliver his gift to the dance studio, he waited anxiously further down the suburban street within the safety of his hired black Mercedes. He broke into a spontaneous sweat as he saw children jump and skip out of the building at the end of the class, to be collected by their hurried parents.

Though he was used to controlling everything in his world with an iron fist, he had to force himself out of the car to follow through on his plan, telling the driver to stay in position until he returned. As he walked over to what looked suspiciously like an old scout hall, he couldn't remember a time when he'd felt more nervous. His heart was pounding violently in his chest as even more children bounced by, utterly oblivious to the fact that he was putting his heart on the line like never before.

Parents looked strangely at his posh attire as he fidgeted awkwardly with his lapels. He felt like he'd just stepped out of a play, compared with the casual beachside apparel of the Australians. He noted that board shorts, T-shirts and short skirts seemed to be the norm, even in winter, as he loosened his cravat, unsure whether it was due to heat or nerves.

Caesar was not a man who was used to the unexpected in life, and he had never felt more out of his comfort zone! He was accustomed to a certain level of luxury, and this all seemed completely alien to him – so much so that he was too flustered even to peek in the door.

Just as he'd told himself it might all be too much, Ashleigh herself came out of the doorway and stood before him, holding the flowers and the note she'd just read, as beautiful as ever with her lean dancer's body and sparkling emerald eyes. They locked onto one another's eyes for a few moments, lost for words and consumed by memories. Tears slipped from the eyes of both as they spontaneously embraced, never wanting to let go.

It was like nothing Caesar had dared to imagine. This moment alone made life worth living once more. He had discovered the love of his life all over again, and this time he would never let her go!

They touched and gazed in awe, as if checking it was all really happening, before words came rushing out.

'Caesar! I can't believe it's actually you, after all these years!'

'I thought you would have forgotten me, Ashleigh.'

'Never! I tried to contact you *so* many times!'

'I know. I left you this note that last afternoon in Paris, but you never received it …' He indicated the message attached to the flowers.

'Your father didn't want us to be together …'

'He's just passed away. I only just discovered what happened. I'm so deeply sorry …'

'You're *really* here, right now! I feel like I'm dreaming!'

'I've never forgotten you, not for a single day.'

'You look amazing …'

'You're perfect, you always have been.'

Caesar passed the next week oblivious to Wimbledon and anything that might be occurring in Britain; it just wasn't important. He spent every waking hour getting to know Ashleigh again and catching up on her life. He apologised profusely, over and over again, for his father's actions, to which she replied that there was no need. They were together again and that was all that mattered.

For the next week they were mesmerised by each other's company, rebuilding their relationship as for the first time Caesar experienced the world through the eyes of a single mother and her two wonderful children. It was busy work, with barely a moment's breathing time: a stark contrast to his own life, which was also busy but in a pampered, hedonistic way. Holding down a full-time job and looking after two growing children was exhausting – which was why he felt so surprised that it was one of the best weeks he had spent in his life.

Amidst the chaos there was love, laughter and lots of hugs. An unbreakable bond united Ashleigh and her two kids, just like the one Gordon had described. Caesar had never experienced anything like it in his all-male world, and to have been invited in to share this world was the greatest privilege he had ever been granted – one that no money could buy.

Their time together confirmed to him that his twenty-one-year-old self had chosen well. Ashleigh was a wonderful mother, whom her children adored, and a beautiful woman, inside and out. Caesar thanked his lucky stars he'd gone through with his plan, for to miss out on meeting up with Ashleigh again would have been to miss out on his sole chance at happiness.

It was only on their last night together that Ashleigh and Caesar shared a bed, revelling in their reignited passion and reacquainting themselves with each other's now more mature and experienced bodies. Though time and continents had come between them, it was as if they'd never been apart. Both knew they would never allow such a separation again.

Caesar had never felt such happiness; Ashleigh had never felt so found. It was a magical time for both as he came to understand that his previously colourful life was subdued compared with the joy of being part of a real family.

Caesar had told Ashleigh regretfully that he had to be back in London for the Wimbledon men's final. They reluctantly withdrew from each other's embrace at Kingsford Smith Airport, but with the knowledge that they would soon be reunited on the other side of the world. Caesar had already arranged for the family of three to travel first-class to New York to join him for the US Open. He was counting the days already as he took off over Sydney with a tear in his eye.

The unimaginable had happened … She still loved him as much as he loved her, even after all these years. Suddenly he was a passionate, reconfirmed believer in love at first sight!

Plans

Noah couldn't believe how cathartic he found running these days. His legs felt stronger as they powered uphill, his stamina greater as he clocked up professional marathon times, his mind unclouded and focused.

He was going to win Wimbledon. Nothing had been clearer or more obvious to him in his life. He could feel it in every part of his body and it felt like the universe was conspiring with him to make it happen. He only had one more man to beat to be the best in the world.

It was this knowledge that had kept him so motivated during his training. There was no doubt or fear, just the simple understanding that all of this was meant to be. He had never been more in the zone when he arrived in England, as if the rest of the world blurred while his own vision remained sharp. His team had never seen anything like it, and did everything to encourage this seemingly transcendental state.

The only moment his avid determination had faltered was when he'd witnessed Stephan, looking as suave and regal as he ever had, officially opening the Gentlemen's Championships as the defending champion. Noah's gaze had shifted from the formal proceedings to scan for any sign of Eloise, hopeful that she might also be in attendance. But his search had proved useless; she was nowhere to be seen. Her absence had only served to ignite the fire in his belly, a fire that wouldn't be extinguished until after he'd won the final.

He was ready. He had beaten the monster to claim the French title and he had every intention of doing the same here. Losing was not an option, and he hoped beyond hope that it would mean Eloise would then be safe from harm.

This was the first time his Australian mother and French father were sitting together in his player's box for the entire tournament, which made him smile. He was surprised to discover they were heading to Spain together for a holiday after the final – wonders would never cease! He knew they'd be proud whatever the outcome, but first and foremost he was playing for his grandmother. Before his first match he silently prayed, thanking his nan for helping him to believe in himself, and for instilling in him values such as compassion and understanding, instead of a desire for material possessions. She'd even sent him a message in Rome right before she died, encouraging him to do his very best. Thanks to her, Noah knew that true happiness came from richness of life, not the accumulation of assets. As he thought these things, he could almost sense her calling him back to her homeland to say goodbye, as soon as Wimbledon was over.

Life had been good to him and he felt truly blessed. He was emotionally grounded, mentally focused and physically prepared – he was ready, even excited, for the battle of his life!

As he progressed through the rounds he was at the top of his game. It was as though his body were insulated from pain, and his shots had the speed and precision of missiles. Crowds watched in awe as the young half Aussie, half Frenchman annihilated each and every one of his opponents, in the most gentlemanly of ways. His fan base had swollen in the past few months. Some put it down to his ethnicity, but most agreed he was a genuinely gracious person, and a wonderful role model for kids. Social media published statistics on how much time the top ten players spent meeting fans and signing autographs – complete with a table indicating average time per autograph. Noah was always top of the leader board, spending up to half an hour with fans at the end of each match he played, with a 3.2-second signature time. (Others – particularly Stephan – preferred to be seen but not touched, spending as little as three minutes with fans before disappearing back into their own luxurious lives.) It was no wonder that when Noah posted something it often recorded more than eighty thousand likes. He had reached the big time, and they loved him – and so did The Edge, as he was increasingly in demand for endorsements and sponsorships, which lined everybody's pockets.

He focused on his matches and his alone until the finals. It was only then that he learnt of a distracted Nordstrom, struggling at times through four-set matches: something that this time last year had been unheard of from the supreme master.

* * *

Stephan was relieved beyond belief when he secured his ticket to the final; it had certainly proved to be more of a fight than he'd expected. He was now so infatuated with his own insular world that he found it difficult to determine whether it was due to his own declining form, or the improved performance of his opponents. Either way, this was his last opportunity to keep Nadia in his life according to Caesar's rules. For if he lost the final, he would lose everything.

Fortunately, he had plans in place to mitigate any risk of losing her should the unthinkable happen. So, win or lose, their future together was secure. Not that he honestly believed losing was an option.

His smile was sinister with the secret knowledge of how his plans had fallen into place when the perfect tiny property became available on Lake Ekoln, in his native Sweden. It was frozen and isolated in winter, and only accessible by boat in summer. It would be Nadia's little private island, and he'd already commenced plans to make it entirely escape-proof. No one else would ever know she was there, only him, and he couldn't think of a more beautiful spot for his Nadia to spend the rest of her life, the length of which would be his choice, depending on whether she pleased him – or not. He decided not to share this news with her just yet, preferring to keep it as a surprise until he had the trophy safely in his hands.

He couldn't wait to see the look on her face when she first saw her new home: the only one she'd ever lay eyes on for the rest of her days. Though he never cared for visiting his parents, no one would ask questions about the time he spent in Uppsala, the town where they lived, which just happened to be the closest city to the lake.

Kipling

The final of the gentlemen's singles arrived. It was a perfect summer's day with not a cloud in sight. The birds were singing and the roof remained open to reveal a brilliantly blue sky. Bright yellow cans of balls were unsealed and checked by the umpire. Ball boys and girls looked smart in their navy-blue outfits. The linespeople were pristine in their piped navy blazers and cream trousers or skirts. All surfaces seemed to have been scrubbed so clean they glistened for the cameras. Wimbledon was aglow.

The smart-casual crowd arrived dressed in pastels or beige, with appropriate hats, designer sunglasses and modestly sized flags to support their tennis heroes. The royal box was full of fashionably attired celebrities and glamorous younger-generation royals with perfectly glossed and groomed hair – at least, those who had hair.

The battle that everyone had hoped for had arrived, as though it had been scripted that way. No one knew which way it would go, but the commentators were being paid for their opinions, and as always, they had many. Anyone who had tickets to the gentlemen's singles final at the All England Tennis Club could have made a small fortune, with prices rising on the black market to tens of thousands of pounds – though most chose to keep the tickets for themselves. There weren't too many battles fought in the modern age that were as epic as this one promised to be. This was it: the two greatest players of their time, competing at the event that stood at the pinnacle of their sport – the Championships at Wimbledon.

Noah was going through his final preparations in the locker room, bouncing around wearing his red headphones, which were in stark contrast to his spotless white tennis attire. As he ducked and wove around the room, he took a moment to reflect on just how far he'd come in the sport he loved. He thought about the one hundred and twenty-eight players thrashing out their skills at unglamorous Roehampton, knowing only sixteen of them would end up with a coveted ticket to play at the ever-sacred greens of the All England Club – only for most of them to be obliterated by a top seed in round one or two. He was one of the very few who had managed to progress through the ranks with ease in his teens, and he felt privileged to have been gifted with the skill to be able to make it to the top level. He had worked hard, but undoubtedly so had many hundreds of others.

Both players were met by the chief locker room attendant, who carried their hefty bags along the beige corridors, past vases of flowers in hues of purple and green, and portraits of notable figures, including Her Majesty the Queen (even though she much preferred horse racing to tennis!). It was as if the long walk were designed to build up the pre-match drama, causing more nerves for players, commentators and spectators alike.

Finally, having walked under Kipling's famous words – 'If you can meet with Triumph and Disaster and treat those two impostors just the same ...' – Stephan Nordstrom followed Noah Levique out onto centre court, to the roar of the exhilarated crowd. Both players would have the responsibility of changing history on their shoulders during the coming hours.

Stephan was agitated, until his eyes focused on Nadia, demurely ensconced between Garry and another member of his security team in his player's box, with the tell-tale blue and lemon scarf wrapped around her narrow shoulders. Seeing her dressed exactly as he had prescribed, in a lemon silk shirt and ankle-length bohemian blue skirt, calmed his nerves considerably so he could prepare for his warm-up. He felt much more comfortable having Nadia in his box rather than with Caesar – who hadn't seemed bothered by this arrangement at all.

He was still in control. Knowing her ankle would be cuffed to the base of the chair for the entire match settled his mind so he could focus on the game. She was secure, she still belonged to him.

There would be no escaping the match. There would be no escaping *him*. Though she seemed tense, with her eyes hidden beneath Jackie O–style sunglasses, she still looked exquisite, and he sighed in the knowledge that she would be his again in a few short hours, after he had decimated the persistent pest of Levique once and for all. All he had to do was win today and his position as Number One was confirmed – she would belong to him for the remainder of Caesar's contract and beyond – no questions asked. She was the trophy he was playing for; he was fighting to protect her from the intrusion of the rest of the world.

He smiled as he saw Levique glance up at her in *his* box, wearing *his* colours – so beautiful and composed, yet totally unreachable – knowing that after this match, Levique would never lay eyes on her again. It would prove the fatal stab in an already bleeding wound. Stephan beamed towards the cameras that were flying around as the murderous thought floated through his disturbed mind.

Meanwhile, Nadia's mind was blank. Whenever she'd been given the time and space to think her own thoughts, it had only served to diminish her world and her choices even further – so she no longer put herself through the anguish.

She had learnt her lesson. The past few weeks had taught her that she was indeed a slave to her Master, and she'd forced her mind to relinquish control so she could continue to exist, which was as much as she could hope for. She had somehow talked herself into believing that her life with Stephan was really no different from what it had been at the Royal Ballet – she had a strict daily regime that she diligently adhered to; she trained, she did what she was told, and in doing so aimed for perfection. In her mind, she still belonged somewhere. In essence, she had been forced to become delusional in order to survive her ordeal.

But even to her depleted mind, there was still one glaring difference between her former and current lives. Stephan had absolutely forbidden her to dance – and had made it abundantly clear that dancing was a privilege she would have to earn over time. It disturbed her that he seemed aware of whenever a thought about ballet slipped into her mind, and every time it happened he took great delight in leaving images from the movie *Black Swan* plastered all over her wall, adding to the other atrocities. Even when she closed her eyes she could see the vivid scene of the ballet dancer in hospital with a broken leg, or the image of the mutilated and bloodied swan as she died.

Forbidding her from dancing was the one thing that spawned a deep-seated hate of Stephan within her – though it did not affect her absolute obedience.

So it was under these circumstances that she found herself sitting at Wimbledon like the pretty, empty mannequin she had become. There was no need for her to think about her past or her future, as they didn't exist. She had no influence over either – including who won the final – and had learnt the hard way how dangerous hope could be. So she simply existed in the moment, a shell of a woman awaiting only the wash of the tide.

Match Point

Tennis at this level was often compared with solitary confinement in front of fifteen thousand people and millions of virtual viewers. A grand-slam match was a personal journey deep into the psyche – and none more so than the gentlemen's final at Wimbledon. In the words of Thomas Paine (and many imitators since), 'These are the times that try men's souls.'

Noah's mindset was evident from the first point: to be Number One. Nothing more, nothing less. And that was exactly what he was here today to accomplish.

Nordstrom won the toss – as if there was any doubt he would – and elected to serve first. From the first pounding strike of the ball, the competition between these two arch-rivals was hot and it was game on.

Each player held his serve for the entire first set, until Nordstrom's formidable cross-court forehand got the better of Levique and the first set went to the Swedish maestro seven–five. It was edge-of-your-seat tennis, and the pace didn't ease when the second set began. The crowd remained glued to the compulsive action on centre court.

Levique seemed to have worked through any Wimbledon jitters, and all of a sudden his game kicked in. His newly improved serve and volley left Nordstrom wondering whether he was playing the same person he'd been rallying against at the baseline just a few games ago. With his seamless serve belting the ball past the service line time and again, Levique clocked up more than three games made up entirely of aces. Attitude, precision and power – he had it in spades. If tennis was a conversation, barely a word was exchanged between the men in the second set, with Levique taking it six–three. Nordstrom looked bewildered as they walked off court for a quick break in the locker rooms, while Levique seemed composed, as if he were just getting started.

The third set began with a bang, both players serving for their lives, for to lose a service game at this level almost guaranteed sudden death. Breaking back serve was never for the faint-hearted. But both players dug deeper than they had in their previous matches because the Wimbledon final was more important than all of the others.

As their aces subsided, the rallies kicked in and every ball was chased down until it could be lethally subdued. When Levique couldn't execute at the net, Nordstrom dragged him all over the court; a less fit athlete would have collapsed by this point, but both players put in a marathon effort. There was no doubting why these two men were the ones who dominated the modern game.

This grand-slam final turned Nordstrom's tennis to brilliant, calculated, cold-blooded warfare, while Levique's skill and passion were reflected in every movement, his athleticism enticingly poetic. The crowd thirstily soaked up every individual point as they attempted to retain decorum in their allocated seats. They were nothing less than awestruck.

The match was the closest thing to Shakespearean theatre in our time.

The third went to a tiebreaker, and it was as though the pair's previous magnificence on court had been a warm-up. It was a good thing they'd both quaffed their liquids and eaten bananas in the break, because they needed every ounce of energy they could summon.

The greatest ego in the game took his time walking to the baseline for the first serve. Then the punishing rallies began again. Precision forehands, topspin backhands, overhead smashes and jumping volleys all featured in the points that ensued. At sixteen all, it was anyone's set. Levique served an ace, giving him the advantage. His next serve triggered an epic rally of brutal intensity. It was unbelievable tennis! Both players couldn't risk taking their eye off the ball for a millisecond. It had been passed over the net a total of two hundred and thirty-two times when Levique's backhand drop-shot skimmed the top of the net, and it was as though time froze as the ball balanced on the precipice, deciding which way to fall. And then it fell, like a feather in slow motion – and was called in, giving Levique the tiebreak at eighteen–sixteen. He was two sets to one ahead. He held up his hand to Nordstrom in commiseration and the look on his opponent's face was akin to daggers flying across the net.

It was rare for the Swedish supremo ever to look dejected in public, but he returned to his seat with his head in his hands, wondering what he could do to break this indefatigable fighter. Meanwhile, Levique bounced back on court for the fourth set as though he were as fresh as a daisy; it was clear to all that his level of fitness was at an all-time high. Spectators could literally sense Levique unleashing his inner beast, physically and mentally walloping Nordstrom off the court.

Until match point.

Levique was leading love–forty and Nordstrom's serve had turned from masculine might to mulch during this fourth set. Had he been playing at Roland Garros, some of his ground strokes could have been compared with an escargot. It was as if Levique's game had crawled under his skin and attacked him from the inside out like an insidious virus. In contrast, every serve of Levique's was almost untouchable, every ball he hit was gold. Compared with the other sets, this looked like it would be a wipeout.

In a last-ditch attempt to worm his way back into the match, Nordstrom inhaled deeply, and with every ounce of energy in his body released a lightning-speed ace down the centre line, reigniting the embers of the match – to the delight of the crowd, who were ever hopeful that Nordstrom might climb back to give them the sizzling fifth set they were desperate for. 'One point at a time' was on the lips of all who were watching with bated breath. 'One point at a time.'

The umpire was forced to call for the hush of the crowd as politely as possible. 'Thank you, quiet please, thank you …' and the screaming voices finally held their collective breath across London and around the world. It was so quiet you could have heard the bubbles fizzing in a glass of Lanson.

Then the unthinkable happened.

Nordstrom served a double fault – and lost Wimbledon!

He slammed his racquet onto the sacred green turf and glared at his opponent with such vengeance in his eyes that even the crowd gasped and recoiled in shock. If they hadn't known better – and they all did, because it was Wimbledon and a certain level of decorum was not only expected but guaranteed – they could have sworn that Nordstrom was about to launch across the net and literally slaughter Levique with his bare hands. It was as though he had temporarily lost all sanity and been possessed by the devil himself as his usually determined blue eyes glazed over with pure rage.

To the relief of all those who had witnessed this unsportsmanlike behaviour, Nordstrom regained control of his mind and pulled to a halt just prior to slamming through the net. Both men grasped each other's hands with such obvious disdain on their grimaced faces that their grip remained frozen for an unprecedented length of time. Which ensured the crowd's eyes were fixated on the big screens to scrutinise their aggression towards each other in detail, instead of on the somewhat miniature real-life version before them.

It was as though the venom between these two tennis gladiators was infusing centre court with poison, something not seen for decades in the hallowed game of tennis, in which the norm was on-court rivalry but off-court camaraderie. The tension oozed around the stadium as neither player relinquished his grip. Levique stood his ground, patiently waiting for Nordstrom – the runner-up – to be the first to step towards the umpire for the mandatory handshake. It took a few loud boos and jeers from the crowd to shake Nordstrom from his fixated state so he could uphold the protocols of the sport – and indeed, the fastidiousness for which Wimbledon was renowned.

Then Nordstrom sat hidden behind the privacy of a towel, trembling with his head in his hands, while Levique was finally free to engage the crowd in his victory. He ran around the court, pumped his fists in the air, ran to his player's box and hugged every member of his team, to the cheers and adulation of the feverish crowd. Then, to everyone's surprise, he stopped right in front of Nordstrom's player's box, placed his palm on his heart and pounded it three times. He blew a jubilant kiss to Eloise as their eyes connected for the first time since the Australian Open, surrounded by thousands of people.

It was as though this year's Wimbledon champion had just jump-started Eloise's heart – and she was alive again.

Request

Before the court officials even began preparing for the trophy presentation Nadia had been removed from Stephan's player's box,

Garry's fingers fastening onto a pressure point in her elbow as he 'guided' her determinedly out of the arena. The entire time her eyes were fixed on Noah as he embraced his team, wishing she could be there feeling his warmth and sharing such a momentous victory with him – until she was wrenched away and could no longer see him.

* * *

All in all, Caesar had had a great day. He had never witnessed tennis like this in his life. And although his mind, and heart, had been elsewhere leading up to the final, he was certainly thrilled he had made it back to London in time to witness these two champions – *his* two champions – battle it out today. It had been invaluable from every perspective. As usual luck had been on his side, along with exceptional planning and foresight, and all of his groundwork over the past six months had paid off handsomely. Things couldn't have panned out more perfectly for him than to have two virile, competitive tennis champions vying for his one ballerina. Spectacular sporting entertainment by all accounts!

His relationship with Noah had developed considerably, and like so many others, he was surprised at how small an ego Noah had for one so driven to achieve. And now the world had a new Number One in men's tennis. Which reminded him: he needed to get on with organising the handover of his precious ballerina, who had indirectly taken tennis to dazzling new heights!

Stephan, on the other hand, walked around with his ego clouding his every action. Caesar couldn't help but wonder about the state he was in right at this moment after his momentous loss; it surely wasn't pretty.

Caesar hoped he could offer him some words of advice and ascertain what his mindset might be for the next grand slam – the

US Open. Making a split-second decision, he resolved to detour via Stephan's manor house before heading back to his house in Mayfair, after he finished the last of his Lanson with his guests.

* * *

Stephan was a mess. He was dreading the press interviews, when he'd be forced to explain losing his title of reigning world champion as civilly and professionally as possible – but not as much as he was dreading obeying Caesar's request to deliver Eloise Lawrance with all of her belongings to the Dorchester Hotel by this evening, which arrived shortly after he left the court with his runner-up trophy.

His stomach churned at the sight of her old and irrelevant name staring up at him. She was his Nadia; she belonged to *him*. He knew better than anyone on earth that Eloise no longer existed; he had seen to it that she had been totally destroyed.

Seething, he ripped the note to shreds and smashed his fists against the wall. The few people around him quickly evacuated to put some space between themselves and the volatile Scandinavian.

Stephan had never allowed himself to consider that such a loss might actually occur, because to think it could happen could well *make* it happen, make him a weaker human being. His mind raced with options as to what his next step should be, his biggest problem being whether he should risk his lucrative career and the global wrath of Caesar should he decide to act on his plans.

His world was crashing around him faster than he could fathom. He couldn't bear to witness the pity in people's eyes at his pathetic loss. Not reaching a fifth set and losing the title with a double fault were humiliations akin to living in a recurring nightmare. He was devastated, he was furious, and under no circumstances would he be handing over what was his most precious possession.

Threats

After the match, Nadia found herself imprisoned in the attic room at the top of the manor house yet again, this time with Garry stationed silently inside her room, as though concerned she might evaporate into thin air. She knew it was useless trying to get any information out of him; he only ever spoke to Stephan.

She was devastated to have missed seeing Noah hold the prestigious trophy above his head, basking in the applause of the adoring, congratulatory crowd. The kiss he had blown her had brought tears to her eyes, tears she thought had evaporated long ago, and she was surprised that they kept coming every time she relived the moment in her mind. He made her feel alive again! Although this also made her life seem even more miserable, since she had immediately been returned to Stephan and the prison he'd created for her. It had been months since she had had any idea of what was going on in the outside world, so she was left to assume that he had remained Number One and she would be his for the foreseeable future. Perhaps she'd been wrong in thinking Stephan had lost the French Open, and her future with him had been set in stone regardless of today's outcome. Either way, she was left feeling utterly desolate being back in this hell so soon.

She could barely breathe in the stifling room, Garry's presence making the tiny space feel even more like a doll's house. 'Would you mind opening the window? There's no air in here.'

Grudgingly, Garry lifted the hefty window a quarter of the way up, not far enough for her to poke her head out should she be silly enough to try to escape that way, and returned to his station by the door. She moved the single chair to the window and sat staring out blankly, the breeze cooling her face as she awaited her relentless fate.

Her heart jumped for all the wrong reasons when she saw Stephan's car swerving around the driveway. Her heart jumped again when she saw what looked like Caesar's limousine arrive a few minutes later. *Maybe*, she thought, *just maybe, he's come to pick me up*. For the first time, she wondered if Noah had finally made it to Number One; maybe *that* was why he had blown her the kiss.

She thought her heart was going to leap out of her chest when she saw Caesar alight from the back of the car. Forgetting herself, she leapt up from her chair and called out to him, waving frantically. 'Hello, hello! Caesar, I'm up here!'

Caesar looked up to the third storey and saw his beautiful ballerina, looking so happy in the window above. He smiled and waved in return as he was ushered inside the house.

As soon as he was out of sight Garry slammed the window shut, gave her a death stare and walked out of the room, locking the door behind him. She honestly had no idea what was going on.

Caesar could sense that Stephan was deeply agitated from the moment he walked in, and did his best to allay his grief, explaining that such losses happened in every player's career and it was how they recovered that determined whether they were a true champion. Although Stephan nodded, his mind was clearly elsewhere.

'You still have a fine future ahead of you, Stephan, and it's not as if your sponsors will have been disappointed by today's epic battle in front of a capacity crowd. Between you and Noah, tennis has never been more popular. You have everything to gain if you bide your time and play your cards right.'

It was this last statement that piqued Stephan's attention. He sensed it could be interpreted in many ways, as was often the case with Caesar; if nothing else, he made you think.

Stephan had every intention of taking Nadia to Sweden this very evening; it had all been arranged – win or lose. But now that Caesar had arrived, he would need to play along, in the hope that Caesar would depart again soon – leaving Stephan free to carry out his plans and whisk her away as soon as possible.

'I want her back, Caesar.'

'I can tell. And you know how to get her back. Her contract with me expires before the French Open; after that, she's free to live her own life and she'll be a wealthy woman in her own right. I'm assuming she has met all the conditions of your agreement, otherwise I would have heard from you?'

He raised his eyebrows, but Stephan couldn't decipher whether it was a question or an implied threat, such was Caesar's skill.

'She has been near perfect, Caesar. That's why I can't bear to let her go.'

Caesar patted him on the back, looking very pleased with himself. 'Well, that shouldn't be too hard for you, Stephan, should it? Win the US and she's yours again. Oh, and by the way, under our terms, I meet any of her medical expenses. You told me she spent some time in Switzerland?'

'She needed to recover from a virus before the French, but it's OK, I covered it.'

'Not at all, a contract is a contract. And I'd lose my reputation if I didn't follow through on such details. I'll have my assistant sort it out.'

The steely look in Caesar's eyes even made Stephan back down. It was perfectly clear that you never messed with Caesar when it came to contractual clauses so he merely nodded his agreement.

Finally he stood up to leave and Stephan felt relief flood through him.

'Listen, I need to make a few calls from the car, but seeing as I'm here, I may as well take Eloise with me, save you organising the trip into the city. It looks like she's already upstairs packing.'

The sudden shock in Stephan's eyes at this didn't go unnoticed but was coolly ignored by Caesar. As far as he was concerned, the sooner Eloise was transferred to Noah, the better. After his week in

350

Australia, he had more than enough business to catch up on, and it would be one less thing he needed to worry about.

'Honestly, I insist. It's no bother at all.' He smiled at Stephan. 'I'm glad we had the opportunity to catch up; it's been a while. Sorry about your loss today, but I'm sure you'll have better luck next slam.'

With that, Caesar's work there was done and he kindly patted Stephan's shoulder and exited through the front door.

Leaving Stephan to deal with his inner meltdown alone. A meltdown that led him directly up the stairs to the tiny attic room.

'So this is it!'

Nadia jumped up as Stephan burst into the room. He towered over the top of her, his face ablaze.

'Sit!' he ordered, and she stumbled back into the chair.

Within seconds, he was kneeling before her with his head in her lap, weeping.

'I can't let you go … No one understands … This can't be happening … You're everything to me … Now I've lost you!' His words spluttered out between pathetic sobs.

Nadia was at a loss as to what to do or say. Stephan's mood swings had become so unpredictable lately that she never knew what to expect or how to respond – but never in a million years had she expected this!

'I've shaped you, moulded you, made you perfect for me – and only me. Don't worry, my sweet, I'll win you back, we'll be together again. You will always be my Nadia. It will all be OK, I promise.'

He went to kiss her lips and she automatically recoiled before she could check herself. He ran his hand through his hair in frustration and fury.

'So this is how it is, is it? The minute I'm not Number One, I'm nothing to you. Is that it?' His face was so close to hers she felt his spittle on her skin.

'Answer me, damn it!' He held her upper arms and shook her hard.

'No, of course not. I just … well … I'm just not sure what is going on … I didn't know …'

'Don't lie to me, Nadia. You and that bastard Levique have probably been scheming for my demise for months.'

'Please, you know that's not true!'

'I'll know *exactly* what's true when I get the report from Karin Klarsson. She's the only one I can trust when it comes to you.'

Nadia shivered in her seat when he looked directly at her with his eyes glazed over in anger. It was this Stephan she feared the most: the violent, vengeful Stephan whose armour couldn't be penetrated by reason.

He hauled her up off the seat, making her stand before the wall of atrocities. She tried not to cry by squeezing her eyes shut, but couldn't prevent the release of a few silent sobs.

'Open your eyes!' he screamed into her ear.

They sprung open on his command.

'I know you, Nadia, better than you know yourself. And I know every single one of your fears, every flicker of your emotions; I can read every thought in your head. I have every moment of your pleasure and pain captured in my photo library, and your notes attached – which is the only reason I can let you go now. They will be my bond to you.'

He dug his fingers into her arm. 'Anything you say about me, I will know. If you mention anything to Caesar, I will know. If you do or say anything to upset me between now and when you are mine again, you will pay.' He pointed to specific photos, leaving no doubt as to his meaning.

'If you say anything to Levique about us, he will pay and you will watch him suffer – long, slow suffering that will end him once and for all. I will make sure of it. Do you understand me, Nadia?'

352

He held her face firmly in front of the images that scared her the most. 'Am I being clear enough for you?'

'Yes, sir,' she stuttered. 'It's clear, I understand. I won't say anything, sir.'

'I may not be with you, but I will know where you are, what you are doing and who you are with until I have you back under my lock and key. And mark my words: I *will* have you back, sooner than you expect!'

He turned her to face him, away from the wall of atrocities, holding her face between his palms and forcing her head up so their eyes met.

'Who am I to you Nadia?'

'My Master.'

'When?'

'At all times.'

'Exactly. At *all* times, whether you are with me or not, so don't ever forget it. This changes nothing. You are my world, Nadia, and if I can't have you, I promise you no one will.'

Nadia shuddered involuntarily as his tongue possessed her mouth in a final goodbye.

Surreal

Eloise was in a state of apathetic shock as she sat in the back of the limousine beside Caesar. Fortunately he was occupied, making phone calls to various business associates and attorneys. Her nerves were spent, and she honestly didn't know whether she was capable of conversation after Stephan's threats began to sink in, never once doubting that he was capable of carrying them out – he had proved that to her time and again. Everything about her life had become surreal; it was as though she could no longer discern fact from fiction. She felt such dissociation from her emotions these days that she could have been watching her own life play out in a movie, idly wondering what might happen next to the main character. That was, until Caesar completed his calls and interrupted her inner monologue.

'Eloise, how are you? You seem tense, distracted almost.'

She stared at him wide-eyed. It felt like a lifetime ago that she had been Eloise, and for a moment she was unsure how to respond.

'I'm fine, thank you, Caesar,' she said way too hastily. 'It's just that it has all come as a bit of a shock.'

'You didn't want to leave Stephan?'

My God, she thought, *how can I possibly answer that?* Her mind was like a vortex; she had no idea what to make of the situation yet. However, her survival instincts soon kicked in and she knew she needed to get a grip, particularly around someone as perceptive as Caesar.

She laughed a high-pitched, nervous laugh that came to a sudden halt in the back of the confined space of the car. 'You know me Caesar, I'm happy to be with whoever is Number One.'

'So it's easy for you to move from one to another?'

That question caught her off guard.

'Not easy as such, but it certainly makes for an interesting life, wouldn't you agree?' She forced her voice to sound happy and light-hearted as she raised her aquamarine eyes towards him and smiled her best smile.

He laughed, which eased her tension a little.

'Well, it's certainly not dull, and if you're young, why not? But what about your dancing? Do you miss the ballet?'

Her eyes clouded over, and she decided to answer honestly.

'I do miss it terribly, but I have no regrets about the opportunity you've given me either.'

The memory of Caesar and Stephan chatting amicably and patting each other on the back in Melbourne sprang to the forefront of her mind. It was clear to her that they were close and she didn't dare make a wrong move that could get back to Stephan and further inflame the dire situation she was in.

'That's good, I'm pleased to hear it.' The limousine pulled up outside the Dorchester. 'Well, here we are.'

The driver opened the door for them both and handed Eloise's bag to a waiting doorman.

'Your suite is ready,' Caesar told her, 'and I suggest you order a meal from room service; you look like you're fading away. I think I'll need to reprimand Stephan about what he's been feeding you – or rather hasn't been!'

'Oh no, please don't, it's my fault,' she said automatically. 'It's just that I haven't had a big appetite lately, but I'm sure it will come back soon.'

'Good to hear. All right, then, unless there is anything else you'd like to discuss …' He hesitated, sensing there was more to what she was saying but unable to put his finger on what it might be.

'No, Caesar, honestly, I'm completely fine.'

'So you say. Well, the lawyers have everything in hand, and as we both know, it's not as if you and Noah aren't already well acquainted, so I'm expecting my meeting with him to be brief and a smooth transition to follow. I assume the next time I'll see you will be in New York!'

'Oh, yes, of course. And thanks for picking me up, Caesar, I really appreciate it.' She spoke with relief in her voice, as she honestly wasn't sure whether she'd be here if he hadn't.

'My pleasure, Eloise. You take care. Enjoy your time with Noah, but don't forget what's expected of you – or that this situation could be temporary depending on the result of the US Open. I know Stephan is very keen to win you back.'

This was her deepest fear and made her stomach recoil in disgust. She had been so focused on meeting Stephan's stringent expectations that she had forbidden her mind to think further ahead than the limo ride with Caesar.

Now she found herself walking into a hotel where her ex best friend was being briefed on Caesar's bizarre arrangement, with her Master's threats hanging over her head. She suddenly felt ill at the entire concept.

Tears

Although Noah had worked out that Eloise was 'assigned' to whoever was Number One, he'd had no idea that Caesar was the mastermind behind the whole scheme, and was astonished to see the long and detailed contract sitting on the table before him. All he had to do was sign and Eloise was somehow his – just because he was now Number One! It was ridiculous, not to mention utterly demeaning. He fleetingly wondered what would have driven her to agree to it – then he remembered their fateful meeting at the pub. This was what she would have been contemplating when he encouraged her to enjoy life's ride – as well as promising to save her if it didn't work out. And here he was, saving her!

He had to acknowledge that it had driven him to work harder and progress faster than he ever would have without it – and Eloise was certainly worth the fight. It was a battle that he had won to prove that he could, and to ensure she was away from the clutches of Nordstrom. There was something about him that gave Noah the creeps, and the idea that Eloise had been contracted to him in this way made him sick to the core.

He pushed the contract away and stared defiantly at Caesar.

'Is this even legal?'

'There is an offer, acceptance and substantial consideration, so yes, of course the contract she has with me is legal or it wouldn't be a contract! The agreement she makes with her Number One is a process of negotiation between her and him, which later forms an addendum. As long as it all goes smoothly, I have no need to be further involved at that point.'

'And Eloise agreed to all this?'

'Yes, of course, willingly. Very willingly, in fact. You should know more than anyone how seriously she is committed to this entire strategy, Noah. To the best of my knowledge the last time you had any interaction was in Melbourne, where she chose Stephan over you. Is that correct?'

'Well, yes … but –'

Caesar interrupted him. 'Then doesn't that prove her commitment?'

'It all feels so wrong, as if she's become Nordstrom's concubine or something.'

'Listen, you might not like Stephan, but I can assure you, she will only have become what she agreed to become, of her own accord – nothing more, nothing less. Otherwise I would have heard about it. And I can say with absolute certainty I am *not* in the business of prostitution!' This last statement was made with resolute authority, the tone he was renowned for.

'Now, I have other business to attend to, so do you have any more questions for me specifically or can I leave you with my more than capable lawyers?'

His eyes had lost all their previous warmth, but Noah was undeterred.

'What happens if I don't want to do this?' He pointed at the document as though it were poison. 'If I don't want to sign it?'

'Good question. Should you not want Eloise Lawrance in your life, the previous Number One has the option of keeping her until the rankings change again.'

'*What!?*' Noah's voice screeched. 'You mean you would send her back to Nordstrom?' His heart nearly jumped out of his throat.

'Yes, it's written in the contract in black and white.' Caesar nodded to his lawyer, who turned to the relevant page and indicated the clause for Noah's perusal.

'That's outrageous!'

'No, it's legally binding. You decide what you want to do and we'll take it from there. Either way, Nad–, I mean Eloise, remains committed to the contract. I spoke to her on the way here.'

'She's here now? Away from Nordstrom?'

'Of course. You are ranked Number One, so she is contracted to you unless you choose not to accept my offer – it's all under "Transferral" in the contract.'

'And it will stay that way?'

'As long as you maintain your current status.'

Noah didn't like one bit of this, but there was no way he would be responsible for having Elle returned to that monster just because he thought the whole contract was preposterous. If he had the opportunity to guarantee her freedom while he was Number One, then that was exactly what he'd do.

He couldn't believe she was actually in the same building as him right now. Excitement replaced any anger and disgust he'd been feeling just minutes ago.

'All right, Caesar, I'm in.' He hastily signed the devious document, declaring that he had no further questions or amendments, except for one. 'Where is she?'

Caesar smiled and shook hands with Noah, congratulating him again on his new world ranking and stupendous win, before handing him the key to Eloise's suite, nodding to the lawyers and exiting the room. He was content to leave these youngsters to their own devices and keen to call his beloved Ashleigh; it had been too many hours since he'd heard her sweet voice.

* * *

Eloise's room was almost identical to the one she'd stayed in when Ivan was Number One – when he had lost and she had happened upon her serendipitous week with Noah. Since then, her life had become an emotional merry-go-round of grand slams.

She ran a steaming hot bath and soaked her tense limbs and exhausted mind for over an hour. Despite her excitement for Noah's win, part of her was terrified about meeting up with him again, after hurting him so badly last time they met. What would he think of all of this? What would he think of *her* for entering into such an agreement with Caesar of all people? She couldn't bear the thought that he might reject her – but how could he not, after all she had done? As Stephan's threats kept permeating her mind she was ever grateful to be finally away from his clutches. All she could do was hope his threats remained unfulfilled as she would never put Noah's life at risk!

Allowing her concerns to consume her, she submersed her entire body in the bathwater, unable to deal with the world any more and the thought of what might happen next.

Eloise basked in the silence of her underwater world for as long as she could without having to surface. When her lungs forced her up for air, her senses were met with loud banging on the bathroom door and Noah's voice yelling her name.

'It's OK, I'm in here!' She hastily rose out of the bath and grabbed a robe to place around her dripping body.

She opened the door to see Noah's face – a smiling face with sparkling eyes that didn't seem to judge her for anything that had happened – and she eagerly stepped into his welcoming embrace. It was only then that tears gushed freely, along with all the tension and anguish that had been pent up inside her. She clung to his warmth as though her life depended on it – and he would hold her for as long as she needed him to.

Smiles

The next morning they sat staring at each other with smiles on their faces and champagne in their hands inside one of Sir Richard Branson's private jets, awaiting their departure for Australia. Noah had been thrilled to accept Sir Richard's kind offer so he could travel to Westen Australia for the sacred ceremony commemorating the life of his beloved grandmother. Obviously winning Wimbledon had many advantages – the most special of which was finally seeing Eloise smile again, instead of the broken and depleted bird he'd found yesterday in the bathroom. If he had been concerned for her health and wellbeing beforehand, seeing her face to face had confirmed his worst fears. Eloise was a shadow of the person she'd been when he'd last seen her, in every possible way.

She refused to discuss Stephan with him, or anything that had happened between them, saying she just wanted to put it all behind her. Noah didn't push her for answers, sensing that it would only drive her even further into herself. But the subject was always at the back of his mind, and he could sense it was the same for her. Figuratively speaking, Nordstrom's presence always loomed near.

'It's great to see you smile, Elle. It seems like it's been a while.'

'I know, my cheeks hurt from not having used these muscles for so long!'

They both laughed.

'I can't believe we are actually here together like this!' He raised his glass in a toast.

'You're right, I feel like I'm living in a beautiful dream; it's almost too good to be true. I can't believe you're still talking to me after everything I said – and didn't say … I'm so sorry.'

'What, for inspiring me to be Number One?' He winked. 'I promise you, I'd do it again. It's not such a bad thing, you know, being Number One and being with you,' he said cheekily, then added more seriously, 'but I'm really pleased you decided to come with me on this trip.'

'I'll do whatever you want me to, Noah.'

'No, I don't want that. I want you to do whatever *you* want to do. Not what someone else tells you to do.'

'It could take a while … It wasn't like that with –' She shook her head, unable to continue and not wanting to even mention his name.

Noah put his hand up, as if to calm her thoughts. 'I know, I understand that. But it's different now that you and I are together. I feel like you've lost the essence of yourself, and I'd love for you to find it again.'

She reflected on his words. 'It's true, I used to be someone else, and now I'm honestly not sure who I am.'

'Well, there's plenty of time to figure that out.'

Or was there? Eloise wondered as Caesar's words in the limo re-entered her mind. All this could change again depending on who won the US Open. She reflected on her relationships with Ivan and then Stephan. At first she had been like their good-luck charm, but ultimately they had both lost their Number One ranking. She prayed fervently that wouldn't happen with Noah.

He spoke again. 'At least I know you can't run away from me now, which is the only good thing about Caesar's dreadful contract.'

'I would never want to run away from you,' she said quietly.

He took a deep breath, as if preparing to broach a difficult subject. 'There's something I still need to tell you, Elle. I had my concerns about Stephan all along, as you know, but more recently I've been contacted by Professor Klarsson, and since then I've been worried sick about you.'

'What! You know her?'

'I didn't, but after the French final I had a message asking me to get in touch with her urgently about you. Of course, that was like a red rag to a bull given that I hadn't seen or heard from you since the Aussie Open.'

She couldn't help but cringe at that.

'We met up for a chat that she kept insisting was off the record, and she told me how concerned she was for your welfare, having met you in Rome with Stephan. She now believes he has megalomania. She mentioned you had been "volunteered" by him to be part of her study of facial micro-expressions, but it was plain that you were being coerced. Is that right?'

Eloise was speechless and only managed to nod in response, remembering the hours she had spent strapped to the chair with the camera directed towards her face.

'I asked her to explain in plain English, and she said the analysis of your expressions suggested fear and shame when looking at an image of Stephan, and a mixture of hope and deep regret when you saw me.' He paused for a moment to assess Eloise's response, which looked to be one of wide-eyed shock, before he continued. 'She talked briefly about dominant and submissive relationships and said she'd witnessed many healthy versions but believed Stephan could have pathological and delusional sadistic tendencies. Essentially, she was worried that you were being pushed way beyond your comfort zone, and subjected to treatment that was bordering on abuse. She wanted to meet up with you privately, but had no idea how to get in contact with you without Stephan finding out, so she contacted me instead. And I'm so thankful she did!'

Eloise couldn't believe what she was hearing; her body was shaking as she absorbed the full impact of his words. She couldn't bear to think of what might happen if Stephan ever found this out – to any of them.

'Noah, I'm so sorry you had to become caught up in all of this ...' Her voice was quiet, edged with nerves.

'Please don't think for a second you need to apologise, Elle.' He looked at her with deep concern in his eyes. 'I think you've been through so much more than you're letting on ... Do you want to talk about any of it yet?'

She shook her head and fought back the tears as Noah wrapped his arms protectively around her.

'Like I told you the first time we met, I'll always be there for you. You know that now, don't you?'

She nodded, holding on to his hand, needing to feel safe as they prepared for takeoff. She sucked in her emotion and closed her mouth tight so no words could escape. It was just not worth the risk – if anything ever happened to Noah she could never live with herself.

Adventure

Word had obviously spread about the imminent arrival of Wimbledon's new champion at the tiny Kununurra Airport, and Noah was greeted with waves and cheers from an array of smiling faces as he stepped off the plane. He returned their smiles with equal enthusiasm. Much to his amusement and delight, the only media outlet that had caught on to his whereabouts was the local paper, as Kununurra wasn't the easiest place to get to on short notice.

It was over an hour before Noah had finished meeting and greeting the locals, signing autographs, posing for selfies and tossing balls with the local kids. He was in his element, and Eloise watched him with pride. He was a natural with people, particularly kids, and seemed to fit in anywhere from the All England Club to the outback.

Finally, he jumped into the driver's seat of a waiting four-wheel drive.

'Are you ready?' He grinned.

'For what, exactly?'

'An outback adventure!' With that, his foot hit the accelerator and they were off.

Eloise had never experienced such a vast landscape. It looked like nothing at first, but the more you looked, the more details became apparent. It was as if your eyes had to slowly come into focus before you could appreciate the real beauty of the land.

Noah had mentioned on the flight that before his grandmother had passed away, she had sent him a message while he was competing in Rome to tell him how proud she was of him. She wrote that he must promise not to return to Australia until after Wimbledon, knowing how important it was to him and that whatever happened, her spirit would carry him through it all. Only then should he return to ensure her safe passage to the spirit world.

Eloise felt a little envious of the traditions Noah had been exposed to during his youth when he stayed with his nan and uncles; they seemed so much a part of who he was. She had never had the opportunity to experience a stable family life, let alone such rich customs developed over tens of thousands of years. There was no denying how special this part of his identity was to him.

'I can't believe I'm here with you,' she told him. 'Didn't you mention bringing me here one day when we were in Melbourne?'

'Sure did. And, true to my word, here you are. Although Nan was alive then.' His mood dampened only momentarily. 'But I don't doubt for a second that she helped bring us together.'

They sat in blissful silence as the road carried them further into the seemingly endless landscape which seemed to soothe the soul.

'Ah, here we are! Welcome to the Gibb River Road. Have you ever heard of it?'

'No, never.'

'Driving the Gibb River Road is considered to be one of the great four-wheel-drive adventures in Australia, but the part we'll be travelling on is pretty much sealed these days so not quite as exciting as it used to be.'

She looked at the road, the vast scenery and back to Noah – and his ever-present grin. This couldn't have been further away from her life of imprisonment less than a week ago with Stephan – and that realisation put a smile on her face. 'Well, let's go!'

'OK, then! Do you think you'll feel like a quick dip on the way there, or are you too tired after the flight?'

'A quick dip?' She laughed; she hadn't heard that phrase since she was a child. She couldn't imagine that a pool would spring up out of nowhere, given that they were surrounded by pretty much nothing, but she wasn't going to argue. 'Sure, I'm not a great swimmer, but I'd love to cool off in this heat.'

'You never swam as a child?'

'I never really had the chance, I suppose, and to be honest, if it wasn't ballet I wasn't interested. Although I did learn to dive a while back …' Her voice trailed off, remembering those early days with Stephan in the Caymans, and as the road took them further and further from civilisation she was left to ponder how terribly wrong things had gone with him in such a short space of time.

Eventually Noah turned off the road and into a car park.

'This is Emma Gorge. Hopefully all the tourists will have left by now. Let's go, it's only a quick hike to the main pool.'

The 'quick hike' was just under three kilometres, and was more than worth it. They scrambled across giant boulders to the most beautiful pristine waterhole, where falls cascaded down sheer cliffs.

'C'mon, what are you waiting for?'

Noah stripped off – exposing buttocks considerably paler than the rest of his body – and jumped in.

Eloise stood for a moment looking at his gorgeous behind, and feeling incredibly self-conscious, until she'd had a good look around to confirm that they were definitely alone.

'You're sure there're no crocodiles in there?'

'Now you *really* sound like a tourist! I promise you, it's safe. The water's beautiful, you'll love it.'

'Oh, what the heck!' She stripped off too, grateful that Noah was now floating under the waterfall away from where she was standing, and tentatively stepped in.

The water was like silk against her skin, deeply refreshing and cleansing. Becoming braver, she ducked under, keeping her eyes open so she could see the sunlight filter through the water to the rocks below.

'This is incredible.' She was full of awe at her surroundings, but wasn't willing to venture in to where she couldn't stand.

'This is home for me,' Noah replied. 'Or at least, the tourist version of home. I'd love to show you even more special places that the hordes haven't discovered yet, and hopefully never will.'

'More special than this?'

'Tip of the iceberg,' he said, with a splash towards her. She splashed him back, their laughter echoing around the gorge. 'Come over to the falls, they're running more than usual for this time of year.'

He went to guide her, and saw the bruises tarnishing her upper arm. She automatically recoiled from the anger in his eyes, quickly swimming away from him to the smaller waterfall in the shallow water, and floating under that instead. Nothing more was said as they enjoyed the solitude of this magic place.

After their refreshing swim, they were on their way again towards El Questro Wilderness Park in the east Kimberley, where Noah's uncles were the traditional guides and some of his cousins Junior Rangers for tourists who visited the massive one million acres of Australian outback. It wasn't until just before they got out of the car at El Questro Homestead that Noah turned to her, tenderly lifted her chin towards him and looked solemnly into her eyes.

'We are not leaving here until you are healed, Elle, both inside and out.'

There was no doubting the care and concern etched on his face and it was clear that he meant every word he said.

She nodded as tears filled her eyes.

Connection

Noah was right: Emma Gorge was the tip of the iceberg when it came to the beauty of this place. Eloise felt like she'd been immersed in a stunning painting, with colours you had to experience to believe. The two of them soaked in natural, bubbling hot springs, discovered even more beautiful waterholes to skinny-dip in, went horseback riding, kayaking, four-wheel driving. One million acres was a large backyard to play in, and they found themselves happily exhausted most nights. As amazing as these places were, there was usually a significant hike to get to them, which gave them both plenty of exercise in the great outdoors.

Noah was ever respectful of Eloise, sensing just how much she'd been through without knowing all the details, and though they hugged and played, their relationship was just like it had been on the canal boat: entirely platonic. Noah didn't want to go further until she was ready.

Finally the evening came for the special smoking ceremony to send his grandmother's spirit back to the great river in the sky, as agreed to by the elders of her tribe; her physical form had already been cared for.

After camping out overnight, the party commenced their hike into the Cockburn Range at dawn, rested during the heat of the day and continued on as the sun began to fall.

The pace was slow and steady, almost trance-like, with few words spoken. Eloise was an obvious outsider within the small band of tribespeople and was ever conscious of the need to behave with respect and understanding. She would never have been able to retrace the path they took, so she made sure she stayed close to Noah and the rest of the group. She didn't know the first thing about bush survival!

When they had set up camp for the night, the men left to get ready for the ceremony. Eloise busied herself helping the women prepare food as she watched the sun set. It was truly one of the most breathtaking visions she had ever seen, and caused a powerful stillness within her. It was as if an artist had flooded a canvas with unimaginable colours, enticing you to stop what you were doing to pay homage to the ever-changing beauty in the sky.

Some time later the men returned with paint on their arms, chests and faces. They led the group to where the ceremony would take place and began their ritualistic dance around the fire. The night had been chosen specifically, for there was no moon, which meant the path of the Milky Way would be particularly visible against the blackened, starlit sky.

The ceremony touched the hearts and souls of the gathered group, Eloise included. The tears in her eyes were for Noah, his nan and the mother she had never known. For the first time in her life she could truly feel the bond of kinship, and recognised the hole in her heart. She was aware she didn't belong in this tribe, but she sensed a deep connection that aligned her with Mother Earth and the heavenly skies above. She breathed this sensation in deeply, allowing it to flow into her heart.

After the ceremony and the sharing of food that had been brought from the camp oven, the tribespeople returned to camp. It came as something of a surprise to Eloise to realise she was suddenly alone with Noah, a million miles from anywhere, under the stars. The stresses of the world seemed to fade into insignificance in this sacred outback terrain. As she watched him leisurely stoking some logs on the fire, she could honestly say she felt content. Not fearful or anxious as she had been, but truly serene.

She moved to sit next to him on a blanket by the fire. 'Thank you for bringing me here … and allowing me to share this with you.'

'I wouldn't have wanted it any other way.'

'This whole place … it's overwhelming in its beauty …'

He smiled. 'I know the word "awesome" is used to describe so many things these days, but to me, this landscape is the real meaning of the word. It's not something your average city folk get to experience, that's for sure. But I need it, I yearn for it if I've been away too long. This,' he indicated the land and the stars, 'this gives me everything I need, the energy to live and breathe. I have my nan, and now her spirit, to thank for it. I can't imagine living my life without this connection to the land.'

Understanding the truth in his words, Eloise hugged him, absorbing his warmth into her body, wanting to feel him close against her skin. She looked deeply into his eyes, and with her palm, guided his lips towards hers, kissing him softly. After a moment she paused to gauge his reaction, and, sensing his eagerness for her to continue, she turned towards his body so they were face to face. Her long hair flowed wildly down her back as she wrapped her arms around his neck.

Eloise had thought about this moment since their time together on the canal boat. Having to say no to him, having to honour her agreement with Caesar and endure the abuse of Stephan. Tonight she wanted to put all of that behind her – to start afresh. To truly be with Noah like she had with no other man. She felt deep within her soul that this would be the beginning of her healing and she wanted it more than she wanted anything in her life. They had waited a year for this opportunity – and it couldn't be more perfect than here under the stars. Their time to be together had finally arrived.

'I want this, Noah ... I want *you*.' She kissed him deeply this time, and he allowed her to lower his body down onto the blanket and remove his shirt – revealing a physique that was more toned and muscled than she remembered from a year ago. And then he let her kiss and adore his body as he lay there before her – and she did so with relish, feeling liberated by her ability to touch without restrictions.

She loved the way he was letting *her* control the pace, only ever responding after she initiated. It was she who removed the rest of his clothes, before she removed her own. His body was dark and delicious beneath her pale limbs, and she explored and caressed him with her fingers and mouth.

Noah looked into her glazed eyes, the glow of the fire merging with the colour of her wild mane. He had imagined this moment so many times in his dreams, but had never envisaged anything as beautiful as this. She felt divine against his body, like an angel sent from the heavens above – yet still he waited.

'Touch me, Noah.'

He sat up, straddling her naked body, kissing her lips, her neck, slowly and tenderly lowering his head to her breasts as she opened her body for him to explore.

She revelled in the freedom she had with him. There were no restraints, no toys, no rules, no punishments, no pain. Just the raw passion and sheer joy of experiencing each other physically, emotionally and spiritually.

Time was inconsequential; there was no rush, they had forever. They kissed with the fervour of having waited so long for the right time, the right place – and tonight, here on top of the ridge, couldn't have been more perfect. He laid her down and his fingers played; she laid him down and her tongue explored. They twisted and turned together – she on him and he on her, over and over – until their bodies intertwined with the earth as the stars and Milky Way gave them their blessing and intensified the passion they shared.

The heat expelled from their perspiring skin burnt into the chill of the night, and then the time came for them to become one. To be completely connected to each other and the elements. Tears of ecstasy removed them from the world and took them on a transcendental journey beyond their physical form that touched the very core of their souls.

Their relationship changed entirely after that night. To be loved by Noah was like nothing Eloise had ever imagined; it was honest and truthful and raw. It was deeply passionate and intuitive, and most of all it was respectful and encouraging; they always drew out the best in each other. To them, their connection felt sanctioned by the universe, and both knew they would be part of the other's life forever. Eloise felt like she was finally 'home' when she was with Noah: something that she had never experienced with any other person.

Their lovemaking was breathtaking – both marvelled at the way their bodies melded together as though they were made to be united. Some days they barely saw the light of day, other days they spent outside, and it was their intimate glances and meaningful touches that announced their love to the world. It was selfless love and provided Eloise with more meaning and connection than she had ever known. Noah wanted to be whatever Eloise needed him to be – her best friend, her lover, her protector. She wanted to be safely nestled in his arms for the rest of her life. In no uncertain terms, as their love for one another deepened by the day – their young love knew no bounds.

Finally she felt safe enough to open up to Noah about her time with Stephan and how unstable he'd become. How she'd loved the excitement of his games in the beginning, but how they'd petrified her in the end, his volatile mood swings causing her to live perpetually on tenterhooks. She could now distinguish her lightness of being when she was with Noah from the heavy darkness she felt with Stephan. She could finally recognise the destructiveness of that relationship now she was on the outside looking in: something she didn't have the capacity to do while she was with him.

The more she disclosed to Noah, the more she came to understand the constant state of fear and pain she had lived in – the restrictions and control, the power and humiliation – all the while being unable to see past her dependence on his approval every minute of every day. She could finally see that her entire life up until this point, ballet included, had been based on the desire to please others driven by her own need for human connection of any kind – something that she had not known enough of since birth. Through her discussions with Noah and her memories of her sessions with Jayne Ferrer in Switzerland, she became increasingly aware of how over time her desire for absolute perfection had ended up making her weaker rather than stronger. Her failure to maintain her status as Principal was no longer something she had to run away from; it was something she needed to learn from.

Eloise had never before been close enough to anyone to discuss her deepest thoughts, but she trusted Noah completely. Regardless of what happened with Caesar and the contract, Noah would be her constant. She felt alive and fulfilled when he was around, and he gave her a sense of her own independence – of discovering and believing in the person she could become, not the person someone else could shape and mould her into. Noah listened compassionately when she shared, held her hand while she wept and embraced her as she slept. And as he lay awake next to her emotionally exhausted and physically abused body, he silently vowed that he would never let that madman near her again.

Their time in this sacred, ancient land was the most special of their lives, and it was with mixed emotions that they said goodbye to Noah's extended family when the time came. Yet there was no mistaking the certainty in their hearts that no matter what happened, they were destined to share a future together.

US OPEN II
August–September

Freedom

Eloise was in her element: she was finally dancing again. When Noah suggested trying something new – at least until her obligations with Caesar were over – she was certainly more than hesitant. He had stated that his tennis schedule would be crazy leading up to the US Open and he'd be much happier knowing she was doing something she loved, rather than watching endless training sessions and being dragged around from one tournament to another as she had been for well over a year. He also just happened to know a 'friend of a friend' involved in a new contemporary dance company in New York City, and said they'd love to meet up with her should she be interested in moving away from classical ballet for a period.

Every reason she put forward to Noah as to why she shouldn't was more or less refuted on the basis of her own insecurities. Until she had to concede that he was right, admitting that she had long wanted to try more-contemporary dance for a change and certainly had nothing to lose in meeting up with his friend's company. Noah still needed (and wanted) to win the US Open to secure his position as Number One and remove any threat that Stephan might regain his previous title – and with it, Eloise.

Noah had tried to persuade Eloise to tell Caesar about what had happened with Stephan, but she wouldn't hear of it. She was petrified he would go straight to Stephan and put both of their lives in danger. It was a risk she was not willing to take. It was better for everyone if they kept their silence, and it would all be over soon enough. It was the one thing that she was adamant about, and no amount of persuasion would deter her resolve.

The director of the dance company, Miguel, was a gorgeous Spaniard and an off-the-scale extrovert, who made Eloise feel instantly at ease. The rest of the dancers were equally lovely, immediately welcoming Eloise into their tight-knit circle. Before she knew it she was having the time of her life. There was no competition between the dancers, as they worked as a collaborative team, rotating their positions based on discussion about who felt most connected to certain styles, roles and pieces of music. Every dancer was encouraged to explore their own ideas, and the company was open to incorporating changes into their routines based on each member's individual strengths.

Working in partnership was something Eloise had never experienced given the strict hierarchy of traditional ballet, and she became completely engaged in the process. While they taught her about the creativity and freedom of modern dance, she taught them about classical techniques and positions. Each week they would teach a class to underprivileged children, and Eloise found that she looked forward to this as much as anything. She saw herself in so many of the little girls and sensed their excitement and love of dance, which reignited her own passion so that she enjoyed each moment in a way she hadn't done for years. Her confidence grew each day in her new world and she felt more grounded than she had in her entire life. She had never had so much fun as they all worked hard in the studio then socialised in the bohemian haunts of New York City. Most of all, she was excited by the prospect of finally performing onstage again.

Though she hadn't seen too much of Noah since they'd arrived in the United States, they spoke most days, even if only briefly. He called, having just won the Winston-Salem Open and loved hearing her sound so happy; her voice was vibrant with energy as she talked about her new life in New York.

'We've just announced all the dates for our concerts, and I really hope you can manage to see one before the US Open begins.' She quickly ran through the list of days and times for him.

'Even if I'm busy, I'll be there on opening night, Elle, I wouldn't miss it for the world. You know I've been dying to see you onstage since we first met.'

'And I love the fact that you want to, though the production is very small-scale and completely different from the majesty of the Royal Ballet; hopefully one day you'll have the opportunity to see me on *that* stage as well. I'm just having so much fun, Noah! Thank you for suggesting this to me; I would never have done it without you.'

He laughed. 'You've done it all yourself. You just needed some encouragement, and hearing you speak like this makes it all worthwhile. I can't wait to see you again.'

'Likewise! And I want to get to as many of your games as I can. Do you have your schedule yet?'

'I do, but they're very similar to *your* dates. I'd rather you not bother watching me and focus on your performances instead. It's been a while, you know, you might be out of practice!' His cheekiness made her smile. 'Anyhow, we'll both be busy at the same time, so it all works out.'

Eloise could tell from his voice that there was more to it than that. He'd mentioned in the past that if he had his way, she'd never be within the vicinity of Stephan again. So she understood where he was coming from.

'OK, if that's what you'd prefer.'

'Even the final – and I aim to be in it – is on at the same time as your last performance.'

'Oh no, it's not, is it?'

'Yep – but it's fine. I'd hate for you to miss your last show, and I'll ask Caesar to send one of his cars around to pick you up straight after your performance. I've organised a surprise for you as part of our post-final celebrations!'

'Noah, you don't need to –'

'I know I don't, but I have, and it's all sorted; it's something we've never done before.' He sounded excited. 'This way you can focus on dance, I can focus on tennis and we can reap the rewards together at the end.'

'Sounds perfect to me then, Sunshine!' She liked using the new nickname she'd invented for him, because that was how he made her feel. Warm and bright.

'Excellent – sounds like a plan! Listen, I have to go in a minute, and I know it's still quite a way off, but Elle, I need to say: just in case something happens and I don't win, I want you to go straight back to my hotel and I'll meet you there. Under no circumstances will you be returning to that monster. We'll sit down with Caesar and work something out. OK?'

He was met with silence. She couldn't even allow herself to think of the consequences if he lost; now that she had experienced life with Noah, it was her worst nightmare. She would rather die than be returned to Stephan.

'Elle, I need you to promise me that whatever happens, after your performance, get straight into the limousine and I'll meet you after the match, either back at the hotel or at our surprise destination.'

'OK, I promise. But please, make our lives a whole lot easier and just win the final.'

'That's exactly what I intend to do! I can't wait to see you again, Elle. There's just one more thing before I go.'

'Yes?'

'*Je t'aime!*'

'I love you too!'

'See you soon!'

Gladiators

Caesar was as excited and nervous as a kid on prom night. This was the second time he had taken Ashleigh to a grand slam – even though more than twenty years had passed since the first – and he couldn't wait to share the experience of the US Open final with her. The family of three had needed no convincing to move to the United Kingdom after their holiday in the US, and Jennifer and David would be starting at their new public school as soon as the US Open was over. They were so excited about their new life, and loved seeing their mother so happy after the tragedy of losing their dad four years ago. Although Caesar wasn't their father, he was interested in their lives and loved doing things with them. They were always tickled pink when he asked them for advice, or when he shared a few more tennis tips; it was a game they were both growing to love. All in all, the four of them were adapting well as a somewhat new family unit.

Caesar was thrilled – and more than well enough informed – to be able to explain the histories, strengths and weaknesses of Nordstrom and Levique, and spoke proudly of the personal relationship he shared with both men. They were being touted as the two most talented players tennis had seen in at least a decade, and tickets to their matches were selling out faster than rock concerts. The stamina both men displayed on court often left spectators dumbfounded and critics wondering whether, as in so many other sports, drugs might have insidiously found their way into the highest echelons of the game.

Today, with so much at stake for both players – more than anyone but Caesar knew – the crowd eagerly awaited the entrance of the sport's two greatest gladiators. For to have any other players in the final would have been a bitter disappointment to both fans and sponsors. Upsets, although beneficial to lesser-known players, basically weren't good for business. In particular, Caesar's business!

Noah had spent the morning meditating, clearing his mind of all thoughts of losing Eloise to Nordstrom and ensuring that his mind, like his body, was truly in the zone.

Stephan, on the other hand, had been waiting for this day since Wimbledon and was desperate to get onto centre court to thrash the living daylights out of Levique and reclaim what was his – Nadia and his Number One ranking. In line with Louis Pasteur's motto 'Fortune favours the prepared mind', there was no question that Stephan's planning had been meticulous and methodical from every angle, including his agreement with Caesar for the immediate return of Nadia to him when he won. As there was no need for contracts to be signed or renegotiated, the transfer – should it occur – would be seamless between both parties.

Like Noah, he knew exactly what he was fighting for and he was more than ready for battle. He'd sooner come off court never able to play again than lose this match. Aggression and adrenaline stormed through him like a tsunami.

It was game on – for their fourth encounter in a grand-slam final, watched by millions around the world!

The first set was taken by Levique seven–five, mainly due to the precision and speed of his serve. Nordstrom made only a few unforced errors, which was all it took for him to lose the set. The second set also got away from Nordstrom, but only just, with Levique winning six–four.

Nordstrom called for a bathroom break before commencing the third – and when he returned to the court he fought back with a vengeance no one had anticipated, playing the best tennis of his life. The number of aces he served quickly escalated into double digits and even his returns of Levique's serves were straight-out winners. It was like he had become a different person. There was nothing Levique could do to upset his unwavering assault as he took the set six–two.

The fourth set went to a tiebreak as both players held their precision serves, and when they entered into a rally the battle was relentless, just like the third set of the Wimbledon final. Just before commencing the tiebreak, Nordstrom called for injury time, indicating his lower back as the area of focus; he was rubbed down on court and swallowed some painkillers. Both players consumed their specialised concoctions, although this time it was only Levique who required a banana before recommencing play.

Levique tried to maintain his focus rather than being distracted by Nordstrom's injury, but when play resumed every serve of Nordstrom's was an ace and he carried out his returns with missile precision. This ensured that he won the tiebreak with complete conviction, leaving a bewildered Levique wondering what had happened. It was as if Nordstrom's form had turned nuclear, leaving Levique looking like he was playing with a club from the dark ages rather than a fully specified racquet.

Fists clamped, sweat pouring, veins throbbing ... the determination in both athletes was absolute. Levique's physiotherapist was called on court to massage his hamstrings. He was continually drinking to replenish his exhausted body after such mammoth exertion, while Nordstrom looked as controlled and smooth as ever.

In the stands, Australian flags were waving and supporters in green and gold were screaming encouragement for Levique to continue, not to become the defeated gladiator succumbing to the lion's roar. He must battle on, he must tap into that Anzac spirit that never gives up, never concedes until the last point is played and the last breath is drawn ... And finally he resurrected himself, to tackle the fifth set with the same verve he had shown in the first, and the crowd was roaring with pleasure (something that would never have been allowed at Wimbledon).

Then the strangest thing happened.

At three games all in the fifth set, an official spoke to the referee, then walked onto the court to hand a document to the umpire, who declared that both players would have a five-minute break off court before play recommenced. Nordstrom and Levique both looked as confused as each other, questioning the umpire, who had discreetly turned off the microphone. Neither player had any idea what was going on, but they were given no choice but to follow the official off court to find out.

The crowd was booing and jeering, and was left wondering, along with the commentators, exactly what had happened to stop play. Such an interruption was very unusual for any tennis match, and had certainly never occurred during a grand-slam final – so something had to be amiss! Even Caesar and his extensive resources were unable to come up with an answer as to what was going on. Everyone sighed with relief when the tennis gods returned, picked up their racquets and repositioned themselves on court.

Such an interruption saw Levique lose the mojo he'd fought so hard to regain, and yet again Nordstrom pounced on him like a wild animal maiming and killing its prey. The damage was immediate and irreparable. Nordstrom won the fifth set six–three – and his second consecutive US Open title. The Scandinavian god was back in full force and the upshot was irrefutable. Levique had been categorically booted back to the Number Two position in the ATP rankings.

As he collapsed in shock and exhaustion, Nordstrom rose in glory before the adoration of the crowd, reclaiming his crown and glory – and silently congratulated himself on executing Part One of his perfect plan.

Surprise

Eloise was thrilled with how all of the performances of the talented group had been received. From opening night to the final show they had gotten rave reviews, particularly for such a new dance company. But she was equally excited to be taking a break and spending some dedicated time with Noah again without the demands of tennis and dancing – something they hadn't done since their time in outback Australia.

As the curtain fell on the group's last performance, they all congratulated each other on a fabulous mini-season. Eloise hugged her new dance family farewell and changed into casual clothes, eager to meet Noah as soon as possible.

Just as they had agreed, Caesar's limo was waiting at the back entrance of the theatre, and she nodded politely to the chauffeur and got into the back seat. It was only now that she thought about the surprise Noah told her he'd planned for her, and began wondering what it could be.

The traffic was flowing swiftly and it was no time at all before the limousine pulled up alongside a marina, where Eloise was escorted onto a majestic yacht decorated with hundreds of white roses. She'd never been on a yacht before, let alone one like this. She was a little taken aback that Noah had organised such an extravagant surprise, so New York and so upmarket. To date, his surprises had included finding a funky underground grunge venue where no one knew them and they could act their own age – which she'd loved just as much. Usually he was a little more grounded in his gestures, but she wasn't going to complain, she knew he'd wanted it to be special – and it was! Everything was gorgeous, including the awaiting glass of champagne with a typed note attached.

Enjoy the champagne while you wait! I'll be with you
soon ...
xxx

Alongside the glass was a snow dome, featuring a tiny yacht and two people sitting at the stern with their legs dangling into the water. Instead of snowflakes, glitter and sparkles floated around in the blue sea. She kissed it and smiled, delighted that she and Noah shared so many special, treasured memories, as she remembered with fondness their canal trip in London, on a boat very different from this one. She sighed into the air at how much had happened in the past year – full of so many highs and lows.

It didn't take long for her to explore the rest of the boat, with its timber master bedroom with cream accessories, a small yet extravagantly accessorised ensuite, tiny, well-equipped kitchen and eating area for two. There were even clothes in the drawers and wardrobe, with a nautical theme that made her smile. Perhaps they were going for a few days. There was a control panel at the front that seemed very high-tech, along with what looked like a TV. It was only then that she thought to turn it on to hear the actual result of the tennis; she'd been so excited about her last show and then the surprise that she'd neglected to check.

Unfortunately the TV didn't seem to be tuned in, as she only saw black and white fuzz on the screen. Instead, she went to her bag to check the results on her phone (bought by Noah to replace her old one) – only to find it wasn't there. She searched the contents of her bag three times, before remembering that she must have left it on a stool near the stage so she could check the score between her performances. 'Damn it!' she exclaimed to no one, annoyed at herself for being in such a rush to leave.

At least she had the comfort of knowing Noah had been up two sets to love when she last looked. Fleetingly she thought about returning for the phone, but the limousine had long since left and she wanted to be here when Noah arrived. Besides, he'd be the only one she'd want to phone, and he already knew she was on the yacht.

So, content to wait as the boat rocked gently, she settled into the cushioned lounge chair, topped up her glass with the bottle of vintage Dom Pérignon that was in chilling by the table and sipped the delicious champagne in a state of bliss as the sun disappeared and the sky darkened over Long Island.

Mission

Even though this tournament had seen Caesar forced to hedge his bets both ways, as the margins were just too close to call, he was still in a celebratory mood, and was even more thrilled when Stephan was able to join his party of five hundred people in the Hospitality Pavilion for a quick drink after his triumphant battle against Noah.

As soon as Stephan arrived, looking like he'd just stepped off the cover of GQ magazine, the party broke into spontaneous, rapturous applause and parted like the Red Sea before Moses, shouting words of congratulation to him as he made his way towards Caesar.

It was with great pride that Caesar introduced him to Ashleigh. Unlike most women Stephan met, she wasn't in awe of him, but was certainly polite and very pleasant. It was obvious that she only had eyes for Caesar and vice versa, and Stephan mentioned as much to him, causing him to beam with pride at his new/old love.

'Never been happier,' he replied. 'It was certainly worth the wait.'

'I couldn't agree more. Speaking of which, I've just popped in to check everything is fine regarding the transferral, as we'll be out of contact for the next few weeks.'

'Everything is in order as discussed. She's all yours – again.'

'Excellent! Oh, and thanks for the offer of your car to pick her up, but everything has been sorted at my end. My girl will finally be back where she belongs.'

'No problem. Enjoy – you seem anxious to get to her.'

'Other than the trophy in my hands, nothing is more important to me than Nadia. My life hasn't been the same without her.'

He spoke with alarming intensity, but Caesar was too infatuated with Ashleigh to notice.

'I understand exactly what you mean,' he said with pride as he pulled her closer to him so he could give her a kiss on the cheek. 'Great match, by the way; you had everyone on the edge of their seat. Your sponsors couldn't have been more thrilled with your performance.'

'A little too close for my liking, but I got the result I needed.'

'You must be a little tired after such exertion, but you certainly don't look it.'

'No, actually, I feel great – must be the high from winning. Thanks for everything, Caesar – I'd love to stay longer, but as you can imagine, I have other things I need to do, so I'll have to get going.'

'Of course. Go and enjoy what's now yours.'

They shook hands as though they were old friends, as Stephan made his way to the nearest exit like a man on a mission.

As they watched him leave, Caesar whispered into Ashleigh's ear: 'So what do you think of our world Number One, darling? Impressive isn't he?'

'As you mentioned, he has an undeniable presence.'

'That he does.'

'But he doesn't bother speaking to anyone he doesn't need to. Obviously you're a firm favourite!'

Caesar glowed with pride.

'So who's his girl?'

'Oh, she's a dancer like you – a ballerina, actually – but it's a long story. Come on, let me introduce you to some other friends of mine ...' Caesar smiled as he guided her towards some of the many people he wanted her to meet.

* * *

Between press interviews in which he had to explain his epic loss, and discussions with Toby and his manager, Noah had been frantically leaving messages for Eloise since the second he came off court, but her phone just kept going through to voicemail. *Why on earth isn't she answering?* he thought in frustration.

Noah began to perspire as much as he had while playing in the final. How could this be happening? He left an urgent message for Caesar, whose phone also went straight through to voicemail. Eventually he found the number of Caesar's secretary, who confirmed he was at his usual US Open final celebration party.

'OK, I'll catch him there.'

Noah showered as quickly as he ever had in his life and made his way to Caesar's gathering. His hamstrings were aching from the exertion of the five-set match and his mind was spinning, not knowing where Eloise was. All he could hope was that Caesar's car had already taken her back to his hotel as planned so they could meet up there before their flight tomorrow.

Spontaneous applause greeted Noah upon his arrival, with condolences and pats on the back for playing such incredible tennis despite his loss. He took some time to chat and thank people while he made his way steadily towards Caesar. He wasn't sure whether he'd bump into Stephan or not, and didn't know what might happen if he did.

'Caesar!' he called out.

Introductions to Ashleigh were made once again, with just the correct amount of small talk about the match, before Noah asked Caesar if he could have a private word.

'Is everything OK?' Caesar asked when they were out of earshot of the other partygoers.

'I'm not sure. I can't get in contact with Eloise, her phone keeps ringing out to voicemail.'

'Well, Stephan left a while ago, so he'll be with her soon.'

'But I thought your car was picking her up …'

'It wasn't needed; he ended up making his own plans.'

'He *what*?' Noah's voice rose above the noise of the crowd.

'You lost, Noah, you know what that means. Stephan's now Number One again, and Eloise belongs with him.'

'*But you don't understand!* She *can't* go back to him, she'll get hurt. It's too dangerous!'

'Keep your voice down! We can discuss this later. I know it was close today, but I'm afraid your loss was his gain. You know that, he knows that and Eloise knows that. It will more than likely be that way until the Australian Open …

'Oh, my God – this can't be happening!' Noah ran both hands through his mop of curly hair, adrenaline heightening his fear. 'Do you know where he's taking her?'

'No – he just said he'd be out of contact for a while, the next few weeks. He was OK, Noah, he seemed really excited about having won her back, said nothing mattered more to him.'

'That's what I'm worried about! He's a freaking sadist, Caesar! You don't know what he's put her through. He's not stable –'

'Noah! We can't talk about this here, and you're not sounding too stable yourself.' He grabbed Noah's arm in an attempt to calm him down. 'Listen, we can speak about this tomorrow morning; now isn't the time. Ashleigh and I will be returning to London tonight, so we can be back in time for the kids' first day of school – but I can call you when we've landed. Relax – you've had a big day and put in a huge effort. Here ...' He got him a drink from a passing waiter.

'I can't drink, Caesar, I need to find her tonight!'

And for the second time that evening, one of the world's current tennis greats made a beeline for the nearest exit.

Fight

Eloise woke up on the bed to find sunshine streaming in from above, temporarily blinding her. She felt groggy as she rose to look out the porthole, but instead of seeing other yachts on their moorings she was surrounded by nothing but ocean – on both sides. Wondering whether she was still dreaming, she fumbled her way up the stairs as she steadied herself against the rhythm of the sea. She couldn't wait to see Noah and was bitterly disappointed she'd presumably slept through their first night together. Maybe all the performing had taken more out of her than she'd realised.

It took her a moment for the face of the half-naked, shadowed body to come into focus at the helm – but when it did, her breath quickened to the point of hyperventilation and her legs buckled beneath her weight.

'Nadia!' The cruel, delighted voice filled her ears.

'I'm ... I'm not ... not Na ... di ... a. Not ... Na ... di ... a.' She stuttered the syllables out, panting uncontrollably.

Stephan hauled her suddenly limp body onto the same lounge chair where she'd sat last night sipping champagne.

'You must try to breathe deeply and relax, my sweet. Finally we are back together, where we belong!'

She threw him a look of pure hatred as she struggled to get her breath back under control, her entire body shaking from shock.

'Now, now, that's not a nice look to give your Master after all I've been through to win you back.'

'You – are – NOT – my – Master!'

'Oh, but yes I am. I must say, though, you *do* seem surprised to see me. You weren't expecting that prepubescent halfwit, were you? Surely not! You must have known I'd never let him win *again*?'

She found her strength when he insulted Noah, and without giving it much thought, she launched herself at him, screaming and scratching his chest so forcefully she drew blood, his tanned skin lodging beneath her nails. Hysterical, she thrashed wildly, belting into his solid chest with her fists and reaching up to yank at his perfectly groomed hair. He let her rain her wrath on him for a moment before grabbing both of her slim wrists and twisting them forcefully behind her back.

'This is not exactly the reunion I had in mind, my sweet. It seems you have forgotten all of your training, not to mention your manners, which is such a shame. It appears we will have to start all over again.'

She continued to scream and writhe against him, kicking madly at his legs, but his strength easily overpowered her.

'You can scream as long and as loud as you want, but as you may have noticed, no one will hear you except me; we are surrounded by ocean, thanks to an excellent night's sailing. So I'd prefer you to be screaming on *my* terms, not yours. What do you say?' The smirk on his face was murderous.

She released an almighty roar from the depths of her chest that grated against her throat as she continued to struggle against his grip. She screamed and screamed and screamed until her throat was raspy, trying to expel every bit of fear and anger racking her body at being with him again. This could *not* be happening – could it?

When her voice had almost left her, he grabbed hold of her hair, twisting it painfully, and forced her to her knees.

'Now, we can play nicely, Nadia, or –'

She sank her teeth deeply into his thigh, forcing him to release his grip as he yelped with pain, and she stumbled as fast as she could back into the cabin and slammed and locked the hatch behind her.

Not believing she had just done what she did, she panted wildly, wondering what her next move might be. Her survival instincts told her to ignore Stephan's fury as he thumped against the hatch, and she fumbled with the EPIRB she had noticed attached to the wall during her earlier inspection of the yacht, and hoped like hell she had managed to activate it. She sent out a silent thanks to Noah for explaining what an 'Emergency Position-Indicating Radio Beacon' actually was. He'd insisted they carry a portable version in the outback, in case they were in any danger or lost. Although this one looked a little more complicated, she hoped it worked the same way. Then she quickly grabbed the CB radio and started screaming.

'Mayday, mayday! Help me! I've been taken!'

A crackled voice responded and she said the words again.

'Mayday, help me! My name is –'

Having torn open the hatch, Stephan crash-tackled her onto the bed, punching her face hard as he straddled her body.

'This is *not* how it is meant to be!'

He took no time in tying her wrists with restraints that were hidden under the mattress as she writhed and kicked against him. She was crazed as he stuffed a sock down her throat and secured it with a Velcro strap. In the struggle to secure her legs she kneed him forcefully in the groin, causing him to crash onto the floor. The fury in his eyes was pure evil when his face reappeared at the base of the bed, having recovered enough to still her thrashing legs, and she honestly thought he might kill her there and then. Her face grimaced in pain as he twisted her left ankle at an excruciating angle.

'Do I have your attention now, my sweet? I know how fragile your ankle is …' His voice was heavy with cynicism.

The burning pain seared up her leg, bringing tears to her eyes as her choked voice begged for mercy.

'You understand how easy it would be for me to break your delicate limbs, don't you, Nadia? Just one twist in the wrong direction is all it would take.'

The fury in her eyes almost matched his, but not quite. His rage was like a torrent beneath his words, and all she could hope for was that he'd release her throbbing ankle. Instead he gave it another twist, so she screamed without sound and thrashed even more violently on the bed.

'Try anything else like that and you'll be lucky ever to walk again, let alone dance.'

His lips twisted into a sadistic smile that scared her witless. She didn't doubt the truth of his words as he finally let go of her ankle. Flooded with relief as the pain subsided, she couldn't help but sob uncontrollably as he left the room.

How could she have been so stupid? Raw fury had surged through her body at the sight of Stephan when she'd been expecting Noah – her rage fuelled by the fear of being under his control once more. She had vowed she would never allow herself to be treated like that again, and she'd put up a good fight, but to what avail? Now she was in more danger than ever, trapped out at sea with a psycho intent on revenge.

Stephan came back into the hull with ropes slung over his shoulder. This time she managed to lie there without moving an inch, her heart pounding hard against her chest and her cheek throbbing in pain.

As he walked towards her he was interrupted by the CB radio, asking for identification and querying whether this vessel had sent a distress signal. In one last-ditch, frenzied attempt, she struggled and screamed with all her might, desperate for her muffled voice to be heard.

Stephan looked over at her with a frighteningly smug face, shaking his head at her useless attempts to be heard before replying to the Coast Guard. He stated smoothly that his name was Richard Warren and that there had been no distress signal sent from this vessel. He confirmed that he was travelling alone and that everything was fine, though he agreed to keep a lookout for trouble. The Coast Guard thanked him and wished him well on his voyage. And then he switched off the entire system.

Eloise knew now she had no hope of ever being found with Stephan, realising that this entire situation was no accident, and that he'd had everything planned in extreme detail for some time – even the idea of lulling her into a false sense of security with the snow dome, obviously sensing she might be resistant. Her previous Master had exceeded all of her worst expectations.

Nightmare

Noah had spent the evening contacting Miguel and the other dancers, trying to piece together Eloise's movements after the performance. He drew a blank, other than being told she'd been excited about catching up with him and had eagerly jumped into the waiting limousine. He was one hundred per cent sure she'd never go anywhere willingly with Stephan after all that she'd been through. Having located her phone at the theatre, he had been desperately hoping for some additional clues when he collected it the next morning, but the last call she had made was to wish him luck for the final right before her performance.

He needed to speak to Caesar urgently, to make him understand the danger Eloise could be in, and get his help in discovering where on earth Nordstrom had taken her. He was left impatiently pacing around his hotel suite waiting for Caesar to call him from London, to sort out this dire mess before it was too late.

Finally Caesar arrived in his office and placed the call.

'You need to listen to me, Caesar. He is obsessed with her; he's abused her physically and psychologically. She was trapped in his house during the entire lead-up to Wimbledon and during most of the tournament. He's crazy, Caesar – a psychopath. The monster took her to breaking point last time they were together and I just can't bear to think of what he will do to her this time round.'

Although Caesar could tell that Noah was frantic with concern, he just couldn't wrap his mind around hearing someone as masterful and brilliant as Stephan being described that way. In all of their interactions, he'd been as smooth as silk. It just didn't seem plausible.

'I'm just not sure what I can do, Noah; the transfer was done exactly according to the contract.'

'The transfer should never have happened. We intended to sort all of this out together with you after the match if I lost.' Noah was at his wits' end. 'Listen, if you don't believe *me*, speak to Professor Karin Klarsson of the University of Uppsala. She contacted me with the same concerns about his personality; she's a qualified psychologist *and* a friend of his mother's. It took ages for Eloise to open up to me about what happened because she feared what he might do – to me and to herself. As long as she was with me, she didn't want to tell you because of your friendship with Stephan, which was so stupid in hindsight and something I should never have agreed to.' He said this as much to himself as to Caesar.

'It just sounds so unlikely – such an incredible athlete …'

Noah was left rolling his eyes, wondering if anyone else could see what he saw in Nordstrom – were they all that blind? He knew he would have to pull out all stops to get Caesar to believe he wasn't just being a bad loser.

'What about the health spa in Switzerland? Did you know about that?'

'Yes, I did. I paid the bill. Why?'

'The psychologist there, Dr Jayne Ferrer, didn't want her going back to him under any circumstances, begged her to stay. She gave Eloise her card so Eloise could contact her whenever she needed to, but Stephan burnt it, cutting off all her access to anyone but him. The staff at the spa saw the abuse; it would have to be recorded in their files.'

'Files that would no doubt remain confidential, regardless of your concerns.'

'Caesar, I implore you! We need to work together to get her back. You are responsible for her. I love her. What do I need to do to convince you? Go to the police and explain that your pathetic contract has put her in danger, enabled her abuse?'

'OK, OK. Let's not be rash.' There was no doubting how rattled Noah was about Eloise's safety; Caesar could tell it was genuine from Noah's perspective at least, though he certainly hoped the accusations had no truth in them. 'I don't understand why this is the first time I've heard any of this. I *know* both of you, my firm *manages* you both, for goodness' sake!' He sounded as disturbed as he did exasperated.

'Nordstrom has fooled *everyone* as to who he really is, not just you. The world wants to believe he is the sporting god he's been set up to be, and he's a monster who would do anything to get what he wants. So now he has. Caesar, if you don't help me with this, I'll have nowhere else to go but the police …'

'Give me the number for this Professor Klarsson, and I'll see what information I can get from Dr Ferrer in Switzerland too; hopefully she'll speak to me, to confirm your story at the very least.'

'This is no story, Caesar; it could be a matter of life or death. And if we don't have a plan within the next few hours, I will be talking to the authorities.'

'Well, that would be a nightmare for everyone involved. I'll be in touch ...'

Hell

Eloise vowed that even in her current predicament, she would never allow herself to become Stephan's Nadia again. No matter what he did to her, she would remain Eloise, she would never go back to that evil place. So she fought and struggled as he tied her ankles so tightly the rope bit into her flesh. And the breath was forced from her lungs when he hauled them over her head and attached them to the bedhead behind her. She whimpered as she tried to adjust to the uncomfortable position. Another yank of the rope ensured that her arse and thighs were lifted right off the bed.

He stood back, admiring his work.

'Oh, Nadia, you have no idea how much I've missed you.' He crouched down to remove the sock from her mouth. 'There's no need for this anymore; I'll take great pleasure in hearing you scream and there's so much you need to relearn. Such a shame, when you were so close to perfection.' He lifted her head and splayed her hair out like a fan, wiping it away from her reddened face as she tried to temper her breathing. His hand gripped her scrunched neck, instantly suppressing both her thoughts and her breath.

'You seem to have forgotten that I own and control you. I decide what you do and when you do it. Without question. But all I have seen is disobedience and complete disrespect.'

Her throbbing face felt like it was going to explode as his hold strengthened, bruising her neck and cutting off all air supply.

'And you think that is acceptable to me? Do you honestly believe I will tolerate such behaviour from you?'

All she could think of as her face turned from red, to white, to blue, was Noah. That she was going to die and she would never see him again. He would have to live knowing that this monster had killed her with his bare hands. This had been Noah's greatest fear, but she had honestly never wanted to believe that Stephen would take things this far. She had walked into his life excited to be with him, enticed by his looks, his power and dominance – until she had become nothing, as if she didn't exist in the world without him.

Noah had made her feel valued again and helped her self-esteem return. He'd given her the confidence to believe in herself like never before. Only for her to be naive enough to fall into Stephan's trap, like a butterfly snared by a patient huntsman spider that has been biding its time and preparing for its final strategic, tragic strike.

She closed her eyes, refusing to allow his menacing face to be the last image she saw, and allowed death in; she had no control over anything else. She had not given in; she had felt more determination in fighting for her independence than she'd believed possible. But it had proved futile. Her last thought was to hope that Noah knew she had loved him, and that she hadn't accepted this fate.

'Every breath you take from this moment on is a decision I make on your behalf.'

He released her throat and her body's reflexes took over, causing her to choke as she struggled desperately for oxygen. The room spun in her dizziness.

He slid her knickers down towards her knees and caressed her skin, as his muffled words pounded in her head.

'No one does what I do to you. Makes you feel what I do. I can tell you've missed this, haven't you, Nadia?'

He reached under the bed and pulled out a cane, stroking it lovingly. She thought she was going to hyperventilate again.

'I asked you a question!' He slid the cane underneath her neck, forcing her chin up awkwardly.

She remained stubbornly silent, refusing to answer this man she now recognised as a lunatic.

'Hopeless!' He roared into the cabin, standing up and raising his cane into the air. If she could have jumped she would have, but all she could do was cringe in fear. Fear Stephan relished seeing in her eyes.

'I will *never* be yours – I *hate* you!' She choked out each whispered word through her burning throat.

This caused him to pause for a brief moment above her contorted body.

'Your words mean nothing to me, Nadia. However, you will receive the gift of my cane – as often as your behaviour requires it. Something I should have done a long time ago. I bought it especially to service you, no one else; it even has your name on it.' He showed her where 'Nadia' had been carved into the wood, and smiled at her lovingly, stroking her face. 'See? There's not a moment that goes by when I'm not thinking of bringing you pleasure or pain. You are an incredible motivator, my sweet; you take me to new heights.'

At these words she spat in his face, her last line of defence given the position she was in.

She didn't know at what point her screams turned into tears, and her tears to whimpers as the cane descended upon her over and over without a shred of mercy.

'That will do as an introduction, my defiant little pet. Welcome to the rest of your life.'

He looked unbearably pleased with himself as he lowered her inflamed legs from above her head. She screamed as they met with the bed, and again when he yanked her ankles, anchoring the rope at the base of the bed.

He walked away, and much to her horror, he returned with a syringe. 'Now it's time for some peace and quiet.'

The sheer terror in her eyes caused a sinister smile of satisfaction to light up his entire face. If she had had any voice left she would have screamed the house down, if she could have moved she would have struggled; instead, there was only a raspy gurgling noise of defiance escaping from her throat as he flipped her body over and took a firm hold of her raw butt cheek. 'Don't ever bother fighting against me; it's a waste of my time and yours. You see, my pet, you are mine to do with exactly as I please.'

She tensed every part of her body as the injection pierced through her skin into the muscle. Stephan flipped her back over so he could watch her eyes dilate as the drug took over her body and closed down her mind. Within seconds, blackness took all of her pain away, and any hint of consciousness with it.

Stephan had been so taken aback by Nadia's violent behaviour towards him that even after her caning he was in dire need of some time and space to work through this unanticipated reaction. So he turned off the autopilot and resumed control of the yacht, letting the sea spray clear his mind of his bitter disappointment and the throbbing pain of his bitten thigh.

He'd had such high hopes for their romantic reunion on their voyage back to the Cayman Islands, where it all began so happily a year ago. He had spent so much time and energy on instructing her, carefully navigating her evolution towards becoming the perfect plaything for his sadistic needs. She had shown such potential as a submissive; he'd known it was only a matter of time before she became fully trained as his masochistic slave – something he'd been searching for since his early twenties. He had come close a few times, but whenever he'd pushed it to a level where it was finally working for him, they had fled.

Then Caesar had miraculously offered Nadia to him, willingly, openly and contractually. His life had been so close to perfection: the power and status of being Number One; the thrill of having Nadia under his complete control. He honestly wondered where it had all gone wrong – and then he remembered Noah, his greatest threat, his nemesis who required permanent rather than temporary obliteration. But first of all Nadia needed to evaporate from the world so that only he could ever possess her.

Stephan had paid handsomely for the chauffeur's silence, and no one else knew they were taking this trip. To all intents and purposes Nadia had literally disappeared from New York City, and it wasn't as if that never happened. He'd sooner feed her to the sharks than give her up again; as he had promised her many times over, if he couldn't have her, he would ensure no one did. It was a promise he intended to fulfil.

However, before making their way to her secluded new abode in Sweden when winter set in she would be trained to within an inch of her life in his new dungeon in the Caymans. He couldn't wait for her to see his latest renovation, which had been inspired by the dungeon they'd visited in Rome, and had effectively replaced her precious dance studio. He had no doubt that it would serve as a particularly poignant reminder of his ultimate power over her, and would more than prepare her for her final destination. Allowing her the freedom to dance in the first place had been an obvious mistake, but he had learnt his lesson and so would she.

Along with the sea spray in his face, thinking this through calmed his riled psyche. Content that all of his plans were firmly in place, he relished being at sea with his prized possession just where he wanted her to be: at his complete mercy. He smiled towards the horizon – knowing that Eloise had sunk to the depths of the ocean, and Nadia was reborn into his fires of hell.

Results

After calling Caesar, Noah returned to pacing around his suite, feeling shaken and exhausted.

His mind was in a spin when a knock on the door startled him. He opened it to be greeted by Sam Wiley, the official from the International Tennis Federation who oversaw drug testing of all the seeded players. He and Sam had become very well acquainted over the last eighteen months, and Sam had been involved in their testing yesterday for the final.

'Hi, Noah – can I come in?'

'Sam, hi. Of course. This is unusual – such personal service for such a dreary task …' He opened the door to let him in. 'I didn't think I needed to do more drug tests, especially not *after* the final, and given that I *lost*.'

His life couldn't get any crazier than it already was. It was only then that he realised he hadn't given much thought to actually losing the final, only to losing Elle.

He opened a bottle of mineral water and poured it into two glasses before they sat down. 'What's up?'

'I'm here on official business, but it isn't public yet, and it affects you.'

'OK …'

Noah wondered what on earth was going on. He had never received an after-hours visit from an official before. He had never had a urine test and hair sample taken during a final before either – which was exactly what had happened during yesterday's unusual intermission.

'Firstly, I just wanted to say thank you for taking the mid-match test without complaint.'

'It was a little odd, but they're the rules; you can test us whenever and wherever, can't you?'

'We can, but we've never drug tested in the middle of a match before, let alone during the final of a grand slam. Let's just say the circumstances were extreme.'

'It wasn't great for my momentum, I can tell you. I lost all my rhythm and Nordstrom gained his … Whatever; your testing doesn't bother me, because I have nothing to hide and it's good for the sport. We don't want to end up like cycling – what a catastrophe!'

'Do you happen to know where Stephan is?'

'I'd give anything to know where he is right now, I promise you. Nobody seems to have any idea.' Concern and anger seeped back into his strained voice. 'All I know is that he spoke to Caesar last night at the celebration drinks and said that he'd be out of touch for a few weeks. Why?'

'Well, he won't like hearing what's happened when we find him. Later today you will be announced the winner of the US Open. Nordstrom has been disqualified for illegal use of performance-enhancing drugs.'

'*What!?*'

'That's right. That's why we had to repeat the tests during the match. Since the implementation of the Biological Passport Program, we've been able to closely monitor blood results against each athlete's baseline, which has proved far more effective than any testing we've used previously. We've only recently established a test for peptides that gives satisfactory results. Stephan had people on the inside, but they weren't aware that we've had access to another completely independent testing lab for the last month or so.

'We found an almost undetectable trace of human growth hormone in his blood sample but nothing in his urine. When he left the court after the second set we finally got approval to test mid-match for the first time in tennis history, and his urine sample conclusively proved drug use during the match. It's taken all night to work through the protocols and legalities, but the Federation made a unanimous decision to move quickly and decisively.'

'This is just unbelievable …'

'We've had our suspicions since just after Stephan played at Wimbledon, but haven't been able to prove anything. He seems to be quite skilled at flying under the radar, and as you know, one of our biggest issues is keeping up with how doping doctors cover their tracks.'

'Good grief! Who knows about this?'

'Everyone will know by the end of today, but obviously we're keen to find him as soon as possible, and issue him with his notice of disqualification amongst other things.'

'Other things?'

'Let's just say there were several substances identified, and a few were illicit drugs, not just banned substances. It appears he had a cocktail of drugs in his system yesterday, obviously believing a test wouldn't happen during a final. So at the very least, he will also be charged with possession.'

'Holy hell!' Noah was aghast. 'Is there anything you need *me* to do?'

'Just get ready for the photo shoot with you holding the US Open trophy – you're now this year's winner. Congratulations!'

'I honestly don't believe this. But jeez, I wish you'd discovered all this yesterday. I need to speak to Caesar urgently. Is that all you need me for?'

'That's it – except of course to confirm that all of your tests were clear.'

'That's something I know for myself, Sam, I can assure you. Thanks for letting me know about this in person, though. Tennis will never be the same again after this.'

'You're telling me. Nordstrom, of all people!'

'Not someone I've ever trusted, I have to say. I'll walk you out. Actually, on second thoughts, do you mind hanging around while I call Caesar, so you can let him know personally? Both Stephan and I are contracted to The Edge, and Caesar will need to know about this to manage the fallout. He's also the only one who might possibly know where Nordstrom is. It would really help me if he heard this news directly from the source.'

'Sure, but I don't have long.'

'No problem!'

Caesar had just finished a call when Noah was put through on speaker phone, explaining that Sam was with him. Sam quickly explained what had occurred.

To say Caesar was taken aback would be an understatement. 'Although congratulations are in order for you, Noah, this is not at all good, for the game, the players, the sponsors, the fans ... anyone!'

The three men discussed the details and what would happen next, before Sam excused himself from the conversation and left Noah's suite.

As soon as he'd gone Caesar continued. 'I agree with you, Noah, about this whole situation. It's a disaster! We need to find Eloise and Nordstrom as soon as possible. Why didn't I know about all of this sooner?'

'About the drugs or about Eloise?' Noah was relieved he no longer had to convince Caesar about Nordstrom, but that didn't bring them any closer to finding Elle.

'Both – but my God, after having spoken to both Dr Ferrer and Professor Klarsson, I just don't understand. It's shocking! Why didn't she say anything earlier? There was *nothing* in the contract that allowed her to be treated that way. You saw it, you know that …'

'But I'm not like that, Caesar, and he is. I believe they agreed on an addendum, and she said she liked it at first …' He was lost in thought for a moment, remembering when he'd tried to get through to her at the Australian Open. She'd been protective of Nordstrom then. He shook his head to get rid of the disturbing thought. 'Let's not focus on the legalities or psychology of it all now. What matters is that you understand my concerns and the danger she could be in.'

'The only thing I've found out is that Stephan used my limousine company in New York and they sent a car to pick up Eloise from the theatre. The driver refused to say where he dropped her off. Apparently Nordstrom paid for his silence but I paid more for his disclosure. She was taken to the New York Yacht Club, where a yacht and champagne were awaiting her arrival. The yacht left dock last night.'

'*Please* don't tell me he has her on a boat, alone! That would have to be my worst nightmare …' Noah felt like tearing his hair out.

'We don't know that, Noah. Let's not imagine the worst. We need to stay calm so we can think clearly. Whenever I heard him speak of Nadia – I mean Eloise – it was with great fondness. It may not be as bad as you seem to think.'

'For God's sake, man, he just cheated his way to winning the US Open so he could get to her! Is there *anything* he wouldn't do? He's just thrown away his entire career, everything he's worked for – so he can have her and I can't. All because of this stupid strategy of yours, thinking you can trade people like possessions. *You've* done this Caesar, you and your stupid agreement. And you'd damn well better fix it before Eloise gets hurt – or worse! I'm holding you personally responsible for her safety and I'm damn sure I won't be the only one when all this gets out!'

Caesar just shook his head, not wanting to register the truth in Noah's words but knowing he must – because he too had been sucked in by the charisma of Nordstrom. 'What about your press conference later today?'

'I don't care about any of that. I'll head over to the yacht club and see if they know any more; it might help if I'm there in person. I just need Elle back so she never has to lay eyes on that monster again.'

'You have access to all my resources, financial and otherwise. I'll do whatever it takes. And Noah?'

'Yes?'

'I'm so dreadfully sorry about all of this. I honestly had no idea what he was capable of. It was never my intention to put Eloise in any danger …'

'All good in hindsight, Caesar – but now we just need to get her back before it's too late.'

Shock

Ashleigh hesitated at the door of Caesar's study when she heard him slam down the phone. 'I'm sorry, I can come back later.'

'No, not at all. Come in.' He forced a smile onto his face.

Although she hadn't been reunited with Caesar for very long, she could tell he was distraught. She went and made some coffee, then Caesar explained everything about the contract and the love triangle, and how he'd never expected any of it to end up like this.

'Everyone was taken in by him. It's hard not to be when you're dealing with a sporting hero the world wants to revere, and he played the role perfectly. Now we know he's actually a psychotic sociopath, and if we don't find him soon, God knows what will happen to Eloise.'

'Should you contact her parents?'

'She doesn't have any. If she did, I can't imagine what it would do to them – given how bad *I* feel right now.'

'Losing a child is something you wouldn't wish upon anyone,' Ashleigh said, as sadness clouded her face. She started wandering around his office to distract herself from disturbing memories, inspecting his gadgets absentmindedly. She was still becoming acquainted with all things Caesar and couldn't get used to the fact that he'd had a portrait painted of her from a photo they'd had taken when they were first together and it was still hanging in his office. Her love for this man was absolute.

'Well at least we know *your* two beauties are safe. It was great seeing them smile this morning as they went off to their first day at school.'

'They were very excited, yes –' Suddenly she stopped dead in her tracks. 'Caesar, what's this? Is it yours?'

'No, certainly not. It's Eloise's. She asked me to keep it safe until the end of the contract. It looks a bit worn, but it seemed to mean something to her so I agreed to look after it. Since she had it delivered to my office I've just left it on my shelf. Why?'

Ashleigh shook her head, attempting to clear it and fearing she was going mad.

'What is it, darling? Now you seem very upset. It's OK, we'll find her and sort this out.' He went over to give her a reassuring hug. 'I'd love you to meet Eloise; I have a feeling the two of you would get along really well.' Caesar's nervous energy kept him talking, which happened on those rare occasions when he wasn't in control of a situation.

'Caesar … there is something I need to tell you, something I've been meaning to tell you for a while.'

She removed herself from his embrace, finished her coffee and placed her cup on the desk. She knew it was now or never. The coincidences were just too bizarre.

'Actually, I know I should have before now, but the time has never felt right …'

'You can tell me anything, darling. I don't want any secrets between us. I've had enough of those from my father; they just lead to pain. Please go on …' He leant on the edge of his desk, waiting eagerly to hear whatever she needed to say.

'When I arrived back in Australia after having been deported … well, I discovered I was pregnant.'

All the blood instantly drained from Caesar's face.

'It was your baby. I know it was, because the week I was with you was the only time I was with anyone in France.'

Caesar walked around his desk and slumped into his leather chair, shocked and speechless for the second time in his life, as Ashleigh continued.

'I was estranged from my parents; they'd never wanted me to go travelling, but I couldn't wait to be free from their clutches. I decided to have the baby, because it was yours and what we shared was so special … and, well, I could never have aborted something we created together. We were young then, but we've proved now that our love was real …

'So I had our baby girl alone in Sydney, but was so unwell afterwards they tried to declare me unfit to look after her. She was so beautiful, but I was terribly sick with dreadful, suicidal thoughts, and I had almost no money. I don't remember too much, except the more they tried to take her away the more I wanted to kill myself. It was a vicious cycle that I didn't understand at the time. I've since learnt that my condition was postpartum psychosis, a far more extreme version of postnatal depression that can put both mother and baby at serious risk. But nobody knew enough about it back then, so I was never properly diagnosed. When Jennifer and David were born I was prescribed medication to control it, so everything was OK; I just couldn't breastfeed. But when I had our baby, the courts just saw me as a young single mother with no job, a mental illness and suicidal tendencies, and declared me incapable of looking after myself, let alone a child. I didn't want to give her up until I contacted you, so I refused to let her be adopted. I wrote letter after letter after letter, Caesar, to tell you about our daughter, and I desperately hoped you would come for me ...'

At this, they both had tears in their eyes.

'When you didn't respond I finally decided I hadn't meant as much to you as I'd thought. I realised I was completely on my own, and our beautiful little girl would be better off with a family who loved her until I could get my life together again – not that the courts ever gave me the option of getting her back.

'I tried to find her again, years later after I married and had my own children; there were some records when she was very young, but others had been destroyed in a fire. It was as though she had simply vanished. I've never told anyone else – but not a day goes by when I don't think of her, Caesar, not a single day.' She handed him a photo from her wallet as tears fell from her eyes. 'It's always with me.'

Caesar stared at the photo of his beautiful young Ashleigh all those years ago and the baby girl he'd never known he had. They embraced each other and wept for their loss, and the cruel hand their lives had dealt them.

'My God, Ashleigh, I can't believe you had to live with this, handle this all on your own! Damn my father forever!' He slammed his fist on the desk. 'He had no right to do this to us!' Fury took over his sadness.

'We're together now, Caesar. I couldn't bear losing you again. You're the love of my life – you always have been.'

'And that love created a daughter – we will find her, I promise you. I'll never let anyone hurt you again, my love. Our sadness ends here!' He said this with such determination it was as if the universe wouldn't dare to conspire against him. 'I only wish you'd told me sooner …'

'I'm so sorry, darling; I was just never sure when would be the right time, or how you'd react. But hearing you talk about Eloise being missing … it just triggered so many memories, since they share the same name … I'm so sorry.'

'First we need to save Eloise, then our focus will be on finding our girl.'

'You see, that's the strange thing. The only gift I ever gave our baby girl was a music box, just like this one.'

'Eloise's music box? Surely there were many of those made; it's probably just a coincidence.'

'Like her name? How old is Eloise?'

'Twenty-three. Exactly what are you saying, Ashleigh?'

'Our little girl was born twenty-three years ago. I named her Eloise and I gave her a music box, just like this one. I left a copy of a photo inside the lining and stitched it up so I would always be with her in some way, even if they took her away from me. The same photo I carry in my wallet …'

She couldn't go on, as the tears of the moment released the emotion of the years. Caesar held her close while he tried to come to terms with everything she had just told him.

'You think she is *our* Eloise?' he asked gently when Ashleigh was a little more composed.

'I need to find out … Do you think she would mind?' She placed the music box on his desk and opened the lid.

Caesar handed her some scissors in answer to her question. They both needed to know.

Ashleigh made a careful incision … and slowly pulled out an aged photo. The same one she had just shown him.

They collapsed into each other's arms, utterly overwhelmed.

Caesar had never felt such consternation. To have discovered Ashleigh was one thing. To find out he had a daughter – and that that daughter was his ballerina – was almost more than he could take in. Yet to know she had now been kidnapped by a megalomaniac sadist, as per the contract he himself had instigated, took Caesar's state of shock to another level altogether.

'If that bastard has laid so much as a finger on her, he will pay for it for the rest of his life!'

All of a sudden, the search for Eloise – his own flesh and blood – became paramount. His emotions ambushed his body as love, sadness and fury simultaneously pumped through his veins and crashed into his heart. If Nordstrom had hurt the daughter he'd never known was his until a few moments ago, he only had one thought on his mind.

'God help him! Because hell hath no fury like Caesar scorned!'

Ego

Eloise became vaguely aware of the warm, wet sensation on her limbs as she came to. She was lying on her stomach with her arms and legs stretched and tied, spreadeagled on the bed as Stephan painstakingly washed her bloodied skin with a flannel, which he rinsed out every so often in a bucket of warm water. It was this sort of tenderness after a punishment that used to lull her back to him, that provided her with the sense of security she longed for. He was singing in Swedish, like a parent might sing to a child, all the violence from before vanished and replaced by loving care. Care she now understood to be disturbingly psychotic.

Her eyes were heavy and her mind was a fog as she lay trapped beneath him. Even the slightest movement made her feel as though she were enshrouded in molasses, and it took every ounce of energy she had to turn her head slowly yet defiantly away from him.

Although she could do nothing to prevent his actions, her revulsion of this man was now so strong she refused to look at his face.

After he'd washed and gently dried her cane-abused body, he brushed her hair with tender strokes, over and over again, until it was disentangled and glistening as it cascaded over her back. Had circumstances been different, this could have been a special moment in their relationship instead of the slow-motion horror it had become.

'To think you almost caused me to cut this off, Nadia,' he said as he continued his languid strokes. 'Now, you'll be able to grow it forever. For there will be no scissors in your new world. You will be like Rapunzel, forever trapped in the fortress I've made for you. You will never lay eyes on another human being, so it's lucky for you I am a patient man. When I take you to your secret new home, you will long to look at me. I will be the only person in your life, the one you will depend on until the day you die.'

Eloise let out a gurgled groan in protest, but it seemed as if her words were tied down as well.

He began separating her thick, silky hair into three parts so he could braid it. 'It is so astonishingly beautiful, I think even more so than your eyes, and you know what I think of them.'

He continued plaiting as she groaned and tried to move her head, all a pointless struggle. 'It will grow and grow, until I can restrain you with your own hair. Would you like that, Nadia?'

He waited for her to respond. She didn't.

'Or I could strangle you with it if you displease me. I think it's possibly long enough for that now. Let's try, shall we?'

He lifted her head and wrapped the braid around her neck twice. And pulled.

'See, you must understand, my sweet pet, that I decide whether you live or die. No one else will ever know or care. For you are dead to them already.'

He pulled tighter, causing her to gasp for breath.

'Your life is no longer about your pleasure, or your pain for that matter. Fortunately we've gone beyond that stage. What your life is about is simple.'

He tightened his grip further, forcing her head upwards so she could see his face.

'It's about *me*! *My* wishes, *my* commands, *my* pleasures, *my* desires. Nothing else will ever need to cross your mind – only *me*!'

He pulled and the braid constricted her throat further. 'I could kill you with your own hair right now!'

He gave one final yank as he watched the veins in her neck bulge and her face constrict, straining for any trace of oxygen. He appeared fascinated by the process of suffocation he was inflicting, as if he were playing with a doll and wondering what it might look like with its head off.

'But that's not what I want.'

He suddenly let go, tucking the end of the braid in so her hair remained wrapped around her long neck like a warm scarf.

She was left gasping and dizzy all over again. This was too much. There were no thoughts left in her mind, other than whether he would let her take her next breath – or not.

'I can't wait to see the look on your face when you see the specially designed home I've prepared for you! It's only small – but then so are you. You'll be able to walk around in your ballet slippers, but your dancing days are over, I'm afraid; you will be too confined for that. There's no reason to give you freedom you don't deserve.'

Eloise couldn't believe the monologue she was being forced to endure; his relentless delusional banter was more sickening than ever before. The smooth rhythm of his voice chilled her to the core, worse to deal with than even his violent anger, as she continued to gasp breath into her battered body.

'Why don't I put them on for you now? I bought a new pair for you for your new home. It's not as though I don't like seeing you dressed as the ballerina you once were!'

He rose from the bed to retrieve the pointe shoes from a storage area under the seat. Her brain sent a message for her feet to kick him, which only made it look like she was aiding him, such was her drugged state. Having just almost choked her to death, he was now stroking her bare legs, gently placing the slippers on each of her feet and carefully tying the ribbons around her ankles.

This torment was unbearable. Every time he touched her she was nauseated beyond belief. She wondered how long the drugs would stay in her body before she was able to resist him again. She promised herself that even if she died in the process of fighting this monster, it would have to be better than enduring the endless living hell he was determined to put her through …

Distress

Caesar had arrived in New York, leaving Ashleigh in London to look after the kids. Noah was able to confirm that both a young woman matching Eloise's description and a man wearing a cap who looked like Nordstrom had been seen boarding the yacht yesterday evening at different times.

There was no doubt in Noah's mind that Stephan had her and it was Caesar who suggested they might be heading towards the Cayman Islands. He agreed to contact the US Coast Guard after Noah received a call telling him that the ATP were ready for him to attend the press conference at which Nordstrom's win would be rescinded and Noah would be declared the men's singles champion of the US Open. News that would take the sporting world by storm – and something he couldn't even begin to think about with Eloise still missing. It would be the most bittersweet victory of his life.

He was in no frame of mind to be cheerful for the cameras, so he tried to keep the entire session as brief as possible. Unable to stop his mind from imagining her possible fate, he forced a smile onto his face and made himself think about what they could do to find the yacht and bring her home – alive. The alternative was unthinkable!

It was late in the evening when Caesar received a phone call with some news. He answered abruptly, then listened intently.

'Oh, I see … No, that's not good news… Any idea where it could be located now? I'll cover the cost of the search; please get your people onto it immediately. Her name is Eloise Lawrance and I believe she would have tried to call it in; she may well be in grave danger … A signal? Yes, I agree, it all could be connected. Thank you, keep me posted.'

He hung up, his face grave as he immediately called Noah.

'Apparently the US Coast Guard received a distress message this morning from a female. It cut out before she stated her name, although it is possible that it was Eloise. They also received a signal from an EPIRB which they are in the process of tracking down. Obviously our best hope is that these two things are related.'

'It *has* to be her, I'm sure of it. I could identify her voice. Where do I need to go?' Noah asked with urgency.

Caesar organised for Noah to go with one of his men to the headquarters of the US Coast Guard.

'Please keep in touch, Noah. I'm as determined to find her as you are, you have my word.' If Noah had known he was speaking to her father he might well have believed him.

Noah was able to confirm that the distress message had in all probability been sent by Eloise. The US Coast Guard commenced the search for the yacht at first light the next morning, after a helicopter search of the Atlantic coast from New York southbound to track the vessel emitting the EPIRB signal. Given Caesar's contacts and his offer to cover costs, Noah had been given clearance to join the vessel.

He was hopeful, but at the same time remained panic-stricken at the thought of what could have happened to Eloise under Nordstrom's control. He silently prayed that she hadn't tried to do anything that would put her life at any more risk than it already was.

Finally they spotted the swaying yacht and Noah's heart lurched. Holding his breath, he watched through binoculars as the smaller craft deployed from their vessel closed in on its target. The wind on his face and the freshness of the sea air did nothing to allay the deep fear in his gut.

Stephan had spotted the ship heading towards him a while ago, and had been listening to the radio messages directed at his yacht. He had immediately checked the EPIRB, and after realising that Nadia had activated it prior to their struggle, he had thrown it overboard. But it was far too late.

As the nimble craft homed in on him there looked to be four Marines on board. The megaphone alerted him to the fact that they had every intention of boarding the yacht, and the larger boat was also steadily closing in.

He waved cordially as the speedboat approached and went round to the starboard side of the yacht, where two of the men alighted.

'Sir, we received a distress signal from this vessel. Are you alone?'

'Yes, I am.'

'You are Stephan Nordstrom?'

The worst thing about being famous was trying to pretend you were someone else. They were obviously expecting *him*, not Richard Warren, as he'd hoped, and now that they could see him up close, it was useless trying to deny it given his fame.

It was at that moment that he noticed Noah Levique staring down at him from the larger boat. He knew he didn't have a hope of denying his identity now, but it didn't deter his eyes from throwing daggers in that imbecile's direction.

'Yes,' he stated simply.

'Mr Nordstrom, we need to search this vessel and tow it back to shore. And the authorities need to speak with you urgently.'

For all of Stephan's meticulous planning, this was a definite obstacle. It appeared his drug use to win back Nadia had finally been exposed. There was not much he could do but go along with them for the ride.

'OK,' he said cheerily, knowing that at least he'd had the opportunity to take care of her before they'd arrived.

The smirk on Nordstrom's face as he got into the speedboat made Noah's blood curdle! He was beside himself as Nordstrom maintained a stoic silence all the way back to the coast.

When the authorities searched the yacht they found no evidence that another person had been on board, and certainly no sign of Eloise. As police officers arrested and cuffed Stephan for possession of illegal substances – methamphetamines, rohypnol and ketamine, not to mention the peptides and anabolic steroids found in the mix – the smirk still didn't vanish from his face. He maintained direct eye contact with Noah and mouthed the words 'She is dead to you' as his head was lowered into the police car so he could be driven to the station and formally charged.

Noah was visibly shaken as the car drove away. The only option left was to search the Atlantic Ocean for Eloise. With each passing hour the light was fading and his hope reducing from finding her alive to finding her body.

Silence

Caesar had sounded like a broken man when Noah called from the marina to update him on what had happened. Noah had never felt such violence towards another human being in his life.

The most experienced police detectives were engaged to interview Nordstrom, but still he maintained his obstructive silence.

Even when a lawyer was organised to represent him, Nordstrom refused to speak to him or make a statement.

From a legal perspective, he could not be directly linked to the disappearance of Eloise Lawrance. And the insidious smile could not be wiped from his face when anyone asked him questions about her, even as he sat in cuffs, detained.

Financed by Caesar's ample coffers, the desperate search continued for any sign of Eloise, either on land or at sea. As each hour passed, the probability of her becoming yet another missing person increased. Caesar arranged to speak with Nordstrom personally, hoping the bastard's ego was big enough to entrap him in his own madness so he would accidentally reveal information that might give them a clue as to whether Eloise was alive or dead. It was a last resort from all perspectives, but he couldn't live with himself if he didn't give it a try. Frustratingly, he had to wait until after the detectives had finished with him, which seemed to be taking an exceptionally long time, particularly when they all knew time was running out.

Minutes felt like hours as the fruitless search continued. Noah couldn't stand being contained within the walls of his suite waiting for his phone to ring any longer. The depths of his heart ached with Eloise's absence. Bewildered, and at a loss as to what to do while he waited for news from Caesar's interview, he made a split-second decision to go back to the marina, to check the yacht for himself. He had been positive that if they found Nordstrom and the yacht, they would find her. He wouldn't let his mind consider that Nordstrom would have followed through on his murderous threats, even though it appeared that was exactly what he had done. Eloise had told him Stephan had regularly said to her that if he couldn't have her, no one would – and his silence meant they might never find out exactly what he'd done with her. Deep down, Noah knew that if she wasn't on that boat, she was probably no longer alive.

When he arrived at the marina it was being patrolled by an officer he had spoken to earlier. Noah asked him if he could board the boat to have one last look around, saying that perhaps he could pick up on a clue others had missed, something of hers that he might recognise to prove Eloise had actually been on the yacht.

A couple of things worked in his favour. The first was that the officer was a huge fan of Noah's. The second was that Caesar had more than financially compensated everyone who was involved in the search for Eloise.

Noah thanked the officer as he boarded the vessel and took his time absorbing the scene in the bedroom. Everything looked in perfect order. Too perfect, in fact. He looked inside cupboards and picked up the fluffed pillows, searching for something, but having no idea what.

In his anguish, he shoved the mattress out of position and in doing so caught sight of a long auburn strand of hair floating idly to the floor. He knew immediately it was hers and fury started shooting through his veins.

He couldn't stop his body from retching in anger and grief, knowing without doubt that she had been here. His thoughts turned feral as he pictured the torture that psycho had surely put her through. He groaned in anguish, slamming his fists and kicking his feet against the wall, utterly distraught after the events of the last day or so. Then his aggression turned to sobbing grief. And it was only then that he heard a thumping sound coming from beneath him.

Thinking at first that it was the banging he had been causing, he instantly stilled his movements, every nerve ending on high alert. He definitely heard another subdued thud from below.

Just then the officer appeared and asked if everything was OK. Noah put up his hand to silence him.

'Elle! Eloise?' he screamed into the air.

He heard the sound again, and so did the officer. It sounded like it was coming from beneath the seat in the small kitchen. As they hastily threw the cushioned pillows off the seat and opened the storage lid, they were met with all manner of nautical equipment, which Noah threw anxiously onto the floor. Much to their disappointment, there was nothing else under the seat.

He paused again to listen. Another thud seemed to be coming from *beneath* the base of the storage area.

'Eloise? Can you hear me?'

Another thud.

'My God! I think she's trapped in there!'

The officer grabbed a knife to lever the base and see if it would open.

The thudding became more frantic and pronounced as he began to prise it unstuck.

Finally, the panel gave way, and lying there was a stricken and dazed Eloise, who had been trapped beneath the artificial base in a very tight space.

Noah was beside himself with joy and relief when he looked into her eyes and they returned his gaze.

Then he became enraged when he saw the state she was in. Lying on her back, with her bleeding legs and thighs folded tight against her chest, immobilised in a straitjacket and gagged, with a bruised cheek, a split lip and her hair braided around her neck. The sick monster had even thought to place ballet shoes on her feet to tie her ankles together.

It was only then that he realised those pointe ballet shoes were what had enabled her to pound against the board beneath which she'd been hidden and trapped. The one thing Noah had heard – the only thing that had saved her life.

They carefully manoeuvred her cramped, fragile body out of the tightly confined space, releasing her from what could have been her tomb. She was dazed, confused, obviously drugged and desperately in need of medical care. As the officer called for an ambulance Noah wrapped his tortured, shivering ballerina in a blanket and held her close with tears flooding his eyes. His heart felt like it was bleeding after what she had obviously suffered; it was as though he could feel her pain in his own limbs.

It was only when Eloise was safely secured on a stretcher in the ambulance that Noah called Caesar; even as Noah spoke to him, he never took his eyes away from hers, still fearing he might lose her again.

Caesar was still at the station waiting for the detectives to finish their interrogation of Nordstrom when Noah called. He was an emotional mess when he met them later at the hospital, and Noah was more than a little surprised at just how anguished – even fragile – he seemed.

It wasn't until later that Noah recognised the Caesar of old.

'I will see that Nordstrom rots in hell for what he has done to our Eloise.'

AUSTRALIAN OPEN II
January

Conviction

How could a man fly to such lofty heights, only to fall so catastrophically? Stephan Nordstrom's entire world shattered after his deceitful, drug-induced win at the US Open. Being stripped of his grand-slam title, banned from professional tennis and charged by the World Anti-Doping Authority merely marked the beginning of the allegations that continued to mount against him. Although the immediate rescinding of sponsorship deals hit him financially, the real crunch came when Caesar vowed to use all his money, power and influence to ensure the full weight of the law came down upon Nordstrom. Distraught and gazing at Eloise as she lay in the hospital bed, Caesar simply couldn't believe that the Nordstrom he knew was capable of such monstrosities to another human being, let alone a woman he supposedly adored.

Psychiatrists diagnosed Stephan Nordstrom with Narcissistic Personality Disorder, describing his behaviour as pathological in terms of being interpersonally exploitive, lacking in empathy, arrogant and aggressive. Essentially people with this disorder were mentally incapable of understanding the destruction they caused to their own and other people's lives through the choices they made.

There was no doubting that Stephan valued himself as inherently better than other people, and the doctors all concurred that his success at tennis had masked his sense of indulgence, entitlement and power over others for much of his career.

Eventually the picture of Stephan's darkness was painted before the courts, with forensic psychologists collaborating with Professor Klarsson and Jayne Ferrer on the process of deliberately layering punishments with moments of kindness and affection, meeting women's needs before inflicting pain and cruelty. His ultimate possessiveness of Eloise was a key element of his deep-seated narcissism and his tendencies towards physical and sexual abuse. The evidence presented in court made it clear that over time, Stephan had created enough moral conflict to tap into Eloise's desperate need for attachment, and his psychological abuse had culminated in hostile threats to her own and Noah's lives, all of which influenced her decision to stay, despite the denial and abuse of her personal freedom.

Stephan's past finally caught up with him as other women, including his supermodel ex-girlfriend, Ava, came forward to provide evidence against him. It added up to an ugly portrait of a dominant predator who manipulated women to gain ultimate control – psychologically and physically. Media commentators and previous sponsors wasted no time in retracting their previous public praise of Nordstrom and labelling him 'an abusive narcissist on steroids'.

Though Eloise could now see the big picture and properly understand what she had been through, she naively felt some sadness, or perhaps pity, for the Stephan she'd known when they first met – for who he'd been rather than what he had become. That was, until she was presented in court with the images of the wretched prison he had created for her on Lake Ekoln in Sweden, and realised with horror how narrowly she had escaped his demented plan.

A final request from Stephan's lawyer that his extensive 'Nadia' photo collection not be destroyed, which was swiftly and vehemently denied by the judge, sent cold shivers down the spines of Eloise, Noah and Caesar – along with the jurors and most others in the courtroom. Finally, any sadness Eloise had felt about Stephan's epic demise was resolutely replaced with relief that he would spend at least the next decade behind bars – well away from her. As their eyes connected for the last time, she saw what most women would have seen. A tall, confident, stunningly handsome man with stylish blond hair, piercing blue eyes and a body that begged to be undressed. But she had learnt the hard way to see behind the façade, and it had nearly cost her her life. Now she saw a man whose arrogance couldn't look beyond himself, a man with a frozen heart incapable of love. Not a man to be revered and put on a pedestal; not even a man to be pitied.

The entire world had their eyes on the outcome of the messy trial. The jury took less than three hours to convict Nordstrom of aggravated assault, kidnapping and possession of controlled substances, and he was subsequently sentenced to sixteen years in prison with a non-parole period of ten years. Conspiracy to commit murder was negotiated via a plea bargain out of court but contributed the additional six years to his sentence.

Eloise, though physically battered and bruised, recovered swiftly under the excellent care she received. Her ordeal on the yacht had taught her that she was stronger mentally than she had ever given herself credit for, and she drew on that strength to make it through the arduous, and at times debilitating, court process. At the end of the final day, Noah seemed to be in more of an emotional mess about everything Eloise had been through than she was; she herself was just pleased it would soon be over, and couldn't wait to have her life back as her own.

When details of Caesar's scandalous contract came to light in court, it had rocked him to the core. He now bitterly regretted every part of his 'Number One Strategy', and vowed never to get involved in anything like that again. He provided endless support to Eloise, but didn't mention anything about paternity, having decided it would be best to wait until everyone was together in London and she was more psychologically settled. The trial was hard on everyone. Caesar certainly didn't want to put any more pressure on her than necessary – being ever conscious that she might choose not to have anything to do with him, given that his selfish contract had been the source of all her sufferings.

Although he was incredibly relieved that she didn't seem to feel that way as he waved her and Noah off on their way to Sir Richard Branson's Necker Island.

Contract

Finally they had the opportunity to fulfil the surprise Noah had planned for Eloise after the US Open – a much-needed break. It was during their magic time together, as they lay on the pure white sand with aquamarine waters washing over their entwined limbs, that they connected more deeply than they ever had before – given everything they'd been through. They touched and explored and kissed as though their lives depended on it, unable to separate or to exist without the other. Their lovemaking was long-lasting and sensual, as they reawakened themselves to each other and the world around them, and embraced the potential of their shared future. Neither had ever experienced such love for another person, a love they knew would unite them forever.

Over the course of their holiday, Eloise convinced Noah to continue with his tennis and work towards claiming victory in the Australian Open – just as he persuaded her to follow her lifelong dream and return to the Royal Ballet. So he proposed that he would return to tennis only if he could support her return to ballet – when she was ready.

They returned to London reinvigorated after their time on Necker Island, having begun to put the horrors of what had happened behind them. Caesar had organised a car to meet them at Heathrow, and was feeling almost as nervous as he had before his reunion with Ashleigh after all those years. He was dressed to the nines in his three-piece suit, as if awaiting a reception with the Queen. Ashleigh too was watching the street tensely from the window above.

The car pulled up outside an apartment in Belgravia. Caesar came out to greet them.

'Eloise, Noah, welcome back! It's so wonderful to see you both. I wanted to show you the apartment, see what you think … please come in. The driver will bring your bags.'

Eloise looked at the street in which they'd pulled up – lined with grand white stucco terraces – knowing that this was some of the most expensive real estate in the world. Even though she knew an apartment in Belgravia had been part of her contract with Caesar, she'd never dared to believe …

Noah wrapped his arm around her as they followed Caesar into the fully furnished apartment.

'Eloise, I'd like you to meet Ashleigh, the absolute love of my life.'

Caesar always introduced her that way as if to make it perfectly clear that she was the most important person in the world to him – which she was. And it made her smile every time she heard it.

The women shook hands warmly, and Eloise noticed the sparkle in Ashleigh's eyes as she stood next to Caesar and could see how much love they shared. He seemed a completely different man from the one who had presented her with the contract twenty months ago.

When the two women discovered they shared the same career it wasn't long before they were talking passionately about dancing.

Eloise felt immediately comfortable with Ashleigh, which was unusual for her even with all her newfound confidence.

Ashleigh offered to show Eloise around the apartment; Eloise was smitten with its mix of classic and functional features. The fireplace was even aglow. The place had been furnished with such style and flair that she didn't want to change a thing; she just wandered around amazed.

'So this is the apartment in the contract?' she asked Caesar when they'd finished their tour.

'It is. Do you like it?'

'I *love* it – but what about the terms of the contract? There's one more grand slam, and fortunately I'm blissfully happy with this Number One or we might have an issue …' She smiled, pleased they could all talk about it openly.

'After everything you've been through, young lady, the contract is done.' He picked it up and dramatically ripped it to shreds. 'This apartment is yours – if you want it, that is – and your first annual payment of £100,000 has already been deposited into your account.'

'Caesar … I don't know what to say.' She hadn't given any thought to the details in a very long time; these days she was just besotted being with Noah, and safe.

'Well, say yes – and it's yours.' Caesar was enjoying this so much more than he'd anticipated. To see the wonder and joy back in Eloise's eyes was priceless.

'Honestly? Just like that?'

'Yes, just like that.' He signed a document and handed it to her.

'Caesar, this apartment couldn't be more perfect. Thank you!' She was beside herself as she signed the document; it felt like all the Christmases and birthdays she had never experienced had come at once. 'I think I'm in shock!' She laughed.

'Well, I also have another letter for you from the Royal Ballet.' He handed it to her. 'Apparently Xavier hasn't worked out as well as Sir Lloyd had hoped so he has returned to Russia, along with his dancers.'

'You're not serious!'

'My sources tell me they are hoping to reinstate their previous Principal ballerina, but you should read the letter for yourself.'

'I don't believe this! What an amazing day.' She showed the letter to Noah confirming her reinstatement, should she choose to accept it, completely flummoxed by such a fortuitous turn of events.

'Well, that's not the only reason we're all here today …' Caesar's mood suddenly became more serious, putting Eloise on high alert. 'There's something else we need to discuss with you.'

Ashleigh went to stand by Caesar and Noah held Eloise's hand, sensing her apprehension.

'You're not going to tell me he's out of jail, are you?'

'Oh, no. You will never need to worry about him again, Eloise, you have my word. I'll see to it that he rots in prison hell until he's an old man.' It felt like the Caesar of old had returned momentarily – the one who wasn't to be messed with.

She sighed, relieved. 'So what is it, then? You're making me nervous.'

Suddenly Caesar became choked up, overcome by emotion.

Ashleigh, a little calmer, walked over to Eloise. 'Perhaps it's best if I show you.'

She guided Eloise towards the mantelpiece, where her music box was on display. Eloise had been so overwhelmed by the apartment she hadn't noticed it sitting there, nor had she really thought about it since having sent it to Caesar.

'My music box! Thank you for looking after it. It's my most treasured possession.'

'May I?'

Eloise nodded, then Ashleigh opened the box and, to Eloise's amazement, pulled the precious photo out of the lining and showed it to her. 'This is you as a baby, Eloise, with your mother.'

Eloise couldn't believe what she was seeing. 'My mother? This has been in there all that time?' She shook her head, astounded. 'How did you find it?'

It was Ashleigh's turn to well up, as she went to her wallet and pulled out her version of the same photo.

'Because I put it there when you were born, and I have carried this one around every day since.'

Now Eloise really was in shock, and collapsed onto the lounge, staring at the photo she had never realised was concealed in her music box.

'You're my mother?' she asked with wide glassy eyes.

'And I'm your father.' Caesar walked over to be near both women, holding Ashleigh's hand as they all attempted to absorb the intense emotion of the moment.

Now Noah too needed to sit down, flabbergasted at such revelations.

'I have a family? After all this, everything that has happened, *you are my parents*?'

Ashleigh held out her arms and Eloise was drawn into her embrace. An embrace she would have never believed could happen – until now. After a few moments, with tears spilling freely from his eyes, Caesar joined them, wrapping his arms around them and wondering if his heart would explode with the love he felt for these two beautiful ladies.

* * *

So it was with Eloise right by his side that Noah became the first Australian in more than two decades to claim the Australian Open

430

as his own. Australian tennis had a new messiah, as did the rest of the sporting world! Eloise was touched when Noah took her to the Southbank Footbridge and gave her the key to their lock, knowing it represented the key to her opening her heart to him.

The key hadn't been away from his body since the previous Australian Open and she felt truly blessed, one year on, knowing he had never, ever given up on her, just as she hadn't on him – even after everything they had been through.

As Eloise bent down to find the one that was theirs, she noticed a beautiful diamond engagement ring attached to the lock. She hastily used the key to unlock it and turned to find Noah beaming at her on bended knee, proposing …

'Yes, yes, yes, yes!'

This year there was no fear of the cameras as photographers eagerly snapped images of the world's Number One and his ballerina's lingering passionate kiss, as the stunning couple embraced this precious moment of their history together, entwined in one another's arms.

Noah held her close and whispered into her ear, 'Now it's *your* turn to be Number One, my love.'

Epilogue

Caesar, Ashleigh, Jennifer, David, Noah and his parents were all gathered around the fireplace of Eloise's gorgeous Belgravia home. They were toasting her success as the Principal in Sir Kenneth MacMillan's *Manon* during the Royal Ballet's winter season at the magnificent Royal Opera House in Covent Garden. Reviews widely acclaimed Eloise Lawrance to be the prima ballerina of her time, acknowledging that her three years away from the company had enabled her to transform the stage, and dance with her soul so much more than her finely honed body. Those who knew what she had been through had no doubt about the tumultuous depths she could tap into to capture the hearts of the audience and take her ballet into the realms entered only by the greatest dancers in the world.

Each time Noah saw Elle perform he fell more deeply in love with her. To celebrate her triumph as Manon, he even surprised her with a new puppy – just like the one adorning the snow dome that had been his first gift to her. He was more proud of all that she had accomplished in the year since the trial than he could ever have been of his own achievements – which were substantial, since he had entrenched his position as the world's Number One. Although their lives were beyond hectic at the top of their respective fields, their Number One status never detracted from being one another's ultimate priority. The world adored seeing them support each other so completely. And they both knew that their lives were about so much more than their careers.

No longer blinded by money and power, Caesar had wasted no time in marrying his beloved Ashleigh in a beautiful and intimate ceremony – a far cry from the extravaganza the media had been expecting. Their daughter had been right by their side. Not an hour went by when he didn't feel blessed by both these women, the most priceless treasures ever bestowed upon him. They were the loves of his life, and he would cherish and protect them until he breathed his last breath on earth. He now felt only sadness for his Papà – might he rest in peace – for never having experienced the true love of a woman and a real family, things that money could never, ever buy.

Strangely enough, the potential gains to be made within Club Zero no longer provided nearly the excitement they once had. Although his passion for ballet and tennis never diminished, they merely became a little more focused, revolving around those he loved – including Noah, who was soon to become his son-in-law.

Caesar and Eloise worked tirelessly together to establish the Nadia Foundation, which suffered no lack of funding given its benevolent founders. The Foundation provided protective refuge and rehabilitation for women and children from abusive relationships.

Eloise's music box still sat at the centre of her mantelpiece – next to the framed photo of her as a baby, being held in her mother's loving arms. Both objects provided a constant reminder that she had been loved from the moment she was born, even if from afar. She would never forget the momentous day when she discovered she had a mother and father. Nearly twenty-four years after the photo was taken, the two women had held each other close and cried for their lost years apart, their tears soon transforming to joy. It was a moment that had changed all of them forever.

So against all odds, Eloise was able to leave the past behind her to live a life she had never dared to imagine. She had the career she always wanted, a mother to share her life with, a father who revered her, a half sister and brother to call her own: an entire family she had never believed possible.

And a lover who would love her to the end of her days.

She finally knew with all of her heart that she belonged.

Acknowledgements

Heartfelt thanks to Selwa Anthony – my agent extraordinaire – and her dedication to covers! To James Kellow, Shona Martyn and Anna Valdinger for their continued support and patience with me over the past two years – and the entire team at HarperCollins Australia and UK for enabling this whim of an idea to become a publishing reality. Particular thanks needs to go to my amazing editors – Katherine Hassett and Emma Dowden – who were completely engaged in the process of evolving *Match Pointe*.

Special thanks to JG for his insights into a world that – until explored – tends to fly under the radar.

And my love and thanks to my family and close friends for their unconditional love and encouragement – I wouldn't be living my dreams without you!

Most importantly, I would like to acknowledge the dedication of all the people around the world who advocate, assist (financially and otherwise), and provide shelter and care for victims of violence – the world would be a dark place without you.

The Avalon Trilogy
by Indigo Bloome

Destined to Play

Dr. Alexandra Blake is about to give a series of prestigious lectures, but the butterflies in her stomach are for a far more exciting reason ...

After the lecture she is meeting up with Jeremy Quinn, esteemed doctor and dangerous ex-lover – the only person with whom she has ever let her guard down completely. After a few glasses of champagne in his luxurious penthouse suite, Jeremy presents her with an intriguing offer: stay with him for the next forty-eight hours and accept two extraordinary conditions, the first of which leaves her utterly at his mercy, and he will give her an experience more sensual and extreme than any game they have ever played before.

This scorching novel is an erotic exploration of trust and betrayal, experimentation and control, lust and love. *Fifty Shades of Grey*, this daring debut will leave you r more ...

Destined to Feel

First he opened her mind. Now she must *really* feel …

Psychologist Alexandra Blake has been awakened sexually by her lover, Jeremy Quinn. But her world is plunged into uncertainty when she is abducted in London.

While Jeremy embarks on a desperate hunt for the love of his life, Alexandra finds herself caught up in a dangerous game being played out in the shadows. Her captors want to use her to explore the darkest enigma of female sexuality and Alexandra is powerless to escape – but does she even want to?

How far will Alexandra be willing to go to satisfy her curiosity and her desires? Is this a game too far, or is there still everything to play for …

Destined to Fly

The thrilling climax to Alexandra Blake's sensual journey

Alexandra has returned to the world after her captivity and is left feeling a heady mix of emotions. Strangely empowered, her euphoria becomes tainted with fear, forcing her to acknowledge how the decisions of her past will now determine her future.

Alexandra understands it is she alone who holds the key to the answers so desperately sought by both her lover, Jeremy Quinn, and her captors. In order to unlock the secrets within her, she embarks upon a quest to explore the long-forgotten sexual and spiritual nature of her ancestry and despite believing that she has experienced everything possible in her erotic adventures, she discovers that there is still so much more to learn.